Cradle of Splendor

Cradle
of
Splendor

PATRICIA ANTHONY

ACE BOOKS, NEW YORK

CRADLE OF SPLENDOR

An Ace Book
Published by The Berkley Publishing Group
200 Madison Avenue, New York, NY 10016

The Putnam Berkley World Wide Web site address is
http://www.berkley.com

Book design by Irving Perkins Associates

First edition: April 1996

Library of Congress Cataloging-in-Publication Data

Anthony, Patricia.
    Cradle of splendor / Patricia Anthony.
        p.   cm.
      ISBN 0-441-00301-X
      I. Title.
    PS3551.N727C73   1996   95-21212
    813'.54—dc20   CIP

Printed in the United States of America

10   9   8   7   6   5   4   3   2   1

To Brazil and all her droll, good-natured citizens.
Com saudades.

Acknowledgments

I would like to thank Braulio Tavares, Clarion grad, science fiction writer, and author of the haunting *A Espinha Dorsal da Memória* for correcting my facts and spelling. And a special thanks to the citizens of Florianópolis, Sta. Catarina, who always treated me like family.

Lying eternally in a cradle of splendor . . .
—From the Brazilian national anthem

CNN, Live

. . . and at the end there, that is the general who six years ago sent tanks into the streets of Brasília to give Ana Maria Bonfim absolute control of the country. General, ah, Fernando Machado. The man on her left, and the boy . . . I'm not sure . . .

Susan? Should we attach any importance to the general's placement at the end of the row, and Director Carvalho at her right hand?

I really . . . Sorry, Bernie. There's quite a bit of blowing dust. It's windy here, as it usually is in this interior desert state. As you can see, the flags are flapping. Uh, in answer to your question, no, I don't think we can read anything into . . . Certainly there's some rivalry between the Army and, I guess you could call O.S. a mixture of FBI and CIA—Ah. And here's the first national anthem.

Short program.

Yes. And right on time.

As usual, President Bonfim cuts right to the chase. We should point out that there is a lot riding on the president's shoulders. But it looks like they couldn't have asked for a better day for a launch. Hardly a cloud in the sky.

Yes, Bernie. A very pretty morning.

1

THEY PLAYED "DEUTSCHLAND, DEUTSCHLAND ÜBER ALLES" AS A SAMBA. They played it *lento*, full of Lusitanian nostalgia and African dreams. A miracle that it was Germany. Dolores could see Pakistan or India taking the chance. Perhaps even Italy. Despite their leap of faith, the Germans on the podium below seemed composed, all but the pudgy CEO of Siemens, whose hands were clasped fervently behind his back. Whose fingers were crossed.

"This is so cool," the young man next to Dolores said. His tenor voice, the American English, carried. Ambassador Crowley frowned a warning from the bottom of the bleachers up, up, up to the ghetto of Third World ambassadors and unoffical visitors from the Economic Seven.

"This is so damned cool. I'm Roger."

An open hand was offered toward her concha belt and thickening midsection. Roger's palm was sweaty. His diminutive size and eagerness gave the NASA windbreaker a high school letter-jacket charm.

"I mean, can you believe? A free trip to Brazil, the weirdest space shot of the century, *and* I get to stand by somebody famous, too. Un-fucking-believable. I usually want paintings to look like something, you know? But I like some of your stuff."

A pro forma smile. She quickly looked away. To her right was a gathering of press and a CNN satellite truck, its dish cupping the heavens. *Order and Progress.* When did the Brazilian motto stop being a joke?

"Whoa, mama! Willya look at that?" Roger peered through a pair of Zeiss binoculars to the silver-green grass and the white pillar in the distance. "First major space mission, and they lose their cherry to the Germans. What a mind-trip. They underbid the Chinese. They even came in cheaper than the fucking Russians!"

The anthem ended too soon. Roger's last two words blared over the gathering. The diplomats, being diplomatic, pretended not to hear.

A-one, and a-two, and the Army Band struck up the Brazilian national anthem. The musicians played it straight, not so much from reverence, Dolores suspected, but out of resignation. It was a Gilbert and Sullivan sort of tune.

Flags snapped importantly in the wind. To the left of the Germans, Edson Carvalho, Brazil's chief spy, listed. One hand gripped a champagne bottle as if for ballast. In direct line from the director of *Operações Sigilosas* stood a sad-eyed child, a stranger with the gawky manner of a farmer, and the president: one small dark woman amid a gathering of men.

Look at me, Dolores thought, but Ana Maria Bonfim faced the band, the wind whipping her skirt about her legs, her gaze riveted to popcorn clouds and the azure Goiás sky. *Look at me, Aninha.*

Eighteen months of phone calls that had never been returned. Eighteen months of seeing her on TV, an empty living room and half a city between them.

The anthem ended. The crowd, except for the podiumful of principals, took their seats. Ambassador Crowley smoothed his hair over his bald spot with a furtive hand. An impish breeze exposed it again.

This should have been the time for a presidential speech, but none was listed on the single-page program.

Why won't you talk, Aninha? Why won't you answer my phone calls? Don't need the dollars anymore?

Roger said in his shrill tenor, "Why not use their base at Natal so they're closer to the equator? A space shot the hard way? Fucking incredible. And look! Those damned tanks are too small. I tellya, that thing's never getting off the ground."

The loudspeakers came to life. "*Sistemas prontos. Começando o countdown.*"

"Hey. So you're just an artist, okay, but how does this look to you?" Roger handed her the glasses.

"*Cinco minutos.*"

Dolores raised the binoculars and studied the side of the president's face—the sagging skin at the jawline, the crow's-feet, the graying black curls near her ear. Ana Maria, melancholy and distracted, wasn't looking at the rocket. But she wasn't looking at the crowd, either. So easy. One marksman with a scope. That's all it would take.

Roger tugged at the sleeve of Dolores's peasant blouse. "So? Whaddya think?"

The whole world is watching, Ana. You took too much of a chance.

Grass bent with the wind, now silver, now light green. And in the distance, the proud little rocket jutted up from the plains.

"A boob," she said.

Roger looked blank.

"You know. A jug. A bazoom. Don't you see it? It's a big white hooter with a gray nipple."

Roger whooped and nearly fell onto the Sudanese ambassador's wife. "God! So cool! I love it when a woman talks dirty."

"*Quatro minutos.*"

Four minutes and not even Saint Ana could stop it. Dolores said, "Useless as tits on a boar."

* * *

Hiroshi Sato was curious. He knew who was laughing at the top of the bleachers. He recognized their voices. He had read every entry in their dossiers. What he didn't know was what they were doing together, the young NASA engineer and the suspected American spy. And he couldn't fathom what they found so funny.

He would not show weakness and look. Instead he watched the ungainly rocket. Brazilian incompetence. He was used to that. But how could the Germans have gotten involved? In less than four minutes, a team of astronauts would burn to death, along with a ninety-million-dollar German satellite.

Over the loudspeakers: *"Tres minutos."*

An anxious flutter in his belly. Hiroshi forced himself to relax. The week before, his CIA contact had studied the data, the photos, then said, "Those Krauts'll find out that you get what you pay for."

Americans might be deluded about the quality of their engineering, but one thing they understood was capitalism. They understood space.

Hiroshi sought comfort in Kinch's pledge: *That lard-assed bird'll never fly.*

Edson Carvalho was very drunk, so drunk that he was afraid he would fall off the podium. At the top of the bleachers, two Americans were laughing: the NASA investigator and the president's oldest and fondest friend. Edson supposed they were laughing at him.

"Dois minutos."

As if his eyes gave him no other choice, he looked at Freitas. Thirty years of espionage. Everything but the hunger in Freitas's face had lost the power to scare him.

Freitas's five-year-old, José Carlos, was quietly and doggedly playing some child's game. An odd amusement. What was its point? Then Edson realized what he was seeing wasn't a game at all. The boy was trying to get his father to hold his hand. He intently folded and refolded the callused fingers over his own. They never held a grip. Freitas never looked down.

Poor little shit. Edson punched the kid in the shoulder. "Hey," he whispered.

And the loudspeakers said, *"Dez."*

"Hey."

The boy's eyes were round and brown with just a hint of slant. Some *Índio* in him. "You see down there?"

A hesitation. The boy shook his head.

"Want me to hold you?"

"Oito."

José Carlos lifted his arms. As Edson hoisted him up, the boy slipped his arm around his neck. His body was warmer than Edson expected, compact and firm. He fit comfortably in his arms, teddy-bear right.

"Temos ignição."

A rumble that tickled Dolores's belly, the soles of her feet. Across the rolling prairie, the rocket caught fire.

Over the loudspeakers an excited, "Liftoff! Liftoff!" Smoke billowed. The white pillar mounted the sky, hemorrhaging orange.

"Not enough power," Roger said, without taking his eyes from the glasses.

Higher, higher, its voice sometimes a roar, sometimes a nervous stutter. The rocket fought to rise as if the earth was determined that it should stay.

When it was halfway to heaven, Roger shouted, "Oh, man! It's not gonna make it!" Gasps of anxiety swept the crowd.

Pity should have shut Dolores's eyes. Macabre fascination widened them. At the top of its arc the rocket was a mere elongated speck in the blue. She saw it stop rising. She heard the engines sputter. She watched as the nose lazily began to tip. The wife of the Sudanese ambassador let out a ladylike scream.

For an instant, the rocket seemed to hang in the sky, suspended by apathy. Then, as if God pulled a curtain on the disaster, a cloud drifted north and screened the spacecraft from view. The engines coughed twice. And fell silent.

Bright flags riffled: the German tricolor, the Brazilian green and azure. A puff of wind turned the sea of grass silver.

Hiroshi heard the NASA engineer shout, the crowd gasp. He saw Trade Counsel Shuma Kasahara squeeze his eyes shut. Saw his mentor's hands clench so hard that the knuckles paled: not with fear, but with hope.

This would halt the meteoric rise of Brazil's economy. They might have stumbled onto room-temperature superconductivity, and an easy answer to fusion. But that sort of success could not be sustained. Space travel required precision. Teamwork.

Wearing his public face, smirking inside, Hiroshi looked at the podium. The president of Brazil was checking the status of her nails.

Edson tickled the little boy's belly, eliciting a giggle. "You had breakfast?"

The child shook his head. *Poor little shit.* "Tell you what. From now on, I will order my men to fix you breakfast. On pain of death. Would you like that?"

"I'm hungry," José Carlos said.

Edson shifted the boy's weight to his left arm. "Just a minute, and this will all be over. Can you wait just a minute, then?"

"Uh-huh."

"Good boy." Edson kissed the top of José Carlos's head. The dark hair was sour from neglect. "That's a good boy. You wait. Then we'll sneak inside to the buffet. They have chocolate."

For the first time he dared look at the silent white cloud, the one that had swallowed the rocket. So this—an engineering miscalculation—would topple *Santa* Ana and send Edson plummeting with her. Strange how anticlimactic and liberating the inevitable was. He wondered if suicide jumpers, seeing the ground approach, felt the same dull relief.

Where was it? Dolores wondered. Where had the rocket gone? The Siemens CEO's head was lifted, but his eyes were closed, waiting. All waiting. The crowd held its breath for the plummet. Even the wind was hushed.

A loud pop. Hiroshi stepped closer to Kasahara, his eyes busy.

There. On the podium. Edson Carvalho was laughing. He balanced a spewing bottle of champagne in one hand, a child in the other.

Crazy countries. Crazy people. And crazy rockets. It should have fallen by now.

That's when he heard the NASA engineer scream, "Jesus fucking Christ! How did they *do* that?"

Of course Roger spotted it first. He had the glasses. Then even Dolores could see the rocket emerge from the cloud, rising soundlessly and fast, no fire on its tail. Up and then up. Mesmerized, she watched it vanish into the blue.

No one moved. No one spoke. A minute or two later, a calm anticlimax from the loudspeakers: *"Orbita."*

The president leaned toward the microphones. "We will go in now and celebrate."

Not even the Germans clapped.

nBC, Live

Right there, Dr. Maynard. Please explain what we are seeing on the video.

Yes. At this point something starts to go wrong with the main engines. I would say they are experiencing insufficient lift. Almost . . . almost without a doubt.

I realize I'm a layman, but still, it almost looks like, at least at this magnification, that the burn . . .

Yes. Definitely, Tom, that—that flicker that you see along the left, that's uneven burn. Very dangerous.

So the rocket shouldn't have—

No. That's why it tips left. And there, just now, you can see the fuselage turn—not normal rotation at all.

Uh-huh. Interesting. Entering the cloud now, and . . . quite long. They're telling me one minute, two point three seconds. Doesn't that seem to be excessive—can I call that 'hang time'?

It does, well, hover. Or seem to.

And there it is again on the screen, headed straight up. The rocket does not appear to be—now, at least—uh, be spiraling out of control. And the engine flame has apparently extinguished. Any thoughts on how that propulsion system works, doctor? . . . Doctor? . . . Dr. Maynard?

Um?

Any ideas on how the Brazilian space agency did that?

Uh, no.

2

Chocolate made a grubby circle about José Carlos's lips. He held a shrimp in one fist, and he was beaming. Speakers piped Villa-Lobos through the tent. Against a blast of "Bachianas Brasileiras," Edson hummed an off-tune, off-beat "Chão de Estrelas," held the boy, and danced.

"Where's *papai*?"

Edson didn't answer. He shuffled close to the table and bent him over a tray of stuffed crabs. His balance lost, José Carlos shrieked and clutched Edson's lapel.

"You don't like the crabs? Let's see what you do like, neh?" Edson dangled him over a platter of quail eggs. He was drunk, and it took him far too long to realize the boy was squealing with terror, not delight. He pulled him up.

"Where's *papai*?"

"Our fun-loving channeler extraordinaire? He's kissing foreign-dignitary ass in the other tent. He'll charm us with his presence in a few minutes." Edson closed his eyes. Drunken vertigo sent him crashing into the table. A papaya and coconut cake fell, whipped cream down.

"*Puta que pariu*," he mumbled, then caught the boy's self-righteous expression, one he must have learned from his father, when his father was still whole. "Don't look at me with those eyes. You're too little to be pious. And too young to know what *puta* means. Come on. Laugh for me." He tickled the child's ribs.

José Carlos twisted away, frowning. "What's this?" he asked and stuck his hand inside Edson's jacket.

"Don't play with that. I shoot people with that."

"Why?"

"For Ana Maria, Our Lady of Economic Development."

Edson shouldn't have closed his eyes a minute ago. Now he seemed to have lost all notion of center. He took a step left, and his foot nearly pulled his body with it. Only a fierce act of will kept him upright. Afraid he would drop the boy, he backed up until his buttocks hit the bar, and waited for the room to stop spinning.

"You shoot lots of people?"

"I'm a *puto*. Another word for 'patriot.' You can understand that, neh? I'm paid to fuck others for my country."

"You shoot lots of people with your gun?"

"Oh." Edson took a deep breath. The room made a giddy half-turn and halted. "Thousands."

Hot sticky hands plucked at his collar. "Listen. Listen."

"What?"

Soft, frightened voice. Breath like moth wings on his cheek. The smells of chocolate and shrimp. "Can you kill it?"

"What?" Edson shook his head, a mistake that nearly sent him to his knees, retching. "Um . . . let you down."

But before he could, tiny fingers seized his jacket, put a stranglehold on his tie. "Please. Can't you kill it?"

Crying. That's what was happening. The boy was crying. And José Carlos's sobs made the room reel until there was nothing, not even dignity, to hold on to. Edson's grip loosened. The child slid to the floor, and the director of *Operações Sigilosas* dropped to the Astroturf.

A tug on the hem of Edson's jacket. "I want my *pai* back."

When Edson understood what it really was that the boy wanted, he muttered, "God have mercy," and the room went round and round.

"This disappoints me," Hiroshi said.

Kinch's eyes, the color of pond scum, were magnified by his Coke-bottle glasses. He wore heavy black frames when gold rims or contacts would do. The tall, egg-shaped, hunch-shouldered vice president of Raytheon Brazil even slicked his dark hair back like Superman's alter ego.

"Yeah, well . . ." His eyes focused on something beyond Hiroshi's shoulder—Dr. Clark Christopher Kinch in search of a phone booth. "We shouldn't be talking here. You're blowing hell out of my cover."

"We are friends. This is what everyone thinks. Smile, Dr. Kinch. Smile and nod as if we are having a good time. I relied on your information, and you assured me the rocket could not fly."

Don't worry. No problem, Kinch had promised. And Hiroshi had promised Kasahara. And Kasahara had promised the ambassador, who in turn promised the prime minister.

"Shit happens. When I find out more, I'll tell you, okay?"

Industrial secrets were Hiroshi's stock-in-trade, political espionage mere hobby. Still, he knew Kinch was in over his head. The CIA had betrayed Hiroshi's trust. Now Kinch treated him like an agent of the Third World country Japan was fast becoming.

Hiroshi took a deep breath. By the green-and-white-striped pavilion, a receiving line had formed. Through the open wall of the blue-and-white buffet tent, he saw Edson Carvalho on his hands and knees, vomiting. A maid was throwing towels on the mess. Caterers scurried in with buckets. Typical Brazilian confusion.

He looked away. "Was the announcement true? Has it actually reached orbit?"

"Don't be a pain in the ass, Hirohito. I told you. When I get word, I'll pass it on."

Kinch started to leave. Hiroshi, expression still impassive, grabbed his arm. Like most Americans, Kinch was all potato-fed muscle. But Hiroshi knew how to squeeze. The American sucked in a breath. His shoulders straightened. His pond-scum eyes grew wide.

Hiroshi drove his thumb into the nerve at Kinch's elbow. He dug until he sensed the taller man's knees going weak. Then he smiled politely. "That would please me very much, Dr. Kinch."

If Dolores hadn't been standing beside Roger, she would never have seen it happen. The American military attaché walked smartly down the outside of the receiving line. His eyes cut neither left nor right. His toffee-brown face never changed expression. His regulation Marine jaw did not slacken. "Can the goddamned color commentary," he muttered. Then he smiled and, as if that had been his sole objective, he stopped to exchange pleasantries with the Latvians.

Roger leaned over her shoulder. "I think I fucked up."

Too late for replies. Three steps. She smiled and put out her hand to the German cultural attaché, who mouthed compliments on her retrospective at the Whitney. Another step brought her to the pale and trembling CEO of Siemens. Next in line was the German ambassador, who had been trained to mask surprise.

"Congratulations," she told him.

A perfunctory bow. The hand shot forward. "We are pleased to be working with our new Brazilian partners." But he had not been trained well enough. Cool in the tent, yet his forehead and palm were damp.

Two more steps. Edson Carvalho should have been beside his president. The mysterious farmer was there, instead. Had Ana found a lover at this late and middle-aged date? A shame. Dolores had fought so hard to win her her freedom.

He was older than she had thought. Anyone's poor country uncle in a borrowed suit. His gaze floated to the tent's ceiling. His grip was awkward, as if he had never quite learned how to shake hands.

Dolores told him, "I don't think I caught your name."

His middle finger traced a clandestine line down her palm. At the unexpected intimacy, electricity arced through her. Her thigh muscles turned to water. She realized, to her chagrin, that she was blushing.

"Dolores Sims," he said. He aimed dark eyes at her. "You are a painter."

He drew her close, loomed over, and engulfed her. His body heat was suffocating; his breath tickled her cheek. "You must tell me about painting sometime." His whisper probed her ear like a tongue. "We can talk together. I would like to—"

"We must not hold up the receiving line."

At Ana's voice, his grip loosened. Dolores jerked free. God. Why hadn't she shoved him away? Damn it, she just stood there and—

"Dolores?" Ana said. "So good to see you again."

Stood there and let him.

She saw the man pull Roger close, and heard him whisper intimately, "Roger Lintenberg?"

"Dolores?" Ana. Puzzled now.

Dolores tore her attention free. "Yes, Ana. Good to see you, too. It's been too long. Why don't we get together? Just the two of us."

Could Ana sense her desperation? Did they pass loneliness,

palm to palm? "We can watch a movie and eat popcorn and then call Jaje. How is the university treating her?"

"I don't know. She doesn't have time for her mother." Bitterness flirted with Ana's mouth. "Strange she hasn't called you, though. Oh, by the way, I heard you suffered a loss." She leaned forward and hissed, "You'll miss him."

Dolores shook her head.

A grip so tight it bruised. "You will. No matter how you hated him. Like me, you now have no one."

Ana coolly moved her attentions to Roger.

The line, inevitable as the tide, pushed Dolores onward. She floated amid a vast sea of guests. The current swept her into the food pavilion, among the whirlpooled cliques and the gossipy eddies. There she drifted, drowning.

A tug on her sleeve brought her head around. Roger asked, "Hey. Couldn't help but overhear. Who died?"

You'll miss him.

"Just my husband," she said.

Crossfire

. . . *as you Americans say, we are along only for the ride.*

So it was—

I'm not finished, Michael. Come on, Mr. Ambassador. Surely you can see the implications of Brazil and Germany together—

No, I cannot see. It was a business decision of Siemens. Germany merely gave permiss—

Your ambassador, sir, was on that podium, right next to Bonfim. I believe his presence constitutes support. We went through this before, didn't we, with Iraq? Isn't this sort of a déjà vu?

May I please to finish a—

German companies got rich selling arms to Saddam Hussein, and all the while . . .

We have not sold—

. . . the German government sat there with its eyes—

Let me explain! This was a bidding situation! Your own press reported on the agreement. I must tell you, I resent—

Resent all you want, sir.

Hey, Bob. Bob! You really believe Brazil's a threat to the security of the United States?

We sat here and saw them do the impossible again, Michael. Didn't it scare you? Power like that in some banana republic dictator's hands should scare the pants off every American.

3

He was there in the dark of the downstairs bedroom, on the stained hospital mattress. He was trapped in the bottles on the nightstand and in the menthol reek of the air.

Dolores flung the window open to the breeze, to the torpid scent of flowering ginger.

"I didn't hear you come in." The maid stood in the doorway, string bag in hand, sweater on, ready to leave for the day. Her eyes were wide with hero-worship. "Did you see her? *A presidente?*"

"We shook hands. She was very busy."

"Oh, don't I know! I watched everything on television. The *Globo* anchor sounded like he was announcing a Botafogo game. Going up going up going up—go-o-o-oal!" She laughed, red-faced with excitement. "And then the rocket went into the cloud and he got very quiet and Iraçí from three houses down—their television is broken—went to crossing herself, and Savio, her sixteen-year-old, gets the remote control and turns to CNN and Iraçí is screaming at him, and right at that moment it comes out of the cloud—such a thing of beauty, neh? The CNN announcer stops talking. I would think there is something wrong with the sound, but I can hear people yelling in the background. He looks upset—the American announcer I mean—as if he has lost his notes." A pause in the verbal deluge. Then, defensively, "But it was wonderful, neh? In spite of the Americans later saying it was impossible. So the rocket flame goes out, so what? Brazilians always make do."

Dolores nodded absently.

"*Presidente* Ana looks tired. She is not taking care of herself. When you see her again, tell her, will you, that garlic is good for the blood. Tell her to drink *maracujá* juice with plenty of sugar. She will sleep like a baby."

"I will."

"And you! You must close the window. It is getting cold."

"Not cold enough." In the garden the guava tree gathered twilight under its branches like a hen gathering chicks. Amid the black-green leaves of a coffee tree white flowers gleamed like Christmas lights. "It's never, ever cold enough."

"Ah." The maid smiled knowingly. "*Saudades.*"

A keen nostalgia that only the Portuguese language dares name. It was a long time ago, and she couldn't quite remember, but it seemed that she loved the memory of Virginia far more than she had ever loved Harry. *You'll miss him.* Dolores's voice was decisive. "I miss the snow."

"It snows in the mountains in Santa Catarina. Maybe this winter you can go there."

"Maybe this winter I can go home."

A long-suffering sigh from the shadows. How many times had they held this conversation?

"Clean this mess up tomorrow." Dolores gestured angrily toward the armoire, toward the bed. "Give it all away. Give it to the Spiritist church. They'll pick it up."

"His clothes? The bed? Everything?"

The house wasn't empty yet. Freezing in the room, and it would never be cold enough. Dolores walked out, pushing her way past the maid. "Everything," she said.

*   *   *

Edson woke with a start. His stomach burned. His head pounded. He was lying on a straw bed in an unfamiliar room. Gilberto Muller stood by the window, looking mildly annoyed. The agent took a syringe from his jacket pocket. "Roll up your sleeve, sir."

"Where am I?"

"The Villanova safe house. You remember the one. East of town. Please, sir. If you don't mind, roll up your sleeve."

The corners of the room were in shadow. An indigo sky peered through the window. Dusk or dawn? "Is it still Tuesday?"

The agent came closer, turned on a bedside lamp. The brilliance drove splinters of pain into Edson's eyes.

"Still Tuesday, sir."

Squinting, Edson rolled up his cuff. "What happened after the reception?"

"You were incoherent for a while, and then you slept, sir."

Too many gaps in his memory lately—a life become defective tape. "Time's a whore, Muller."

"Yes, sir. I quite understand."

The needle stung. The vitamin B-complex ached exquisitely going in. Muller sat at the edge of the bed and waited. He waited until Edson began to gulp for air. Until his muscles spasmed and his skin slicked with sweat. Until he was sober.

"Better, sir?"

Edson couldn't move his arm without groaning. "You fuck sheep, Muller. All you dim-witted gauchos fuck sheep."

"Thank you, sir. Are you feeling well enough to talk to the president?"

"No. Send the mulatta cunt in."

Muller got up. Rusted springs squealed. He returned with two wooden chairs. Two. These days she never went anyplace without him.

"So. Edson. How are you feeling?" The president's drowsy contralto preceded her. She bent down and peered into his face. "I can invite several hundred guests over for dinner. We can watch you puke."

"Sorry."

"Don't lie," she said pleasantly. "You're not sorry at all. When God was kind enough to answer my prayers, he was cruel enough to give me you."

She sat. More footsteps. The creak of worn floorboards. Edson swallowed hard as Freitas came up and stood over Ana, his belly pressed to the back of her chair. When he stroked her shoulder, Ana gently pushed his hand away.

Freitas's jaw knotted, his fists clenched. Muller started to rise, to do what? Surely he wouldn't dare stop him.

But petulance overcame fury. "Everyone was impressed today. Didn't you see that?" One last glare, and Freitas crossed to the window. In the dusk, beyond a stand of bamboo, a rooster crowed a death omen.

"Oh, everyone was certainly impressed." Edson sat up and patted his pockets in vain search of a mint. "We surprised the Americans mute, terrified the Germans, and awed the Japanese—things not easy to do. I warned you, Ana, that engineering team would make a mess of things. Let's send them up in one of their own rockets. We'll make bets on how far above five thousand feet they can get. And while we're at it, let's put those damned astronauts in with them. We told them not to turn on the antigravity before they were out of sight of the cameras, didn't we? Didn't we? Now look what has happened. We should shoot them all for cowards when they land."

Freitas said, "Tell him."

An instinct that must have taken years to develop, one that she had learned first from her husband: Ana ducked her head between her shoulders to shield her face. "They want someone else."

Edson sighed. "Who?"

Freitas's gaze caressed the curve of Edson's cheek with detached, generic longing. "We invite Dr. Lizette Andrade de Morais."

Light was dying. The clay road was a glimmering path into limbo.

You think there's more? Harry had asked her.

More what?

More than life. He'd been afraid of death. Afraid of Dolores. Afraid of everything.

At the corner, in the pool of light near the streetlamp, an empty Coke can lay. Nestled among the dun weeds, its crimson was shocking. Dolores hurried her stride, and she didn't look back. The Company had been trying to contact her for days.

Somewhere in the darkness cowbells clanked. Birds chirped vespers. Past the shuttered corner store. Ten more steps, and she halted.

She didn't know what to do, but she knew how she would paint it: cobalt for the night; jet black, straight from the tube, for the bridge and the waiting figure.

She should have brought her gun. The silhouette was small, but lithe. If she ran, he'd catch her. A knife, to make it look like a robbery? A garotte? They were used to working that way. Or a silenced .22, an American finger on the trigger, a Brazilian bullet? All because Ana Maria refused to talk.

She took a breath and walked forward purposefully. Not as Harry would have. Not afraid.

The shadow shifted its weight. "Dolores? That you?"

She recognized the voice and her heart sank. She reached him. Stood beside him in the gloom of the bridge.

Roger said, "I gave the taxi driver your address, and he left me here. I couldn't see any houses. The store's closed. There wasn't anyone around to ask. Christ, it's dark out here. I thought I'd have to spend the night in the road."

"*Ponto final do ônibus*, Roger." He knew that. And if she hadn't come to him, he would have come to her later, tiptoeing through the silence of the house.

"Yeah. Right."

"Our mailing address. The last bus stop in Quedas Brancas. We pick up our letters at the store."

No "we" anymore, she remembered. Just her. Marriage, like lying, was a difficult habit to break.

"Oh. I get it. Anyway, you haven't picked up the Coke can. You're blowing their minds."

"I know what they want." She walked away fast, her back tensed for the shock of the bullet.

"Hey!"

At the edge of the bridge she halted. In the darkness below, a rainy-season stream hissed over rocks.

"Can I call you Dee? They tell me your American friends do."

"I don't have any American friends."

"Hey, look. I'm just an engineer, okay? I work for NASA, but I'm on loan. The Company's not so bad, really. They knew you were tired of the spook types." A pause. "You mad?"

She sat on the cement guardrail and looked down the road to the streetlight. Her vision blurred. Not tears, but the foggy aftermath of fear. She heard him sit beside her.

"Wow. Look at the stars. You can't see stars like this in the States. Not even in the desert. Brazil looks right into the fucking Milky Way."

The reverence in his voice made her lift her head. Her eyes traced the dazzling stars in the Southern Cross.

"It's in orbit," he told her. "Satellites tracked it. You know? When I was in college I used to go out to the black mailbox and watch lights zip around Area 51. When I graduated, and NASA hired me, they sent me right smack inside Dreamland. But all I found there was good human engineering."

She heard him shift his weight. Heard him sigh.

"God, Dee. Ever since I was a kid I've wanted to see a UFO. I finally saw one this morning. And it had a Brazilian flag on its fat white butt."

She got to her feet. "I'm going in."

He reached for her. "Listen." Strong fingers clamped her wrist. "Just listen, okay? A year and a half ago Brazil patents room-temperature superconductivity. Fourteen months ago they come up with cheap fusion, and pay off their foreign debt. Then Bonfim tells us to get fucked just about the time the CIA starts hearing rumors that she's developing orbital weapons. And today a Brazilian rocket makes it into space without benefit of any goddamned technology we know. This is scary."

"Brazil? Scary? Isn't that a punch line?"

His grip hurt. "'Order and Progress' used to be the punch line, too. But people are disappearing, Dee. Over a hundred Brazilians and counting. Everything's starting to unravel, just like fucking Argentina in the 70's. What's Bonfim doing? She's your friend, damn it. What is she, a saint or some kind of nutcase? You're the only one she'll talk to. Come on. You're still an American, aren't you?"

Slate gray skies. Cold humid scent. The dreamlike fall of white. It was so long ago she couldn't be sure what part was memory, and what imagination. "Leave me alone, Roger."

She wrestled out of his grip and started walking. Near the streetlight he caught up with her. He was lugging a suitcase and a huge camera bag, and panting. "They told me to stay with you."

"Go home."

"Come on, Dee. Have a heart. Don't leave me out here. There's no taxis."

"The bus comes at six-thirty in the morning." She strode through the puddle of lamplight. She walked until she noticed that she was walking alone. At the edge of the glow she paused. Roger was sitting on his suitcase under the flood of light, staring into the dark dry plain. A waif.

"Where are you from?" she called.

He lifted his head, eyes shorn of hope. "Houston."

"No, damn it. I mean where are you *from*?"

"Minnesota."

Heavy gray skies. White flakes falling like blessings. "It snows there."

"Like a motherfucker."

Not able to leave him, she called Roger in from the snow, and knew one of them would live to regret it.

From PBS's <u>The New Brazil</u>
Filmed Three Months Prior to Launch

. . . her campaign platform was to lease huge sections of the Amazon rain forest and the Mato Grosso pantanal to pharmaceutical companies, a move she promised would protect the environment as well as pay off Brazil's staggering foreign debt. Four years later, facing reelection, Bonfim apparently tired of waiting and ordered troops to expel the ranchers. When the opposition party pushed for impeachment, she used her power as the Army's commander and chief, and forcibly disbanded both congressional bodies.

The Brazilian people accepted this turn of events with their usual aplomb. After all, wild swings from dictatorship to democracy have been the accepted trademark of Brazilian politics since Dom Pedro the First. Congress had been historically corrupt, anyway; and Ana Maria Bonfim at least made good on her promises.

Today, Brazil leads the world not only in the development of new drugs, but in the creation of groundbreaking technology. It boasts the highest standard of living in Latin America, a sophisticated workforce, and streamlined import/export laws. In the six short years since Bonfim seized full power, she has single-handedly revived Brazil's moribund economy, and made it one of the most stable countries in the hemisphere.

4

A KNOCK ON THE FRONT DOOR SHOCKED HIROSHI FROM SLEEP, AND HE fumbled for the pistol on the nightstand. His wife rolled over, taking the covers with her, muttering in her dreams.

Quietly, so as not to alert the visitor, Hiroshi slipped on his robe, put the pistol in his pocket, and crept acoss the cold tiles to the den.

So quiet he could hear his own heartbeat. So dark that dots swam in his vision. Right index finger on the trigger, he unlatched the lock with an awkward left hand. He aimed the hidden gun muzzle at what should be the visitor's stomach and flung open the door.

Kinch. "Hey. You already asleep, you dumb motherfucker?" The American was drunk. And loud.

Hiroshi's eyes indexed the background shadows; then he ushered him in. "What time is it?" he asked, turning on the floor lamp.

"Time to wake up and smell the coffee. Rise and shine! Oops. Got the little woman up."

Hiroshi turned. A sleepy form stood in the gloom. He glared at his wife until she withdrew.

"Satellite's in place," Kinch said.

"You should not come here." A wail from the back of the house. Kinch's noise had awakened the baby. Taguchi, head down in shame for her intrusion, shuffled through the den to the hall.

"Oh, jeez," Kinch said with drunken sorrow. "Baby's screaming. I hate when that happens."

Hiroshi hissed in an exasperated breath. "It is dangerous for us both that you come here."

Kinch's eyes cut to his, and he realized with a start that the American was stone-cold sober. "*Tora, tora*, Hirohito," he whispered. "The nigger cunt's going down."

Hiroshi's mouth went dry. He pried his cramped finger from the trigger.

Kinch nodded toward the hall, cocky-drunk again. "Hey. Sweet dreams and everything. Sorry I woke the kid." He left, closing the door with a bang behind him.

Taguchi came in, holding the baby. "Is everything all right?" she asked.

He didn't dare look at her. "I will buy plane tickets for you and the baby tomorrow. You will visit your sister in Osaka."

"When will I come back?"

"I don't know." The gun felt heavy and useless in his pocket. War was coming. There would not be one target, but a hundred and fifty million. And the Americans would make a mess of it.

Something soft pressed down on her mouth, her nose. It shut off her air. Dolores woke, flailing. The bedroom was empty. The clock shone a bilious green 1:35 A.M.

Heartbeat booming in her ears, she rose, shivering in the dry high-altitude chill. She felt for the cheap homemade alarm she had placed by the door. With both hands, she picked the Coke can up and set it aside, her palms softening the clink of the nuts and bolts inside. She crept downstairs.

The guest room door was ajar, she saw to her surprise. The inside was dark but for a sliver of light that angled from the floodlamp outside the window. It glinted against the aluminum walker, the oxygen bottle. A form sprawled across the bed where Harry had died. The glow illuminated a trouser cuff, a single herringbone sock.

Quietly she took a blanket from the armoire and tucked it around him. Even more quietly she took the suitcase and camera bag from the room and carried them into the kitchen. She shut the door and turned on the light.

She searched the outside of the suitcase for simple traps: a hairthin wire, a telltale thread. Nothing. The snaps of the latches were loud as twin gunshots. Dolores froze, alert. The night was so silent she could hear the creak of the lemon tree in the wind.

Pants. Jockey shorts. Shirts fresh-folded from an American laundry. She gently squeezed the rolls of socks. Shook his can of shaving cream. Peered through his amber bottle of Aramis, opened the cap, and sniffed the liquid. She was careful to return everything to its place.

She ran her fingers through his pockets. Searched by touch for hidden compartments. Unzipped the camera bag. Opened the back of his Canon AE1.

Her thighs ached from crouching. Grasping the edge of the kitchen counter, she pulled herself stiffly to her feet.

Maybe they were cleverer than she thought. Maybe Roger was trained in hands-on wet work. She was getting old, and it wouldn't take much: a karate chop to the back of the neck, strangulation. Smothering.

That's right. She'd had the dream again: Harry, holding a pillow to her face. She lifted the receiver from the wall phone and dialed.

"Palácio da Alvorada," a voice answered.

"President Bonfim."

"The president is asleep and cannot be disturbed. May I ask who is calling?"

Dolores looked at the black square that was the kitchen window. Snow, she thought she remembered, always made the nights bright. "A friend. Give her a message, will you? Tell her she's wrong. Tell her I don't miss him at all. Ask if she spoke from experience." A pause, then. "Can you remember all that?"

"I'll tell her." There was a click, and the hum of an empty line.

Dolores replaced the items in Roger's suitcase the exact way he had packed them. The spy game honed short-term memory. It was in long-term memory that she failed. Ice storms. Leafless twigs dipped in glass. If she closed her eyes she could hear the sound-stage quality of snapping branches, like walking through a winter war movie.

The phone rang. Dolores lunged for the receiver before it could ring again. "Hello?"

That familiar sleepy voice, a burble of laughter in it. "You lie, you bitch. I know you too well."

Dolores sat cross-legged on the floor, her back against the cabinet, and pulled her robe about her knees. "If you loved me, you'd make it snow."

"It's snowing now. Go to the window and look. The Germans brought it with them. I think, *querida*, that I made a mistake."

Dolores twisted the phone cord around her fingers till it cut off circulation. She held onto it for dear life. "It'll be all right, Ana, I promise. You don't have to tell them everything."

"Too late. It's snowing already."

"No, listen! They just want some assurances. Throw them a bone. A little bone. Something to chew on, something to keep them . . ."

"Did you kill Harry?"

. . . to keep them away from me.

The tick of the clock on the kitchen wall. The slow dirge of a dripping faucet. "I didn't need to kill him."

And a single soft noise. A chuckle? "You lie. You hated him, and couldn't leave him. You didn't have the courage. I speak from experience," she said.

"Staying with someone because they're helpless is one thing. Clinging to someone because you can't live alone, Ana—that's different."

"Clinging. Do you think that's how Jaje feels?"

"I didn't mean . . ."

A sigh. "I saw snow once. The nice thing about it—it eventually covers everything."

"Ana . . ."

"Go to bed," she said, and hung up.

When Dolores walked out of the kitchen, the suitcase and camera bag in hand, she saw Roger standing in the darkened dining room.

"I can take the bags from here. They're pretty heavy."

She put them on the floor and started up the stairs. He called after her. "I'm sorry they dropped me on you like this. Without warning and everything, I mean."

"Not your fault."

"I met a guy at Camp Pearcy who knew you. He said you killed somebody once."

She halted, her palm on the cold metal of the bannister, her fingers clenched.

"He said you did it against Company orders." He stood in the rectangular glow from the kitchen, his expression innocent.

She forced her cramped fingers to relax. Took a breath. "A tire blew. That was all."

"They told me you put something in that tire. Were they lying?"

"Everybody lies, all the time. They tell us assassination is never authorized; then they teach us wet work."

"Hey. Not me, okay?" He spread his hand over his chest as if she had shot him in the heart. "Six weeks ago I didn't even know what 'wet work' meant. I was at Pearcy for two days—two big deal days—and it rained the whole time. I just came to Brazil because I'm curious about the UFOs. I'm from fucking NASA, Dee."

But an innocent would have been irked at the invasion of his privacy. A poorly trained spy would have asked what she had found.

"See you in the morning," she said.

Without another word, Roger carried his bags back to the guest room. He was a good Company man.

Crossfire

. . . just because I treat Bonfim like any other politician—

Really, Bob? You criticize Newt Gingrich's hairdo?

Can I please make this one point? And just because Bonfim's a woman—a black woman—all of a sudden I'm a sexist and a racist. Well, that's politics. She knew how the game worked before she got in it. And if you can't stand the heat . . . Besides, Bonfim went to Palmer Bank for her campaign money, Martha. Palmer Bank. You remember Palmer Bank? The CIA? The Contras? Sort of tarnishes her liberal, feminist halo.

Give me proof.

When are you going to admit this is no saint we're talking about? She puts tanks around Congress. She halts Brazil's democracy in its tracks. Her goons are snatching people off the streets. If a conservative did that—

There go the innuendos.

Talk to the Brazilian students, then. Hear why they're protesting. Gee. And I thought you were fond of the 60's. Which is more important to you: feminism or freedom?

I don't see Brazilians sleeping on the streets.

Which means?

Which means I don't see Brazilians sleeping on the streets. I don't see Brazilians beating their wives anymore.

Are you saying tyranny is acceptable?

I don't know, Bob. What are you saying is acceptable?

5

THE SÃO PAULO AGENT—EDSON COULDN'T REMEMBER HIS NAME—
leaned across the car seat to put that morning's *Folha* into his lap.
"This story here," he said.

Four column inches below the fold on page eight. No byline.
Palmer National Bank Contributed to Bonfim's 1987 Campaign.

Edson put the newspaper on the velour and opened the window. The alley of Butantã Reptile Institute was dank, red brick
walls to either side pied green with mold. Silent, of course.
Snakes were silent. But still, it smelled like a zoo. "I want monkeys."

"Sir?"

"And tigers. And birds. Birds make a lot of noise. They feed the
snakes mice, I suppose. Mice don't make noise, either."

Endless brick buildings, sun-dappled by overhanging trees.
Near the eaves, long barred windows. A calm morning in
Auschwitz. Were they afraid the snakes would escape? Or robbers
would try to get in?

"What do you think about the story, sir?"

Dr. Lizette Andrade de Morais, who studied snakes. Edson

hoped she wasn't pretty. Wasn't young. It was harder when they were young.

He felt light-headed, as if the car was still moving. That flight from Brasília—what did the Americans call it? Oh, yes. A red-eye.

"I think that no one has the experience of the Americans when it comes to managing political scandal," Edson said. "I think that in a few days we'll see the story move from four inches on page eight to sixteen inches on page one. Find out who the reporter is."

The São Paulo agent, really just a boy, nodded. "We'll contain it."

Ana had committed the unforgivable sin. Jealousy had been loosed from the deep—no one could contain it. Edson closed his eyes. When he opened them, he saw Muller coming, a woman in tow. Young. Dark cascades of curls. Nice legs. A shame.

"Where's Donato?" she asked when Muller opened the car door.

"We're taking you to him." Muller firmly helped her inside.

She turned around in her seat to look at Edson. "Where's Donato?"

Muller got behind the wheel. There was a quiet, well-oiled slam from the Volvo's door.

"In Brasília. Is Donato your boyfriend?" Edson asked.

"No." She whipped her head to Muller. The car drove down the alley, picking up speed. "Yes. Brasília? Who are you?"

"Friends of Donato," Edson said.

She stiffened as the Volvo left the gates and turned into the morning traffic. "Is he in some sort of trouble?" Her voice was reedy, her movements agitated. Angry? She would cause a scene at the airport. Or hysterical? She might try to jump from the car.

"Are you gangsters?" she demanded. "Is that what you are?"

The São Paulo boy laughed.

"Donato was injured," Edson said.

Her coffee eyes widened.

"Don't worry. He was just a little injured, working on a government project. He asked for you. We thought we would take you to him."

"He never told me about a government project."

"Of course not." Edson winked. "It's a secret."

*   *   *

Too dull. The new painting should look brooding, but it simply looked dull. Gray. More gray. Dead leaf brown. Colors she barely remembered. Was that the truth about winter?

A sound from the living room. Roger was up, studying the photos on her walls. Finally he wandered into the studio.

"Morning." In one fist was a coffee mug, in the other a Coke. He tossed the can to her. A poor throw, but she caught it left-handed. The can was empty. No rattle of bolts. So it wasn't the one from her room.

"I thought you might want to read the message."

She crushed the can, top to bottom. "You're kidding, right?" When he didn't answer, she threw it back hard. "I told you: I know what it says."

Roger didn't make a move to catch it. The can hit the plaster with a sharp clank. "Great arm. You don't throw like a girl. I was noticing the pictures . . ." He tipped his head toward the living room. "Hiking through the jungle. Boating down the Amazon. Was that the Andes you were climbing?"

"In Bolivia. A long time ago."

"Hey. You were a good-looking chick."

"Up yours, Roger," she said tiredly. She jabbed a paintbrush in his direction. "You know the problem with men? They have tunnel vision. It comes from looking at everything through their dicks."

"Oh. Oh, hey, I didn't . . . I mean, well? You have that great bone structure, you know? They say you never lose the cheekbones." He grimaced charmingly. "Have I dug myself out yet?"

"A little bitty hole, Roger. The penis has this little bitty hole. The Amazon jungle. The Andes. And all it lets you see is a good-looking chick in khakis. You have a girlfriend?"

Red-faced now, he shot back, "No. Do you?"

She felt her own face go hot. So, back at the Company, the rumors about her and Ana were still flying. Roger, hands in his pockets, was studying her sculpture as if gauging how much strength it might have taken to lift the blocks of peroba wood and the granite to their perches.

"I was never very good at it," she said.

His eyes met hers. He hadn't been thinking of sculpture at all, but of relationships.

She laughed. "Jesus. Let's call a cease-fire."

He sat on a paint-splattered stool. She liked the careless, childish way he plunked himself down, neglecting to check if the paint was wet. Roger would be interesting to draw: his face a simple circle, with complex intelligent eyes.

He said, "The bus comes every hour, right? I'm supposed to meet with the embassy people today. What do you want me to tell them?"

She squeezed crimson onto the palette and brushed it, a swatch of bloody anger, down the right side of the canvas.

"Oh, come on, Dee. It's not a big deal. They just want you to talk to her. That's all they want."

Her hand twitched, an involuntary muscle spasm, as if somewhere a puppeteer had jerked a string. Funny. She thought when Harry died, she'd be free.

"They'll have to bring me home afterwards," she said.

"What?"

"Safe passage out of Brazil. And I'll need a house, a nice one on a few acres near Richmond. A million in the bank. No, two million. You tell them that's my price."

*   *   *

Hiroshi bent into a forty-five-degree bow, hands on his knees. "Tell Tokyo that I am to blame. I relied too much on CIA information."

Ambassador Mitsuyo waved the apology away. "Ah, Hiroshi. This is understandable. You have not been trained in political espionage. Join us."

Kasahara kept his gaze tactfully lowered. But the eyes of Kengo Fujita, the head of covert operations, followed Hiroshi as he walked to the opposite end of the table and sat.

Kengo said, "My contacts indicate that Brazilian resistance to partnerships may be softening. Perhaps we can invite them to enter the downscaled fusion project with us. Nissan is willing."

Hiroshi stiffened. How long had Kengo been double-checking his work? And who had misled the man?

A cough as Kasahara drew attention away from his beleagered protege. "Yes. But to take away the need for petroleum would mean breaking the back of the American economy."

The ambassador grunted. "If things go on as they are, that is destined to happen, anyway. This antigravity already makes Nissan's fusion prototype obsolete. We should offer ourselves as partners for the new technology before the Americans do."

Hiroshi felt sweat bead his upper lip and fought the urge to wipe it away.

"An excellent idea," Kasahara agreed. "Still, I wonder at the fear I saw yesterday in the Germans' faces."

Kengo laughed. "My contacts tell me that the astronauts landed, this time without news coverage. The satellite has begun transmission. The Germans got what they wanted, and cheaply. Still, what is it the Americans say? A tiger by the tail?"

"Yes. A tiger by the tail. We must never forget that." Hiroshi met Kengo's glare. "The CIA created Ana Maria Bonfim. Now they can no longer control her."

Ambassador Mitsuyo pulled a Winston from a crumpled pack.

Hiroshi said, "The Americans will overreact and topple the government."

"The technology will be lost." Kasahara's voice was soft, his words measured. He shot Hiroshi a cautionary glance.

The ambassador took smoke deep into his lungs, let it out in a sigh. Kasahara folded his hands over his belly. Following his mentor's lead, Hiroshi sat back. They waited for someone, anyone, to speak.

It was Kengo Fujita who broke the silence. "The Americans are vital trade partners."

Mitsuyo ground his cigarette out in the ashtray. "And we know them better than the Brazilians. We can predict their actions."

Hiroshi nearly came out of his seat. "But we also know their failings." They looked surprised. Had he protested too vehemently? He struggled to control himself, but the words had been pent for too long. "Because the CIA has forgotten tradecraft, the Americans will be forced to bring in troops. In the meantime, the CIA ignores the important question: Why are Brazilians disappearing? Why kidnap professors of French, and herpetologists, and housewives? It does not make sense. The Americans watch with their satellites and listen from a distance. They are deaf and blind."

A strained silence, then Kengo's "Best to play both sides."

"Safer," Toyoko Chiharu agreed.

"I . . ." Hiroshi began, but stopped himself. The other four men were nodding, one big happy family.

Accepting the consensus, Ambassador Mitsuyo got to his feet. Once more Kasahara had yielded to group pressure. Once again the agreement was to do nothing. Hiroshi stood and bowed.

He could not meet Mitsuyo's or Kasahara's eyes. Duty demanded obedience. Survival demanded more. He must work alone now, no matter how the prospect terrified him—and knowing full well that the nail which sticks up is hammered down.

White House Press Conference

. . . *true that the president has spoken today with the other G-7 members, including Germany?*

Yes, but I have not been informed as to what was said. Brett?

What about the link between Palmer Bank and Bonfim?

Uh. We're looking into that, uh, what connection the Reagan Administration might have had. You'll be briefed as soon as I am, I promise. Yes? No. I'm pointing to Joan.

Thank you, Dan. What about that leak from NASA about radioactivity being detected at the Brazilian launch site? Is the radioactivity connected with the new propulsion system?

That, or a secondary payload. Next?

Secondary payload? Something other than the German communications satellite?

Ah, possibly.

A secret military payload?

I would have no more information on that. Next? Hugh?

Thank you, Dan. As to the American naval presence suddenly building off the coast of Rio . . .

Naval exercises.

Isn't it in response to the radioactivity that was found?

Um. My information has it that the exercises have been planned for some time. That's all I know. You, uh, Donald?

6

THE MERCEDES HANDLED THE MOUNTAIN DIRT ROAD ADROITLY BUT, Edson imagined, with a touch of stoicism. He put his hand over the doctor's small red-nailed one. As expected, she stiffened when she saw the sign over Cabeceiras's unimposing gates: QUARANTINE—ANTHRAX. ENTRY STRICTLY FORBIDDEN.

"Nothing to worry about. Just a cover. Have a Guaraná." He took the soft drink from the limo's refrigerator, watched carefully as she drank.

Past the gates. Cowless fields to either side, the complex so far away, its profile so low, that it couldn't yet be seen.

"You were telling me about the coral snake?"

"It's passive." Her voice was tight.

"Yes? And?"

"They bite only when they're hurt. Friendly, really. You can play with them."

They topped a rise. Ahead, a cluster of buildings.

Her knuckles paled against the bottle. "Where are you taking me? I thought Donato would be in a hospital."

"He wasn't hurt badly. You're very brave," he said, "to play with snakes."

44

"I hear rumors. People disappear. Nothing ever heard from them again. One day they're there, and—"

"All working on the project. Dangerous, isn't it, to play with snakes?"

"No. The corals, they have tiny mouths. Tiny teeth, for killing small animals. Between the toes or the fingers, that's where they pierce the skin. They have to chew very hard. It's not easy for them to kill a human." A mad rush of words. Frightened already. She knew something was wrong. "They don't mean to bite. Not their fault. But people step on them." She turned to meet his gaze. Her eyes were wide, but already sleepy. He took the half-empty bottle and set it aside.

"Corals. They're beautiful."

"Yes." An intake of breath. "Listen. I don't know anything."

The car stopped. She took in the blank wall. The parking lot. Muller got out of the front seat and opened the passenger door. She clutched Edson's hand so hard that her nails dug into his flesh; an accidental bite.

"Come," Edson said, and helped her out.

The three of them walked into the building and down a long faceless hall.

"Where is Donato?"

Edson hooked her arm, drew her close, and said, "I have lied to you a little."

He felt her knees weaken, saw her eyes glaze. Fear? Or the sedative?

At the end of the hall, soldiers. She saw the guns and made a sound deep in her throat. Muller grabbed her other arm before she could bolt.

"I don't know anything," she said.

The soldiers swung open a door. Edson walked faster, so she would have less time to think. Beyond the entrance lay an echoing hangar, and the small steel chamber that two years ago Freitas had ordered built.

"Donato isn't hurt. Not at all. He's inside, in the chamber, wait-ing."

Her voice rose. "No. Tell him to come here. Tell him to come talk to me."

"He says you have to go in."

"But I don't know anything!"

Light spilled into the tiny chamber, across the floor, and bent toward a pencil point at the center. The interior stretched to a dim otherworldly infinity.

Her legs gave out. Muller put his arm around her waist. He was whispering into her ear in a fast, cajoling voice.

"Donato says he has something to show you," Edson told her. "I've heard it's wonderful."

Her eyes were starting to close. She whipped her head back and forth. Her breath went in and out in sucking sounds, like sobs. She fought desperately, but without coordination.

Edson didn't want to watch another one. "Wait until she's nearly asleep. Don't hurt her," he ordered, and walked from the hangar.

There was no air-conditioning in the embassy's sound-hardened room. Three people in it, and the atmosphere was stifling. Smooth white walls, overly smooth. To make it more bearable, perhaps, someone had furnished it with two overstuffed chairs and a sofa.

"So I wake up when the phone rings . . ."

"Who called?" The major's question, his words as hard and fast as bullets.

"I don't know. Anyway, I walk out and she's got my luggage. She went through my goddamned luggage. And then this morning she starts in with the male-bashing. A weird chick," Roger said in summation. "She scares me."

Kinch, the tall guy with the dork haircut and glasses, laughed. Roger wanted to slap the shit out of him.

"Come on, guys. She as much as admitted to me that she kills people."

McNatt sat even straighter, a hundred and ten percent Semper Fi. "As they informed you at Langley, Dr. Lintenberg: Dolores Sims is not reliable."

"In other words, Roger, don't believe a thing the bitch says." It was obvious Kinch thought he was cool. What ruined his image was that doofus grin and that nerdy way of adjusting his glasses. "She might be playing doubles."

Nudge nudge. Wink wink. Kinch leered at McNatt, who, Roger noted, did not smile back.

"No reason to be afraid of her, Dr. Lintenberg. Dolores Sims is just your ordinary, run-of-the-mill dyke."

Roger snorted. "Not politically correct, Major McNatt, seeing as how you're just a nigger."

McNatt started to his feet.

Kinch put a warning hand on his shoulder. "We're all on the same team here, aren't we? Let's just put the ball in play."

Roger slumped into his chair. "I want to see the UFOs. I thought that's why I was sent here. That's what I'm an expert on. Not this spy shit." The spooks scared him, like Dolores Sims scared him. Working with spies was like using a computer after someone took a couple of bytes out of its operating system.

Kinch said, "Real soon, Roger. We'll get you out to Cabeceiras real soon."

"For now, you will put the transmitters in her purse, in her billfold, in whatever you deem essential," McNatt said.

"Yeah. Okay."

"And you are not to be seen doing so," he added.

"Yeah. Right. And am I supposed to deliver the two mil, too?"

"Best to forget you ever heard that." Kinch warned amiably. He elbowed McNatt. The major didn't change expression.

"Yeah?" Roger asked. "That's a shitload of money. What'd she mean, 'safe passage out of Brazil'?"

Kinch shook with silent laughter. McNatt sat back, his shoulders relaxing.

"No. You guys . . . You're fucking with me here. You and Dee. Everybody's fucking with me. All this 'wet work' crap and everything. 'Cause—crazy, right?—but what it sounds like to me is she's supposed to, you know, off the president."

"Oh, Dr. Lintenberg." A twinkle came into the major's eyes. He didn't look like a recruitment poster anymore, but a ten-year-old kid who'd just put one over on his teacher. "There are laws against that."

The waiting room was empty except for José Carlos, who sat cross-legged on the tile floor, somberly playing with a radio-controlled car.

The boy looked up when Edson walked in. The car, unsupervised, ran into a chair leg and stopped. "Where's *pai*?"

"Have you had lunch?"

He nodded, a lock of dark hair spilling into his eyes.

"Well, then. Have you had chocolate?"

The eyes widened in anticipation.

Edson opened the door and caught the attention of the agent on guard. "Get chocolate," he said. "Lots of it. The president's Belgian chocolate, not the Brazilian crap."

"Sir," the guard said, nodding.

To the agent's retreating back, he called, "And her Chivas Regal."

Edson sat beside José Carlos and watched him deftly back the car away from the chair leg. "You ever had Belgian chocolates? No? Ever have Chivas Regal? That's a pretty car."

"A Corvette."

"Americans build pretty cars that go very fast for a very short while. Tell me about your mother."

He didn't look up from the controls.

"Is your mother pretty? Is she sweet? My mother wasn't pretty, but I think sweet is better, anyway. My mother sewed all my clothes. She made me *canja* and rice pudding when I was sick."

"*Mãe* fell down."

"Oh?"

"Uh-huh. *Mamãe* fell down and hurt herself. And *pai* couldn't fix her anymore."

The agent came in, toting a silver tray with the Chivas and chocolates. When the agent left, Edson poured himself a drink. "Eat the chocolates. That is an order."

He looked over. José Carlos was crying, and wiping his face with his sleeve.

"How fast does your car go?"

Another shrug, sullen this time.

Edson drained the glass. Lead crystal. The presidential seal etched on its side. He took a mouthful of Chivas from the bottle, leaned over, and put the empty glass on the car's hood. "Now," he said. "Let's see how fast. Back it up so you get some speed. Aim for the wall."

"It will break."

"Sometimes men must break things, even when they don't wish to." He handed the bottle to the boy. "Take a drink. Go on. It makes it easier. You can play with coral snakes, José Carlinho. Did you know that? I don't suggest you should do so. It takes an expert."

"*Pai* broke *mãe,* but he didn't mean to, either. I guess he had to, then." José Carlos lowered the bottle and stared at the car. "I don't like the thing that lives in *pai.* It hurts me. The doctor used to come in before him, and he spoke funny, and I liked him. I think sweet is better, too. Doctor Singh would leave *pai* after the patients were over, and when *pai* was *pai* again, he would read me funny stories. He would take me to the *venda* and buy me an ice cream." A tear slid his cheek.

"Say 'fuck you.' "

José Carlos turned, shocked.

"That is what men say to life when nothing can be done. Fuck you. Never say it in front of a lady. Now. Break the glass."

The boy bent over the controls. The car rushed toward the far
wall. When it hit the plaster, it flipped. The glass arced up, tumbled down, exploded into a glistening spray of shards. José Carlos
squealed.

A drowsy contralto from behind: "Boys' games."

Edson didn't turn. "Fuck you, Ana Maria. What would you
know of it?"

The tap-tap of high heels. A slower man's tread. Edson saw José
Carlos look up, saw the boy's face change.

"Zé Carlos," Edson said. "Take your car and go out into the hall.
Take the chocolates, too. Ask the guard outside for another glass.
A dozen of them."

A good boy. He got up and quietly left the room.

"Dr. Lizette loved snakes," Edson said.

"I don't want to know."

"*Santa* Ana, patron of the vanished. You never do."

"You look ridiculous on the floor, Edson."

Edson lifted his head. Freitas was watching him, and behind the
channeler's human eyes Edson could sense . . .

"She loves snakes," Freitas agreed.

"What do you do with them? Where are they, really?" Edson
asked. "Are they dead, like your wife?"

"They love being with us." The man bent, picked up a piece of
broken crystal, and studied it. A line of blood ran down his finger.
"They never want to leave."

Suddenly Freitas hunkered beside him, hands cupped on his
knees. One palm was full of blood. "They have bright colors in
bands, and small mouths, and tiny teeth. She loves being with us,
you see? We make it so pleasant, they all love it there." The dark
eyes met his. "I could show you things."

Edson started to get up, but Freitas caught his wrist. His blood
trickled down Edson's arm. Hot, damp lips brushed Edson's ear.
"You're not such a bad man."

A yank, and Edson was free. He clambered, stumbling, to his feet.

Ana was regarding him, her eyes narrowed. "I've ordered Jaje moved to the Petrópolis house," she said. "They were demonstrating at the universities."

Freitas remained squatted, watching his own blood drip. Edson took out his handkerchief and daubed at his cuff until the hankerchief was stained red.

"Edson? Are you listening? I had to pull my little girl out of class so she wouldn't hear me called a murderess. You promised me you would take care of everything." Her voice was sharp and high-pitched. Not at all like Ana.

Edson forgot his disgust. Suddenly he was aware of how tiny Ana was, as if he was seeing her for the first time without the aid of a telescope. And it scared him. "No, Ana. I never promised you that."

Roger was waiting for the bus when he felt a hand grab his elbow. He turned. A fiftyish black man in a blue knit shirt, with a duffel bag over his shoulder.

Velvet baritone and American English. "Don't look." Friendly chestnut brown face, and a muscular fireplug of a body. "The next bus. Get on."

JARDIM ZOOLÓGICO, the sign on the bus read.

"But I'm not—"

The man hissed, "Just do it."

They boarded. Roger took a seat near the front. The man passed him, and sat next to a woman with a straw basket. He didn't look Roger's way.

Roger considered getting off at the next stop, but the bus had turned down a broad avenue and picked up speed. Soon he was lost.

When they arrived at the zoo, the man exited with a group of schoolchildren. Roger followed. He bought his ticket and went through the gates. The children were clustering around the concession stand. The black man in the blue shirt was gone.

A nearby peacock gave him a sharp black stare. Hands in his pockets, Roger walked on. Except for the animals, the park was empty. The bears slept indolently in the midday heat. A lion, belly to the concrete floor of his cage, lifted his head off his paws as Roger passed. A band of monkeys hooted and screamed and chased each other across a rocky island.

Someone bumped his back. A mumbled, *"Desculpe."*

Roger flinched. The man in the blue shirt was regarding him. *"Você é estrangiero, não é? Americano?"* he asked so fast that Roger's confusion and Berlitz Portuguese left him mute.

"Alemão? Inglês?"

"Americano."

"No shit. I'm an American, too." The man's smile was irresistible.

Roger found himself smiling back.

"I love watching the monkeys." The man propped his elbows on the steel bar and looked across the moat to monkey island. "Look at that guy. Look at him run."

A trio of monkeys was chasing a fourth. The three were screaming murderously.

"There's a gun in the duffel. Play it casual."

Roger's grin failed.

"Hey, you like penguins?" Challenging dark eyes met his.

He swallowed hard. "Love penguins."

"Come on," the man said.

They walked the sun-dappled path side by side.

"What's your name?" the man asked conversationally.

"Roger."

"I'm Jack. Jack Jackson, actually. Youngest of eight children, born just as my mom surrendered to tubal ligation and redundancy. Glad to meet you, Roger." He was occupied with his duffel bag, and didn't offer to shake hands. "What do you do?"

They passed the cheetahs. Roger looked at them for help, for clues. "When?"

Jack's laugh, too, was engaging. "You know. For a living, I mean."

"I'm with NASA."

"Must be interesting. I'm a librarian."

"A librarian?"

"Uh-huh. With the American library. Pretty boring stuff. I taught at Arizona State until the wife left me. Did the middle-age crazy. Lost myself. Found myself again. Found my lady. You?"

Roger glanced at him uneasily. "What?"

"Got somebody waiting for you at home?"

"Uh, not yet."

"I tell you, Roger. It's worth waiting for. I didn't marry until I was thirty. Now I can't imagine a life without. A lady makes things home. Upper midwest?"

"Excuse me?"

"Your accent. I'm kind of a linguistics nut. I'm originally from south central L.A., although Columbia muddled my homeboy idiom. Columbia University, that is."

"Nice place, south central L.A."

Jack looked at him.

"Nice place, Columbia University."

"So. Roger. You're from the upper midwest, right?"

"Minnesota."

"Oh," Jack said, nodding. "Then you'll like this."

The inside of the penguin building was dark and cool and empty. A shove. Roger stumbled forward, hands outspread. He caught himself against the glass. Penguins peered at him in mild interest.

Jack's voice wasn't conversational anymore. "Don't turn around. Who are you?"

The glass was chill against his cheek. "I'm Roger Lintenberg. I'm with NASA."

A hand patted his jacket, rummaged in his jean pockets. Took out his passport, his wallet. Slid down his pants legs. Disconcertingly ran up the inseam. "Hey! Hey!"

Cold metal pressed the back of his ear. "Don't move."

Roger gritted his teeth as strong fingers probed his genitals. Suddenly Jack stood away. "Unzip your pants."

"What? What did you—"

"Unzip your pants."

Roger's zipper stuck halfway down. He tugged at it frantically. Giggles and chatter from the far doorway. The schoolchildren. Roger froze, imagining small corpses on bloody concrete, the mute witness of penguins. But Jack's gun was back in the bag. Confused, Roger stood, hand gripping his fly.

A little girl pointed. "Is that man going *xi-xi*?" And the chaperon, in a fluster, hurried them out.

When they were gone, Jack laughed and shook his head. Then he gave Roger back his passport and wallet. He lifted a red plastic bag. "See what I found in your pocket? Small round things. Feels like . . ."

"Transmitters."

"I thought so. Did you know that silencers don't make a lot of noise? Hence the name. Did you know that if you shoot someone in the heart, they don't bleed much? I like that shirt, Roger."

Roger looked down at his maroon shirt anxiously. "Please. Come on. I don't know anything."

"What are you doing with these transmitters?"

"The CIA gave them to me."

Jack sighed. "May we get right to the point? We don't have much time."

"I'm getting to the point. Really. Gimme a hint."

Jack took the gun from the duffel. Long barrel. Silencer. The gun took forever to emerge. "Who were you sent to kill?"

"Oh, no. Aw, Jesus. Please don't." Roger's stomach tightened when the muzzle touched it. He went tiptoe and squeezed his eyes shut. "Please. I'm a member of MUFON, the Mutual UFO Network. About a year ago I started leaking some NASA information:

video clips, photos. The CIA found out. Threatened to tell my boss if I didn't do a little UFO investigating for them in Brazil. I didn't want to be fired. That's all. Swear to God. But . . ."

"But?"

"If you're with the Americans, didn't they say?"

The gun pressed harder.

"Okay, okay, okay. They want me to be a go-between for that painter, too. You looking for a hit man . . . uh, person? Well, it's her. It's Dolores Sims."

The gun went away. Roger opened his eyes a slit. The barrel was still aimed at Roger's belly. "Who was the asshole who told you that?"

"She was. I mean, she told me. No. No! Don't shoot! Don't shoot, okay? Just—oh, please—can't we chill here?"

"You're shitting me, son. Don't shit me."

"Wait. See? She told me to tell the CIA that she wanted two million dollars. And then . . . lemme get it straight. Uh, McNatt and that dork from Raytheon . . . Oh, right. I don't know if this is important, but they said she was a dyke—"

The pistol barrel punched a neat round bruise in his belly. Pain took his breath away.

"Ow. Hey. I'm just telling you what they said. And then they said she killed somebody once. But she seemed okay to me. I kinda like her, lesbian or not. Personally I don't have anything against, you know . . . In fact, some of my best—"

"Stupid-ass white boy. You don't know dick." Jack put the gun in the bag and walked out.

Roger could breathe again. He slid to the raw, stained concrete, among the gum wads and candy wrappers. Above his left shoulder birds in formal dress paraded, flapping their flightless wings.

By the White House Helipad

Mr. President! Mr. President!

Nice tie, Kurt. Hi, Joan.

Mr. President, is it true that you're on your way to meet with members of the U.N. Security Council?

What? Sorry. The rotors . . .

Mr. President! Please, Mr. President! Won't you . . . thanks.

Only a minute. Hey, Freddie. How's the golf game? We filming? Okay. I'll have some news for you very soon concerning Palmer Bank. President Bonfim was involved, and I believe CIA employees have overstepped their bounds. I'm ordering the CIA to turn over all files to Congress—we'll be working very closely on this, uh, Congress and the White House, to get to the truth. Probably a hearing's in order. I'm sure there'll be indictments.

And the radioactivity reported, sir?

Well, that one's a no comment.

Are you—sir. Sir! Mr. President! Nothing at all?

Okay. I will say this: I will do everything in my power, and that means everything, to preserve the safety and well-being of the American people. Thank you.

Does that include possible military action, sir?

Mr. President!

Mr. President! Does that include war, sir?

7

A SHORT TWO-HOUR BUS TRIP NORTH FROM FLORIANÓPOLIS AND YOU WILL arrive in Blumenau, the jewel of the Itajaí Valley, famous for its porcelain, towels, and crystal . . .

Hiroshi put the guidebook in his pocket and opened the door. A bell chimed overhead. The man behind the gift shop counter didn't look up.

Could he have guessed wrong? The storekeeper had a sweet, grandfatherly face. His gray head was bent over his work. Reading glasses were perched on the end of his nose. From behind the wooden barrier came a sporadic click-click. Cleaning a gun?

Ignored, Hiroshi wandered the aisles of expensive breakables. When he looked at the counter again, the man was looking back. His eyes were a disturbingly brilliant blue.

"Paraná?" the man asked. "São Paulo?"

"Sorry. I am from Japan."

The man returned to his work.

"The porcelain is very fine."

Gray eyebrows lifted in disbelief.

"Japan has fine porcelain, too. But not so many happy colors." Hiroshi approached the counter and, with a bow, presented his card. His heart sank. The man wasn't cleaning a gun. He was darning a sock.

The storekeeper dropped the card carelessly on the counter. He bent over and adjusted his glasses. "Yes, Mr. Shinobu, is it? What may I do for you?" Then he returned to his darning, the needle clicking on the marble egg.

"I am in the import business, as you can see."

The man nodded. "You will want directions to the factories."

"Yes, Mr. Piehl, that would be fine, but there are certain matters that only you, personally, can do for me."

Blink. That sudden. The blue eyes were focused on him again. The face was soft; but the fingers were strong and deft. Reinhard Piehl had killing hands.

"Japan is in dire need of imports. We seek other countries to work with. Countries which are in need, as ours is."

Piehl put down his darning, looked at a porcelain wall clock shaped like a passion flower. "I will be closing the shop in two hours. Why don't we meet for dinner?"

Before Hiroshi could respond, Piehl went on. "There is a restaurant, a quiet one. *Die Blaue Gans.* Or *Die Blaue Ente.* I forget which. When you leave, turn right. Seven blocks until you see the construction, and turn right again. Three blocks and you will come to a winding street. A half-block down, you'll see a small yellow building with a blue goose—maybe a blue duck?—painted on the side. You can't miss it."

"Six o'clock, then?"

"Six-thirty."

Hiroshi bowed, but the man was darning again.

Outside, the sun was bright, the air pungent with car exhaust. Hiroshi walked to a nearby cafe and sat down, wishing his mentor, Shuma Kasahara, was there. Yet that very loneliness made him feel heroic—like one of the masterless samurai. He opened his guidebook. No listing in the restaurant section for a *Die Blaue*

Gans or *Die Blaue Ente.* An out-of-the-way spot, then. A perfect and very romantic place for espionage.

A waiter approached who spoke such limited Portuguese that Hiroshi ordered by pointing to the bottles on a nearby table.

. . . founded by Dr. Hermann Blumenau in 1859 . . .

The waiter returned with a Brahma Chopp. Hiroshi nursed the beer and watched the front of the store.

. . . World War II. Laws were passed forbidding German to be taught, and even to be spoken . . .

At six o'clock a chubby middle-aged woman—Piehl's wife?— turned the OPEN sign to CLOSED. She walked back into the shadows, and didn't emerge. Neither did Piehl. A back door, then.

Hiroshi tossed money onto the table and hurried out. The construction, the only spot of dirt on the immaculate sidewalk, was five blocks down, not seven. He halted in confusion. Turn right, or walk the other two blocks?

He turned, and soon found himself in a residential area.

. . . traditional Alpine gingerbread houses set amid native tropical vegetation. Notice the boats in every garage which, before the dams . . .

Two blocks of garaged boats later, the street dead-ended at the river. Panicked, Hiroshi retraced his steps.

Six-fifteen already, and Piehl would not understand if he was late. At the construction, he stopped a blond-headed couple. "Pardon me." He bowed hurriedly. "I seem to be lost. I am looking for a winding street and a small yellow restaurant."

They smiled and shook their heads.

"Do you know of a small yellow restaurant? *Die Blaue* something?"

"*Blaue, ja?*" The woman looked to her husband for help.

"*Bitte? Ich spreche nicht,*" he said apologetically.

Hiroshi bowed. "Sorry. So sorry." And he rushed on. Ahead of him, emerging from a bank, was a pin-striped, round-faced burgher. "Excuse . . ."

The man shot him a look. Waved a hand. *"Nein, nein."* He strode purposefully down the sidewalk the opposite way.

Hiroshi looked around for help, but at early evening the mercantile section of Blumenau was nearly deserted. Time was running out. He quickly walked two blocks past the construction and turned right. Three blocks of gingerbread houses and palm trees, and he ended up at the river again.

No. It couldn't be. Had he lost count? He started back to the main thoroughfare, his thighs aching, his back dripping sweat.

There. Ahead. A pair of black men, strolling loose-limbed and graceful. Hiroshi trotted to them. "Please!"

They stopped. Turned.

"Please! So sorry to bother you!" He bowed.

After a confused pause they bowed, too.

"I am lost, you see. I am supposed to meet someone at six-thirty at a little restaurant and the town is unfamiliar." He glanced at his watch. Six-thirty-eight already. Could Piehl trust someone who couldn't follow directions? "It is a little yellow restaurant with a blue bird."

They shrugged helplessly. Looked at each other. *"Auslander,"* one said.

"Ich spreche nicht Portuguese," the other told Hiroshi.

The name of the restaurant came in a blinding gestalt. *"Die Blaue Gans? Die Blaue Ente?"*

"Die gans?" They smiled broadly. *"Ah, ja! Ganse."* Pointing now. Rapid spurts of German. One man took a notebook and pen from his pocket and scribbled a map.

One block. Turn right. Two blocks.

Map in his fist, Hiroshi ran. He ended up at the quiet riverbank. Tall grass to either side. A tumbledown boathouse. And a flock of geese.

"Raise your hands. Turn around."

Hiroshi did as he was told, dropping the map, slipping a bit in the mud. Piehl stood a few feet away. There was a lead pipe in his fist.

A deserted spot. A blunt instrument to make it look like robbery. The river to dump his corpse. And no one would guess the truth. Hiroshi knew that he had only himself to blame. The nail that sticks up is hammered down.

The man sat on a fallen log, panting for breath. "A good chase, that. It proves you don't know what you are doing. How did you find out who I was?"

Behind Hiroshi, the crackle of a shoe on dead leaves. He fought the urge to turn, struggled to keep his voice from shaking. "Indirect information only. From letters sent to England. About a girl from Santa Catarina that Vyacheslav Lavinski met. MI5 did not recognize the signficance in what was said in the letter. I did. I tracked you through your mother."

A hand slid around him, patted pockets, reached inside his jacket and brought out his passport. "Hiroshi Sato, Japanese embassy," a voice behind him said.

Piehl smiled. "Why would the British share the letters with you?"

"The letters had been declassified. I told them the truth: that my hobby was collecting spy stories. They had me fill out forms, and pay a small copying fee."

Two laughs: a baritone from Piehl, a tenor from the man behind.

Hiroshi's arms were beginning to ache. "An interesting man, your father. To be shipwrecked and live for weeks on what he could kill with his bare hands. To die in a plane he himself sabotaged. An explosion that also killed two suspected moles in the PZPR. That is how I knew he was working for the Soviets."

Piehl tipped his head to the side, inquiringly. "Maybe Papa hated Poles. Maybe he hated planes."

"Please hear me out. If I am right, Mr. Lavinski, there is not much time left. I believe President Bonfim has made a fatal mistake allowing the space launch to be televised. Americans are jealous, and they are heavy-handed. The CIA is asking all the wrong questions. I wish to find out why Brazilians are disappearing. I must solve this riddle first, in order to save the new technology."

Late sun slanted through the trees. From the river came the honking of geese.

Finally: "Why me?"

"Because your father was so good at his job that both the Americans and British dismissed him as a joke. And because the KGB is not hampered as the American CIA is with silly rules."

Piehl pulled pensively on his lower lip. "Japanese trust no one but Japanese. Are you working naked, Mr. Sato?"

"You will forgive my bluntness, but I think you are not completely under the umbrella of the KGB, either." Hiroshi relaxed and, at last, let his arms fall. "I believe, Mr. Lavinski, that your father did not die in that plane crash in 1960. I believe that he brought you into the business and taught you tradecraft. Now Russia lacks money, and Japan is fast becoming poor. Work with me. I promise you that both countries will benefit. And we will let America go begging."

"Interesting proposition." Piehl got to his feet. "I'll think about it."

"But . . ."

Someone walked past Hiroshi, bumping his shoulder. A lanky teenage boy carrying a machete. He looked back, grinning. His eyes were that same hot blue.

"By the way," Piehl said. "Some advice my father gave me in '82 just before he died: Do exactly what people expect, and you'll blend into the background. The guidebook is a nice touch, Mr. Sato, but Brazilians expect to see Japanese tourists with cameras."

Hiroshi felt his face stiffen into an automatic public mask. He bowed—more a brusque nod. The spy's son and grandson walked away together, leaving Hiroshi mired sole-deep in the mud.

*   *   *

Dolores tucked an edge of the fitted sheet in place only to watch the opposite corner pop loose again. She gave up and refilled her wine glass.

The squeak of a soft-soled shoe against tile brought her head up. She set the glass on the nightstand and, patting her sweater pockets, crept toward the living room. What had she done with her gun?

Only Roger. He stood by the sofa, looking worried. "Why'd you put my furniture on the front porch?"

"That's not your furniture. That's Harry's furniture. I'm getting rid of Harry, Roger. I'm exorcising Harry."

He ran a hand through his hair, leaving a lock of it standing on end. "Oh. Good. I thought . . . So where am I supposed to sleep?"

"Can't sleep. It's an exorcism party. Get yourself a glass and come on." She retreated into the guest room.

The corner of the sheet had pulled loose for the eighth time when Roger came in and looked around. He was holding the crushed Coke can. "Where'd this bed come from?"

"Storage."

"The room's all different. I *hate* this. I thought I'd come back to the house, relax a little . . ."

"The only way to get rid of the monster, Roge: redecorate his lair."

Somehow the sheet ended up as an amorphous lump in the center of the mattress. Dolores sat down to study the problem.

"I suppose you wrestled everything out on the porch by yourself. God. Macho shit. Just like that guy today at the zoo. You'll never believe—"

"No choice, Roge. The Spiritists told me they'd pick up everything tomorrow, but I wanted Harry out of my house. I wanted him out of my goddamned house."

He sighed, monumentally.

"Hey, Roger? You know what's strange? I was around thirty-five,

I think. Harry was almost forty. Just before he got sick. So . . . what was I saying?" She looked up. Roger had sat down on the over-stuffed chair she had brought in. He was still holding the Coke can, and he looked put out. She couldn't remember if she had checked the furniture for spiders. "Oh. Leaving Harry. That's what I was trying to do. And I was holding the car keys when he grabbed my hair with one hand and forced the key into a wall socket with the other. Direct current: one side nothing, the other 210 volts. Harry was surprised we lived. Asshole thought the socket wasn't working. Roger? You see what I'm talking about? Harry told everyone it was my career that stood in the way of us having kids. But it was him. You can understand why. Well? Can't you? Have you seen the evening news?"

Roger was staring.

She got to her feet, slapped the sheet on the mattress, yanked the corner down. When the opposite end gathered in a roll, tears sprang to her eyes. "I just want to make the goddamned bed! Is that too much to ask?"

"Okay. Okay. Don't get upset." Roger rose, fumbled with the other end of the sheet.

She tore it out of his hands. "I can do it myself!"

"Right. No harm, no foul." He held his palms out in capitulation.

"Why did I let him ruin my life? I hate leaving things unfinished. Let's dig Harry up. I need to kill him."

"Hey, I know! Let's have some coffee."

"No. Put the Coke can down. Get the shovel."

"Sure. Okay, we'll do that. But you gotta tell me the truth now, all right? Promise me, 'cause I'm on your side." He held the crushed can toward her, gingerly. "Just . . . okay? Just tell me what this means."

She flapped the sheet over the mattress. The elastic in the hem made the material ball, like a spider touched by a flame. "God. You're such an amateur. The Company puts a can at a drop to tell the field agent to call the office. Haven't you seen the news? The bank scandal? The demonstrations? I've been trying to call Jaje, but no one's answering. What's wrong with me?" She spread the top sheet and threw on the quilt. Not too bad. The bottom sheet was a lump in the center now, a poorly buried corpse. "Am I *that* neurotic?"

Roger sat in the chair and regarded the lumpy quilt.

"I'd lie about it, you know, Roger? I'd say, like, 'He needed me.' But half of me learned to blank out—divided the world into light and shadow, form and space, simple unemotional crap like that. And the other half believed I *couldn't* leave him, because he'd come after me in his walker, dragging his oxygen bottle. He was a monster, right? So you couldn't kill him. Not easily. I'd have to—I don't know—pour gasoline on him and set him on fire. Throw him in a tree shredder. Stake him. That's what I have to do: dig him up and stake him."

Roger looked morose. "Is that it? Call the office? That's all? What's the deal about the two million dollars?"

"Two . . ." She remembered. "Sorry." She sat down, patted his hand. "Life's just a cover story. That's my philosophy. Come on, don't pout. Have a glass of wine. Or two. Or eight. That always worked for Harry."

"God! Nothing is fucking *real* around this place! And to think I used to believe I was a cool undercover kinda guy: fixing the Xerox machine at NASA so it wouldn't count my copies, sneaking the stuff out of the office in my Jockeys. Then this morning you convince me we're rerunning '63 Dallas. Kinch and McNatt take a long lunch to jerk off my brain. And, oh yeah, this guy pulls a gun on me. A gun! At the zoo! And he groped me. A librarian. Let's see what's hiding here in the stacks—"

Adrenaline ice shot through her, tingled down her arms. She squeezed Roger's fingers together so hard he yelped. "The librarian—was he all right?"

"He's goddamned nuts. He told me to unzip my pants. We looked at penguins. I *hate* penguins."

"Shhhh!" An engine was purring up the drive. Roger cowered as a car door slammed.

"Probably just the Spiritists coming early." She went to the window and peered out. Men were stepping up on the porch, eyeing Harry's sickroom furniture. Three men, dressed like police officers.

"Roger." Before he could answer, she clapped a hand over his mouth. "You never saw that librarian."

An officious knock on the front door.

"Keep your head down. Don't let them know you're here." She released him. Pulling her cardigan tighter, she went to answer the knock.

All three men eyed her, then "Dolores Sims?" one of them asked.

"What do you want?"

"You are Dolores Sims?" He had dark curly hair, a swarthy complexion. Looked and acted Brazilian. Spoke in the fast-talking mumble of a Goiás native.

"Yes."

He hiked his gunbelt, stepped forward. "Come with us, please. You are under arrest."

CBS Evening News

I'm standing here in front of the science building at the University of São Paulo. As you can see, Dan, everything is quiet now. There on the steps just a sprinkling of lights—red candles—for the missing; but it was not so quiet earlier today when students clashed with police.

So far, President Bonfim's popularity has held among blacks and those of mixed race, and of course among women. That is the majority. According to recent polls, however, her popularity is swiftly eroding among the young, such as the students here behind me, and among the country's white population, located mostly in the south.

The consensus among Bonfim supporters seems to be that the space weaponry is an American fantasy; and that the missing Brazilians are somehow, too, our fault.

Well, Robert. I'm sure your interviews are met with resentment . . .

Not really, Dan. Brazilians are, above all, pragmatists. Even in the rural areas you get a sense of 'seen it, done it, and who cares?' No, Brazilians think America is naive and somewhat gauche.

Naive and what?

Gauche.

8

Ana Maria slapped the manila folder closed. Her tone was the one Edson had long ago learned to catalogue as fury. "Close the universities."

General Fernando Machado's frown made him resemble a congenial frog. He folded his arms over his girth and looked at Edson, who shrugged.

"Do it," she ordered.

Perhaps too many drinks for dinner. Perhaps only because it was three in the morning and Edson was exhausted—he came to the general's defense. "Don't overreact, Ana. That is what the Americans hope to force you into. They expect another Tiananmen Square."

Through the glass wall, Edson saw Freitas in the neighboring atrium. The man was looking out the window where the northern district of Brasília arced, the wing of a glowing albatross.

Ana made an irritated *tsk*. "I'm talking about a handful of soldiers. No violence. The students are the same age as my own daughter. Do you think I'm some sort of monster?"

Edson met her gaze. She rubbed her temples as if a headache plagued her, not guilt. He imagined the heft of the gun in his hand, the sound and the smell of the shots, the heavy-rain patter of blood against the polished table. Should he? Could he? Edson took a breath, and wondered how history would remember them.

"Don't let the CIA push you into doing something rash," he said. "If you send in soldiers to confront those students, I guarantee there will be more than unarmed Brazilians in the crowd. This is what the CIA does, Ana. They agitate. And no one is better at it. Now. Please. Let us not compound our mistake. It was stupid enough to cut the Americans out of the technology, but keeping people prisoner in the other universe is insane. Tell him to bring them back."

Her eyes darted to the atrium. "I've asked."

The way Freitas stood there, unmoving. Edson wanted to grab him by the shoulders and whirl him around, to see the look on his face. "Ask again."

She picked nervously at the folder. "If the Americans want to play games, so be it. We'll officially blame the disappearances on them."

The general waggled his hand—not outright disagreement, but . . .

"What?" Ana asked.

"You would have to declare war to make it look believable."

Ana leaned her head back, closed her eyes. "God bless."

"And it would look as if you are accusing them only to distract from the bank story—"

"I have plugged that leak," Edson said.

Ana kept to that annoying silence she had picked up lately. Damn her. Friends for almost thirty years, yet she didn't ask if Dolores was still alive. "Ana? I said I've—"

"I heard you. So. For the time being, we will ignore the demonstrators. Let the CIA go broke paying them to carry signs. People go missing all the time, don't they? Edson, release a statement saying the police believe the disappearances are linked to a rise in crime."

The back of her neck, that niche where graying ringlets strayed from her bun. Or between the eyebrows, the bullet's angle down. Ana was a small woman. If he jumped to his feet right now, caught her sitting, looking up . . .

In the atrium, Freitas suddenly turned. Did he know what Edson was thinking? Assassinate them both, maybe. Hope Nando didn't try to stop it.

Nando coughed. "Your decision, of course."

"Worst-case scenario," she said. "If the Americans take over, how will they do it?"

The general yawned and loosened his collar. "The U.S. won't act unilaterally. But they will not have to. Success has made Brazil enough enemies. The Americans will charge us with civil rights violations. Intervention will become a moral imperative. The U.N. will order bombing runs. They will destroy as much of the infrastructure as they can."

Like coming out of anesthesia—Edson's discomfort slowly blossomed to agony. He had never realized how fond he was of Brasília's desert-sculpture buildings. His vision blurred, and with it, his judgment. Assassinate Ana? Only because he'd been awake for thirty-eight hours straight.

"What about the new aeronautical system?" she asked.

The general nodded. "I like it. It's pretty."

"And?"

"We use it to tease the spy planes that are coming over from Bolivia and Paraguay."

"You told me last month you had armed our Air Force planes."

"Well, we had to. The lights are only attracted to them if they are armed. But if our pilots try to fire their missiles, their antigravity systems fail and our planes explode. It's some energy bubble design problem. I don't know, Ana. Ask the engineers. Better yet, ask Freitas, since the engineers don't seem to understand how some of his technology works."

"The Army has always been completely yours, Nando. I have

never meddled in such matters . . ." Ana's voice trailed off. Considering repercussions or loyalties? No sense in that, Edson knew. They would all share a coffin. "But how in the world do you plan to protect us?"

The general massaged his eyes. His voice was a rumble. "Pray they bomb on a weekend."

Laughter burst from Edson, loud and cathartic.

"Here is my plan." The general shoved his thumbs into his belt, leaned back, and spoke to the ceiling. "We will evacuate Brasília on a Friday evening. Everything will appear normal, and the Americans will not know what has happened until no one shows up for work on Monday. We'll desert those belligerent assholes the way the Portuguese did Napoleon."

Edson, overcome with merriment, wiped away tears.

Ana touched his arm. "Please, Edson. Please, Nando. Tell me what to expect."

Nando patted his pockets, looked around the table, and finally picked up the ornate silver sugar bowl. "The Americans, and whoever is opportunistic enough to join the action, will bring a small tactical force into Brasília. To distract us, they will pound the coastline. A war on at least two fronts, you see? They have the manpower." With the spoon, he drizzled a line of sugar. "Rio," he said, and incredulously Edson was looking at the wide sands of Copacabana.

"It's in range of their navy guns. São Paulo is close enough for their cruise missiles." A sparkling pile south, and inland. The quiet alley of Butantã. Pacaembu Stadium. That little Japanese restaurant Edson always went to when he was in town—what was its name?

An anticlimactic chime as Nando dropped the spoon back into the bowl. Edson battled the urge to rush to the phone, to call Gilberto Muller. To ask him the name of that restaurant.

"Luckily Brazil is a big country. Expensive to overpower."

"I see." Ana's face was pale, her cheeks so taut it seemed the bones would pierce the skin. "I see." Her voice was very soft. "And you could win such a war?"

"Win?" Nando roared, and slapped his knee. "The Americans will whip our ass!"

They didn't handcuff her. In the squad car no one spoke. They drove Dolores down a discreetly lighted street that was identical to all the other residential streets, and past apartment buildings that were ultramodern clones of each other. At an elegantly understated police station they stopped and got out.

Gilberto Muller was waiting by a potted palm in the mosaic-tiled booking area. "Come with me, please."

She followed him down a hall that smelled of gardenia potpourri. He ushered her into an interrogation room, and they sat across a table from each other. Muller pulled an envelope from his jacket, slid it across the Formica.

"A statement that is to be videotaped. Memorize it."

She pushed it back. "Tell me."

He ignored her, folded his hands.

"Tell me what it says, Gilberto. Tell me now while I'm drunk."

"Years ago you became Ana Maria's friend and gave money to her campaign. Now that Brazil is rich and the United States wants our technology, you have finally disclosed to her that you are an American spy. You tried blackmail. Poor Ana. She had no choice but to arrest you."

The ground free-fell from under her. She clutched the table's edge. "Paulinho's accident?"

A startled pause. "No one is—"

"Are you going to blame me for Paulinho's death, too?"

He took a quick breath. "I don't think it's—"

"You know that yearly photo op of her putting flowers on his grave? What everyone calls 'Visiting the First Corpse'? Well, the First Corpse was a pig. I should know: I made Paulinho what he is today. I see you're not surprised. Edson must have told you. Get me a cigarette."

He got up and went to the door.

"And a bottle of something. Scotch or vodka. Something."

Ten minutes later Muller returned with a bottle of *cachaça* and a single *palha* cigarette. "All I could find. The officers are trying to quit smoking. This came from the property room."

He lit it for her. The smoke from the cornhusk paper was as pungent as marijuana. The first drag of unfiltered tobacco made her choke; the third made her ears ring. She pulled an ashtray close and stubbed the cigarette out. "I confess to Paulinho's murder. Put that down."

Muller sighed. "Dolores . . ."

She drank from the bottle. Cheap *cachaça*. The policemen must have taken home all the confiscated liquor worth stealing.

"I confess to making her president of Brazil." She lunged to her feet. The chair toppled, and its crash fragmented her anger. She blinked, confused. The lights in the room were too bright, the peach walls too cheerful. She cleared her throat. "I confess to betraying my country for her. Damn it. Aren't you filming yet?"

For the first time she noticed how tired Muller looked. The butt of the *palha* cigarette still smoldered, unsupervised. A layer of blue smoke settled at decapitating height. "You tell that bitch to come here and ask me herself."

"These were Edson's orders. And he had no choice. You saw the stories about Palmer Bank, Dolores. You know the Americans purposefully leaked that. The truth is, the CIA sees you as a liability. They plan to destroy you, and use your destruction to bring down Ana."

She righted the chair. Its metal legs shrieked across the linoleum. "I'm just a painter."

"No one blames you for what has happened." Muller wouldn't meet her eyes. "And Edson has given strict orders to make certain you are comfortable."

"Comfortable? Kiss my ass. I'm fifty-three years old, Gilberto. I'm somebody. I'm an important goddamned somebody. My shit's hanging in the Guggenheim, in the Whitney. Go ask that dick-brained Edson Carvalho if he's ever been in *Newsweek*."

He nudged the paper closer. "Are you going to read this?"

She slapped her palm against it. "Comfortable? Who the fuck does Edson think he is?"

He got to his feet. "This wing of the station is empty. We've ordered that you be given the run of it. The officers will get you anything you wish, within reason."

She rose, too. "Who ordered Jack activated? He's not ready. He won't survive."

"Books, whatever. They'll bring a television in." His eyes locked on hers. "I'm fond of you, Dolores, but just like your country, I can't trust you all the same. Tell me when you're ready to make your statement." He walked out the door, not bothering to close it behind him.

Hiroshi sat at his desk. Anxiety flash-froze his spine. Something was wrong. The stapler was out of place, jarringly so. And his acrylic cube of photos sat with the nighttime skyline of Tokyo up—meaning the one of his father was facing down. Had a Brazilian maid been hired without his knowledge? Two women were security cleared to clean his office, and they were native Japanese. They would never be so sloppy.

Or would they? Perhaps something had upset one of them, and she was too shy to approach.

He quickly booted his terminal and searched his files. Nothing seemed disturbed, but he was no expert. He got up and walked into the hall, turning right—the direction of security.

He would check the log. That is what he would do. Faster than reviewing the videotape of the night before. And the incident was so subtly worrisome that he wanted the answer quickly.

"Hiroshi!"

He halted. A beaming Shuma Kasahara stood in his doorway, waving him inside. Hiroshi had no choice but to comply. His mentor's office was bright, the windows open to the brilliant April sun and the eastern prairie, still dressed in autumnal green. "How are you? Is anything the matter?" A frown of concern creased the cherubic face. "You look pale."

"Thank you, Kasahara-san. I am fine." Even to Hiroshi's own ears, his voice sounded strained. Would Kasahara realize he wanted to hurry the obligatory civilities? "And you?"

Kasahara patted his belly. "Brazilian food, and too much beer. A bad stomach keeps me awake. So I do not drown, Sunada holds my head above the toilet last night and sings to me." He looked woeful. "Poor Hiroshi, who has no one to take care of him. We missed you at the restaurant last night. You must take care not to work too hard. Remember the directive from Tokyo: no embassy personnel are allowed to work longer than sixty-five hours a week. Let the big noses from America and Germany drop dead from heart attacks." He laughed. "Come tonight. Promise you will come."

Hiroshi smiled back, hoping ambiguity would save him from the burden of the request. "Thank you, Kasahara-san. It sounds pleasant. I would very much like to."

Suddenly Kasahara reached past him and closed the door to the hall. He wasn't smiling anymore. "Please. I have no one to rely on but you." As Hiroshi watched, appalled and helpless, the old man lowered his head. "Please," Kasahara whispered to the floor.

"What has happened?"

"The beer talked through me last night. I made a small joke: Americans are jealous of Brazilian space travel, so they will conquor Copacabana's firm, brown moons. See, Hiroshi? I said nothing that the Brazilians themselves do not already laugh about. But afterwards, when we go to the parking lot and it is just the ambassador and Kengo and myself, Kengo becomes very haughty and says that because of our friendship you have told me too many secrets. He calls me 'loud-mouthed' and 'foolish' and 'indiscreet.' What could I do?" Kasahara looked up, and Hiroshi caught a glint of mischief. "Right there in front of the ambassador, I lower my head and agree: 'Oh, yes, Fujita-san. You are so right. I am a stupid old man.' Now Kengo is left wondering if I did so to shame him in front of Mitsuyo, or if I plan revenge. But as you can see, it is not me he wishes to destroy. It is you."

Hiroshi felt his face burn. "Why?"

"Don't you know? Kengo is jealous. Ambassador Mitsuyo thinks your assessment may be right."

"But in the meeting he—"

"Yes, yes. But he has no choice. Washington is about to make its move, and Japan will back the Americans. Keep your opinions to yourself, Hiroshi. And promise me you will do nothing, at least for now. Kengo is smooth-talking when he wishes to be. But 'Honey in his mouth, a sword in his belly.' We will protect ourselves by sticking together. Agreed?"

"Yes. Of course."

Hiroshi took a hurried leave and headed straight for his own office. It was Kengo who had left his desk disordered. And the disorder was a message: I have control over you.

Hiroshi ignored his computer. He put nothing sensitive or private there, and Kengo must have already found that out. Sitting in his leather chair, Hiroshi bent, and after three nervous and fumble-fingered tries, tapped the combination into the keypad. The tiny light on the lock changed from red to green, and he pulled his bottom desk drawer open.

What he saw made him hiss in a startled breath. His diary was missing.

The Today Show

. . . sounds like a spy novel.

Yes, Katie, it most certainly does. As you can imagine, all this has caught me very much off guard. Oh. Oh, yes. Here. This one is my personal favorite, 'Zebu Triste.' I hope I'm saying that right. She fusses over my pronunciation.

Beautiful. She uses Brazilian subjects a lot, doesn't she.

She's lived there since she was twenty-six, and met President Bonfim around that time. I have met the president, too, actually, on one of my visits down there. Very striking woman.

Dolores's husband recently died, didn't he? I think I remember reading something about that.

Yes. Harry died about a month ago.

Al, as her agent, you probably know her better than anyone in the United States. Is what they're saying true? You . . . You're shaking your head. Is that a yes or a no?

Simply unbelievable.

Have you talked to her?

No. The Brazilian government will not allow her phone calls.

Well, do you think she spied . . . You're shaking your head again.

I cannot begin to imagine her predicament, how it must feel to have your own country turn against you. And, for sheer political expediency, have a lifelong friend put you in jail.

9

A NO-NONSENSE HAND SHOOK ROGER AWAKE. MAJOR McNATT WAS leaning over him. He was wearing jeans, a *Visite o Maranhão* tee shirt, and a scowl.

Roger sat up, rubbing his eyes. Late morning light flooded the small bedroom, and the breeze through the open window already smelled of dust. "So, you get my message? I left that code shit on your answering machine like you said."

"Get dressed," McNatt said.

Roger yawned, swung his legs over the side of the bed, and froze. Two men were standing in Dee's living room. Like McNatt, they were dressed Brazilian casual, except for the pistols stuck in their waistbands.

"Uh . . ."

He looked to McNatt for clues, but the major was wearing his CIA-approved expression. Roger took his last clean pair of Dockers from his suitcase. Laced his bare feet into his Reeboks. One-upped McNatt with a *Baja California '91 Eclipse* sleeveless sweatshirt.

"All right, Dr. Lintenberg. Let's go."

"Uh, I gotta take a whiz."

"Jerry?" McNatt called.

Jerry was the one with the greasy ponytail, the earring, and the convicted-felon eyes. He tagged along. In the bathroom Roger turned his back, held what had become the world's tiniest dick, and tried to ignore Jerry. It took the piss a long time to arrive; and when he was finished they all walked outside, climbed into a Toyota sedan, and took a little ride.

"Where are we going?" Roger asked.

McNatt rolled up his window, leaned forward, and tapped Jerry on the shoulder. "Turn on the air."

A blast of cold from the vents. The tires thrummed the clay washboard road. The car fought for traction in the dust. Desert flashed by.

"Dee was arrested. You know that, right?"

"Let's try our best not to talk, shall we, Dr. Lintenberg?" McNatt hiked his hip, took a partial roll of Tums from his jeans change pocket, and popped two tablets into his mouth.

They turned off the road onto a grassy track, and the driver slowed to a crawl. In the resulting quiet Roger could hear Jerry humming. It took him a mile or so to realize that he was hearing "New York, New York."

"We could talk in your office, right?" Roger asked. "I mean, you could have asked me to come in. I would have done that, you know: come to your office."

McNatt checked his watch.

They slowed to a stop beside an unpainted shack. Kinch was there, leaning against a nearby Chrysler, eating a hard roll. McNatt took Roger's arm and helped him from the back seat. Kinch finished his breakfast and dusted his hands. "We fluttering him?"

"Yeah."

Roger's legs went rubbery. Fluttering him. My God. They were going to flutter him. What the fuck was that?

Kinch opened the shack's front door and ushered everyone inside. Roger blinked fast, trying to adjust to the dim. Living room/bedroom combination. Kitchen to the right. Table in the center of the scarred wood floor. A single straight-backed chair. McNatt pushed Roger into it.

"They came and got her," Roger said, talking fast. "Three guys—maybe four. They looked like cops. I called you right then. There was that beep on the other end of the phone, like you said. And I used the code: *Buzina.* Right? *Buzina.* That's what you told me to say if there was trouble . . ."

McNatt shot him a disinterested glance.

Something was going on behind the chair. Roger fought the urge to turn and look. He squeezed his eyes shut.

"Sit up. Raise your arms."

When he opened his eyes, he saw McNatt holding an elastic garotte. Roger yelped and curled into a ball.

Laughter from Kinch in the form of piggy snorts. McNatt said, "Are you afraid of taking a lie detector test, Dr. Lintenberg?"

Roger sat up, quick. "No."

McNatt snapped twin straps around Roger's chest.

"Not afraid at all."

He put a blood pressure cuff around Roger's arm, settled metallic bands over the ends of his fingers.

"No problema. Really."

McNatt stood away.

A new voice, flat and unemotional. "Is your name John Davis?"

"What? Are you . . ." Roger looked at McNatt.

"Yes or no," McNatt said.

"No."

From behind the chair, a mouse-in-the-wall scratching. Roger cleared his throat. Through the open doorway he could see an expanse of prairie and the bright red front fender of the Chrysler.

"Are your eyes blue?"

"No."

"Were you born in Meridian, Mississippi?"

"No."

"Do you work for NASA?"

He stared hard at the Chrysler and tried to convince his heart-beat to slow. "Yes."

A flurry of rasping.

"Do you work for NASA?"

His pulse jumped. "Yes! Christ, yes!"

Papery whispers. He licked his lips. The belt under his arms felt too tight.

"Do you currently reside in Houston, Texas?"

"Yes."

Outside a black speck—vulture? hawk?—sailed the wide sky.

"Are you in the employ of the Brazilian government?"

Panic exploded in Roger's stomach. "No!"

Crazed scribbling sounds. Only McNatt's eyes moved. They flicked to something, or someone, in back of Roger. The black speck in the sky circled closer.

That uninflected voice: "Are you in the employ of the Brazilian government?"

"You can't believe . . ." He sucked in a mouthful of parched desert air. "Christ, you can't . . ."

McNatt said, "Yes or no."

"No." The strap was too tight. Too damned tight. He started to pant.

"Do you want a cup of coffee?"

Trick question. Shit. Sweat rolled down Roger's forehead and dropped, stinging, into his eye.

A bang. A hand put a thermos top full of coffee down beside him. Another hand slipped off the finger cuffs.

"Just relax a minute," McNatt said. He stretched and everyone took five.

The coffee was lukewarm. Roger spilled as much as he drank. Kinch crouched beside him. "Hey, look, guy. If you get upset like this, you mess up the test results. We'll think you're screwing us around. You don't want us to think that."

Roger swallowed coffee the wrong way. A moment's panic when he couldn't catch his breath. Kinch slapped him on the back.

"Let's try it again," McNatt said.

Kinch put the metal cuffs on his fingers.

"Have you ever stolen anything from the United States government?" the voice behind the chair asked.

"No!" Roger took a shallow breath, looked at McNatt, and said, "Yes!"

By the kitchen Jerry was humming again.

"Have you ever committed an act of treason?"

Roger opened his mouth to answer, and halted, confused.

A huge silence. McNatt's gaze slid to his. Jesus Christ. How did the CIA train people not to blink?

"Have you ever committed an act of treason?"

"No." Behind him pens scratched wildly over paper. A single male grunt. Roger's throat was dry. He swallowed, and it was like swallowing grit. "Not as far as I'm concerned."

McNatt rocked back on his heels. "Yes or no."

"Give me a break! It's not a yes-or-no question."

Kinch said, "A little treason is like a little pregnant."

"I let MUFON see NASA documents, remember? I don't know how you'd ask me the question around that, but . . . just . . . okay?"

He waited for someone to say something. "Cabaret." That's what Jerry was humming. Maybe he dreamed of retiring from the Company, buying a sequined jacket, going Vegas.

"Other than the release of NASA documents to MUFON, have you ever committed an act of treason?"

Roger let out the breath he had been holding. "No."

"Do you know a man named Jack Jackson?"

The question snapped him bolt upright. "Wait," he gasped.

"Do you know a man named Jack Jackson?"

"Time out! Time out, okay? I followed him to the zoo. I thought he was working for you guys. He took the transmitters you gave me. That was all. Look, Major. I don't know how to answer the damned question. I know him, but I don't *know* him, see what I mean?"

McNatt popped another Tums.

The voice said, "Other than that single meeting at the zoo, have you ever spoken with Jack Jackson?"

"No."

"Do you currently reside in Houston, Texas?"

"Yes."

"Are your eyes blue?"

"No."

"Did Jack Jackson relay any information to you during your meeting?"

"Not only no, but fuck no."

McNatt sighed. "Dr. Lintenberg . . ."

"No. Sorry, I'm tired."

"Have you relayed any classified information the CIA has given you to the Brazilian government?"

"No. Can we stop now?"

"Do you believe in spirit communication?"

Roger's heart knocked his chest wall once, hard. He listened for sounds behind him: the threading of a silencer, the well-oiled click of an automatic's slide. Through the doorway, the broad blue sky was empty.

"Do you believe in spirit communication?"

The sun on the prairie was too bright. Roger's eyes watered. "No."

"Do you intend to give the Brazilian government any classified information?"

"No."

A pause, then, "That's it." The voice sounded resigned. McNatt unhooked the strap from Roger's chest.

"Did I pass?"

McNatt took off the blood pressure cuff, folded it.

"Hey. I passed, right?"

"Get up," the major said.

His knees wouldn't lock. Roger dropped into the chair again. "What are you going to do?"

"Take you back to Dolores Sims's house."

Kinch gave Roger a glass of water. "Just relax. We're taking you back now."

His throat was tight. The water wouldn't go down. "Look. Okay? It doesn't matter what the test showed. Please. I'm telling you the truth. Swear to God."

McNatt helped him to his feet. Two steps past the door, Roger wobbled. His knees gave way. He sat down hard in the dirt.

"See you around," Kinch said to the other three agents. He waved, got in his car, and drove off, the Chrysler raising a rooster tail of dust.

When Kinch was gone, McNatt asked Roger if he could get up.

"Yeah." But three steps later, Roger collapsed. McNatt, Jerry, and the interrogator walked over to the car and waited. Jerry was humming "The Love Boat."

If he could just get his legs to work, Roger would run. Still, they'd shoot him before he got twenty yards. The middle of Brazil, and there weren't any goddamned trees.

"You ready now?" McNatt asked. He opened the door.

Roger felt absurdly proud that he made it up and to the car. That he didn't beg for mercy. Because for each second of the forty long minutes it took to drive to Dolores Sims's house, he believed he was about to die.

"You comfortable?" The uniformed woman standing in the cell's doorway was short and broad and warm sienna brown. She was holding a box in her arms. "Are you listening? I asked if you were comfortable."

"The door to the entranceway's locked," Dolores said.

A spark of amusement in that impassive face. "But you're under arrest."

"I'm being ignored."

"They didn't feed you." The woman put the cardboard box on the table, and for the first time Dolores saw the uniform's insignia: police captain. "Mother of Christ. My officers didn't feed you. Together they have the sense of a turd." She wiped her huge hands down her pants legs. "Muller, too. I told him you needed some things. The ass said he'd pack your toothbrush and a dress. Chicken all right?"

The captain left. Dolores got up from the cot and peered into the box. Faded, shapeless jeans. Smudged sweatshirts so worn by washing that they felt like flannel. She touched her painting clothes piece by soft, aged piece. Held a cotton shirt to her face to breathe the smells of lye soap and linseed oil. Memory nearly sent her to her knees.

A discreet cough. The captain was in the doorway with another box. "I'm Madalena."

The name didn't suit her. It was a willowy, delicate name. "Captain."

The smile ignited slowly and faded, light without warmth, like a defective match. "Yes. Captain Madalena Correa Prado, Domestic Violence Division." She put the carton she carried beside the first. "Muller tells me you're a patriot. That if it were known what you were doing for us, we'd raise a statue in your honor."

"I'm hungry," Dolores said.

"I sent a boy to the restaurant. I'll bring you a beer." She walked out of the cell.

Dolores pulled the second box close and looked into it. Everything that mattered was there: a plush stuffed frog from Jack. The note her agent sent after the Chicago Museum of Fine Art's acquisition: Now you're too big to spank. Her first invitation to a State dinner, and across it Ana's scrawl: Wear shoes!

She heard Madalena walk in, and kept her head down, stroking the purple frog. The frog wore a silly, hedonistic grin. How many years ago? They had been outside, she remembered, in the shade of the orange tree. Harry, as he had been for a decade, dying on the hospital bed within. The smell of dust and citrus. The buzzsaw of cicadas. Jack spreading his jeaned thighs, forcing her palm over his erection. *I grin like that frog when you pet me.* Her whispering *We're too old for this* even as her resistance surrendered.

Footsteps of Madalena's exit. Another entrance. The smell of oil paint.

Dolores looked up. Madalena had set two recent paintings against the wall and was studying them. What would she call the newest: *"Futile Attempt to Capture Winter* and *An Old Woman's Rage?"* The brown and white didn't look cold, merely dingy; the red was more candy cane than blood.

"I like this one," Madalena said, stroking an edge of the second with a blunt brown finger. Then she shrugged. "But I don't know what it means."

Two shapes, two colors: beige desert cupping cobalt heavens, like the bowl of the National Congress building. Dolores painted it in a single frenzied afternoon, and only vague impressions remained. What the hell *did* it mean? Something about the masculine sky, the feminine earth. Oh, no. Had she really? What banal crap.

"Do you want it?"

Surprise altered Madalena's face so much that she looked like another woman. "Your paintings are expensive. I couldn't—"

"Yes or no. If you don't want it, I'll regesso the canvas."

"Why? It's so pretty."

"Too romantic."

Madalena, brow furrowed, was searching the canvas for romance when a barefoot urchin arrived with the package of chicken. "The news people!"

Absently, the captain rummaged in her pants pocket, came up

with a handful of hard candies. "Here," she offered without taking her gaze from the painting.

The boy took the candy. He didn't leave. "Hundreds of news
people! And they asked me questions, but I didn't answer. I could
hardly get to the restaurant."

"I paid for salad, too."

"I dropped it when they shoved me."

Madalena searched her pockets again, came up with a palmful
of varied aluminum coins. "The change from the chicken and
this. No more." And she shooed him away.

The chicken was wrapped in pink paper, spotted translucent
with grease, fragrant with lemon and garlic. Dolores untied the
string and pulled a roasted leg free of its socket, loosening an
avalanche of toasted mandioca. She took a sip of the beer.

"You're friends with the president." Madalena was sorting
through the box of mementos.

"Those are my things. Put them down."

A brief, wry glance. "What's left to hide? Tell me about *Presidente* Ana."

"Why?"

"Look at my color. And don't I have breasts? Ana is a particular
hero of mine."

"She owes everything to me. Didn't Muller tell you?"

"I know what the reporters are saying. Dirty money to her political campaign. Everyone in bed with the CIA." Madalena didn't
sound impressed. "And there are rumors around *Operações Sigilosas* about you and a murder."

Dolores walked out of the cell, picked up the vacant chair from
the guard station, and brought it back. She sat down and began
on the chicken and stuffing in earnest. "You believe everything
you hear?"

Madalena sat on Dolores's cot, leafed through a picture album.
She shrugged.

dson Carvalho will eventually have to kill me. I know too much."

Madalena flipped the page.

"The CIA will leak more dirty little stories about Ana to the press."

Madalena snorted. "What do I care? *Ô.*" With the tip of her forefinger, she pulled down her lower eyelid. "So *Presidente* Ana is shrewd. Everyone has secrets. Especially women have secrets. What matters is that I'm a police captain. What matters is that I don't have to take crap off anyone anymore. You think I care she took money? That she was involved in murder? She can fuck pigs at high noon at the Palace of Itamaraty if she wants."

Madalena went back to the photo album; Dolores to the chicken. When Dolores glanced at the captain again, the woman was looking at an 8x10 black and white photo. The disappointment in her face was wrenching.

They'd been so young, Ana and Paulo and Dolores and Harry. The men sat shoulder to shoulder in the first dim-witted, cheerful phase of inebriation. On Paulo's right sat Ana, a tense smile on her face, her eyes panicked.

There are stages to drunks, like stages to grief. Ana pled from the picture: save me from what comes next.

Of course. This photo. This was the painting she'd given to the captain—parched beige soil and thieving blue sky. The earth wasn't cupping herself to receive; she was recoiling.

The time we went to Rio together. That was the way Harry remembered it. He looked at the photo album a great deal, especially in the last year, but had never seen Ana's eyes. He'd reminisce, and he would cry—never for Ana, who had been terrified for so long; not even for Paulo, who from that photo-instant on would have three months to live. Harry couldn't be tender; he was simply maudlin.

Madalena had seen enough brutes, enough cowed women. She

knew. The captain ran a forefinger up and down Paulo's hand-some, grinning face, gently rubbing him out.

"He died three months after that photo was taken."

Madalena's head rose, her expression under control.

"The car crash," Dolores said. "On BR-351."

"History."

"No. Ana prettied him up. I knew them when he whored around. When he gave her the clap. When he beat her. He was drunk and doing nearly two hundred kilometers an hour when that tire blew. It took him five hard hours to die. The asshole de-served every minute of it."

What was it the captain had said about secrets? Women held them best. For every William Casey who went to his deathbed si-lenced by patriotism, a thousand women died silenced by dis-grace.

"Give me that picture!" Dolores snatched the book from Madalena's hands and finally, after forty years, tore Harry into shreds. From the ruins her own face fell intact, a study in calm gray.

That's why she'd had to kill Paulo. Because Ana couldn't. Turn the painting upside down, and it was dirty sky and blue eternal sea. Harry spat on Dolores, shit and pissed, and had not altered her one drop. He'd envied her vastness, feared her tran-quility. Married a lifetime, he never explored more than her shallows.

"I hear he died of *Chagas.*"

Dolores sat, photo confetti in her lap, her fingers plucking at Harry's corpse. "So?"

A sniff that wasn't quite laughter. A somber shake of the head. "You never recover from *Chagas* once the worms start eating the heart. A slow, terrible death. If someone put him out of misery with a pillow, is that murder? I don't care, and I don't want to know." Madalena picked up her painting and left the room.

Dolores looked down at Ana's single frightened eye. *Did you hear that? She thinks I killed Harry. But I've always been so god-damned self-sacrificing. If I had to set someone free, of course it would be you.*

She brushed the tatters of the photograph from her lap. They landed on the floor willy-nilly, pieces hidden, pieces revealed. Because it's easier, sometimes even men take disgrace to the grave. Sometimes for women silence isn't compliance, but complicity. She *had* killed Harry—that was her secret. He died with each and every rendezvous in the garden: her hands on Jack, his on her. Something pale as death at the window. Yet she never warned Jack they should move out of sight. Never told him to stop.

Presidential Press Conference

Thank you all for coming. I will read a brief statement first. I have, ah, been informed by intelligence sources that, at 3:02 A.M. today, Eastern Standard Time, the Brazilian government placed a nuclear device in orbit—Wait. Please. I'll answer your questions in a moment—an allegation that President Bonfim vigorously denies. I have spoken with the members of the U.N. Security Council, and we are in agreement that Brazil must, without delay, open up its secret military base at Cabeceiras to U.N. inspectors. President Bonfim has refused.

Therefore, we are issuing an ultimatum. As time is of the essence, this ultimatum will expire four days hence, midnight, Brasília time. Now I'll, um, take questions. Only a few. Sandy?

Are you saying the United States is in imminent peril?

No. Intelligence is pretty sure that the Brazilians need more hardware up there, uh, before the satellite becomes viable.

What is its orbit, Mr. President?

Ah . . . classified.

But does the orbit send it over the U.S.?

That's three, Sandy. Bob?

Are we talking air strikes? Invasion?

Yes.

Which? Air—Mr. President?

Thank you. No. No more. Thank you.

10

ROGER PERCHED ON THE CAR FENDER TO WAIT. CABECEIRAS REMINDED him of Nevada: the big lilac sky, the breathless dry air, that rim of gold at the horizon. Now that the sun had set, the wind was turning chill. Anxious, he rapped out a fast finger rhythm against the Zeiss binoculars while the percussion of an *escola de samba* thumped from the radio.

Sounds of footsteps in the dry grass. In 1990 by the black mailbox, Roger had been rousted by Wackenhut security. No one would scare him away, not this time. He turned.

It was a farmer, probably the owner of the frame house whose lights Roger could see in the distance. The man bobbed his head in greeting. "Doctor." The title wasn't a good guess—merely generic respect. "Read the sign?" He leaned on the sagging wooden gate. There was just enough of the day's afterglow to pick out the seamed face; enough of a smile to see the gap of a missing incisor.

"Government thinks they'll scare us with anthrax. I got cows. They don't scare me much. They usually come on weekends. Tourists." He took a pouch from his shirt pocket and deftly rolled a *palha* cigarette. Struck a match. "Today's Monday. Lots of spies

94

come through here. I can tell." He dropped the conversational ball at Roger's feet.

A pause, and Roger picked it up. "How?"

Quick grin. "Foreigners don't like music."

The samba ended and another began. "*Aaaah-maaah-zooonha,*" the *escola* sang exuberantly, accompanied by what sounded like a band of kitchen utensils.

"And if they like it, they have no rhythm."

Roger stopped tapping the binoculars.

"Every night the Chinese set up a tent a kilometer or so south of here. The British park a van north. They have telephoto lenses, and the Chinese have big guns. Helicopters fly over once in a while. I suppose the helicopters are ours. I like Americans." The farmer pointed his cigarette at Roger's chest. "NASA. Florida. Lots of ocean."

Roger slid off the fender, walked over, and put his elbows on the gate. "Houston."

"Eh?"

"I work at NASA in Houston, Texas."

"Why? Don't you know the ocean's magic? Florida has ocean on three sides."

"Well, there's sort of an ocean near Houston, too. Dry as this place is, you guys must be shit out of luck."

The farmer laughed. "Juscelino knew better," he said, as if he and the long-dead president were best buddies. "He knew lights come out of the ground here. And spirits speak."

Roger's pulse quickened. He wondered if his Portuguese had suddenly failed. "Lights?"

The farmer touched a fingertip to the side of his eye. "Flying saucers. Turn off your radio and come. No need to lock your car. I'll show you."

During the walk to the house, Roger wanted to talk about the saucers. He never had the chance. The farmer announced that his name was Flavio, that the boss would put another chicken on

for dinner—no, no, he insisted on it—and that they were keeping
the kids for his daughter who worked in the city—no one farmed
anymore, although to be truthful, there wasn't much farming to
be done in the desert, and he'd been thinking lately about
dates—Moroccan dates.

"What do you think?"

"Well—"

"Here we are. It's not much. Humble people; a humble house."
They walked up the steps, through the front door. "It's nice that
you learned Portuguese, even though you talk it funny. The Chinese squeak like cockroaches. The Brits mumble out their assholes. Like I said, Americans are easy to get along with."

"Thanks, but—"

"Wait here. I'll take care of it." Flavio walked into a neighboring
lighted doorway, leaving Roger standing in the dark living room.
Uncomfortable, Roger looked around. Framed Sacred Heart on
the wall next to a glow-in-the-dark cross. Woven rug, swaybacked
sofa. Couple of straight-backed chairs. Clean, but excruciatingly
cheap. All but the new Mitsubishi television. On its gleaming top
sat something odd. It looked like the television had sprouted.

A child screeched in the back of the house.

"Guest for dinner," he heard Flavio say.

From the bright kitchen a woman's reply went on and on,
higher and higher, louder and louder.

Then Flavio said reverently, "He's from Florida."

Roger closed his eyes. Aw, jeez.

Kids' shouts. A resonant bang that shook the thin walls. Neither
grandparent went to check.

Roger cleared his throat, shifted nervously on his feet, bent
over and studied the object. It was a faithful reproduction of a
television, right down to the channel changer. Instead of a screen
there was a terrarium of plastic flowers. A statue of Ana Maria
Bonfim stood in the center of that never-wilting garden. Her arms
were spread in welcome; her smile was beatific.

Over the hiss of a faucet Flavio offered to kill the chicken.

The woman said no, she would.

Roger prayed: *Please, God.*

The woman: "Florida? Mickey Mouse?"

"And Donald Duck."

Not even the Cape. A chicken dead for his sake and he'd have to eat and talk Orlando.

Flavio came into the living room with two water glasses. There was half of an orange-fleshed, green-skinned lemon in each, and the bottom third of the liquid was pearly with sugar. Roger took a cautious sip. The rest was pure *cachaça*.

"See? A heaven on earth, Doctor: Christ on the wall and *Presidente* Ana on TV."

The play-television was pathetic. "You must like her."

"Boss does. I guess she's okay. More honest than we're used to, than maybe we deserve. And she speaks well to the spirits, have to give her that. So, life changes. We have more money. Gas stove, washing machine, a refrigerator."

Confused, Roger's attention drifted. He tipped the dime-store glass back and forth. The juiced rind waved tendrils, an undersea creature. At the bottom, sugar syrup rolled like mucus.

"I used to beat her." It was a moment before Roger realized he hadn't meant the president. "When the Women's Rights were passed, she had me arrested." He shrugged. "I suppose things are better now. Maybe the women are happier, I don't know. I was getting too old to beat her, anyway."

Chickens in the backyard squawked in alarm. Aw, jeez.

"Tell the boss all about Disney World."

Behind the house a sudden ominous silence. Roger took a steadying sip of his drink. "I've never been to Disney World."

"Make it up."

Flavio, a bottle of *cachaça* tucked under his arm, led the way to the front porch. They sat down together on the steps. "Disney World is a place of magic," he said.

"Uh-huh." A plane, landing lights gleaming, lifted off from the nearby Air Force base. It rose thirty degrees into the purple evening and suddenly, precipitously tumbled out of the sky. Roger's stomach fell with it. "Jesus! Oh, Jesus! You see that?"

No fireball. No sound of sirens. The sky was empty again. Still shaking, Roger took a gulp of his drink. Then another. Flavio re-filled his glass.

"I've seen them five times the size of the full moon and eight different colors."

Roger drank, swallowed a lemon seed.

Flavio said, "They were all in it together. Padre João came from the spirit world and told Juscelino. And Juscelino told Oscar Niemeyer. That's why Niemeyer built those buildings—so the space people would feel at home."

From the house the sizzle of something frying, the smell of gar-lic and peppers.

"So. Oscar Niemeyer tells Lúcio Costa, who plans the city in the form of an airplane. Why?" Flavio pointed a finger at Roger's nose. "To invite the space people down. And how could they re-sist?"

On the horizon something glittered. Something breathtaking. Roger got to his feet.

"Destiny. Padre João prophesied that from this spot a city would rise which will rule the world. And three generations later—just as promised—Juscelino built Brasília with *Presidente* Ana in mind."

A huge golden ball, shimmering in the thin desert air. Too bright for the moon. Wrong color, and too big, for a plane. "Aw," Roger breathed. "Aw, jeez."

Flavio said, "A conspiracy. Christ was in it, too. He vowed the meek would inherit the earth; then *Presidente* Ana gives black peo-ple power, frees the women, and makes Brazil rich so that I can buy a refrigerator."

Forty-five degrees into the spangled sky, the light swelled to twice its size and exploded into sparkles of red. The sparkles shot off to the southeast.

"Shit!" Roger tore his shirt pocket trying to get to his miniature camera. His glass toppled and bounced loudly down the steps.

"Early," Flavio said and, retrieving the glass, poured Roger another drink.

An emerald delta wing rose and sank before Roger got the binoculars to his eyes. "Aw, jeez." He leaned his head back, spread his arms. Flavio put the glass into his hand.

"I'll put in a good word for you, Doctor. Could I have your jacket?"

Roger walked out onto the hard baked clay of the front yard. "What?"

"I want your jacket. I'm not of the ruling class yet, but it's only a matter of time. When judgment comes, I'll speak for you. I figure that's fair."

Roger upended the glass so far that the lemon rind rolled down and hit his nose. He gave the empty glass to Flavio. Then he gave him his jacket.

"More *cachaça,*" Flavio mumbled, and went into the house.

Arms out, Roger spun around and around in the barren yard. A flock of amber squares flew heavenward. Roger snapped their picture. "Aw, jeez."

Flavio came back and they drank some more. Crystalline globes iridescent as peacocks. Pentagons of blue flame that changed in an instant to pink.

"Come sit down. Boss has the chicken ready. We can eat on the porch."

"Aw, jeez, Flavio. Look at that." Roger couldn't eat. Barely noticed when the son-in-law arrived. Laughing like a kid, hands snatching, he chased UFOs like fireflies.

He realized he was cold when Flavio brought him a blanket. "Eleven o'clock, and you're too drunk to go home. Besides, drive south and the Chinese will shoot you. Let's go in."

"It's so fucking pretty." He'd never go inside. Didn't dare close his eyes. An apricot moon swung lazily back and forth over sixty degrees of sky.

Flavio brought him a pillow. Made him lie down on the porch. The night was so bright. So quiet. "Will you be mad at me when I take over the world?"

"God. Look at that."

Lights whirled. The day's dust settled, the hot-metal air turned sweet.

Flavio took a deep breath. "Nice out here. Sometimes I think death's like this. That maybe it's a good thing, really. A magical thing. Something to look forward to. Do you think?"

"Oh, man." In the dark of the desert a nightbird chittered. Tears welled in Roger's eyes, scattering the light. "It's so damned beautiful."

Nando stood teetering on the jeep's seat, arms flailing for balance. His right hand jerked, aiming Edson's revolver first toward the sequined sky, then toward earth.

In the passenger seat, Edson ducked and threw his arms over his head. "Watch out! You will shoot me. Every cow in *O Vale do Amanhecer* is in danger."

"The cows here are good Spiritists. Maybe they will reincarnate as my wife's housecat." No warning stillness, no obvious aim. The .45 barked loud and deep. The orange strobe from the barrel lit up the night. At the turn of the road, another streetlight blinked out.

Nando said, "Eight to six. See? Drunker than you, and I have only missed two shots. We never made it to the Valley."

Edson drank from the Dewar's bottle. "I don't know why you wanted to talk to a fortune-teller. I can see our future without a crystal ball. Sit down. You're lethal."

Nando dropped behind the wheel and gave Edson the gun. "But the score is eight to six."

The barrel was hot, the grip still damp from Nando's palm. The air was spicy with gunpowder. They drove toward the gleam of the next streetlamp, the headlights sweeping the brush.

"I have been thinking about Ana," Edson said quietly.

Nando stopped the jeep and set the emergency brake. "What about her?" The general's voice was suspicious.

Edson lost his courage. "Look where you parked!" He clapped a palm to his forehead. "You always bring yourself in close for a good shot. You think I'm too drunk to notice."

"Liar. Complainer. We're one tenth of a kilometer from the last light pole." A grunt as the general bent over and felt his way along the dash. The siren whooped. "Shit," he whispered.

A light went on in a nearby farmhouse.

One last mechanical sob from the siren, and it hushed. Nando fumbled. The under-dash lamp clicked on. Light lapped at their ankles. "There. Can you read the odometer?"

"I've lost count." Edson clambered up on the seat. He let go of the door and stood unsteadily. His left hand was occupied by the bottle, his right by the gun. One-armed, he aimed, thought of Ana, and squeezed the trigger. The report made his ears ring. The recoil nearly flung the gun from his fingers.

"Still eight to six," Nando said.

When Edson dropped into his seat, Nando grabbed the bottle. He shut off the engine, the headlights. "I have been learning English. I think that is prudent."

Edson cleared his throat. "Closing the universities played right into the Americans' hands. I warned her. Now no one in the U.N. supports us. We end up trying to counter CIA lies about radioactivity and space weapons. Now we face an ultimatum."

No answer. Not even a grunt. Edson took a breath and went on. "Her first blunder was disbanding Congress."

A laugh. "Yes. The people would have been happier had I aimed my cannons and shot them."

"But don't you see, Nando, what a predicament that put us in? Americans hear 'dictator,' and they think of death squads and brutes in uniform."

Nando took the gun from Edson's lap. "The brute expropriates." He planted a knee in the jeep's seat, and shot out the final streetlamp. When the sharp clap had died away, and the fire was a violet afterimage on Edson's retina, the general said, "Somehow I don't think I frighten the American Army. Is it the uniform, you think? Maybe more medals. One for when that jeep ran over my foot. A big one with a death's head for flying in Air Force planes. Now *that* scares me."

The road was black. Only two lights burned: the faint 10-watt bulb under the dash, and the far yellow square of the farmhouse window. Odd how lonely, how wide, the darkness seemed. "Does Freitas scare you?"

Lit as it was from beneath, the general's affable face looked eerie.

"I imagine killing him sometimes," Edson said.

"Um. The devil arrives with roses, and poor Ana can't send him away. Some women are like that." He took a drink. "You know how we climb up on the jeep seat to shoot, and there is nothing to hold on to? Ana can't stand by herself."

"She must."

The rotund general was slouched, bottle snug in his crotch. His head was lowered. Abruptly he leaned forward and turned off the under-dash light. Edson felt vertigo, and a fleeting panic, as darkness leaped at him.

Nando said, "The thing in Freitas loves her."

Not the insurgency Edson had hoped for. He peered into the black rural night but saw only Freitas's hands on Ana—that strange listless passion in his eyes.

The wind stroked hair from Edson's forehead, then moved restlessly off through the roadside brush. He might have thought he was blind if it hadn't been for the yellow glow from the farmhouse and the sky's ice-blanket of stars.

"It loves the way my brother-in-law loved before he killed my sister," Nando said in his gentle bass. "I blew his brains out afterwards, you know. My brother-in-law. He said it was her fault that he stabbed Rosinha sixteen times. He said she should not have tried to leave him."

Movement in the house. Someone walking between the window and the light.

"We have to do something, Nando. The technology we get from the other universe is not worth letting the Americans take over. If Ana is too weak to handle Freitas, here is what I think—"

"Shhh," he ordered. But it was the other sound that made the words stick in Edson's throat: the precise, metallic sound of a hammer being cocked. "I know what you have been thinking."

Edson strained to see Nando's face. Was he angry? Did he wear a teasing grin? The general was merely a hulking shape, the quiet sounds of breathing, and the smells of whiskey and sweat.

"Nando . . ."

"Shhh. I have been watching you. I see how you look at Ana."

Not angry. Deadly serious. Edson's faint, questioning smile died.

"Nine years, and I still miss my sister."

Someone was standing motionless at the window now, looking out, too far away to be more than a blot in the light. Perhaps the gunfire had awakened a baby. And the cries had roused the wife.

"I figured out what is wrong with love," Nando said. "I had to, in order to sleep. Women's mistake is giving, even when the man doesn't want what she has. Men's mistake is taking, even when they have no right."

Did guilt keep the one in the window awake? If so, that was the husband.

The under-dash bulb came on. Edson had been fighting to see, so even the dim glow was dazzling.

Nando sat back, the gun cradled in his lap, and regarded the dark road. "I will tell you a secret, one that I have known for some time: there is nothing but the Freitas-thing on the other side of the Door. I know because I saw that same emptiness inside my brother-in-law. He called it love. My sister wasted her life trying to fill it. She thought that was love, too. I suppose women are happiest when they give. And I suppose that when men have an emptiness, they can't help eating things. My brother-in-law ate his future, his mother's heart, the happiness of his family. Strange, isn't it?—how they let him."

Nando met his gaze. "So, Edson. I will not help you take over the government. And I will not let you hurt Ana." He eased the hammer down, handed the gun back. "When the time comes, let me kill Freitas."

Nightline

. . . has been trying for years to ruin President Bonfim.

Ms. Ambassador? This is getting us nowhere. If you'll—

What about the photos? You see the—

Ms. Ambassador? Congressman? I'm tired of playing referee.

Ted, in a few hours we will prove what we say. That CIA agent, the American painter, will confess how the CIA has conspired to ruin Ana. It is dangerous for the United States government, for all governments. In other countries, men are in power. Yet here is a black. A woman—

Oh, give me a break.

She makes you afraid.

. . . makes me sick, you guys fall back on this female-as-victim routine. This is a political question, not a gender one. Why don't you let the inspectors in?

You want to control us.

Who's wanting to control you? Look. If you don't have anything to hide, just let the inspectors in.

I must agree with the congressman, Ms. Ambassador. It seems simple enough. Why not allow the inspectors in?

Everything must be as the United States wants it. Latin America is tired of complying. Women are tired of complying, of being kept silent.

This is getting us nowhere.

11

HIROSHI AWOKE DURING THE HUSH OF THE NIGHT. THE BEER HE drank at the restaurant with Shuma Kasahara and the others was a dull pressure in his bladder. The *vatapá* he had eaten smoldered, sending up fumes of shrimp and *dendê* oil. He should get up to relieve himself and take an antacid, but he was too sleepy, and his nest in the blanket too comfortable.

Then he noticed the smell. Oily. Familiar. Recognition made gooseflesh break out beneath his sweat. Candle wax.

He opened his eyes to slits. The room was dark but for the sapphire shimmer of the open window. The balconies of the neighboring apartment building were limned by the amber glow from the streetlamp three floors below.

He listened for extraneous noises—heard his own breathing, the quick-step march of his own pulse.

Had he locked the door? Fastened the chain? What if there was a burglar? What if the man was in the shadows now, knife in hand? Would Hiroshi have time to reach his gun?

But he clearly remembered locking the dead bolt, hearing the tumblers click.

Kengo. Only he had the opportunity to make a key. Only someone from Covert Ops would know how, with a wire, to free the chain. Of course. It was Kengo Fujita standing in the dark, waiting to make his move. He had stolen Hiroshi's diary without leaving a trace on the embassy videotape. Now he had entered Hiroshi's apartment without making a sound, just to frighten him, just to burn a candle . . .

No. Absurd. Hiroshi lifted his head. And screamed.

Something was perched on his hip. Something winged and black. Hiroshi vaulted out of bed. The sheet tangled with his legs. He hit the floor shoulder-first, still shrieking.

He clawed at the nightstand. Alarm clock and gun and lamp came crashing. What was it? Had a vampire bat flown through the open window?

His grasping fingers found the gun. Once his hand was around the grip, he felt silly. Shoot, and the neighbors would hear. The police would come. Kengo would find out. *Let me tell you how Hiroshi killed an intruder.* And he would relate the story again and again, like a *rakugo* comedian telling a favorite joke, until the audience knew it by heart.

Hiroshi swept his hand over the floor, found the lamp, and switched it on. He peeked over the edge of the mattress, studied the rumpled sheets. The bed was empty.

Then he spotted it in a corner—an explosion of glossy ebon, like a dead crow. He crawled across the hardwood and crouched, afraid to touch it. A thing of black feathers, white paint, and red beads.

Gun held high, his left hand steadying his right wrist like they did in the movies, Hiroshi crept out of the bedroom and around the next blind corner. He was trembling so hard that his breath came in staccato snicks.

He stole into the living room. The candle smell was stronger here. From where he stood, he could see that the front door's chain was still fastened, the dead bolt securely locked. The window, overlooking a sheer drop of four stories, let in a sluggish night breeze.

Onward. Down the short hall into the dining room. The jackhammer beat of his heart. An air-thieving tightness in his chest. An oppressive silence, as if the air was too thick for sound. Walls, floor were a dim, flickering orange.

Gun leading, he crept around another corner to the kitchen, where yellow light tongued the walls. A single black candle sat atop the counter, guttering in the draft.

Hiroshi's sweat turned to ice. His eyes teared. He forgot how heroes in movies acted. He waved the pistol wildly into each corner. Nothing. No one.

Vatapá and beer churned. He backed out of the kitchen and down the hall toward the bathroom, where a cloying odor brought him to a halt. He turned on the light.

The toilet was clotted with blood.

Captain Madalena awakened Dolores before dawn and brought her to the interrogation room where Muller was waiting. He pushed a paper across the tabletop. "Memorize the confession." And the demands started again.

This time the discussion was subdued. They drank coffee and even laughed a little. They ate guava paste and white cheese and bread. Madalena leaned against the closed door, her arms folded, and watched.

"Why not?" Muller sounded so reasonable. "You can't expect to go back to your house. The press would never leave you alone. Neither would the CIA. To both countries you are now a traitor. Do you think you could return to the States without facing a congressional subcommittee? Or, now that you have been arrested, we would be able to free you from jail?"

Odd how bureaucracies murdered. They rarely stabbed, they stung: the death of a thousand paper cuts.

He sat back in his chair. "You've been a spy for over twenty years. You know how the game is played. Don't tell me you have become an idealist now. Or an American patriot."

She stopped herself before the automatic "Of course not." Answers were never that easy. The tawny sweeps of Montana; the autumn seclusion of small-town New England; the Smokies rising to the morning like humpbacked whales from the sea. Was love of country why she had gone into espionage? Or the titillation of having a secret she could keep from Harry?

When Dolores didn't answer, he told her, "I have been ordered not to let you leave this room without recording the videotape."

At the edge of her vision Dolores saw Madalena's arms drop. Dolores reduced Muller's face to strong, downturned pencil strokes, then to planes of light and shadow. The room simplified into space and form.

"Do you understand what I am saying?" Muller asked.

The ceiling's fluorescents washed the shelf of Muller's cheekbones in bluish light, and threw shadows of ash. The wall behind him was oyster-beige. Muller needed a cigarette, a single contrasting dot of crimson.

A sigh. "I am a reasonable man. Edson Carvalho is not. And when he tells me to come back with a videotaped confession, I will do whatever it takes. There is nothing personal, neh?"

Captain Madalena tugged fretfully on her ear, took a step forward. She looked at Muller, then at Dolores.

Muller didn't turn. "Leave the room, Captain."

A hesitation. Madalena walked across the floor noiselessly, shut the door behind her.

"Dolores?" Muller asked.

Sometimes Dolores felt if she tried hard enough, she could walk out of the three-dimensional world into one whose depths were harmless illusion.

"You must hate Ana Maria a great deal, if you would destroy Brazil to hurt her."

Destroy Brazil? Hate Ana? No. Dolores's emotions didn't run that deep. "You're asking me to stop painting."

"You can still paint. Don't be silly."

"Paint where?"

A neat fold of confusion between Muller's eyebrows. She fought the urge to reach out and feel of it. He would think the gesture affectionate, or worse, seductive. "Here. We will bring you anything you want."

Her work would flatten into rectangles: walls and ceilings and floors. "I can't."

"I will help you through it. It's a short statement, really. We can do as many takes as you . . ."

"I can't paint here."

He let go his breath in a *puh* of exasperation. "Of course you can."

"I can't paint in here."

"You just haven't tried it. Great works of art have been done in prison." Poor Muller, trying so hard. His forehead knotted again. "All I can think of is *Mein Kampf*. I'm sure there are more. Didn't Dostoyevsky . . . ah! I know! Solzhenitsyn! And maybe Pasternak. The Russians do well in custody, don't they? You could do a series of paintings like—"

"I have to be able to see."

"Dolores. Edson wants a statement."

"You named writers. I'm a painter. I have to *see*!"

His voice rose. "I will get you a *window*!"

"The same view, day after day—"

"Dolores. Dolores. I don't trust you. You know that. But I've always liked you just the same. If you do not cooperate, Edson would have me kill you, and then what?"

She shrugged.

He shook his head. His fingertips patted a melancholy rhythm against the tabletop. "Edson is not himself lately. He drinks too much. His mind wanders. Please. Just help me, and we will work something out."

Dolores opened her mouth. The words that emerged surprised her. "If I can't paint, I'll die."

Hiroshi shuffled down the wide aisle of the *mercado,* string bag in hand. His head was lowered so as not to draw attention. He looked neither right nor left, walking like a conscientious wife.

He listened for footsteps behind him. Under the tin roof, sound carried: laughter, the bang of wood against metal, the whine of a butcher's saw on bone. The air was heavy with the smell of raw meat and fish and coffee.

He stopped where flounder basked wide-eyed on an ice beach. Looking into the stainless steel sides of the bin, he indexed the hazy reflections. Nothing.

He walked on, confused by the household chore. He was accustomed to meals being handed to him, ready-made: cafe plate lunches; upscale restaurant dinners. Taguchi always served fruit for breakfast, but now the fruit was all soft rot.

He passed scalloped *fruta-do-conde.* Pudgy finger bananas. Red candy oranges. A box of *carambola,* like a gathering of translucent orange stars. What would Taguchi buy? How much? What would she pay? Knowing he must have something fresh to eat, he stopped to purchase half a kilo of grape-purple *jabuticaba.* This time he could feel someone watching. He whirled. Nothing seemed out of place.

"You all right?" the stall keeper asked.

"Fine, thank you. I am fine." But Hiroshi's hand shook as he accepted his change.

Because of the candle left in his kitchen that morning, he knew that he would be followed. And not by Japanese.

The CIA would play first. Then kill him.

Holding the string bag tight, he hurried past a fringe of skinned, dangling rabbits.

Kengo's doing. He had told the CIA what Hiroshi said. How he had made light of them. Now they would prove that they were not so stale in tradecraft, after all.

Stalls of baskets. Of pottery. Of cookware. Suddenly Hiroshi noticed he was alone. The lighting in this aisle was dim, the stalls too narrow.

A cold adrenaline-rush of alarm. He took refuge inside the next doorway. "Hello?"

Whispery flutters from caged birds.

"Hello? Please? I would like to know how much is a parrot."

Odors of seed and shit. In its bamboo house an *azulão*, feathers a supernatural black, chirped sweetly. An owl, no larger than a sparrow, blinked somber yellow eyes.

The scrape of shoe against concrete.

Hiroshi spun. "Hello?"

"Hello. Hello. Hello." A scarlet macaw cocked its head, spat out a sunflower husk.

"Please? Who is there?"

A dry snap, a rustle. The huge parrot spread its wings, bobbed its head, and anxiously paced its perch.

Hiroshi would leave. Push past whoever was there. They wouldn't dare stop him. Wouldn't be crazy enough to shoot him. Or would they?

The *azulão* twittered and hopped like a jolly demon. The macaw abruptly craned its neck, peered over the neighboring cages. "Hello."

He would make a run for his car. Then what? Did he dare put the key into the ignition?

Beyond the stall the sound of something small, something fleshy, hitting the floor. The macaw agitatedly began to preen.

Hiroshi grabbed the hooked wooden pole used to raise and lower the cages. He should have brought his pistol. He was a diplomat, wasn't he? The police wouldn't search him. Next time, then. Yes. If there were a next time, he would bring his gun.

He put down his bag and stepped quietly into the aisle. Two meters away a boy sat eating a mango, a knife in his hand, a *sagüi* astride his shoulder. The bandit-masked monkey held a guava in its dainty black fingers. A second guava lay, fallen, at the boy's feet. Aloof as a Siamese cat, the *sagüi* bit into the fruit's pink meat.

Then the boy looked up. His chestnut hair was filthy. His clothes were ragged. His eyes were a hot blue.

Hiroshi's thighs weakened. He had forgotten Piehl.

The anxiety that had rumbled all morning in his bowels eased. Everything would be all right now. The KGB would know how to protect him.

"Are you ready to discuss terms?" Hiroshi asked.

In one fluid motion, the boy was up and striding quickly down the aisle. Hiroshi put down the pole and followed, afraid he would walk too slow and lose him, afraid he would walk too fast and be obvious. They strode past reaching hands of green bananas, past tomatoes and okra and flats of quail eggs. Then Piehl's son stopped, bent, and put the monkey down. He swayed, clapped. In a bell-like tenor he began singing *Odilé, Odilá*.

The *sagüi* tugged on passing trouser legs, its other hand begging for coins.

Hiroshi spotted the father. Piehl was sitting at a counter, back to the wall, hat pulled low, a *cafezinho* in his hand. So professional, Hiroshi thought in admiration. The KGB agent looked as if he had not bathed in a week. Piehl grinned an inane grin. Flashed artificially discolored teeth. "*Ô*, Doctor." The slow, dim-witted cadence of the *caipira*. A nod toward his son. "*Ô*." As if all that could be said about singing and dance was contained in that one syllable.

Piehl's son had gathered a crowd. He spun, slapping the rhythm against his bare belly. His open shirt flapped. Exuberant samba darkened, became a deadly, high-kicking *capoeira*. The monkey gathered coins in a pile, hugged the five-and ten-cruzeiro bills to its cream-colored chest.

Hiroshi sat down at the counter, leaving a stool's distance between himself and Piehl. He could play the professional, too. He bought his own *cafezinho* and waited.

When the barkeep walked back toward the center of the U-shaped counter, he heard Piehl say, "I found out."

Expression impassive, Hiroshi pulled the small white cup close. He poured sugar into the dark roast coffee until it became syrup.

"I cannot work for you."

At first Hiroshi thought that he had not heard correctly. Then, for a comforting moment, he was certain that the words meant something else.

"But I believe in the courtesy of a yes or no."

Hiroshi fumbled for the child-sized spoon. Into his cup he whispered, "Please. I need your assistance."

"Ask in the Valley."

"The Valley?"

"The president's friend is a medium."

"I don't understand."

A man in a maroon-smeared butcher's apron sat at the opposite bend of the counter's U, mumbled something, gestured. The barkeep nodded, poured cashew fruit juice and *cachaça* into a blender. The motor ground and whined.

Piehl said, "Blood gods."

What was Piehl talking about? The butcher? Or did he know about the black-red gore in the bathroom? Hiroshi was paralyzed by fear. He couldn't go on alone; it was too late to go back. "I don't understand. Please."

Piehl's son halted the whirling dervish of the *capoeira* and, slapping an upbeat rhythm on his chest, began singing, in a clear falsetto, "Vem Morena"—the song for Brazil's most famous "brown girl," Ana Maria Bonfim.

Two dozen spectators, two dozen reactions. Half were singing along. A sad-faced business-suited woman clutched her toddler's hand. A man in a knit shirt played matchbox percussion. A teenage girl laughed and danced, clinking a ballpoint pen rhythm against an empty Coke bottle. The *sagüi* climbed a very ancient, very black woman's skirt, and her laugh echoed to the rafters.

"I will pay you anything. Please."

"Afraid." Piehl abruptly slapped the flat of his hand on the counter, boomed out a laugh. The song ended. The KGB agent hoisted himself to his feet.

As he limped past Hiroshi he muttered, *"Quimbanda."*

How long had she been in the darkness? Dolores wasn't sure. Madalena had confiscated her watch; Muller had stolen the light. She sat in a corner of the interrogation room, staring at the glowing strip that lined the underside of the door.

She always wondered what it would be like to be blind. Painting was so splendid a gift, in fact, that she feared God would demand her sight as payment. But lately creation had become drudgery, and she didn't know why.

Early in her career, she became bored with the representational; now she wearied of the abstract. What was left but blindness? At least that would give her an excuse not to work.

Then what? Pray that her hearing would be taken to save her from chatter about children and grandchildren, cooking and fashion? Dear God, how she disliked tedium, and the squawling of infants.

Dolores smiled when she realized that, aside from wanting to paint again, she probably most wanted to die.

I don't know you anymore! The enfeebled Harry had complained.

Dolores long ago accepted that she was two-dimensional. Odd how Harry had problems with that. Still, she had gestured toward a stack of paintings being readied for shipment to the States. *There I am, stark naked. What else do you want to know?*

As Harry often did in the years just prior to his death, he burst into tears. *We never talk.*

Of course not. If she could talk, why would she have to paint? Harry never discussed things, either. He lectured. "Why the United States Needs a Third Party" or "Why Brazilians Can't Make Decent Wine" or "Teal Is Green, Not Blue." After a few years of marriage, she gave up trying to exchange views with her art critic vintner political analyst.

There had been no last words between them, although she had had the opportunity when the respirator finally shut him up. Now she drew Harry on the blackboard of her imagination, and told him, "I'm in jail. But you're *dead.*"

Guffaws became chortles. Chortles softened to chuckles. Merriment went the way of all things, even of Harry. Dolores sat, glum. And when she figured out the one thing that would save her from videotaping the confession, she knelt and fumbled her way through the darkness to the table. She ran her hand up the steel leg to the metal-cased Formica corner, and froze in indecision.

Don't be a girl. Isn't that what she had said to Ana, and Ana had said to her, for courage? *Suck it up and be a woman.* Still, thinking about what she was about to do made her wince.

So don't think. That's what Ana would have told her. Dolores brought her head down on the table corner fast.

A crack. A white-hot explosion of pain. When she could catch her breath, she hissed, "Shit, shit, shit."

A feverish throb above her right eye. A rush of sticky warmth. "Shit," she said, and aimed her forehead at the table again.

She misjudged, hit mouth-first. Impact came too soon, too hard. Her bottom teeth dug into the meat of her lower lip. Pain blinded her. Her mouth filled with blood. Spitting, choking, she flung her arm out to grab the chair, knocked it over instead.

Startled noises in the hall. A clank of keys. The click of a lock. The overhead lights were so bright that Dolores squeezed her eyes shut. Through her split lip, she mumbled, "Get the video recorder," and received silence in reply.

Had it worked? Dolores opened her eyes. Muller stood in the doorway, caught between fury and shock. Madalena was frowning in consternation. And the drab room was festive with red.

C-SPAN, Live Coverage of the Senate

. . . *review the situation. Let the president hand over these intelligence reports.*

Time! There's no time! Nuclear bombs are hanging over our heads. We've got to do something! We owe it to the American people.

Come to order. Chair recognizes the gentleman from New—

Senator, all I'm saying—

The Soviets never put arms in space. Well, hell. With what we know about their state of technology, they probably couldn't. The Brazilians can. Look. If they don't have anything to hide, they should let the inspectors in.

Order. New York has the floor.

All I want to do—

Imagine nukes in the hands of Perón and his ilk. Nuclear missiles in El Salvador during the 80's. Think about it. If Bonfim would murder her own people, how do you think she'd treat us?

Sit down, Senator.

Well? Answer me.

Sen—

Don't turn away like that. Come back here. Answer my question. If she'd murder her own people, how do you think she'd treat us?

12

FRIGHT BROUGHT ROGER TO A STANDSTILL. TWO MEN IN SKI MASKS WERE sitting on Dee's sofa. At his entrance, they stood. Black tee shirts, high-top Adidas, jeans with pistols in the waistbands. The CIA was back for mind games, and wanted Roger to come out and play.

Cold fear warmed to simmering irritation. Roger's head throbbed, the aftermath of the previous night's *cachaça*. His back was stiff from spending the night passed out on Flavio's hardwood floor. The F of his "Fuck" was a violent, bespittled aspirant; the U a groan of exasperation.

Silent panic. One man waved his hands wildly. The fat one held up a Bullwinkle Sketch-A-Lot. Roger squinted to bring the message into focus.

HOSE IS BUG!!!!

"What?"

The thinner man crumpled in Marcel Marceau despair. Fatty frantically erased his Sketch-A-Lot, and printed in huge, clumsy letters:

CIA BUG HOSE!

"CIA—?"

And Fatty shot his own brains out with an imaginary pistol.

WE MUFON, ESTUPID!

They waved Roger outside. Once on the brick patio, they took off their masks. Older than Roger had thought. Marcel Marceau was bald; Fatty's graying sweat-damp hair stood up in spikes. They looked tired and hot and annoyed.

"You was gone all night. We think they kill you," Marcel grumbled.

"You suppose to call!" Fatty clapped palm to forehead in frustration. "Jerry promise you call."

"Jerry?"

"Shhh."

"Directionals." Marcel screwed a forefinger and thumb into his ear, cupped his other hand into a dish, and scanned it across the dusty yard.

"Jerry," Fatty said. "Tucson conference. Talk about Gulf Breeze."

"Who *are* you guys?"

Marcel Marceau shook his head, tapped his lips with a forefinger.

Fatty translated: "No names."

Roger looked around the empty drive. The autumn sun's glare made his eyes water. "How'd you get here?" he asked suspiciously.

"Walk. From Savio and Irací house." Fatty pointed east. "Neighbors see police. They—" He rolled his eyes. "*Puxa vida! Qué merda, esta Inglês!* They call attention? Dolores maid. And maid, she . . ." Fatty's English ground to a halt.

"She . . ." Marcel's gaze wandered the sky in a search for vocabulary. ". . . get from town . . ."

"Hey, guys?" Roger said in Portuguese. "You don't have to speak English."

A pause for thanksgiving, then:

"We were scared to contact you—"

"The CIA! But the people in Houston told us you were reliable. They said the CIA must have put pressure—"

"They have been following you closely. At least until today. It has been difficult for us to—"

"Jerry told us—"

"Jerry! A genius! He predicted everything. He would travel to Rio once a year—"

"That's how we met him."

"*He* said when they finally landed, it would be here."

A smug grin from Fatty. "Our Air Force did not bother them."

Marcel grabbed Roger's arm so hard it hurt. He leaned forward. "Your military wants to shoot one down."

Roger tried to pull away. "I've been out to Cabeceiras. I've seen those things. The technology is light-years ahead of ours. We don't have weaponry good enough for that."

"Yes? What about Roswell? What about Aztec?"

"Grow up, man. There aren't any bodies in Hangar Eighteen. Roswell was a weather balloon and Aztec never happened."

"Are you that stupid? You believe everything they tell you?"

"Hey." Roger shoved Marcel in the chest. The man stumbled backward but held on, his fingers digging into Roger's arm. "Who qualifies here as the dumbass? I'm with NASA. I've been to Dreamland. I know what the military has and what it doesn't. I've seen the fucking inventory, man, and every piece of weirdness we have comes from Brazil. The American military—"

"Will kill anything that stands still."

"Hey."

"And they always shoot well. After all, they have the smart bombs, and war is only a game, neh? They killed thousands for oil. What do you think they would do for antigravity?"

"Hey. You shut your fucking—"

Marcel shook him. "I think you are lying to us. I think you are a CIA plant."

Fatty snapped, "Let him go!"

Marcel stepped back, glaring. Roger retreated gingerly, palms out. He'd just remembered that the pair had guns. "Look, guys. Let's chill. I don't know who you are. I don't know any Jerry."

"Oh?" Marcel's eyebrows rose. "Then why did Jerry tell us he got in contact with Matt?"

"Not Matt Nagel."

"Yes!" The tension left Fatty's face. He beamed with relief, then turned to Marcel Marceau, who actually smiled. "Yes, Matt Nagel! So you talked to him? Jerry told us that if you have any questions, we are to tell you to call this Matt. He will verify everything."

"Matt Nagel died in a car accident three weeks ago."

Color drained from Fatty's cheeks.

Marcel said, "I cannot take any more," and began walking fast down the driveway.

A wave of panic washed over Roger. He wanted to tell Marcel Marceau he was full of shit. He wanted to fall on his knees and beg him for help. Jesus, he wanted to catch the next flight home.

Fatty dug in his pocket, came up with a slip of paper, pressed it into Roger's hand. "You must memorize that number, then burn it."

"What's he talking about, he can't take any more?"

"Eighteen MUFON investigators have died in the past six weeks. Please. There is not much time left, Dr. Lintenberg. Call us when you find out something, and we will get the word out."

"Word of what?"

Fatty started after his friend, then turned to look back. "America plans to go to war with the aliens. And I tell you this: you may be familiar with your country's arsenal, but I have seen alien weapons. America will lose."

*   *   *

Edson walked across the hangar, his footsteps loud against the polished floor. He walked until the gaping Door of the chamber stopped him.

Ridiculous to think it could be seen. Emptiness was so private it could only be felt. He drank from the bottle of Dewar's and contemplated the spot on the floor where darkness squeezed out the light.

Emptiness felt like gravity. He had met it first in the mountains. It was what threatened to suck him down when he stood too near the abyss.

He craned forward, listening for voices and hearing none—not even Dr. Lizette's amorous croons to her Donato. So Edson sang a love song for her into the steel-walled chamber. "They died of thi-i-irst, my cattle . . ." The cottony gloom absorbed sound. "Died of thi-i-irst, my heart."

Was that right? "Asa Branca" was such an old song—he couldn't have forgotten the words. *Coração. Sertão.* Heart or land? Certainly he loved the land—he'd killed for it. He loved Brazil so much he stepped over the brink.

Edson had been born near Diamantina. Shoeless, he'd walked the clay roads of Minas, tending his father's lyre-horned cattle. He'd been raised to live the sun-scorched life of a *caipira,* so Edson knew that one day the land would dry him to bone.

And would God welcome him when he arose, soul parched and weightless? Edson wanted to believe in Ana's all-forgiving spirits, but lately when he thought of God he couldn't imagine a form at all. He saw instead that emptiness inside thick-walled, baroque churches. God was chill, heavy with damp. He smelled of candles and stone and incense. His voice was merely echo.

This time it was whiskey that made Edson step over the edge and into the chamber. His eyes searched the dark. The inside was as dim as God, but smelled of nothing.

Where . . . The word wriggled past, and was gone. Edson took another step and was suddenly caught up in a teeming school of murmurs.

. . . go home, want so bad to . . .

. . . was a teacher once.

Dark here . . .

Please. Can you see where I am?

He stretched his arms wide, but he wasn't substantial enough to catch them. The babble flashed by, quick and bright. "Don't be afraid. I won't hurt you anymore."

A whisper flicked near his cheek, barely stirring the thick air. *Where? . . . can't see . . .*

He said, "Touch me."

A current nudged his fingers, slithered through.

Then something caught him, jerked him toward the light. The Dewar's bottle dropped endlessly. Edson stumbled backward and fell. Kept falling. He watched himself, jacket billowing, body tumbling, growing small, smaller.

Someone was calling his name. The lights in the ceiling were bright. "Sir?" Muller's face was close to his.

Time to awaken now. Past time to stop falling. He had to tell Muller. It was the most important news in the world.

Muller helped him to sit up. "What were you doing in there, sir? You all right?"

Edson scrubbed his hands over his face. So short a time ago, yet he couldn't quite remember.

"I have the videotape you asked for. And some bad news. The São Paulo police overreacted to the demonstrations. It's pretty bloody."

"Um. How many killed?"

"No word from the hospitals yet. Are you sure you're all right? They said you were in the hangar, and I didn't see you. Then I looked inside the chamber, and you were just standing there. Just standing. What were you doing?"

Glass shards from the Dewar's bottle sparkled in the shadows beyond the door.

"Sir?"

"It isn't what I thought. They are right by the doorway." Late afternoon of a long day, and the whiskey was getting to him. Edson's eyelids felt heavy, his forehead felt packed with sand. "Take me to Alvorada."

"Alvorada, sir? But it's only three o'clock. I'm sure the president will be in her office—"

"No. I want to talk to Freitas."

The agent helped him to his feet, led him outside, put him in the Mercedes.

Edson reclined the leather seat and closed his eyes against the afternoon sun. The heat was stupefying, and he found himself drifting off. Falling.

He roused himself. "Muller? Wake me up when we arrive." The car door shut with a quiet, understated sound. The engine started with a roar. Edson loosened his grip on consciousness, embraced oblivion, and let himself go.

Hiroshi had seen the gaudy temple. Had been greeted by mystics dressed in silly costumes. Vale do Amanhacer was poor, crude, and pathetic. And even though it wasn't a day for public visits, everyone in the Valley was gracious. And they oh-so politely avoided answering his questions about the president's friend.

He ate a late lunch at the larger of the town's two restaurants, and started back to his car. A block later, he realized a young boy was trotting at his side. "She says she wants to talk to you."

Hiroshi stopped at his Honda's fender and looked around. The town napped under a thin blanket of dust. Windows and doors gaped, open-mouthed and snoring. A dog, comatose or dead, sprawled in the shadows of an overhang. "Who?"

"*Mãe* Xuli. She can call the spirits of *Bispo de Pará* and *Preto*

Velho. She said, 'Go out into the streets,' she told me. 'And you will find a man who is lost.' "

Exhaustion hummed through Hiroshi's body, buzzed through his brain. It took him three tries to slot the key in the door lock, and he wondered if it was safe for him to drive home. "I'm not lost."

"You're the only person in the street, so you *must* be lost."

"Go away now." Hiroshi fished in his pants pocket for change, came up empty.

The boy tugged on Hiroshi's sleeve. "She says to tell you, 'Samurai.' "

A bluebottle fly landed near Hiroshi's half-open mouth. He absently batted it away.

"Did I say it right? Samurai? What kind of stupid foreign word is that?"

Hiroshi relocked his Honda. "Take me to her," he said.

Nothing moved in the small town but Hiroshi and the boy, and they walked wordlessly. A flaxen haze of dust shimmered in the late afternoon. Sun gilded the cottages, flooded the streets with gold. The pair walked until town ended and wide desert began. At the last house, the boy entered. In the kitchen an enormous woman with skin like the hull of a Brazil nut was stirring a pot of black beans.

The boy stopped behind her. Hiroshi stopped with him. Xuli didn't look around. Her voice was laconic, her Portuguese musical Bahian. "Samurai. I been told to make you welcome."

Careful. He mustn't let his imagination run away. Of course she didn't need eyes in the back of her head to know that Hiroshi had arrived. The boy was barefoot. She'd heard the click of shoe heels. But "Samurai." That was daring.

"Maria Bonita comes to me three nights ago," Xuli said. "Since then, she pulls my hair. She won't leave me be, and it's your fault." The beans steamed their disapproval, perfuming the small kitchen with garlic and bay leaves.

Hiroshi smiled, and decided to prove that he, too, could tell the future. "How much for a reading?"

She whirled so fast that he backpedaled. "Jackass! Slant-eyed clown! I don't know what Maria Bonita sees in you, but she tells me to throw the *búzios*. I can't charge. You want her to snatch me bald?" Xuli wiped her hands on a dishtowel and left the room.

Hiroshi wasn't sure he should follow. The boy stayed, so he did as well.

Rustles from the neighboring room. A thump. "Here!" Xuli called.

Hiroshi pushed aside a flowered curtain. Xuli was seated cross-legged on the living room floor, a white towel spread within her reach. She grumbled, "Lucky for you this is Thursday. The *búzios* speak clearer on Thursday. Still, ô." With a fingertip, she pulled her lower eyelid down. "Watch yourself. Don't believe everything. I don't throw the *búzios* for years. Hurts my knees, but what does the bitch care? She was young when she disincarnated, so. Sit! Sit!"

He sat on the floor across from her. The afternoon was so silent he could hear a one-note drone of fatigue in his head. The living room was ripe with foreign odors: cooking beans, the ghost of old incense, Xuli's pungent sweat.

A flick of leathery hands. Shells tumbled to the towel. She grunted. "Your *orixá* is Oxum. Serve him at rivers and waterfalls. Around here in autumn always use a stream; in winter you can make do with a fountain. Oxum likes mirrors and aftershave lotion and earrings. Make sure they're expensive, mind. Oxum, he's a vain little prick. You settle things with Exú first, then he calls Oxum for you. A little *cachaça*, some cigarettes, that's what Exú likes. Better get all the gods on your side, 'cause you fighting a powerful hex. *Quimbanda.*" She raised her head. Her eyes were amber beads. "Somebody done told you."

He kept his face impassive. "Maybe."

Her eyes swept over the pattern of shells. "So. You don't like that? I tell you something else: you go off on your own, *pô*. Since you're a little boy, you dream of this. But now you living this dream, and it's not how you thought. Little Samurai don't like being lonely."

Hiroshi went cold.

"Something scare you bad. Fear keep you up at night. Can't tell your friends, neither. And *búzios* say you need to be afraid, 'cause this enemy of yours, he make a bad *trabalho* against you. He killed the goat and brought you the gift of blood."

He sucked in a breath. The long muscle in his leg went out of control, began a galvanic, crazed tic. The drone of exhaustion crescendoed.

"You know this enemy."

"Yes." He caught himself. "I'm not sure. But I have been told the president's friend is a medium."

She laughed. A gold incisor flashed. "Henrique Freitas? That lily-white Kardeckian Spiritist? Our Father No Salt–No Meat–No Fun? Freitas, he take out cancers with his fingers. He straighten bones with his hands. No, little one. Doctor Singh comes through Freitas, and he don't have time for no low spirits. You, now. You got three enemies. One is black, and he destroys for love. One is white, and he destroys for pleasure. One is brown, and he destroys for envy." She jerked her head toward the door. Her chins quivered. "You go."

"But . . ."

"Can't read no more. My knee hurts. You come back some other day, I tell you more."

"Tomorrow?"

"Can't throw no *búzios* on Friday. Monday, neither. You buy a *figa*. Wear it. Funny. Your hands are soft like you work in an office, but the *búzios* say there is danger, like a construction worker who walks the high girders. This make sense to you?"

He nodded.

"Huh. Well, even with the *figa*, there be danger of the evil eye.

When you at work, don't look at nobody face-to-face, mind. 'Cause somebody there at work stole something of yours. And he got power over you now."

Muller woke him so gently that Edson came to consciousness still befuddled by sleep.

What was this place? Edson rubbed his eyes. He was in the car, that much he knew. When the power seat lifted into upright position, Edson recognized the underground parking area. The residence of the president: Palácio da Alvorada.

"Sir? On the way here, São Paulo called again. The story is already out on CNN. Three dead, one a woman. The president is still in her office, and I expect she will be there for some time. I understand from the guards, sir, that Pastor Freitas is in his bedroom."

The confusion must have shown in his face, because Muller said, "Was I wrong to bring you to here?"

Something bright. Slippery. Almost . . . The thought darted from his grasp, minnow-quick. Then: "Yes. I remember! They were still in there. Right near the doorway."

"Who, sir?"

"Hand me the bottle from the map box."

"Perhaps you've had enough for today." Even as he was protesting, Muller obeyed.

Gentleman Jack, Edson saw with surprise. Had he known that, he would have raided the map compartment sooner. "I have to do it. She won't push the point. Where did you say he was?"

"In his bedroom."

Edson climbed out of the car, slipped the pint into his pocket. "Go to Palácio do Planalto. Keep her there in her office."

Edson strode into the elevator, exited on the first floor, and took the marble stairs two at a time. On the second floor, a single plainclothes officer was manning the corridor station. Three people dead in São Paulo, one a woman. The guard was watching a game show and drinking a Coca-Cola.

He looked up. His smile failed. "Sir."

The TV's sound was off. On the screen a swimsuited blonde was bouncing on a trampoline, trying to catch a plastic ring between her knees. She had enormous American breasts, the kind that looked as if they could be used for pillows.

"Don't," Edson ordered as the boy reached out to turn the television off. "Not for my sake. When Ana comes up, it would be best, though, if you weren't watching that."

The guard grinned: boy's-club camaraderie. "Big, neh? See how they bounce?"

Edson watched the instant replay. In slow motion, the blonde woman was falling. Falling.

The guard looked up. "What, sir?"

The woman disappeared without ever hitting bottom. A Varig commercial blinked on. The guard was waiting for an answer, but Edson couldn't remember making a sound. "I said she has a fat ass. I'm going to see Pastor Freitas now. See that I'm not disturbed."

The fourth door from the end of the hallway—the room next to Ana's. Edson took another drink, but his hands still shook. There was not enough whiskey in the world.

He put the bottle in his pocket and opened the door. Freitas was staring out the window into the dusk. Edson halted just behind his chair.

"I went inside the Door."

Their eyes met in the windowpane. It was like stepping over the brink again, walking into the dark.

Edson folded his arms, cleared his throat. "I heard the voices of the people we sent in. They are right by the entrance, not scattered across your universe as you said. So you can let them go. It would be easy. They can talk to the press. If we are lucky, and use the Disappeareds skillfully, we can defuse this entire situation."

Freitas reached out to the window, stroked Edson's reflected cheek.

"Listen to reason, my friend. The Americans have issued an ultimatum: Brazil allows U.N. inspectors into Cabecieras or they will bomb. Your little collection game is over. The Disappeareds must come back."

The fingertips squeaked as they moved, leaving a contrail of condensation on the glass. Down Edson's chest, his belly, following the line of his zipper, to stop at his groin.

Freitas's hand dropped. Outside, Brasília's science-fictional buildings glittered. A jet, red light winking, sailed the wide violet sky.

Edson said, "If you do not bring them back, the Americans will discover that something else has taken up residence in Henrique Freitas's body."

Three auras of moisture lingered on the glass between Edson's spread legs. Freitas leaned over, put his mouth to the spot.

A shudder. Edson brought his legs together fast. Dropped his arms. Stepped away.

Freitas's hushed voice: "When you came to me, I had you. Did you feel it? I whispered in your ear. Did you hear? Dark, so dark here. I was a teacher once." Abruptly Freitas turned, looked him full in the face, and it was as if the air had been snatched from Edson's lungs. "I don't know where I am."

"Turn around."

"They died of thirst, my heart. How could you forget the words?"

Edson put his hand into his jacket. No matter what he promised Nando, Edson had to shoot while he still could. "Turn around."

A sly grin. Freitas looked away. Edson studied the neatly clipped gray hair. That spot. That sweet spot at the bulge of the skull. And if you hit it right, death came so quickly that they never even quivered. How many? Under the rule of generals, he had made chronic thieves slumber. And under the uneasy dominion of civilians, he had tucked murderous children into their beds. Edson had tried to be gentle, and if not gentle, fast. Their faces were serene, their bodies so still.

"They forgive you."

Edson's fingers lost their grip on the pistol.

"If you had walked in farther, you would have heard the people you forced inside telling you that. Farther, and you would hear the forgiveness of dead children. You see, when you go all the way into the shadows there is no dark. When you go all the way into emptiness, you'll find it full. Isn't that what you came to ask?"

Edson couldn't remember.

"And if you fall far enough," Freitas said, "I'll be there."

The click of the door latch drew Edson's attention. Ana stood, clinging to the knob for support. He realized his hand was still in his jacket and from her expression, an expression he had seen countless times, he knew she expected to be shot. He showed her his empty palm. Only then did he realize he was crying.

"Edson. What are you doing? You know I don't allow anyone to be alone with him."

Freitas ordered: "Come here!"

Edson was appalled when she obeyed. A step from him, Freitas seized her wrist so roughly that her face went taut. He jerked her near. Kissed the inside of her arm.

She touched the graying hair—appeasing? or already forgiving? "Let me go, please. I need to talk to Edson."

A savage twist. Before she could cry out, Freitas released her. Ana walked quickly to the door, the white imprints of his fingers marring her skin.

Freitas whispered, "Everything I do, I do for you," and Edson wondered which one of them the words were meant for.

Ana led Edson into the hall, shut the door. "Damn you. I have forbidden this. How dare you talk to him alone?"

"I had a question. I—"

"If you have a question for him, you go through me. Is that understood?"

"But—"

"Answer me. Is that understood?"

Edson held his breath for a ten-count, looked at the baseboard. In a controlled voice he said, "Yes."

"Because it is dangerous. I understand him. I can handle him."

"No one can handle him, Ana. He reads minds."

She laughed. "See how little you know? He asks questions, that's all. He pries. He's curious about us."

"I walked into the chamber today."

"Oh? Did you hear them?"

So Ana knew. Could she hear the pleas of the Disappeareds when she lay her head on his chest? When Freitas came, did he cry out in other voices? "The Disappeareds—they're close to the Door. Almost within arm's reach. Maybe we could call them out. If we do, they could talk to the foreign press. You would not be seen as a—"

"They won't come."

"How do you know?"

"Leave them alone, Edson. They are happy."

"How can you say that? Freitas lies to us, Ana. He tells us what we want to hear. The other side isn't like he told us at all."

"And how do you know? Because one time you stepped inside and thought you heard something? Those beings in the other universe have our best interests at heart. Otherwise they would not have given us the tech—"

"Other beings? Are you absolutely sure there are others? When I look at him, I feel something lonely. I sense a hunger. You must have felt it from him, too."

Ana was shaking her head as if, by moving fast enough, she could dodge Edson's words. "Only one of him? No. How could he have developed the technology alone?"

"I don't know. He talks of happy people beyond the Door. All so friendly. All so delighted to meet the people we send in. It sounds like the little animal books I used to read my children. I am not myself a believer in such things, and I know you aren't either, but . . . Ana. Only the devil could be such a liar."

"That's enough!" Her words rang down the quiet hall. The venom surprised him.

"I sent those people inside, and they sound so afraid."

She sighed tiredly, rubbed her arm. "Go home, Edson." The place Freitas had grabbed her was already purpling. "Everyone's afraid."

CBS News Special: <u>Standoff</u>

. . . here on the deck. Commander Surry? This certainly is impressive, sir, how quickly the Navy has pulled this together.

Thank you. This is all part of the Rapid Response Force, uh, the capability to move our troops in quickly, aggressively, and then mop up. It's something we've been working very hard at.

Amazing. Just amazing. Commander, there has been some speculation that certain top-level Brazilian officials may be charged by the U.N. with committing crimes against humanity. Would your command here be capable of, say, bringing in a squad and arresting those officials as well?

We're prepared to do whatever the president asks.

Uh-huh. Just one more . . . Thank you. The Brazilians have not fought a war since 1870, except for a handful of soldiers they sent to the Allied side in World War II. Uh, so do you think this will all go down pretty easy?

They teach us in OCS to never underestimate the enemy. No military engagement is ever easy, sir. Brazil is large, and people tend to fight tooth and toe nail to protect their own country. Also, don't forget that the Brazilians have been major arms manufacturers for decades. We have to assume they know their weapons. And we have to assume their defense will be rigorous.

Uh-huh. Well, good luck to you, Commander.

They teach us not to count on luck.

13

ROGER RATTLED AROUND THE EMPTY HOUSE, WATCHED A LITTLE NEWS, noticed that the U.N. deadline was fast approaching, and that the demonstrations had spread. Bonfim's smiling picture flashed on the screen—file footage from happier times.

By ten-thirty the news was off, and the barometric pressure of the silence grew unbearable. Roger decided it was time for bed. He went into the downstairs bathroom, set the nozzle heater on MEDIUM HIGH, and while his shower warmed he picked up his toothbrush, ran a line of Tartar Control Crest down the bristles, put the brush in his mouth, and looked into the mirror.

McNatt was behind him.

Roger bounced as if spring-loaded. Dollops of toothpaste flew. "Je-sus!" He foamed at the mouth.

"We need to show you something."

"Couldn't you *call* first?" Roger toweled the mirror free of steam and toothpaste, rinsed the sink free of traumatized spittle.

McNatt turned off the shower heater and then the water, in that order, leaving Roger wondering if the man lacked a grasp of electricity or if he liked living life on the edge.

"Let's go," he said.

The usual four-door sedan was waiting in the drive. The night air was chill on Roger's wet shirt; and by the time McNatt climbed into the backseat beside him, Roger was shivering.

"Hey, guy." Kinch turned around, regarded him cheerfully from over the top of the seat. "You cold?"

Roger replied, "Up your rosy red one."

The driver inched the car down the driveway.

"Turn on the heater, Mike," McNatt said in a quiet voice. He got out a small paper bag, the kind used to carry a lunch. He opened it, took out a cloth and a can of oil, and started cleaning his gun. Kinch paid no attention; Mike, the driver, didn't either. McNatt cleaned his gun the way some men whittle, and some pick their noses.

Roger thought that cleaning the gun was completely, totally cool. He thought that it would be sort of great to be a real spy. He'd like to learn how to handle a pistol as nonchalantly as he folded his socks. But Roger was realistic.

McNatt, now. McNatt probably got off on danger. Probably was an endorphin freak. Stateside, the major'd be into hang gliding. Bungee jumping. Precision skydiving. Roger wondered what the guy's sex life was like.

Suddenly McNatt hiked a hip, took some Tums out of his change pocket, bit two tablets off the open roll.

"Where we going?" Roger asked.

McNatt went back to cleaning his gun. "Eyes only."

"Right. My eyes, right? I mean you said you wanted to show me something."

"That is the operative word. *Show* you."

Roger sighed and looked out the window. A half moon sailed the cloudless heavens. He let his eyelids droop, his mind drift. Air from the dashboard heater warmed his face, his chest.

Then McNatt asked, "Dr. Lintenberg? What religion are you?"

Oops. Roger stirred and took a long breath. But for the spectral glow of the moon, the desert was dark and bleak. The perfect place to hide a body.

"Well?"

"Episcopalian."

"Um."

Was that a good "um" or a bad one? The slide went back onto the barrel with a precise click. The rag, folded neatly, went back into the paper bag, the oil can with it.

Maybe McNatt wasn't a James Bond type. Maybe there was a Mrs. McNatt and two-point-five kids at home. If so, McNatt would be an ideal husband, always cleaning up after himself—trained to leave no clues.

The major leaned over, stowed the paper bag under the front seat, put the gun into the holster. "That's good."

"What?"

"Episcopalian."

"Does it for me," Roger said.

McNatt nodded, not getting it. "So you believe in life after death."

Whoa. What was this? A bit of idle conversation to make Roger feel comfortable? He wondered how fast the car was going. Wondered if he'd survive jumping out.

"In my business you really shouldn't dwell on religion. But there are times, you know?"

Roger studied the door handle. "Uh-huh."

"I'm not such a bad guy, Dr. Lintenberg."

"I'm sure. Not, I mean. I'm sure you're not."

"I've enjoyed working with you. Reading your file. You have an agile mind. I would suspect that if one accepts a supernatural occurrence as being valid—UFOs, for example—it's probably easier to accept another—oh, say channeling. Don't you think? Take Brazil. Odd mix of what Mama called 'hoodoo,' and Catholicism, and Victorian table-rapping. You ever wonder about salvation, Dr. Lintenberg? Or what constitutes evil? To my belief, the unforgivable sin is not murder, but stealing another's free will. The worst thing I ever saw, however . . ." McNatt paused for another Tums.

Don't tell me, Roger thought. *Please. You don't need to . . .*

"Iraqis down in a foxhole kept plinking away at us. Captain called in the bulldozers. Must have been air pockets, because we could hear them for a long, long time. We laughed about it then. Later I had nightmares. I dreamed for years that we had turned those Iraqis into demons. Fascinating transference symbolism. Your mama raise you to be a good Episcopalian?"

Roger began to sweat. "I suppose. Salvation, huh? I don't, ah . . . My church is kind of laid-back. Sort of hard to tell a good Episcopalian from a . . ."

The car slowed. Ahead was an old airstrip, a dilapidated hangar running to seed. And a brand-new helicopter.

"Oh," Roger said.

The car stopped. Kinch and Mike got out. McNatt leaned toward Roger confidentially. "What you're about to see is beyond Top Secret."

"Huh."

"I've stuck my neck out on this one, Dr. Lintenberg. I told the Company I thought you could be trusted. Truth is, we need you. Few respectable scientists accept the existence of UFOs. Fewer still have actually studied them. And even fewer have your facility for foreign languages. You are a valuable man. Ready?"

Without waiting for an answer, McNatt got out of the car. Roger followed him across the packed clay field. The air inside the hangar stank of burnt insulation. Plastic tarps trailed from the ceiling like gauzy falls of rain. Rubbernecking mainframes crowded scorched-metal accidents. Roger recognized part of a landing gear.

"This him?" A lab-coated man with an aging linebacker's build ran a deft pattern through the machinery. "Dr. Lintenberg?" A hand extended toward Roger. There was a pair of needle-nosed pliers in it. The man looked at the pliers, momentarily disoriented, then shoved them into a pocket. "Sorry. Things have been pretty hectic. Capture was, oh . . ." A quick glance at his watch. "Twelve hours, twenty-two minutes ago. The bodies are still in situ. If you'll come this way." And he started off across the hangar.

Roger stayed. "What's going on here? That's a plane, right? Isn't that part of a plane?"

Lab Coat seemed irked. "Major McNatt? Was this man not told?"

"You are to tell him, sir."

The man sagged so thoroughly that it seemed the white jacket was emptying. He ran a hand across his bald pate. "You were with him in the car . . ."

"Not authorized. Only you, sir, are authorized."

"Bodies?" Roger said.

The pair looked at him.

"Bodies? Of the guys in the plane, or . . ." Roger's voice went out from under him like those movies where the Indian tears ass across the prairie and—bang—his horse gets shot. Shit. He was going to cry. Right here in front of McNatt, career tough guy. McNatt, who talked salvation, but who laughed as men were buried alive. Aw, jeez. He was going to cry in front of this Ph.D. stranger, a little peer review. "Just what are we talking about here?"

Lab Coat parked his hands on his hips. "Nothing to worry about: our pilot ejected in time. UFO got off one good defensive shot before it was downed by the wingman. Damage was pretty extensive, I'm afraid."

Roger swallowed hard. Aw, please, no. "You shot one down?"

"Finally." Lab Coat was boyishly proud. "Since bringing our jets into Bolivia, we've been toying with each other. Interestingly, most of the UFOs we've sighted over Brazilian airspace are decoys. And—I know you'll be intrigued by this—the illusions actually have mass, enough mass to give a good radar return. The few manned UFOs themselves seem to be capable of disguising the size and shape of their crafts. Nothing was like we thought. But this time the pilots were able to acquire a good target—"

"So we shot first?"

A hesitation. Lab Coat looked at McNatt, who popped another Tums.

"Any of them survive?"

Lab Coat nodded. "Well, yes. One."

"Where is he?"

"Unfortunately, he succumbed to his injuries."

Roger felt sick. It was probable the creature never understood the reason the teasing game turned deadly.

Lab Coat coughed into his hand. "We have a tape you can view later. I know you'll be disappointed. He spoke a few words, but died before he could say anything meaningful."

Spoke?

"We need your input, Dr. Lintenberg. Washington is waiting. Are you ready to view the cabin now?"

He spoke.

"Come this way. Careful of that monitor. I read your article in *World UFO Magazine,* the theories on possible propulsion and guidance systems. That's what we're looking for here, and you would be the man to spot that."

The alien fucking spoke.

"Surprised? I can see by your face you're wondering how I knew. Oops. Watch those cables. I read your *Scientific American* article first. The style in the anonymous *World UFO* piece was identical, the ideas mere extrapolations. In fact, I was the one who originally brought you to the attention of the Agency. Ah. Here we are."

The man swept back the plastic curtains. At first glance, the wreckage might have once been a spaceship, or could have been a Chevy. One occupant was a bloody smear. The other corpse was still strapped in, the chair and part of the instrument panel around it left intact.

Incredible that the pilot had survived at all. It had a mouth, one eye, no legs, no hands; but before impact it had been a human male. And the spaceship a two-seater Cessna.

Edson leaned back in his favorite easy chair, remote-controlled the television to a mumble, and ran through the tape again. He didn't need to hear the words—after all, he'd written them.

A terrified Dolores Sims peered out from the screen, one eye swollen shut, lip split—pathetic as a whipped dog. Edson shook his head. "You lying bitch," he whispered in admiration. The brief tape ended, automatically rewound.

Something else had happened today . . . What was it? Ah, yes. The return of CNN reminded him. Nando had put the entire São Paulo police department on leave. He brought in militia from Curitiba, from Congonhas, from Caxias do Sul. Young soldiers from small towns, their first time away from home. All experts in traffic control who could write parking tickets, who could step in when red lights malfunctioned. They looked so overwhelmed, their rubber bullet-loaded rifles slung forgotten over their shoulders, their faces lifted to the tall buildings, their expressions awed.

Edson got to his feet and wove an unsteady path to the kitchen. He filled another glass and wandered back. His eye lit on the only legacy from his family: a baroque crucified Jesus.

"I did *my* job," Edson protested, but knew he had failed the test for heaven. He leaned against the wall and brought his head down close to the cross. "Forgiveness is *yours.*" He pushed himself upright and shuffled to the easy chair. When he sat, he could see Jesus watching him out of the corner of His eye, watching his every move, like the thing in Freitas—only Jesus loved the sinner, and the thing in Freitas loved the sin. Fondled it. Pressed his lips against the glass.

Edson heard the whistle of wind in the eaves, the squeak of fingers down the window. On the screen a somber American announcer was mouthing something. Behind her shoulder was a map of Brazil, and letters the color and shape of panic: ULTIMATUM DEADLINE.

He pulled the phone closer, and dialed the number by memory.

A woman answered on the third ring. "Hello?"

"He home?"

"Um," she replied. A thick-voiced male query in the background, and the woman's "Edson Carvalho. Drunk."

Outside Edson's picture window wind muscled into the patio, whipped the potted palms, battered the glass.

The line clicked as the extension was picked up. "Edson?" Another click as Nando's wife left the line.

"I'm not mad." Wind kicked at the orchids, pushed the patio chairs. Jesus, that look in his mahogany eyes—Maybe Jesus was mad.

"It's two o'clock in the morning, Edson."

"Is the deadline passed?"

"I don't know. Why don't you call the White House?"

"Don't hang up."

"No. I promise I won't hang up. Is someone there with you?"

Jesus on the wall.

"Edson?"

"Yes, someone's here."

Bass laughter that became a smoker's cough. "You keeping them awake, too?"

"I walked into the chamber."

The silence went on so long that Edson wondered if Nando had fallen asleep. Then, "Where are you?"

"Home. I heard voices. The Disappeared are still there by the Door. You were right. He's lying to us. Today, just today, I talked to him without Ana. And now afterwards, I feel—Nando? Tell me the truth. We are good friends. Aren't we?"

"Edson, the exchange of police was Ana's idea."

No feeling in his body except for that bullet of ice in his heart. He forced himself to laugh. "The militia doesn't look at all deadly."

"But what rhythm when they march. Besides, that's the point, I think. Who would want to bomb children?"

"Ana doesn't trust me anymore."

A pause. "She just thinks you're tired."

"If I were in your position . . ." Edson closed his eyes. "I want you to know I won't fight."

He sighed. "Oh, Edson. When the time comes, I promise we will face the end together. I will teach you English. Then we will go to Itamaraty and burn an American flag. I will shoot you first. Then I'll hand you the gun, and you can shoot me."

Edson had the glass to his mouth before he understood. He smiled. The wind pounded the window. Jesus chuckled softly from the shadows of the hall.

"Edson? You still there?"

"Yes. Did you ever wonder if Hell is full or empty?"

"Interesting question. Phone the White House. Ask them. Perhaps tomorrow you can tell me what they say."

Nando hung up. Edson cradled the receiver to his chest. On the screen the American president thundered a warning. Children in uniforms milled, lost in São Paulo streets. Edson felt an overpowering urge to call Freitas and ask him the question, but was terrified of what the answer might be.

Morning. Gray light seeped through the window, made a high-tide line on the wall. From the corridor wafted the smell of coffee, the cheerful squawk of the station's parrot. Dolores, forehead and lip throbbing, pulled the blanket snug to her neck, cocooning against the early chill.

An avian shriek. *"Opa! Policia!"* The parrot whooped like a siren. Close by, a man laughed.

Dolores bolted up in bed, bringing the covers with her. Jack was standing in the open doorway of her cell.

His expression changed from surprise to empathy before becoming woeful. "Oh, sweetie. Bless your—"

"Stop." Her swollen lip muddied her words. She couldn't remember when she had been so relieved to see anyone. When she had been so furious. "Go away."

"Go away?"

She grunted, straightened her nightgown, beat the blankets around her into submission. "Don't need pity."

A raw and painful quiet. She hadn't the heart to raise her eyes. Poor Jack suffered Harry's sins.

"Let me get dressed, Jack. Turn around."

"God bless, girl," he said softly. "We've seen each other naked."

"Without glasses. In the dark. Doesn't count."

He turned his back.

She got out of bed, began gathering clothes. "Arrest you, too?"

"No. They just wanted to talk. God, I'm disappointed. I didn't expect this Presbyterian prude shit. They told me what you did. Said you refused a doctor. Why don't you let me call one for you. Please, baby? You should see somebody about that."

Talking was agony. Her whole face ached. "I'm fine." She turned her back on him and slipped her panties on under her nightgown. Shimmied into her jeans. "Talk about what?"

"Ana asked Fernando Machado to track me down. She wants to deal."

Dolores pulled the nightgown over her head. As if self-inflicted wounds weren't enough, she felt an arthritic complaint in her shoulder. "Carvalho know?"

"I get the feeling he doesn't."

"Um. Offer?"

"Canadian passports. Money. Lots of money."

"Plural passports?"

"Both of us. We'll go away to Vancouver together. With new identities, Dee."

She put her arms into her shirtsleeves. Stared blindly at the floor. "Where are my goddamned shoes?"

His voice was soft. "I know what you'll be leaving behind, hon. I can't make that up to you, but I'll always be there. Always love you. You never had that."

"What did I do with my goddamned fucking shoes?" The scab on her lip popped open, and she tasted blood. She kicked a nearby cardboard box, stubbed her toe. "Shit!"

"Dee?" He sounded so sad. "Not just for me, honey. Ana wants us to get Jaje out."

Dolores fumbled, suddenly numb-fingered, at buttons. The world fogged. She couldn't feel her bruised and throbbing toe, her battered face, her hands. Couldn't make her muscles work. Her arms dropped, forgotten and useless at her sides.

"Dolores?"

Streaks of light in the air, as if the room was crowded with visiting angels. "Has to ask."

"What?"

She formed the words carefully. The wound on her lip stretched and stung. "She can't saddle me with saving her damned daughter, unless she comes and asks."

Good Morning America

. . . we should take a moment here to review her accomplishments. She passed the Women's Rights Law. She began groundbreaking educational reforms which became a blueprint for other countries. Ana literally pulled a nation up from its knees.

I understand that you, personally, were her friend. And that you stood by her even through the takeover six years ago.

I saw the takeover as necessary, Joan. Tragic, yes. But necessary. Had Ana not acted decisively, the entrenched power structure would have resisted her legislation. It was at this time that, well—that I believe she made the mistake of relying on the advice of those around her.

So you're saying . . .

A few of those men, if you'll forgive me being blunt, are strong-arm goons with long histories of civil rights violations.

Part of Brazil's old death squads.

Yes.

What about the soldiers currently stationed in Brasília?

The militia?

Yes. They seem so . . . poorly trained, I suppose is the word.

I hate to think this. I really do. But it puts me in mind of the Iran/Iraq war.

The—

When the Iranian Army sent innocent children out into the field, thinking the Iraqis wouldn't fire.

Um. But they did fire, didn't they?

Yes, they did.

14

AMULET HIDDEN BY WHITE SHIRT AND SUBDUED TIE, HIROSHI WALKED the morning corridors of the embassy. He kept his head down, his eyes averted, just as the black woman had instructed.

He knew what was wrong with his life. It looked like *Quimbanda,* but nothing was ever as it seemed. The *on* his family carried opened him up to danger. When his grandmother died in the earthquake, no one, not even Hiroshi's father, offered as much as a cup of tea to soothe the place her blood polluted.

If Hiroshi were in Japan, he would perform *owabi* for the unhappy and vengeful ghost of his grandmother. He would walk the proper shrine one hundred times each morning. He would give *kuyō,* and rinse the site clean with hydrangea tea. He would leave her offerings of rice cakes and milk. Maybe then she wouldn't wander. Maybe then she would not punish him.

He halted when he thought he heard his dead father call his name. No. Just Shuma Kasahara. Hiroshi looked into the beaming, round face, then remembered, and quickly lowered his eyes.

But Kasahara would not have stolen his diary, would never use that to gain the evil eye over him. What was Hiroshi thinking? Still . . .

The old man had asked something, and was waiting for a reply. But since his trip to the Valley, the drone in Hiroshi's head had grown louder. He had not heard a word Kasahara said.

"Hiroshi. What is wrong?"

A quick bow. "Thank you for your concern, Kasahara-san." He cast around for some excuse for his behavior, could think of none.

Kasahara's worried frown deepened. "You are ill."

"I . . ." Hiroshi almost blurted out the ugly secret of his family's debts. How his father had abandoned his own mother's ghost. How Hiroshi was destined to bring ruin on Kasahara.

"Please. Come into my office."

Hiroshi went. And that was destiny, too. Since his trip to the Valley, Hiroshi had stayed up at night, his lights burning. Thinking, putting things in order. That's when he recalled the grandmother the family never spoke of. That's when he remembered the family's *on*. Realization of that sin had given him a sense of destiny, how all things fit together, everything but Hiroshi. Hiroshi, who, by disobeying orders, had lost his sense of place.

Kasahara closed the door. His hands fluttered, first toward Hiroshi as if he wished to touch his arm, then toward a lacquered table as if offering a poor gift. "Please. Please."

They knelt on pillows, facing each other. The old man poured tea from a thermos, offered a sticky cake. Hiroshi picked up the cup to be polite, put it to his mouth, and set it down.

The old man's face was as ritually tragic as a *kabuki* mask. "You eat and drink as if your stomach plagues you."

A quick nod. "Yes." There should be more he should say. Instead he propped his hands on his thighs, and waited.

"We complain when women nag us, and pamper us with food, but they are our strength. Don't you think it is so? It seems that when we are left to our own devices, we skip meals. We eat unhealthy things."

Kasahara had graciously given him a way out. Hiroshi nodded

in relief. "Yes. Surely that is all that is wrong with me. My wife is not at home, and I have acquired an indisposition."

The old man sipped from his cup. Waited.

"And if the indisposition continues, of course, I shall go to the doctor."

"Good. Good." Kasahara put his cup down. Eyes lowered, he braced his hands on his knees as if he would bow an apology. "I have wronged someone. Judged them unfairly."

"Ah?"

"Yesterday, Kengo came to see me." Gaze still averted, Kasahara picked up his cup again.

The warmth of humiliation washed Hiroshi's face. His skin tingled. Kengo. The brown enemy who destroyed for envy.

"He is worried about you."

Hiroshi was suddenly so hot that he wanted to tear off his tie, his jacket. The flesh around his eyes prickled. Did Kengo know Hiroshi had gone to the Valley? Did he know what was said there?

"Kengo tells me that it is his habit to wake three hours before dawn. He likes to walk then, he says, when the city is quiet and cool. And he tells me that for the past two mornings, when he passed your apartment house, he has seen your lights on."

Like the dead of Nagasaki, he would burst into flame. "But Kasahara-san. Why should Kengo know where I live? Why should he watch me?"

"That is his job. He means nothing by it."

"He sees my light on, and thinks . . . all this because of my indisposition. Why doesn't he come to me directly? I would tell him. Of course I can't sleep, so indisposed. There is nothing sinister in that."

"No one said that it was sinister."

It was the heat that made his voice rise out of control. "Have I done something to offend?"

He saw the truth in the old man's face. But, being kind, Kasahara shook his head. "No, no. Noth—"

"Kasahara-san, forgive me." Hiroshi's words emerged as a strangled cry. "I shamed you. I shamed myself." That's when the tears came. Kasahara knew Hiroshi had begged help from the KGB. Everyone in the embassy knew. There was no way to escape it— the nail that sticks up is always hammered down.

He couldn't have made this mistake. How had it happened? *Baka!* his mother would have shouted. *You stupid!* From the time he was two years old, she would lock him out of the house when he had done wrong. He would sit on the porch and sob, just as he sobbed now—the same grieving pain in his chest. To think that once he had longed for the romance of being a masterless samurai. *Baka! Stupid!* He should have remembered what loneliness was.

What was left for Hiroshi to do but write a note: *Shinde owabi suru,* and then to throw himself in front of a train. Jump from his office window. Put the muzzle of his gun in his mouth. *My death is apology.*

"Please, Hiroshi! Do not upset yourself so! Kengo now agrees with you. Yes. Don't look so surprised. This is true. He has told the ambassador that it was not your fault that the information about the space launch was incorrect. Kengo distrusts the CIA, and thinks they purposefully misled us. At least he has told me this. If he has not yet told you, it is only because he feels shame at his mistake."

Hiroshi was so tired that he couldn't think. Who was lying now? The Americans, or Kengo? No. They were in it together. And they had seduced Kasahara.

Kasahara clucked in concern. "So bad an indisposition, Hiroshi. Very, very bad. You must take a few days off."

The hardest thing Roger ever had to do. He picked up the receiver, looked around. The phone was in an estuary of the shopping center, at this early hour empty but for a pair of teenagers sailing cardboard signs upwind, and an old guy with dark glasses and white cane, seated on a bench.

The teenagers passed, laughing. Roger turned his back in case the blind man was trained to read lips, and the dark glasses some CIA one-way trick.

Roger dialed the number from memory, dropped change in the pay phone's slot. There was a flat, ugly buzz. On the other end of the line, the phone was ringing.

A click. Then, *"Sim?"*

He cupped his hand around the receiver and whispered, "Hello?"

"O que? Quem é? Fala, pô."

Sounded like Fatty's voice. Aw, jeez. Roger didn't even know their names. *"Sou eu."* Oh. That was brilliant. *It's me.* That was good.

Fatty was determinedly affable, the kind of guy who would always play along. *"Pois é. É você."* He agreed: Right. It's you.

"From NASA."

Silence.

Oh, man. Maybe Roger memorized the number wrong.

"Dr. Lintenberg?"

Roger let his breath out in a long sigh. "Yeah. Something's happened. Something big. I'm gonna speak in English, okay? You can talk Portuguese. There's a guy maybe within earshot, and I don't—"

"Where are you?"

"Shopping center."

"What block?"

"Uh . . ." He pulled the map from his pocket and unfolded it.

"What block?" Fatty was breathless.

The map wasn't any use. "I don't know. Everything in this damned town looks alike. I got off the bus—"

"Which bus?"

"Shit. I don't know."

"Look around you, Dr. Lintenberg. Tell me what you see."

"Just that blind guy." The man was smiling, talking to himself, rocking back and forth, while a jazzy Elis Regina number drifted from a nearby music store. He looked like a white guy from Duluth trying to do Ray Charles. "I don't *think* I was followed."

"No, no. Tell me what you *see*. Read the names of the shops."

"Oh. Right. Uh . . ." He looked around, could see nothing from his alcove but some foliage, the bench, and the blind man. "There was a book store . . ."

"The name?"

"Started with 'Th.' Thant? No . . ."

"Thot?"

"Oh! Oh, yeah. That's—"

"Stay right there. Right there. No matter what happens."

"Uh, what's going to—"

But Fatty was off the line.

Roger hung up. The two teenagers hurried through the alcove, this time signless, moving in the opposite direction. From the main part of the complex came the scent of brewing morning coffee and the cheerful cacophony of Brazilian retail.

Roger imagined he could hear the moans of the dying UFO pilot, *Maria Teresinha . . . Seguro.*

Telling her that something was "certain"? Or that he was "safe"? Five last words, and the pilot spent four of them saying her name.

Lab Coat had told Roger, "At first glance it seems like an ordinary Cessna, but look at this."

In the instrument panel were bird's nests of wires, miniature cities of microchips, copper tubes, pumps, and jars of mercury— Rube Goldberg variations on the theme of propulsion. And yet, if Lab Coat was to be believed, they allowed this single-engine Cessna to hover soundlessly, to outmanuever and outfly an F-22. The CIA had radar tapes showing the Cessna traveling Mach 9, making ninety-degree turns without slowing down. God. Roger wanted to get the word out. But who was going to believe it?

He paced. Nibbled on a fingernail. The blind guy stopped rocking, leaned his head back, and sang along with Elis.

Crap. Fatty was going to want to hear about hairy aliens with
claws, a Latin American favorite. Or the little grays with the big
black eyes, the Worldwide Best of Show. Or maybe Roger's own
choice, the pale, winged, beanpole Mothras who smelled like rot-
ten eggs. Oh yeah. MUFON was going to expect a little more than
some thirtyish guy in a flight suit with DELORENZO stenciled on
his breast.

Suddenly a man in a business suit walked around the corner,
grim-faced, moving fast. He looked at the man on the bench, then
looked at Roger. He slipped his hand into his jacket pocket.

Oh, Christ. Run.

Too late.

Then the guy who should have had a gun was somehow holding
a walkie-talkie. He paused, whispered into it, and left.

The CD of Elis Regina ended, and in the lull, Roger heard
sirens whoop. Oh, jeez. What was going on? The blind man was
starting to look worried.

Get out quick. That's what Roger should do. But which way? He
was still trying to decide on a direction when he was spun around
and captured in a rib-crushing *abraço*.

"Let's leave," Fatty said into Roger's ear.

Roger hurried to keep up. Fatty's car, a sun-faded Volkswagen,
sat three blocks down, engine running. Marcel was in the driver's
seat.

Fatty pushed Roger into the back, jumped in next to Marcel,
slammed the door. "Go! Go!"

Marcel peeled rubber. Roger checked the rear window. Despite
the sirens, Roger could see no danger behind. But the front seat
was suddenly a battleground.

Fatty snapped, "Slow *down!*"

"Oh, pardon me. I somehow got the idea you might be in a

hurry. If you wish me to, I can stop right here. We can let the riot catch up with us."

"Riot?" Roger asked.

Marcel said, "It was your choice to meet him at Edifício Eldorado, when the demonstrations were beginning not three blocks away. We could have had him meet us someplace safer . . ."

"He does not know the city."

"He could not find something easy, like the cathedral?"

"The cathedral? Every dope dealer in Brasília meets there."

"Then by all means, let us sacrifice ourselves on the altar of the off beat." To underscore his irritation, Marcel took a corner on two wheels and sped toward a yellow light, scooting under it just as it turned red.

Roger searched frantically for a seatbelt. A taxi honked.

Marcel took both hands off the wheel to give the taxi driver a cupped-palm fuck-you gesture. "I find it so *upsetting.*"

A *tsk.* Obviously Fatty found it upsetting, too. "So you will do a Paulinho Bonfim against the next light pole."

Roger found half of the belt. He dug his hand into the gritty rift between the seats for the rest.

They raced a bus and won. Marcel shot in front of it and abruptly turned right. Roger looked out the side window. For a heartbeat all he could see was grille.

"Well," Fatty said dryly, "I have lost last night's dinner into my pants, and I suppose you have outrun the rioters who, after all, were on foot."

The sense of velocity was terrible and exhilarating. Major McNatt would have loved it. Roger symbolically girded his loins with as much as he had found of the seatbelt.

"It was *your* idea," Marcel said.

"Guys?" Roger said. "Don't you want to know?"

They turned around. Both of them.

"Watch the road!" Roger gasped.

Marcel passed a truck by pulling into the wrong lane. Oncoming traffic blared. "So what have you found out?"

Fatty turned around in his seat. "Yes. Go on. What is it?"

"The UFOs you've been sighting . . ." Roger raised his arm in an oh-well gesture, then let it fall. "They're Brazilian."

A screech of tires. Roger flew forward, tumbling onto the floorboard. When he sat up, he saw that the car had pulled to a stop at the curb in front of DeutschBanc.

Marcel peered over his seat at Roger. "What?"

"Brazilians." Roger said. "Piloting Cessnas."

To his surprise, they didn't laugh.

Voices woke Edson. He sat bolt upright, and a headache met him like a wall. Pain made his vision blur. Even through that fog, he could see soldiers in his bedroom. Panicked, he lunged to the right side of his headboard. His holster was empty.

"*Puxa vida.*" Playful Carioca Portuguese, the spoken singsong of Rio. A colonel in full camouflage gear parked his hands on his gunbelt, walked to the bed, and smiled down at Edson. "Good morning to you, too. Fortunate for me, neh? That I took your pistol."

The room spun. The bed rocked like a boat. Edson tried to steady himself by holding onto the headboard, but motion sickness won. He leaned over the side of the bed and threw up.

"*Opa.*" Cheerfully, the colonel stepped out of the way. "Too bad we sent the maid home. Private, clean this up." He put his hands to his chest in a theatrical display of candor. "Oh, please, *Senhor* Director. Don't stare at me so. It pains me to see you distressed. General Fernando sends his apologies, and says to treat you with the utmost cordiality. Therefore we stopped on the way here and bought sweet rolls. Sergeant, make us a pot of coffee."

Edson unwound himself from the sheet, and sat hunched, head in his hands, over the clean side of the bed. He squinted at the clock. 10:15. Sun glared through the blinds, made his head throb. "I'm under arrest."

The colonel sat down beside him, patted Edson's knee. "Just until the Army is in place. Consider this an enforced brunch."

"Have the Americans invaded?"

"Only a little."

A private came into the room, carrying a pail, looking resigned. Over the stench of bile and last night's whiskey, Edson could smell coffee brewing.

The colonel said, "This morning there were more demonstrations, complete with signs. When have Brazilians ever organized anything more than Carnaval? Well, all right. To make the invasion go smoothly, General Fernando has us learning English; but that's less organization than pragmatism, *não é?* So. Now rocks are being thrown at armed soldiers. That is *anything* but pragmatic. We caught one of the rock-throwers—a Panamanian. Imagine. We get rich, and everyone hates us but Peru. Yes! Peru. And I know you will sleep easier, knowing they are on our side. By the way, it was your own agent—the one from Blumenau—who arrested the Panamanian and interrogated him. You see? We continue to work together. General Fernando has no doubts about your loyalty."

Edson coughed so hard that he gagged.

The colonel prudently inched away. "So. We told the foreign press about the Panamanian, but do they care? CNN compares us to Argentina and El Salvador—as if we would line up for the honor of dying for politics."

"Am I allowed to take a shower and get dressed?"

"My dear Director, I hope you will take this in the manner it was meant: I wholeheartedly wish you would. The private will accompany you—won't you, Private?—but he promises not to watch, and never to compare."

Edson got to his feet, watery-kneed. His whole body ached. The young private, still resigned, dropped the sponge in the bucket and got up with him.

As Edson started toward the bathroom, the colonel called out happily, "General Fernando told me to keep your pistol. Nothing personal, neh? He says he beat you by a score of eight to six even when he was drunk. He fears you may not miss if the target is closer."

CNN, Live

. . . press was abruptly moved into the hotel. But I must point out here, Bernie, that if worse comes to worse, there are no bomb shelters in Brazil. Not even any basements. The hotel is converting a food locker, but . . .

Susan? What's the mood there in Brasília?

Ah . . . Not quite panic-stricken. A great deal of confusion, though. Most seem to view this sudden switch to martial law as a simple inconvenience.

I have the results of a recent poll. Susan? Can you see it there?

Uh-huh. Yes, Bernie. I can see it now.

A full sixty-three percent of Brazilians want Bonfim to step down. However, if you'll notice, only thirteen percent believe that she acted illegally, or that Brazil has actually put weapons in space.

Well, Bernie, Brazilians are nonconfrontational. They worship compromise. In fact there's a term here, 'Dar um jeito,' which fits the mood here very well. If you'll forgive my free-wheeling translation, it means something like, 'There's always a solution,' and it's understood—and silently agreed upon—that the solution might just bend the law a little. Law is far less important here than order. We Americans simply don't think that way. No, Bernie. Brazilians don't want to be bombed. They think their president is completely in the right, and that the U.N. is dangerously paranoid, but leveling the city to prove that point just isn't worth it.

15

When Hiroshi walked out of the pharmacy holding his pink-wrapped parcel, he saw militia in the street: confused-looking children with angelic faces, automatic rifles in their hands. A knot of them stood at the corner, arguing about what was meant by "a defensive position." They didn't bother to look up as Hiroshi passed.

What had happened? Was the American military already invading? The Americans would bomb, and Brazilians would be helpless. There were no sirens. No basements. No shelter.

He clutched the package to his chest and walked quickly on. Around the next corner was another squad. The officer with them shot Hiroshi a suspicious look, then ordered him to stop.

Hiroshi obeyed. The gun holstered at the back of his belt felt extraordinarily heavy. The tip of the short barrel dug at his kidney. He kept his eyes lowered so the officer would not see fear on his face, and search him.

"What's in the package?"

That single-note drone in Hiroshi's ears returned. "Please. Only medicine. Has some—"

"Open it."

Tremendous pressure against his temples. It felt as if his head would explode. Hiroshi tugged the string free. His eyes stung.

"Nervous?"

The officer knew Hiroshi was hiding something. He would make him take off his jacket. Would see the gun and—diplomat or no—would stand him up against the nearest wall and have him shot. "Sorry. Please. I am only tired."

The man sorted through the bottles. "Um. Yet there is something here for nerves, I see. And for the stomach." A pause that Hiroshi did not have the words to fill in.

The officer prompted, "Aspirin. Vitamins. A lot of medicine."

"Yes. I have been ill. Has something happened?"

"Papers."

Without raising his eyes, Hiroshi handed them over. He heard the officer leaf through his passport. Then leaf through it again. "I am a diplomat."

"Yes. I can see."

He couldn't breathe. "If something has happened, I should return to the embassy."

A noncommittal grunt.

"I said I should return to the embassy, perhaps." He looked up. The man was comparing passport photo with Brazilian ID. "Do you find my papers in order?"

"Nothing, Mr. Sato, is in order. You were on your way—?"

"Home. But . . ."

Down the street, the squad had stopped a car. The driver, a Brazilian, was swearing.

"Then go there at once. And stay inside until instructed you can leave. President Bonfim has declared a state of emergency." The officer handed the medicine and the papers back. He waved Hiroshi on.

The package was in tatters. Hiroshi let the wind take it. He grappled with the armful of bottles. Half a block later he lost the vitamins, and didn't stop to pick them up.

Hiroshi made the turn into the breezeway of his apartment building. He would go inside and listen to the news. He would have a beer, and then another. He would call Taguchi so her voice could drown out that drone.

Someone lunged from the bushes and grabbed his elbow. Medicine bottles fell, exploded. Pills scattered like roaches in the light. Hiroshi's gaze moved up—sandaled feet, smudged work shirt—to be stopped by hot blue eyes.

"My father does not know I came here," Piehl's son said. "I did not want him to worry."

"What—"

The boy dug his fingers into the meat of Hiroshi's arm. "Damn you," he hissed. "You are the one who asked the questions that will kill my father."

Hiroshi shook his head, trying to make the words fall into place.

The boy misunderstood. "No. You listen to me! You put him into the hands of the CIA. They have turned everything around!"

Hiroshi stepped back. Pills crunched underfoot. "I am afraid. You must hide us!" the boy urged. "You are a diplomat. Give me and my father political asylum."

"Sorry. So sorry." Hiroshi pulled away.

A huge troop transport truck growled up the street. Piehl's son withdrew, crouching, into the shadows. "They will kill you. Like us, you know too much."

Mid-morning the soldiers came: three flak-jacketed commandos and a tense captain.

During her life's more melodramatic moments, Dolores pictured herself facing a firing squad. Her fantasies were wrong. It was the captain's comical search for his wallet when Madalena demanded ID. It wasn't stiff-upper-lipped courage, but the passivity of shock. It was trivial decisions: take her purse? a sweater?

A polite hostess, Madalena walked her to the door. Once there, they might have kissed cheeks. Madalena offered her hand, instead. Then the captain took Dolores outside. The reporters were gone. Soldiers lined the streets. And a Jeep Wagoneer was waiting.

Dolores didn't balk when they ordered her to get in. She didn't try to jump from the car. She thought they would go to the Urban Military Sector. They didn't. The Wagoneer headed south, picked up the highway, and sped past the zoo and the airport.

Disorienting, how the city always abruptly ended and the desert began. She'd meant to paint this, but had never really understood it before.

She wanted to ask the captain if the trip would be long. She didn't. And it wouldn't have mattered. He sat in the front next to the driver, staring stonily ahead. The commando beside her took a comic book from his flak jacket and began reading. No one spoke.

The Wagoneer slowed. The driver steered off the asphalt into the dry grass and scrub brush. When they were far from the witness of the highway, they stopped. The commando put his comic book away. The captain stepped out of the car.

She got out, too, cradling her purse like a infant. They were so young. Just soldier boys. The commandos looked uncomfortable. The captain didn't seem to know what to do with his hands.

Time for last words, but she couldn't say them. Let her progeny, color and form and light, say them for her. As last testament, words were too theatrical, yet not emotional enough. She and Harry. What a pair. Neither of them had ever understood sentiment.

Dolores looked away. *Aim right,* she thought. *Make life leave me as suddenly as city leaves the desert.* She took a breath that tasted of dust, and tried to imagine snow. The humps of distant hills were a bruised violet, the sky a deep, drowning blue.

The sound of an engine startled her. A Volvo drove up and

stopped. A rear window lowered. A major in full dress uniform beckoned. "Please."

The Volvo was scarab green. The interior a tan leather wound in its carapace. She climbed in the backseat beside the major. He reached across her and shut the door.

"Comfortable?" the major asked. "I can turn up the air-conditioning."

She didn't know how she felt. She stroked the soft plump belly of her purse. The driver eased the heavy car across the prairie floor. Once on the highway, they sped south.

"Not too long now," the major said.

No. Not too long. Soon, a small town. At the end of a rutted road, a frame house. The outside was royal blue; the slatted vertical planks inside, turquoise. Worn hardwood floor. A small kitchen. One bedroom.

"Would you care for something to drink?" the major asked.

A bed with a rusting iron headboard. A scarred nightstand.

"Juice? Mineral water?" he persisted. "Coca-Cola?"

She shook her head, and heard the door quietly being pulled to. Outside the window lay a barren yard surrounded by a living bamboo wall.

Dear God, not this. She couldn't take this. Better to die than be imprisoned in this claustrophobic world. If she crawled out of the window and ran, would they be kind enough to shoot her? Maybe if they killed her quickly, it would be like walking into the light.

Because there was not enough light here. Not enough form or space.

Behind came a click, and a familiar contralto voice. "I should have expelled you years ago."

Dolores turned, tears streaming.

A fleeting slip in Ana's expression; a quick recovery. "You look a mess. You expect me to feel sorry for you? I heard the truth from

O.S. You beat your own face into a table." She took a breath.
"Well?"

Pigeon's blood-red suit, terra-cotta skin. Ana was a glowing
ember in the shadows.

"Well? Didn't you?"

Dolores looked out the window.

An explosive *puh* of exasperation. The resolute click of heels on
hardwood. "I don't care who did it. I should have had you shot.
Edson Carvalho would have killed you gladly. Life would be easier, don't you think? That is the trick of politics: someone gets in
the way, you rid yourself of them. I learned that from you." A
pause. "Well?"

Something Dolores had not noticed before—movement in the
air above the yard. A whirling galaxy of gnats, drawn each to each,
never touching.

"You killed my husband because he beat me, but you—you had
to prove you were strong enough to stay with yours. Poor little
Ana. Wasn't that what you wanted me to believe? That I couldn't
take care of myself?"

The gloom beneath the bamboo shifted, and a tomcat wove his
way from the dark. He sat and, with bubblegum pink tongue,
began washing. His striped coat was a study in brown.

"I loved . . ." Twenty-five years, but the words not yet worn
smooth. Ana's voice snagged on their edges. "You had to take
Paulo away, didn't you? You were the one who had three abor-
tions. Then you spoil my child and take her away, too. My fault. I
should have remembered that you were only my handler, not my
friend."

Dolores pushed herself away from the window. Ana stood, legs
apart, hands on her hips. "Oh, now *that* looks presidential. Didn't
I teach you that women in politics can't afford to whine?"

The frown wavered.

"You know, Ana? I saw Paulo beat you once. Harry was a crazy
asshole, but he never hit me like that." Dolores propped her arm

against the window frame, rested her head against it. "It's too late. I can't help you anymore. The Company's changed, or maybe it hasn't. Maybe I just got smarter. Anyway, it's all about running the game. That's all there ever was."

"You never did get smart," Ana said. When Dolores laughed, she added sadly, "I didn't, either."

Outside, the cat prowled the yard, lithe, muscular. Massive masculine head, the self-assured eyes of a predator. "Is it him?"

Silence. A direct hit, then. Had the question confused Ana, she would have said something.

"God, Ana. With you, it's always a man. At least Paulo was pretty. So was that married one—what was his name? Remember? I sent that anonymous letter to his wife? And the truck driver you met in '83, the one with the great ass. The one I did the bag job on. But *this* one? What do you see in him?"

Still nothing—not a sharp word, not a joke. Dolores looked around and saw how frightened Ana was.

"Shit."

"Dolores, you can't understand . . ."

"You're right. I can't. Three times I jumped into that fucking river and pulled you to shore. Now you turn around and crawl right back in. Jesus God, Ana. Why? What makes you addicted to assholes? Wouldn't it be easier just to buy yourself a dildo and a whip?"

Ana's eyes glittered, a dark spark of anger.

"Okay. So tell me. How did you let things get so out of control? And what are you doing with all these missing people? You never got rid of your critics before—sensitive, suddenly, in your old age, Ana? You going to make me disappear like that, too?"

"The CIA is doing it. They want to make me look bad."

"Bullshit."

"You don't know what the CIA does, Dolores. You are expendable. They would have destroyed you, had Edson not put you under arrest. So. Here you are at age fifty-three, trying so hard to be strong that most men think you are lesbian. You have no family left. No friends." The pain in Dolores's face seemed to satisfy her. She smiled. "You coerced me here. Now are you telling me you won't take Jaje?"

"I'd never tell you that."

"Good. It will be safer to send Jack with you. Lucky you have one person you can't push away. Besides, you will be less conspicuous as a family. Nando has booked you on a Varig flight to Lima. Remind Jaje, when she gets to Canada, that she mustn't be careless. Don't let her stay out late. Tell her not to drive fast. Tell . . ."

Ana's face contorted, the face of someone just informed of a devastating loss. Dolores started to her. Ana brusquely waved her back.

"You tell her that for me."

"I will."

"You remind her to eat right."

"Yes."

"And to balance her checkbook . . ." Air exploded from Ana's lungs. Her legs seemed to give out, and she sat down hard on the edge of the bed. "Jaje's missing. Nando says . . ."

Dolores sat down, put her arm around Ana's shoulders.

"Nando doesn't think—well, the CIA . . . no point in hurting her. She is just a little girl, and it would look bad for them, wouldn't it. Wouldn't it?"

"Yes, sweetie, it would."

"She ran away. Ran away! I could never control her. Even when she was a baby. And she was too much like you, always selfish, always did just what she wanted. You know her."

"I know."

Ana was so tiny that, as usual, Dolores felt cowlike. If Ana was anything, she was a bird. The bones of her hand felt hollow.

"She'll turn up."

Ana nodded, burrowed her cheek into the nook of Dolores's

neck. She held on tight to her sleeve, as if begging to be pulled from yet another river. "Nando felt so badly. He tried . . . Still, men aren't good at such things."

"Shhh." Of course men weren't good at it. Not their fault. Only mothers could give comfort like that. "Ana." Dolores held her, rocked her, smoothed stray curls from her forehead. "Who's named for all good endings. Jaje's fine. I know it. I see it in my crystal ball."

"Dolores." Ana clung to her as she had in the hospital, at the funeral home, at Paulo's gravesite. "My Lady of Sorrows."

Tonight Show Monologue

Well, folks, taking a poll here. How many of you ever thought we'd fight a war with Brazil? Huh? Is that wild or what? You see the film clips of those, what do they call them? Not soldiers. Militia? Huh? Definitely not soldiers, ladies and gentlemen. See old World War II clips of the German Army, and you knew—hey—am I right? This was going to be a war. Anybody who has the thighs for goosestepping . . .

But these guys . . . They got lost on their way to summer camp.

Seriously. Where do they hide the real Brazilian soldiers—Paraguay? Think about that. All of a sudden we're back to the duck and cover, and it's Brazil. Jeez. Brazil. I don't know. You want to just give up now? Show of hands. How would it be—a Brazilian invasion? I hear that if we let them take over, they promise string bikinis on every beach . . . Oh. Guy back there's ready for a takeover. Watch it! Wife's got an incoming . . .

And Bonfim promises to wear that same dress she wore to the State Dinner here four years ago. Was that hot? Huh? Proves you don't have to have a bad bod to be . . . don't . . . no, don't groan, ladies. It's only sexist if you girls don't have a thing for Kennedy. What? Gore? Naw. Not Gore. He's too much trouble for a fantasy life. You have to imagine winding him up first. But seriously . . .

16

AT THE LOUD, PERSISTENT KNOCK, ROGER OPENED THE DOOR. NATALIE
Wood was standing there. Not Natalie Wood like she was before
she died, but Natalie Wood like she was in *Splendor in the Grass,*
which besides *Close Encounters,* was Roger's all-time favorite movie.
He'd seen it first when he was twelve, and even though he didn't
quite understand everything, he knew the sad parts had something to do with her being horny.

What a flick.

And here she was. Taller, okay? And maybe thinner. And black.
Well . . . not *black.* More tan—the kind of peachy-bronze color
girls can only achieve before they're thirty. But this Natalie Wood
was tan all over, even in those hard-to-reach places like the insides
of her elbows.

And she had on a red tube top. And short shorts. White short
shorts. Oh, jeez. And she had on sandals, and her little bronze
toes had little pink toenails, like shells.

She spoke. *"Titía Dolores está?"*

Roger knew what the words meant. He just couldn't put them
together.

She rolled her eyes. And then she said in perfect English, "Oh du-u-uh. Like, are you stupid, or just deaf?"

Roger couldn't decide.

She shoved past him. "Aunt Dee?"

A terrific butt. A religious experience of a butt.

"Aunt Dee!"

Whatever she wanted: her aunt, a car, the moon, his life's blood. He stood behind her, his hands out in silent but heartfelt offer.

She whirled. Instantaneously, he lifted his gaze to her face.

"Her car's here," she said.

"Yes."

A huff. She parked her hands on that tiny brown waist, tapped her foot. Her hip went up and down. "So? Is this like a *test*, or something?"

"Uh, you haven't been watching the news, have you?" How could he tell her what had happened to dear, sweet Aunt Dee? It might break her heart. Ah. She might need comforting. "A bunch of guys came and took her away."

She cocked her head. Frowned, prettily. Her hair was a brown cloud.

"In the middle of the night. Guys with guns. Policemen. Probably secret police. I tried to stop them, but . . ."

"Dee was ar-*rest*-ed?"

"Great big guns."

She was going to cry. Any second now, she was going to cry. And he'd take her in his arms. Stroke her back until she melted into him like toffee. He had to remind himself to stand up straight, though. She was tall for a girl.

"Bummer." She walked into the kitchen.

He tagged along.

She opened the refrigerator and bent over. God. Bent over. And those white shorts rode up high, higher, and—

Suddenly he was looking into her face. Uh-oh. She was angry.

"Come on. Get real. There's no *food.* Eighteen hours on the bus, and there's no *food.* Everybody was all shoved together. The john got stopped up. Kids screaming. I mean, nobody could get any sleep. Who ever thought I'd do eighteen hours of hell to get *into* Brasília? So anyway, I get to the only truly un-happening place in the country, and, like, I can't find a taxi. The busses aren't running. The soldiers are stopping all the cars. Sure. Like the American Army's gonna come down the Rodoviária in a fleet of Hondas. And then I get here, and there's no *food.*"

So soon. Already Roger had disappointed her.

She started searching cabinets. "I can't *believe* Aunt Dee doesn't have some cookies or something. She always makes cookies for me."

"My name's Roger. Uh. Dr. Roger Lintenberg, actually, although you can just call me Roger. I'm with NASA."

"Uh-huh."

"You know the shuttle? I work on that."

She reached up to the top shelf, and her right nipple started pulling out of the tube top and any second and oh my God any second now Roger was going to find out if it was pink or tan or please please please please . . .

Crap. She brought down a box of crackers, turned it over in her hands, speculatively. Straightened her top.

"I'm very important to the Hubble, too. You know, the Hubble? The telescope?"

She looked at him. "I nearly have a degree in communications, okay? I'm not, like, you know, a ditz."

"Yeah? Communications, huh? I met Forrest Sawyer once."

"Um."

"And I work for the CIA." Oh! Fuck! How could he have said that? Stupid! So stupid he felt the urge to slam his forehead repeatedly into the refrigerator. The goddamned hose was bug.

She smirked, went back to reading the package. "For sure."

"I could maybe fix you something."

Finally. A spark of interest. "What?"

"Let's see." He searched the refrigerator. The cabinet. Then he slumped. "We could go out."

"Hello-o-o? Anybody home? You hear what I said about the taxis? The busses? Mom, like, imposed martial law, okay? You really work for the CIA, huh."

"Uh . . ."

"I mean, 'cause that's what they're saying about Mom and Aunt Dee, but give me a break. Mom? She goes ballistic if I stay out too late. She has guys follow me, you know? Like on dates. Last year? I'm the only junior at UCLA who has her own chaperon. So there's some guy from O.S. watching me, and some FBI guy watching him. I mean—get a life. And she never lets me talk to reporters. 'Low profile,' she always says. I don't know. She's got this overprotective thing."

"Uh . . ."

"So she put Aunt Dee in jail, huh? Is that Mom, or what? Things get tough, she blames somebody else."

"Can we . . ." Roger's mouth went dry. His tongue ran aground. "What?"

He waved toward the door. Waved again. ". . . go outside. Just— you know, maybe for a minute?"

She opened the package. Put a cracker into her mouth. Searched the refrigerator.

"There's food out there. Outside."

She looked around, expression challenging. Ritz cracker protruded from her lips like the tip of a tongue.

"We could catch one. Fried chicken, mmmm, sounds good. Or not."

The cracker disappeared into her mouth. She chewed. "Gross."

"Eggs! Okay, eggs. Come on. We can look for them together. Just like Easter, you know? Easter eggs."

She made a face, but followed anyway. They walked out to the yard: Roger, Natalie Wood, and the box of crackers.

"So where do we look?" she asked.

He licked his lips. The tube top and the white shorts were enticing, but scary. "Are you, uh, Ana Maria Bonfim's daughter?"

"Yeah. So where's the eggs?"

Oh, no. Had the Company overheard? Was she already being followed? What would some stone-cold killer like McNatt do to her? Or worse—that dork, Kinch? Kinch was the kind who would tie her up. Probably the only way he could get his fun. Kinch wouldn't be standing here like a gentleman, staring at that tube top. He'd be ripping it off. Oh. Roger was in big trouble.

A louder, more exasperated, "Are we gonna look for eggs, or not? And then who's going to cook them? You don't expect me . . ."

Roger told her to wait right there. Right there. To not say a word. It had to be love, he guessed—because even though he knew the consequences, he tiptoed into the house and gathered Dee's car keys and gun.

During brunch the colonel's cellular phone rang. "Ah, yes, General!" he said into the receiver. He poured himself another cup of coffee and winked at Edson. "He's right here. Do you wish to speak with him?"

Edson pushed his plate away, the sweet roll half eaten.

The colonel eyed Edson, shrugged. "Excuse . . . ? But of course! Your orders were very explicit . . . what? Oh. Sweet rolls. From that little bakery in the Diplomatic Sector. Yes, General. I have been practicing my English every chance I get. I'll be ready. Um? I'll tell him. *Ciao.*"

He thumbed the disconnect, folded the phone, put it back into the voluminous pocket of his camo jacket. "General Fernando says to tell you hello. And so I must now tell you *ciaozinho.* An agent of yours is here to see you. I'll let him in now, shall I?"

The colonel gathered his men and left. Reinhard Piehl walked into the room. "The Army held me out there for two hours!"

Everything is *schiesse*." Piehl dropped into a chair, sorted through the cups on the table until he found a clean one. "This country is going down the shit hole and everyone makes jokes. Brazil is a nation of two-year-olds. There is no organization here, Edson," he said as he poured. "You don't understand the concept of organization. My father didn't understand it, the KGB didn't understand it. My German mother, now, she understood organization. Fernando Machado will find out the American Army understands it, too. The goddamned coffee is cold."

Edson sighed, shoved his hands into his pockets. He looked out the window at the dusty blue sky, and wished for rain. A soft rain, not a tropical afternoon downpour. Edson wanted to be buried under goosedown clouds, dripping trees. Someone, somewhere should cry for him.

"*Schiesse*." Piehl rested his head in his hand, and with the tip of a finger slashed a series of X's across the tabletop. He sighed, stuck out his lower lip. "The Army took my pistol away. 'Nothing personal,' they told me. So, anyway. What do you want me to do with the Japanese?"

A ghostly X of moisture evaporated from the polished wood. Edson thought he heard the squeak of glass. "What?"

"The Japanese we're doing the bag job on. If the embassy maid is still reliable, our target is on sick leave. My guess is that she *is* reliable, and that she will stay that way. She has the face of a mud road, and da Silva's her raven. I hear the man could make a rubber fuck-toy come. So. On his way home today, our target Japanese boy stopped in a pharmacy, bought a bunch of pills. He's not malingering."

Piehl lifted the cup to his mouth and drank. The way his lips met the porcelain. How Freitas—Jesus. What was he thinking? Edson quickly looked away. "I don't . . ."

"The target who works for the Japanese Trade Ministry."

"Ah." Edson couldn't remember.

"Sato. Mr. Spy Hobbyist? The one who knows Kinch. Edson. For God's sake. The one who went to Blumenau and flushed me out."

Edson ran his fingers through the change in his pocket, found a coin, held onto it for dear life. "Yes, yes. That one." Edson looked at the clock. Five-thirty already. Ana would still be in her office. Freitas would be alone. Edson wondered what the man was doing. He could go there. To Alvorada. He needed to talk to him. That was all. Just talk. Find out about the Disappeareds and—

"The more I see of our target, I doubt he's with the Americans. He may be out of the Japanese loop, too. Makes him a waste of manpower. Although—one never knows—he could come in useful some day. What do you want me to do?"

Not the abyss Edson longed for. No bottomless black eyes. Bright summer-sky blue.

"Edson? Are you listening?"

Edson turned the coin over and over in his pocket until the friction against his thigh made his skin tingle, made his chest feel tight. When Piehl left, he promised himself, he would have a drink.

"Goddamn it. You brought me all the way from Santa Catarina to run this boy. You want us to keep up the bag game or not?"

That question again. Edson wished Piehl would leave. He took his hand from his pocket and looked down at the coin in his palm. Tails.

"Keep it going," Edson said.

She hated the gun. "Do you have to, like, do the Clint Eastwood thing? And where are we going, anyway?"

Roger hunched over the wheel. He'd been heading northeast for almost an hour. Not even a farmhouse in sight. And the sun was going down. "I don't know."

She *tsk*ed. Crossed her legs. Jiggled a foot. "You're not CIA."

"I *am*."

"For sure."

"I *am*."

She gave a world-weary sigh. "I've been *around*, Roger, you know? People fit their jobs, okay? I mean, one look and I *knew* you were an engineer or something geeky—nothing personal. And spies all have these Mafia kind of eyes, just like Edson Carvalho. Can we get something to eat now?"

Dee's Toyota squeaked and rattled over the washboard clay road. He checked the rearview. Nothing but sand and scrub brush. A dying sun set the tops of the hills aflame. The valley floor was violet. Night was coming on fast. What if they had a flat tire? Roger looked at the gas gauge again. Still half full. Couldn't be. What if the damned thing was broken? "Look for a farmhouse," he told her.

"Why?"

"We're going to call your mom."

"Like, I don't think so."

"Jaje, the house was bugged. The CIA heard everything." Roger clenched the steering wheel so hard that he could feel the vibration of the road in his shoulders. "No telling what they'll do."

Her foot went up and down. The sandal flapped. "Roger," she said in a tone of consummate boredom. "Spies are only dangerous in the movies."

"Why can't we just call your mom and tell her where you are? She's probably worried."

"I don't *want* Mom." No ennui this time. An unsettling quiver in her voice. "I want my Aunt Dee."

He took his eyes from the road. Her hair was windblown, her makeup streaked. She was pouting at the window. He allowed himself one pang of longing, then looked out the windshield again.

Whoa. Was that lights ahead? He touched the brake, let up when the tires lost traction in the dust.

"What?" she asked.

"That a car?" Oh, shit. What if that was a car? What if it was Mc-Natt? How many bullets did Roger have, anyway? He hadn't even bothered to check the round thing that held the . . . cylinder? Was that what it was called?

Jaje uncrossed her legs and leaned forward. "A town."

It was. Thank God. It was a town. The sun paraded behind the hills with red fanfare, flourishing banners of gold. The town shimmered on the horizon.

It was smaller than Roger had hoped. A few shacks, a one-room store, an attached pool hall. The store was closed, but warm light shone from the windows next door, cast brass rectangles on the hard-packed yard. Inside, men were shooting pool and drinking beer.

Roger and Jaje got out of the Toyota and walked up the weathered wooden steps. The pool games stopped. Silence greeted them. The men weren't big, but they were tough-looking. A lot tougher than Roger. Tougher than even McNatt—because where McNatt had grown up, whether in some upscale neighborhood in Seattle, or in the projects of Chicago, Domino's Pizza delivered. A short walk past the drug pushers in South Dallas, and you'd get to civilization. This little town, wherever the hell it was, was an hour's drive from noplace.

Roger put his hand in the pocket of his jacket, slipped his fingers around his gun. "You got a phone?"

They might not have civilization, but they had a satellite link to it. On the wall was a mounted television tuned to CNN.

The men looked at each other. Did they recognize Jaje? Roger didn't think so. Christ. What a stupid mistake! It was such a killer of a mistake that Roger broke out in an icy sweat and his stomach went into free fall. What had he done? Jaje was just a kid, and she wasn't dressed to go out. Roger wondered how many he could shoot before they overpowered him and raped her.

"You lost?" one of the men asked. He took a swig from his Antarctica longneck. His cheap cotton shirt was unbuttoned. He had a knotty, skinny-looking chest and a hard washboard of a stomach.

"I'm hungry," Jaje said.

Oh Christ, no! She was walking toward them, right within their reach, stepping into Roger's line of fire.

"Twelve hours on the bus. Then I get to Brasília, and he," she waved in Roger's direction, "didn't have any food."

Before Roger could shoot, there was an outpouring of noisy sympathy. "Oh, 'tadinha!" One man brought her a chair, another searched the refrigerator. "Poor little thing." They threw admonishing looks at Roger. They apologized for their inadequate hospitality. "We don't get many visitors here." They brought Jaje the remains of someone's sandwich, painstakingly cut off the tooth marks.

Buried under the avalanche of cordiality, Roger took his hand out of his pocket. And this time when he asked to use the phone, they told him the lines were down.

"Some trouble in Brasília," a man understated.

While Jaje ate three pickled eggs, Roger watched CNN. An American State Department spokesperson was discussing secret atomic weapon plants and Cabeceiras and U.N. inspectors.

While Jaje ate coconut ice cream, Roger saw aerial photos of launching pads. Heard talk of payloads and space weaponry.

He put a handful of ten-cruziero bills down on the pool table, and sipped on a Brahma Chopp. Jaje ate a sugared avocado while she played a game of pool.

A man said to Roger, "Young girl like that, she shouldn't be out here. There's bandits." A neat white scar ran from the man's chin to his hairline. It looked as if sometime in his life, he'd gotten up to go to the bathroom, and run into a razor.

"Right." Bandits? Who cared about bandits when there were bombing runs, cruise missiles, and Special Forces?

The man asked, "You got a gun?"

The question confused Roger. A gun? Shit. He'd need a tank.

"Because you'll need a gun," the man said. "You a foreigner?"

"I'm . . . Yeah. Australian."

The man nodded. "Want to stay here?"

He wanted to. More than anything. But if he didn't keep moving, McNatt would find him. "I need to get back on the road."

"Be careful," the man said.

Around eight o'clock Jaje put down her pool cue and yawned. Roger said his goodbyes, the men waved, and he led her to the car.

"Where to?" she asked when they drove off.

Roger didn't know.

"I'm cold."

He turned on the heater. He stowed the gun in the map compartment, then stripped off his jacket, and gave it to her. Blackness ahead but for the tunneled glare from the headlights. Roger wished for gravel shoulders and double yellow lines.

"It's not true what they're saying about Mom and Aunt Dee."

Roger's vision blurred. He rubbed his eyes.

"It's just not true. Mom's won the Miss Boring pageant forty-eight years in a row. She'd *never* have people murdered. She'd *never* take money from the CIA."

The road ahead went double. Then fuzzy. Roger took his foot off the accelerator.

"What?" she asked.

He steered off the highway, drove a short way into the scrub brush, and parked. "Get in the backseat."

"In your dreams."

"I can't drive anymore. Get in the backseat."

"I'll drive."

"No." He got out and walked to the trunk. Just as he had hoped: Dee packed for survival. There were bottles of water. Bandages. A blanket. He took the blanket to Jaje.

She got out, wrapped herself in the blanket. "I know what American guys are like. Don't you try anything. You'll be sorry."

"Yeah, yeah." Roger slipped behind the wheel, held the gun in his lap, and shivered. So dark. The horizon was just a place the stars ended, and absolute blackness began. Roger wished he had his own blanket. Some coffee. He looked at his watch. Nine. It would be a long wait for dawn.

From the backseat a tiny voice. "You gotta promise not to take me to Mom, okay? 'Cause I need to talk to Aunt Dee. She'll tell me what's going on. I just want to know what's happening here. And why people are saying these things."

The night was silent but for the chitter of a nightbird. Roger felt her presence as a prickly, melting warmth between his shoulder blades. The feeling made him want to tuck his body around hers, to keep her safe. And it wasn't just the tube top or the short shorts. Or the funny way she cocked her head to the side when he said something dumb. Or her laugh. Or even that she smelled of coconut oil and perfume.

Unbelievably awesome, what he realized he was willing to do. He'd step in front of a train for her, in front of a bullet.

"Promise," he said.

ABC News Special: <u>Confrontation</u>

. . . *behind me you would normally see Corcovado and the huge statue of Christ, the Cristo Redentor. But tonight the floodlights have been extinguished. Rio, which lies along the Brazilian coast like a thin jeweled belt, is dark. Closing the universities, imposing martial law and a curfew have effectively ended the demonstrations, but at a cost.*

The mood here, so close now to the deadline, is subdued. The quiet is eerie. And still the clock ticks. While Americans await death from the skies, so do the Brazilians. Peter?

Thank you, Jim. A small personal note: I've been to Rio several times, and always enjoyed my visits. It's one of the world's most beautiful cities. And certainly one of the most lively. Shocking to see it like this. And now we have ABC correspondent Tomás Fuentes standing by in Brasília. Tomás?

Well, as you can see, Peter, the busses are running, but they're running fairly empty. Everyone's keeping their heads down. No word from President Bonfim as yet, whether or not she will allow the inspectors in. The Brazilians I've spoken to think it is incredible that the two presidents aren't communicating. They just don't understand it.

Tomás? You were in Haiti and Panama, and . . . well, you've covered a number of military actions in this hemisphere. Is it just me, or is this confrontation somehow different?

Very different, Peter. There's no grandstanding on either side, for one thing. Just a silent, terrible anxiety.

17

"COMING, COMING!" EDSON STUMBLED THROUGH THE DARKENED LIV-
ing room to the foyer. He turned on the light and opened the
front door.

Muller. "Sir, I'm sorry. I did get your message. They released me
at six, and it took me this long to get through the roadblocks.
Things are easing a bit now. Are you all right?"

Edson ushered him in, set the half-empty bottle of Jack Daniels
on the hall table. "Where is she?"

Muller's gaze strayed. "The Villanova safe house."

"Look at me. I need to see if you're lying."

The eyes snapped to Edson's. They were angry.

"Tell me again."

"The president is at the Villanova safe house, sir. She's with Dolores Sims."

Anger, and nothing else. "Why?"

"Jaje is missing." They had worked together long enough.
When Edson's face tightened, Muller knew. "No, sir. Not the CIA.
Machado thinks she simply wandered off."

"Um." He started out. "Take me to Alvorada."

"Sir?" An apologetic voice at his back. "It's about Henrique Freitas, sir. Something I think you should hear."

Muller stood in the fall of light under the chandelier, his blond hair white-hot against the living room's dark.

"The Valley is an isolated place, sir. You know that. Two simple country police officers, no coroner. Still, I found out how Freitas's wife died. A fall, sir. In a one-story house, she died of a fall."

Muller was too radiant, too disturbing, to look at. "Take me to Alvorada."

Without another word, the agent walked to the car. Edson got in the backseat. No more roadblocks, but every kilometer, a knot of soldiers.

Edson noticed Muller watching him in the rearview mirror. *Not that I want this,* he thought.

"From what I learned, I think the boy saw everything," Muller said. "What sort of man would beat his wife to death while his child watched?"

"He's not a man," Edson told him.

"Sir . . ."

"Don't."

Muller didn't speak again, not even when they drove down the parking garage's ramp and through the gates. Edson got out of the car, and walked past the soldiers.

"Good evening, sir." The guard at the first-floor desk sounded surprised.

The lonely click of his own heels on the marble staircase. Five steps. Ten. Then down the parquet hall. Twelve. Fourteen. Edson halted at Freitas's room. He could go back now. Go home.

Edson turned the knob.

Dark. So dark that Edson nearly fled. No, not quite black. City lights shone through an opening in the curtain. And a ruddy glow from a corner, steadier than a candle.

Edson closed the door behind him. Someone was quietly laughing. He walked closer. A night-light. A Porky Pig night-light.

And it wasn't laughter that he heard.

In the glow from the night-lamp, in front of a wingback chair, a little boy sobbed. Hair straight and black as an Indian's. His pudgy hands covered his face.

And more hands. Ones that reached out from the chair's shadows. Fingers sliding down, down, past where knit shirt ended and taut warm flesh began.

"Freitas," Edson called.

The hands stopped.

"José Carlos." Edson knew he should look away. He couldn't. "Pull your pants up."

A whisper from the dark. "Time for bed."

The boy fumbled with his clothes.

Freitas helped with a button. "Give *papai* a kiss good night."

A chaste kiss. José Carlos was gone in a flash. Edson walked around the chair.

"Taking his place?"

The man's fly was unzipped. The last two buttons of his shirt were open.

"You'll have to get on your knees."

The room tipped. Edson couldn't catch his breath. It felt as if he was falling.

"You've always wondered what it would feel like—a child's body."

"Never." Edson couldn't look—not at the open zipper, not at the man's face. He went to the window, thought about his own children. Had he . . . ? No. Not once.

"Wondering doesn't mean you're bad, Edson, only curious. You just want to feel things, like the times you felt the corpses."

Edson looked into the glass. His own startled reflection looked back.

"You see, I know you. I know, for instance, that you closed your eyes the first time you pulled the trigger. And I know that you watched the fourth man twitch. By the sixth, curiosity got the best of you, didn't it? You're an inquisitive man, and that was inevitable. You put your finger on the corpse's open eye."

Impossible. He'd been so careful. No one could have seen. Edson's breath fogged the pane, and he watched himself disappear.

"Don't be ashamed. You and me, we're explorers. The bullet hole: so perfectly round. Did you know the nine millimeter makes an opening in the skull the exact size of your index finger? Of course you did. The wound is dark, isn't it? Mysterious. You always wanted to stick your finger inside." Freitas said, "Come here."

Edson turned. Freitas was watching him. Had they touched yet? Surely he would remember. He walked closer. It didn't have to go this far. He could run away. He would have. But his legs felt weak.

"Kneel down."

In Freitas's eyes, the heavy gravity of the abyss. "I know what you want."

Edson didn't want it, but he couldn't help himself. It was only because he felt weak, and his thighs wouldn't hold him. He dropped to his knees between the V of Freitas's legs.

Suffocating body warmth and the salty smell of him. Edson couldn't look at . . . there. Look at the wall. That was safe. Porky Pig. Round flesh-colored head, smooth as a child's belly.

An exploratory touch on his hair. Edson squeezed his eyes shut. If he wasn't so weak, he would get up and walk away. If he wasn't so numb, he would fight that hand's pressure.

Lips against his. The kiss surprised Edson, that was all. Freitas's mouth moved. Overripe lips and an assertive tongue that tasted of beer and garlic.

The shocking scrape of a late-afternoon beard against his cheek. A whisper: "You think I'm a devil." Freitas shoved him back. "You're wrong."

It couldn't be disappointment that Edson felt. Please. Maybe it was only confusion. He blundered up and hurried to the door, scrubbing his mouth with his sleeve.

Freitas's voice followed. "I'm what you touch when you stick your finger in the hole."

Hiroshi stayed awake past sundown, past the time the dust settled and the air turned sweet. Seated at the kitchen table, he fought sleep as if he had hired on as wakefulness's soldier.

As Sunday ticked into Monday, his head became so heavy that his neck could not support it. The drone in his ears was deafening. *Just for a moment,* he thought, and laid his cheek on his arm. He shut his eyes, and dreamed.

Lost in a market amid flats of spiked berries and translucent bananas. Boxes of green raisin-sized things that could have been fruit, that might have been spice. Monkeys climbed braids of purple chiles. Their screeches echoed the rafters.

Hiroshi wanted to ask the shopkeeper the names of things, but was shamed to discover that he had lost Portuguese. All the words came out English, and the man behind the counter began to cry.

Outside, lush vines bloomed and twisted across the desert. The Southern Cross glowed in the daytime sky. Hiroshi tried to find his way home, but the buildings had been stolen.

Something wicked was about to happen. Hiroshi felt it. He started to run. American bombs began thudding to the ground like rotting oranges from a tree. Hiroshi looked up, saw incoming missiles high overhead, small as grains of rice. They tipped with the weight of their warheads, fell faster.

He ran, afraid. So afraid of burning.

A gasp. Hiroshi's eyes popped open. His heart knocked his chest wall, not the feel of meat against meat, but that of iron bell against clapper.

His living room was dark.

The gun was on the table, and he found it by feel. Perhaps there had been a power outage. Perhaps that was all.

No. The darkness had a smell. A pulse. Holding the pistol, he got up and crept to the kitchen. The room was empty; whoever had been there was gone. But the furtive visitor had left behind a reminder of his control: another burning candle.

Baka! It was no more than he deserved. Hiroshi had betrayed his mentor, the good name of his *bun*. *Baka!* You stupid! When they came the next time, Hiroshi's dead eyes would be left open, the candle left burning in his mouth. There was no one he could turn to, no one to protect him. And that was his own fault.

Hiroshi slid to the kitchen floor, the muscles in his chest and arms twitching. Had he the energy for it, he would have put the muzzle to his head and pulled the trigger himself.

Sometime during the cold predawn, Ana fell asleep. Careful not to wake her, Dolores turned the lamp off and sat quietly in the rocker beside the bed. A strip of light shone from under the door where soldiers stood guard.

This was the bright part: the comfort of mothers, the protection of sentries. This was the doorjamb light, the way things should be.

Dolores let her eyes fall half-staff. Black dresser hulked against blue-black wall. The gray bed, with safe shadows under. Never given guards, Dolores learned to be a little mouse. Interesting how mice could hide anywhere. How if they didn't move, and if they breathed softly, they could disappear.

Strange how a woman could save a country, could start a war, and be such a tiny, tiny thing.

Dolores yawned. Her eyes felt grainy, and there was a dull ache at her temples. What time was it getting to be? They had taken her watch: Harry, Edson Carvalho, Gilberto Muller, the CIA, they had taken everything. She got up, her back stiff, and shuffled into the neighboring room.

She expected a group of soldiers playing cards, telling jokes. There was only one man. The major who had brought her here.

He sat at the kitchen table, his head in his hands. Asleep sitting up? Then she saw his Adam's apple bob. He was silently crying. And not so much protection, after all.

She whispered, "You want—"

He recoiled.

Dolores gave him an off-center smile. "Sorry."

A flustered, "You startled me. So quiet . . ."

"I'm CIA-trained, remember? Want some coffee?"

He nodded.

She ran water into the pot, searched the cabinets until she found the coffee—things the major had never thought of. Funny. When she was younger, she believed Harry would learn to cook if he was hungry enough. By the time he was forty, she knew she was wrong. He would starve to death before it entered his mind to put food in pot, to put pot on stove.

"Is the president all right?" the major asked.

She turned the knob on the burner. Flame sprang into being. "Asleep," she said.

He asked, "How will it be to be invaded?"

Dolores sat in the chair across from him, placed her hands in her lap. "I don't know. I've never gone through it."

"I received a call twenty minutes ago. Planes incoming from Bolivia. Do you think this is it? The bombers?"

In the shadows of the kitchen, that pure blue flame. "How many radar returns?"

"Six."

"Then probably not."

He scraped his forefinger across the emerging beard on his jaw. "Should I awaken *a Presidente*? The colonel said I was not to worry her, but . . ."

"Then don't."

An anxious nod. "I have forty-two boys outside. This night is the first they have spent away from home. The first dinner they have not eaten at their mother's. We teach our militia to direct traffic, to keep order at soccer games. They don't understand war. Do you think the Americans will consider that?"

The coffeepot began to sputter. The fire blazed orange; it danced and hissed.

"I doubt they will," she said.

The brightening horizon startled Roger, sent his head banging into the car window, sent Dee's pistol sliding off his lap.

In the shadows of the backseat, Jaje muttered. Her eyes were puffy. Mascara had run. Her hair looked like a bird's-nest wanna-be. God. She tore his heart out.

"Ready to get up and get at 'em?" No matter how encouraging he sounded, he himself was not. His back was stiff, his sinuses stuffy, his mouth furred.

She groaned and pulled the blanket over her head. He fumbled around on the floorboard until he found the gun.

"I'll drive up the road. Bound to be a town. We'll get some breakfast, how's that?" He received a grunt in reply.

Roger rolled the window down. The morning breeze tickled his cheek, ruffled his hair. It stirred a layer of dust on the dash. He yawned. Thirty degrees above a golden horizon hung the search-light that was Venus, and above that, silent and smooth, six con-trails sketched the sky.

"Jaje?" he breathed.

He heard her sit up.

How could the morning be so hushed? The white contrails against the bowl of the heavens so beautiful? To have struck mois-ture, the planes had to be high, far higher than a commercial jet. The dull thunder of a sonic boom followed them—they were moving fast.

"Look." She sounded awed.

He started the car, headed back to the highway, and followed the planes east, toward dawn.

"What does *that* mean?"

They were already gone, the chalk marks of their passage growing fat and gauzy. "They were too high for bombers," he said. "Fighters? I don't know. Maybe it was a warning." He thought: *Maybe it was scouts.*

His hands shook. Ten kilometers. Twenty. Winds in the upper atmosphere pulled the remains of the contrails apart.

Over the next rise lay a small town. Roger parked and they got out. The *venda* door was open. Bare dangling lightbulb. Music from a radio. A *periquito* in a bamboo cage. Everything was so ordinary.

The one-room store had bread and fresh cheese and soft drinks. Roger bought toothpaste and toothbrushes, deodorant, jeans, and knit shirts.

Carrying her toothbrush and new clothes, Jaje walked behind the counter, pushing through a curtain of onion braids and frilly little-girl dresses. She went to the bathroom to change.

The storekeeper said, "I saw the planes early. Heard a boom."

"Sonic boom. They were going faster than sound."

"Ah. The Americans invading?"

The store was flour-dusty, fragrant with sugar and cinnamon, sour with vinegar and lye. "I don't think so." Roger took a breath. "I don't know."

She wrapped the cheese. "You American?"

"Australian."

"Kangaroos," she said, and nodded.

"Yeah." Roger dropped his eyes. "Kangaroos."

When they had changed, Roger and Jaje went outside. While the sun rose, and before the dust came up, they ate. "I know you want to talk to your Aunt Dee," he told her. "But I just don't see how you can do that. I mean, she's in jail."

The expected argument never came. Jaje nibbled absently on a piece of cheese.

"Jaje, you have to get out of the country."

She hugged her knees. "Those could have been our planes."

He reached out and took her hand. She didn't pull away. "You can come back when it's over." He knew she couldn't. At least, wouldn't want to. Not to what was left. "Let me just call somebody, okay? You can trust them. They can take care of it all."

"The CIA?" The sarcasm had deserted her voice. Roger already missed it.

He squeezed her fingers. "MUFON," he said.

CNN, Live

. . . rumors that a coup has taken place.

Their embassy here is vigorously denying that. You're familiar with the situation, Susan. What do you think?

Bernie? It's true that Bonfim hasn't been sighted for a couple of days. And the way Brazil historically hands over the reins of power is during a quiet palace coup, not a bloody revolution. Portugal works the same way, as a matter of fact.

Who would have taken over, then? Machado and the Army? O.S. and the police?

Well, I'm not sure anyone has taken over.

So . . .

Um, but I think they'd go for a coalition government, one set up simply to expedite . . . you know how that works, and then there would be some behind-the-scenes backstabbing, and either the Army or the police would come out the eventual victor.

Bets on?

Army. Let's face it. They have the tanks. They have the trained troops. Machado's had experience. He's been through a power struggle before. And Carvalho's got too much bad history to be effective. I don't think the Brazilian people would go for him. I know the United States would find him a problem. And the one thing Brazil wants to avoid now is problems.

18

Day broke, gold and royal blue. To a fanfare from the valley's roosters, chickens paraded the yard. From the center of the village, the temple bells rang. Hiroshi sat huddled in his blanket on the cold hard clay.

The sun was a hand's span high when a yellow hound limped out from under the steps, regarded Hiroshi suspiciously, and then lay down, one paw to each side of his water bowl. By the time Xuli emerged from her house, it was mid-morning.

"Why you here?"

Hiroshi rose and bowed. "Please. I have no one else to turn to." His joints were stiff. His back ached. He unwound himself from the blanket. Only then did he notice how hot the day was, and how he was sweating.

"Why you got the gun?" A face like a scowling dark moon.

He had forgotten he was holding it. "They are after me, and soon they will kill me." His knuckle had cramped around the trigger. "Please. You must tell me what to do."

She nodded. "Come in."

The house stank of old garlic and beans and of the rank foreign smell of her.

"Sit down," she told him.

He wanted the clean taste of green tea, but she served him dark syrupy coffee. The white bread she gave him stuck like paste in his throat. "There is nothing left for me. I have turned against my own people," he said. "I have betrayed my position. I cannot pay the debt of my father."

She nodded. "Maria Bonita says you don't sleep anymore at night, and that it is the Americans' fault. Eat your breakfast."

He lowered his head. The wood tabletop was worn smooth by years of scrubbing, bleached bone-white by lye soap. On it, tarnished silverware, cracked crockery plates. The kitchen smelled of dust and mold and strange spices. Hiroshi felt such a rush of homesickness that it brought tears to his eyes. "Sorry. Please. I cannot eat this food."

"You eat what I serve you," she told him. "This is the road you take now, the way to your destiny." She spread a roll with butter, stuffed it with cheese, with sausage.

He ate, gagging. The food lay heavy in his belly. When he was finished, she took him to the living room, lit candles, and closed the shutters. She pulled the curtain at the kitchen doorway to.

"Kneel down," she said. "Don't sit, Samurai. You kneel. There's gods watching."

Warm in the room, and close. Yet Hiroshi could not stop shivering. Candle flames leaped in the shadows. It might have been night, but for the incandescent wedge of sun between shutter and jamb.

"Close your eyes. I been talking to Exú about you," she said.

A scratching at the window, like a curious cat. The smell of incense. Afraid, Hiroshi opened his eyes. The room had changed. It was darker, most of the candles out. Before him squatted the massive form of Xuli.

"Don't look at me!"

A strange, youthful timbre in her voice. He obeyed. The blackness behind his lids terrified him. The drone in his head returned.

No Bahian anymore. No African lilt. Xuli spoke in the hard-scrabble accent of the northeast. "I am that spirit which enters the body of the entity you call Xuli. I fill her like water. You are to be a vessel for a spirit called Brazil. It will fill you to bursting. Do you understand?"

"Yes."

"Now." A rustle of clothes. She leaned close; breath warm against his face, voice intimate as a kiss. "Tell Maria Bonita what makes you afraid."

His throat was tight. He swallowed. Maria Bonita, the pretty one, who fought and died alongside the bandit Lampião. A spirit with the voice of an angel. He wanted to open his eyes and see. "I am afraid to be alone."

"And tell Maria Bonita what makes you ashamed."

The question rocked him back on his heels, made him want to howl with grief. "I am ashamed to have forgotten my place."

"Shhh." A touch on his knee. "Maria Bonita knows someone has betrayed you. I want you to call this someone's name."

The scratching shook the window. He had to open his eyes now. "Please, I—"

"Say it for me!"

"Kengo Fujita."

"And someone has lied to you," she said. "Tell me his name."

"Dr. Clark Christopher Kinch."

"When you have someone's name, Samurai, you cannot be alone. When you have someone's name, you steal their place. Now. Someone is standing behind these two, in the shadows. Someone dangerous. And what I want you to do is, call his name."

The hand crept up his thigh. Such a small hand, like a child's. Hiroshi let his breath out. The floor seemed to sway like the sea. "Major Douglas McNatt."

She grabbed his fingers. Hiroshi could feel a vibration pass flesh to flesh. She squeezed so hard it hurt. "You have done well. And now Maria Bonita will prove to you how much Spirit is pleased."

The window rattled fiercely. There was a thud, like a small body falling.

"Open your eyes." Bahian. Tired and old.

Only two candles were left lit. He and Xuli were kneeling, holding hands like schoolchildren. On the woven rug between their knees lay Hiroshi's diary.

Marcel Marceau seemed to find Roger's telephone call disconcerting. "But there are *troops*."

"No big deal. The Army's letting people through. The soldiers hardly paid any attention." Roger propped his elbow on the pay phone and winked at Jaje. She stood against the wall of the appliance store, twisting a lock of hair.

"Still . . ."

"Look. I got somebody with me, guy. Understand? I can't say the name over the phone, but this is big. You gotta help us get out of the country, okay? You gotta do this for me. Shit. You gotta do this for Brazil, man. Are you listening?"

From the receiver, mutters. Suddenly Fatty was on the line. "Okay. You can come."

They got back into Dee's car and drove to Marcel's apartment. Jaje's nearness made Roger's chest ache from shoulder to heart. They could go away together. Roger would give her some time. Then they'd buy a house in the piney woods near Houston. He'd take her skiing at Telluride in the winter, snorkeling in the summer at Cancún.

And so what if rednecks gawked? Jaje was sexier than a movie star, prettier than a model. For once in Roger's life other guys would envy him. And if the racism got too much, well, they could avoid those NASA barbecues. Jaje was all the company he needed.

"Just a few blocks more," he said.

She sighed and then—oh, Christ—she curled a lock of hair around that tiny finger, and this time the gesture knocked life right out from under him, demolished everything Roger had been, rearranged his future. The loss made him feel like he was falling.

I love you. But the words were too new, too big to say.

Roger found a parking spot a half-block from Fatty's and helped her out of the car. He couldn't tell her, but maybe she could feel it. He gently took her arm, led her past a knot of pre-occupied soldiers, and into the apartment building.

Fatty opened at Roger's knock. And froze. *"Nossa."*

Marcel Marceau pushed Fatty aside. He saw Jaje, and his eyes widened.

"Let us in," Roger said.

"Kiss my ass." Marcel slammed the door shut.

Roger knocked louder.

Fatty jerked open the door. *"Nossa Senhora,* Roger. Do you know who that is?"

"Let us in."

Marcel said, "No."

When Fatty stepped back, Roger put his arm around Jaje's waist, pushed past Marcel, and steered her inside. Parquet floors shone. A painting of nighttime Rio hung above the sofa, a beef-cake poster over the dining table. In the corner was a new stereo system with waist-high speakers, big enough to woof and tweet the building down.

Fatty let out a long breath. "Ah . . . Have a seat."

Two open doorways: one led to a tiny kitchen, another to a single cozy bedroom. Oh. Roger was finally starting to get the picture. "You gotta help us get across the border to Peru."

Easy magic. An abracadabra wave of Fatty's hands. "All taken care of." His cheeks were pasty and he was sweating. "We called some people. They're on their way over."

"These guys know what they're doing?" Roger asked.

"What? The people? Oh, yes. Relax." Fatty snatched a section of newspaper off the couch, crumpled it, dropped it on the parquet. "Mineral water? Beer?" Fatty was all smiles—an airplane steward on his last, fast ride down. "Coffee?"

Jaje collapsed on the sofa, crossed her legs, jiggled a foot.

Roger stood guard over her. "Get her a Coke."

Marcel clapped his hands to the sides of his head. "The president's daughter wants a Coke. Oh. By all means. The president's daughter, who is sitting on our couch, with her mother's soldiers outside, the whole world but Peru against us, the Americans about to invade, and she wants a Coke."

Jaje crossed her arms. Her foot went up and down. "So are these the guys who are, like, going to save me and everything?"

"It's okay." Roger sat beside her. "I got the gun. All we need now are forged IDs."

Marcel cried, "He has a gun!"

Fatty put out his hand to Roger. "Give it to me."

"What? No way."

"Listen to me, Dr. Lintenberg. Guns are dangerous. Nobody, uh . . ."

Marcel: "We—we just hate guns. It . . ."

"It is customary. Like visiting a Japanese," Fatty explained. "You know how you must take off your shoes? Well, at our house—"

Jaje asked, "Would it, like, be too much of a *bummer* for somebody to get me a beer?"

A knock at the door. Marcel whirled. Fatty said urgently, "Roger. Give me the gun. These people are the nervous type, you know?"

"Who . . ."

From the hall, the scrape of a key, a click of the lock. The front door opened.

And Major McNatt walked in.

It was weird how, in that instant, Roger noticed everything: that

McNatt was wearing a jacket, even though it was hot. That Jerry's baggy shirt hid his waistband. McNatt looked more sad, really, than angry. And that's when Roger knew that the CIA had kept him on a short, short leash. And that he was about to die.

Roger pulled the gun out of his pocket. Marcel leaped. The impact of Marcel's shoulder knocked Roger back hard into the sofa. Roger pulled the trigger. Again. Again. No bangs, just muffled thumps. And Marcel was screaming.

Wait. How did the two things become intertwined: Marcel's hand and the revolver? Then Fatty was pulling Marcel one way, and Jerry shoving Roger the other, and McNatt was holding the gun.

McNatt looked at Jaje. "*That*, I believe, is Teresa Solange Bonfim. I don't like this."

Roger sat back, breathing hard. Fatty prattled a string of apologies. McNatt said to shut up, that he had to think. Marcel Marceau rocked back and forth, cradling his hand, sucking on the bruise left by the revolver's hammer.

McNatt shook his head. "This is trouble."

"God. Don't hurt her." Roger didn't even know he had spoken until the words came rushing up his throat. "Please. This is all my fault. She hasn't done anything. I haven't told her about . . . you know. Not a word."

Jaje asked, "Who *are* these bozos?"

Finally McNatt seemed to come to a decision. "Hey, Jer?" he said. "We'll need three." Jerry left, and returned a few minutes later with an intense-expressioned guy.

"God. Please don't," Roger said.

McNatt put his arm around Fatty's shoulder. He led him into the bedroom, and they closed the door.

Roger tried to comfort Jaje, but she pulled away. He wanted to tell her how sorry he was. Wanted to tell her how much he loved her, but Jerry and Mr. Intense were watching.

McNatt came out of the bedroom holding a pair of handcuffs. "Mind if we use these?" he asked Marcel.

Marcel didn't mind at all.

"Aw, Jesus. Please." Roger held Jaje's hand so tight that she yelped.

McNatt asked if Marcel wouldn't mind showing him how this brand of handcuffs worked.

No problem. Marcel stood up. Two snaps. That easy. McNatt had pulled Marcel's arms behind his back and cuffed his wrists. Before the man could protest, Jerry put a bag over his head.

Roger couldn't believe it. He sucked in a quick breath. Marcel couldn't believe it, either. He sucked in a mouthful of plastic.

Oh. And Roger was suddenly looking down the barrel of Mr. Intense's gun.

On the parquet in front of Marcel's cheap couch, the three men struggled. "Get him into the bathroom," McNatt said.

Jerry grunted, tried to wrestle Marcel toward the door. The Brazilian was stronger than he looked.

"He's going to shit," McNatt warned. "Pull his pants down, Jerry, before he shits."

Marcel's stocking feet slid on the polished wood. He went down—bang—on one knee.

Mr. Intense never took his eyes off Roger, even though there was life and death going on. He backed to the stereo and hit the power button. António Carlos Jobim sang a song about March waters and the ends of roads and being a little bit alone, while Marcel fell the rest of the way to the floor and flopped like a fish. His mouth opened and closed. Opened and closed.

"He's gonna shit," McNatt said.

Jerry fumbled with Marcel's zipper, and jerked the pants to his knees. Marcel's muscles knotted. Some autonomic reaction had made him half erect. He gulped in plastic, made a gargling sound.

Then Jaje ordered them to stop, to let him go, let him go goddamn it, and Mr. Intense was pointing the gun and telling her to shut up.

Roger wrestled Jaje to him, warm against him, forced her head onto his shoulder and stroked her hair. She tried to sit up, but he held her down. "Shhh. Shhh. Everything's going to be all right." *Please, God,* he thought. *Don't let them do that to me.*

Marcel's feet whipped back and forth. His back arched. His veins bulged. And, aw jeez, he was crying. Roger could see that even through the foggy plastic bag. Face as blue as a West Texas norther. Dying in front of an audience. Bare-ass naked, with half a hard-on, and tears streaming down his cheeks.

"Shhh," Roger crooned while Jaje fought to pull away and Jobim sang that it was a toad, a frog, a forest in the morning's light. "It's gonna be okay."

Let him die now, Roger prayed. But Marcel sat up again.

When life left, it left catastrophically. Marcel's eyes rolled back in his head. He went loose-limbed. Jerry let go; McNatt danced backward. Marcel's head collided with the floor, and the crack could be heard over the speakers.

"Shit," Jerry muttered.

Oh, Christ. Marcel had. "No paper towels," McNatt ordered. "Just enough toilet paper to flush. And turn that stereo off."

Mr. Intense bent over the CD player. Jobim went silent.

McNatt said, "Jerry? There's some amyl nitrate in the bedroom on top of the nightstand. And a jar of petroleum jelly." He drew his gun. He stepped over Marcel's sprawled body, perched on the edge of the coffee table, reached into his shirt pocket, and, one-handed, popped a Tums.

Roger put his body in front of Jaje's. She elbowed him painfully in the side. "Just . . . don't . . . I don't want it to hurt."

"Dr. Lintenberg, really." McNatt shook his head. "We're not going to hurt you. I *am* disappointed, however, that you were so predictable."

"But everybody's been lying to me."

McNatt looked surprised. "Of course."

The gun lay loose in McNatt's hand, as if he had forgotten it was there. Jerry, humming now, brought a towel from the kitchen. He bent, wiped the handcuffs clean.

"Ms. Bonfim," McNatt said. "I'm sorry you had to see this. We had no choice. And no time to deal otherwise with a pair of rogue agents."

Jaje shoved herself free in time to see Mr. Intense painstakingly wipe Marcel's ass.

"I'm afraid I have some bad news."

Even considering what had just happened, McNatt looked far, far too solemn. Roger's body went hot, then cold. His bowels cramped.

"I wish there was an easier way to tell you, but there has been a coup by the Brazilian Army. Your mother is dead."

"Oh, man," Roger whispered. "Man. Man." Relief left him guilt-ridden. It looked like Roger was safe, but Jaje's mom was dead, Marcel was dead . . . and, hey. Where was Fatty?

Mr. Intense picked up the toilet paper and walked into the bedroom. Roger waited for the sound of Fatty's voice. Wanted to hear him say something, anything. Jerry dragged the bare-assed, purple-faced Marcel after. He was humming "Oklahoma."

"The United States government has instructed me to offer you political asylum." McNatt started to put the roll of Tums back in his pocket, reconsidered, and bit off another. "The thing to do now is see you safely out of the country. General Machado may quite possibly see you as a threat. The good thing is, your presence at this apartment came as a complete surprise. Believe me. A complete and utter surprise. And these two didn't have a chance to pass the word along to the Brazilian Army. Well." He slapped his knees. Looked expectantly at Jaje. "That's settled. As soon as we clear the area, we'll be on our way." He stood, put the Tums in his pocket, tucked the pistol in his waistband.

Jerry stuck his head out of the bedroom. "Hey, Mac? Scenario's

fag accident, right? One heart attack, one erotic suffocation, isn't
that what we planned? Well, would you tell Artie, please? I already
greased down the fat coronary, but Artie's got a load of K-Y in one
hand, and the other guy's cock in the other. It's so *wrong*."

So McNatt killed Fatty so quietly that only murderer and victim
had marked the passing. Odd. Roger wasn't sure which was worse:
Marcel's battle or Fatty's quiet surrender.

"Right. Coming." McNatt bobbed his head apologetically to
Roger. "I'll just be a moment, then."

Roger leaned toward Jaje, kept his voice low. "Hey. I'm sorry
about your mom. You can come to Houston with me. Stay as long
as you want. We could, you know, maybe buy a house later and
everything. Don't worry. I'll take care of you."

McNatt came back into the room. He was dusting off his hands.
"Artie. Don't leave your prints on the popper capsule. Ready?" he
asked Roger.

Poor Jaje, upset about her mom and about seeing Marcel killed
like that. She was shaking and crying just like a kid. She stumbled
a little, getting up. Roger helped her to the door.

The street was clear, the car parked at the curb. Roger started
to climb in the Buick when a deep-throated roar tore the door
from his hand. Wind blew him face-first onto the seat. Store windows rattled. Roger sat up in time to see a flock of pigeons explode skyward.

McNatt shouted, "Come on, Ms. Bonfim! Get in!"

The northern sky was a wall of black. McNatt caught Jaje's arm
and pulled her into the car. Artie slammed the door. Jerry
gunned the engine and sped east.

Artie said, "Well. More great USAF timing. A day too soon, and
there goes Brasília's whole goddamned military."

McNatt tugged on Jaje's arm. "Stay down!"

They took a corner too fast. Roger poked his head up to look
out the rear window. Brazilian soldiers were standing, mouths
ajar. Roger asked, "When did the deadline expire?"

"Get *down*," McNatt said.

The car swayed as they took another corner. Roger heard a click, heard McNatt's grunt of surprise, felt him lurch left. And then the door was open and, oh Jesus no, Jaje was hanging halfway out, and McNatt was holding her wrist.

"Jerry! Stop!" McNatt said.

Artie was reaching over the seat. "Get her inside, Mac. Right now. There's a squad up ahead."

A fierce rattling sound. Jerry said, "Fuck!" and floorboarded the accelerator. The car leaped forward.

Roger flung himself over McNatt and grabbed Jaje's other arm. She kicked and screamed.

Over the stutter of gunfire, McNatt shouted, "Get in the car, you stupid little bitch!"

Jaje kicked him in the face. His head snapped backward. The car whipped around the next corner, threw Jaje into McNatt, tossed McNatt into Roger, sent Roger tumbling toward the door.

Blood gushed from McNatt's nose, his mouth. He crumpled. Roger couldn't lose her, couldn't, and so he pushed McNatt the rest of the way onto the floorboard and crawled over his back. Suddenly he and Jaje were face-to-face, inches apart.

No sign of tears. Her eyes were bright with fury. "Let me *go!*"

"I can't. Oh, God, Jaje. I can't . . ."

"Roger! Let me *go!*"

Roger was too weak, his palms too damp. His grip loosened. She struggled—Christ—then she was dropping. Dropping under the wheels.

Her hand slipped from his. Roger shut his eyes. McNatt pulled Roger back into safety, and slammed the door to. Roger knelt up on the seat. Jaje was lying on the sidewalk. Part of him wanted to run to her. The rest of him wanted to close his eyes again.

"Get up. Please. Get up," Roger urged under his breath. He was watching Jaje so intently that he didn't notice when a soldier fired. Didn't realize at first that the thumps he heard were rubber bullets hitting the Buick.

That sound. The thumps. He should have heard the thump of tires passing over Jaje's body.

Then the soldier and Jaje grew small. Soon they were far away. And when they were gone from sight, it was like Jaje was too beautiful to have ever been. But Roger's arms still ached from trying to hold her. His chest ached from letting her go. The street swam. He wiped his eyes. *My whole life*, he thought.

McNatt daubed blood from his nose. He looked dazed. "Jerry? She jump?" His voice was muddied by a split lip.

"Yes, sir. Too bad."

Gingerly, McNatt touched his face. "Oh, just as well."

I've lost every fucking worthwhile thing in my whole fucking worthless life. Roger couldn't stop himself. Right in front of the tough guys, he leaned his cheek against the car window and sobbed.

CNN, Live

There, Bernie!

Ye—

God! Incredible! Thick column of smoke. Up from the Military Sector. The whole area's burning. I felt the hotel shudder, and we must be—oh—several miles away.

Um. Preliminary report coming in now from the Pentagon, Susan . . . ah, they don't know what to make of it, either.

Awesome, Bernie. The noise. The windows here in the room rattled so hard I thought they'd break, and I have, and I have some binoculars with me, and can see . . . I don't know if we can get a picture from this distance . . . glass-sided buildings down in the Commercial Sector, um, just shattered. Some panes simply shattered by the force of that explosion.

The Pentagon is saying this was not a U.N. strike. I repeat, ladies and gentlemen. What you are seeing on the screen, the aftermath of that explosion, was not caused by a U.N. bomb.

Bernie! Can you hear the sirens?

Yes, I he—

So many fire trucks. All headed up Via N1.

Totally unexpected.

Down on the sidewalk, there's a squad of militia. The officer with them is trying to . . . but they're just milling around in complete confusion. And, I suppose, a bit of panic.

19

"I REMEMBER THE FIRST TIME WE MET." DOLORES, HAVING DRUNK HER own beer, deftly appropriated the rest of Ana's. "You just won your first election, and there was a party—remember? A lot of the Congress was there."

Ana pushed her luncheon plate away, half eaten. "Elected officials at a party. Coca-Cola? General Motors? Some American company with shallow slogans and deep pockets." She sat back and looked wistfully out the window.

Strange. So many years together. Dolores had forgotten how beautiful, how tiny, Ana was. She should have painted that face while she had the chance. No. Sculpted it in clay. Run her fingers along those ovals and hollows, so that her hands would never forget.

"It's quiet here," Ana said.

"Um. The party . . ."

Ana nodded. "Always the same: Barry Manilow, whiskey, blank checks, bad food."

The refrigerator, an ancient round-shouldered Climax, buzzed as the motor kicked in. "I can't remember the year . . ."

Ana said, "Nothing changes but the dates on the checks."

"Early, though. Several years away from the CIA approaching me. I was still trying to learn Portuguese, I think." A time when the hollows in Ana's face were fuller. Dolores closed her eyes, heard the beep of a car horn. The far, happy screams of children.

And Ana's sad chuckle. "You never stop learning. I wish . . . But things come too late, don't they? Knowing what would make you happy. Mountains and beaches and a little quiet."

Dolores kept her eyes shut so that Ana could be voice, something to hold onto, something she couldn't disassemble into visual component parts. "The band was playing the National Anthem, and you came up beside me. 'Lying eternally in a cradle of splendor,' you said, and then you asked if I thought Ford—that's right. It was Ford who gave the party—if Ford would be on top. I was scandalized that a government official could make jokes like that."

"Um. Our anthem is immensely lampoonable. Pretty words. Not such a pretty tune. Yours, of course, is impossible. I must tell you: I've heard all the anthems now, and only Germany's and Japan's and France's are worth hearing."

"Ana. Are you going to let me tell my story?"

"I thought it was over."

"No. I'm trying to make a point. Where I grew up, everything was sacred: high school history, the Pledge of Allegiance, football games, the goddamned nightly news. America's a place where everybody tells everybody else what to do. Which reminds me, you're not as irreverent as you were."

A tapping sound. Dolores opened her eyes. Ana's perfect, small head was lowered. No music, at least none that Dolores could hear. Yet Ana was counting rhythm with her fork. "Serious. Yes. I was elected to be Brazil's designated driver."

"Please. Don't make me leave."

Ana dropped the fork. "You should have known what would happen."

"The CIA was a lark for me, Ana."

A slight shake of her head. "I should have known better, too."

"What will I do in Canada?"

Ana finally looked up. "You will ski. Take care of Jaje. Have snowball fights with Jack. Live your life."

"There isn't any life except painting. I don't have any home but Brazil."

Ana seemed startled. "You will do this for me, Dolores. Jaje is *my* life."

"You're her mother."

"She doesn't need me. She was always more your child than mine. My fault. I should have taken up painting or some other woman's work instead of—"

A noise at the door. The major burst in. He had a cellular phone in one hand. "*Presidente,* General Fernando has just called. Your daughter . . ."

Ana's face didn't change, but her hands clenched. Dolores reached out and held onto that small, trembling fist. Held it hard.

"Oh." The major must have noticed the melancholy tension. He shook his head. "No. I meant that they have found her. And she's all right. A little scraped from a fall. A doctor is seeing to her now. Then she is to come here with the man from the American library and the passports. They must leave for Peru at once." He took a breath. His voice shook. "It pains me to inform you, but there has been an explosion in the Military Sector."

The guard saw him approach and came to rigid attention. "Director."

Edson hurried through the lush garden and into the shade of the triangular roof. "Any news?"

"Just the one explosion, sir. Perhaps it was a mistake, do you think?" The lieutenant opened the church door.

"They here yet, son?"

"No, sir. On their way."

The chapel of Our Lady of Fatima was shadowy, despite its architect's enchantment with light. The air smelled of incense and wax. José Carlos sat alone on the floor near the wall, playing with a toy airplane.

The plane dipped and rose, carried along on the boy's zooms. José Carlos's fly was open, his other hand busy.

"José Carlinho," Edson said. "Don't touch yourself like that."

The hand pulled. Pulled. The plane soared and dived.

"José Carlos!"

Hard, fast motions. The boy's whole body jerked. "You promised you would shoot him."

"Your father?"

José Carlos slammed the plane into a pew. The wing broke.

"Stop." Edson dropped to one knee and pulled the boy's hand free.

José Carlos drove the toy hard, painfully into Edson's shoulder. "You kissed the thing in *papai*." The hand went back into the pants.

"Don't, Zézinho. That's dirty."

"You're the one who's dirty. You kissed it. It told me you did. And it hurts me. And it never lies. You want me to kiss you, too." The boy pulled Edson's zipper down, squirmed his small hand inside.

Desire came on so fast that it outraced good sense, and even humiliation. "Damn it!" Edson knocked José Carlos against the wall. "Damn it! Don't ever do that!" He fastened his pants.

José Carlos looked up, bewildered. Fearful. "But that's what love is."

The boy was on the floor, pants to his hips, so defenseless that he frightened Edson. Edson was afraid, too, of the shadow at the bottom of that open zipper, and what was waiting for him there. He wanted José Carlos to touch him again, wanted it so badly that he doubled up his fist and punched the boy, hard, harder, just to make the need stop.

José Carlos crawled away until he fetched up against the corner.

God. No. How could he have done that? Had he hurt him? Oh. Had anyone seen? Edson knelt by the pew, terrified. He knew he should check to see if the boy was all right, but he was afraid that if he touched him, one touch wouldn't be enough, just like one blow hadn't been enough.

"Zé Carlos?" A safe two meters distant, the boy sat, doubled up with pain, and rocking. "I didn't mean to do that."

Nossa Senhora. What was happening to him? Edson had never wanted to touch a child like that. Never felt a hunger as sick.

We are explorers, you and me.

From her niche, Mary looked down. Could she understand that Edson had no choice? It was either shove his fist into the boy's stomach, or else his cock into his mouth? The fist was not unthinkable.

After all, Edson had killed children before. Older ones, predatory adolescents. And then it was only a job. Nothing but duty. Something to do quickly and right. Oh, but this . . .

All the boy's fault. He had wanted to be fondled, hadn't he? Hadn't he begged for it with his eyes? That was it. And Edson had merely felt the pull of gravity: dark appetite to dark.

A sound at the door brought Edson upright, his cheeks burning. Bracing himself against a pew, he stood.

Nando was striding down the aisle. "A whole barracks gone. We are still pulling out bodies. And you know what the reporters say on CNN? That it was an accident. Oh, yes. Our accident. And they can prove it, can't they? American Army intelligence has satellite photos. Therefore a barracks becomes an armory. And a cruise missile becomes our own damned fault."

Edson's eyes moved to the corner where José Carlos was hiding. Would the boy talk? What would Nando do then?

In his passing, Nando battered a pew so hard that the wood boomed like a drum, hit it so hard that Edson flinched and, in his corner, José Carlos shook. The general's bellow pounded the silence. "God help me! Little children in uniform, Edson. With legs gone. With arms missing. What will I tell their mothers?" He halted when he caught sight of José Carlos.

The boy's pants were still down. God bless. Nando would know. Because however gentle Nando was, like everyone, he had grown up touching himself under the covers, thinking childhood's nasty thoughts. Yes, Nando knew how iniquity felt. And perhaps if he had murdered more than his brother-in-law, he would learn to love killing, like Edson.

"Come out of there, boy."

José Carlos got up, holding his side.

Nando said gruffly, "Pull up those pants, José Carlinho. Little boys play with their *pauzinhos*, but not in church. And especially not in front of Our Lady. Oh. Look what you did with your pretty airplane." He bent, gathered up the bits of the toy, and gave them back.

Such kindness that it made Edson ache. Nando had more innocence in him than Edson had ever had, more than was left in José Carlos. What sort of monsters was Freitas making?

"Nando," Edson said. "I want my gun."

The general straightened, ruffled the boy's hair. He turned, and Edson realized Nando knew not only what had happened, but the penance Edson had chosen. "Not yet," he said.

A noise at the door snagged Edson's attention. Ana was walking in.

When she was halfway down the aisle, Nando shouted, "I will *not* fire back!" His voice echoed along the high pitched ceiling. "We could not see the missile coming! They have stealth bombers, and we will not see them coming, either. Young boys, Ana. Young girls, nineteen and twenty—who only know parking tickets and directing traffic. You have given me an army of children, and I tell you what I will do with it: I will surrender."

"No, Nando. You won't."

"Is that man of yours more important to you than this city? This country? Please. Please, Ana. The technology he channels to us is not worth this. Let the inspectors into Cabeceiras."

She spoke, and Edson had never heard such a soft voice. The answer brushed past the shadows, breathed along the banks of candles: "I can't."

Nando closed his eyes, pressed his palms against his temples, as if her voice had been too loud to bear. "Then let me destroy it."

"Not yet."

"I warn you: if I can't make the Americans fear me, I will send them to their knees with pity. I have taken the guns away from the militia. Even from the officers. The Americans will shoot, and when they see what they have done, they will weep, and put their weapons down."

God help the people of Brazil. Nando's plan would kill them all. For Edson had discovered how good hurting the defenseless felt; and so he knew that once the Americans started killing, they would not stop.

Jack came, dragging suitcases, huffing and puffing enough to blow the frame house down. "Jaje's on her way."

Dolores and the major fought a tug-of-war over who was going to help him. The major won possession of a makeup case and a pink overnight bag.

"Stole this stuff." The largest suitcase, a red Samsonite, hit the floor with a thud. Jack leaned over, put his hands on his knees, and tried to catch his breath.

Dolores said, "You're too old for this crap."

Jack laughed weakly. "The airport's a mob scene. I stole these from a departing American Airlines flight."

The suitcase Dolores had wrenched from the major was leather, with earth-tone fabric inserts. The name on the tag read: Mrs. Nelson Albright. Mrs. Nelson Albright, as if marriage had absorbed her. Inside would be Family Value dresses, a June Cleaver strand of pearls, unliberated undergarments. God. And if she complained to Jack, he would look surprised. Then he would look hurt.

He collapsed into a chair. "So. Red case is mine. You and Jaje can fight over the rest. Maybe the stuff'll fit, maybe not, but at least Peruvian customs is going to see native American products."

The major was impressed by what Jack, the hunter, had brought. He squatted to pull the tags off the cases. "La-uuu-reu?" he read off the makeup bag. "La-u-reu Es-ski-nar. *Puxa*. A woman, neh? Everything smells like perfume." He wiped his hands on his trousers. "They must be nice people. They must all be nice people. Myself, I think the explosion was a mistake. Whitney Houston. Bugs Bunny. *E.T.* It is not in your nature to slaughter. That is why General Fernando has ordered us to give up our weapons. I have even locked my sidearm—"

Jack sat bolt upright. "What? He what?"

The major was on one knee by the pile of bags, looking so small. Not brave like a soldier. Frightened, suddenly, like a mouse.

A clatter at the door. A loud laugh. Jaje came limping in. "*Titía* Dee! Oh, look. You got banged up, too." She had a bandage on one ankle, a scrape on her arm, and a wide smile. That small, perfect face could have been her mother's when she was young—if Ana had led a sheltered life.

"The CIA, like, captured me and everything? And they told me Mom was dead, and that the Army took over, but I knew Uncle Nando wouldn't ever do that, so I jumped out of the car. And they tried to stop me? But I, like, kicked him real hard in the face, this guy. The CIA guy. This *moreno* hunk. He's American, so maybe you know him and everything. A real to-die-for *pão*. And then they— oh, yeah—the hunk? So he like kills this guy right in front of me. Strangles him and everything. Really gross. And this guy at your house, Roger something? Some kinda computer guy or something, not the hunk, but I think he was CIA, too. And we drove around together, and he was, like, you know, trying to save me? I mean, Captain Geek-o to the rescue. But then the CIA found us . . . Oh." The flood halted. She looked confused. "Maybe he's sort of in trouble now."

A militia colonel, a redheaded woman, came in the door behind Jaje. The major shot to his feet. Saluted.

"Let's go," the colonel said. "The flight crew to Lima is pretending they have problems with a tire, but they can only stall so long."

Dolores got up, gathered her purse. The major picked up the big leather suitcase before Dolores could grab it.

"Lima?" Jaje stood in the center of the room, the center of attention, her hands on her hips. "I mean, I'm supposed to go to *Lima*? I don't get to say anything about it? Isn't this just like Mom. She never cares how I—"

The slap was so odd. Dolores never felt her arm move, didn't even know it had—until that sound. Until the skin on her palm tingled. Until that too-familiar cheek went red.

And after the slap was over—it hadn't been much of a blow, not really—the room went very still.

Then the colonel said, "Ready?" and Jack picked up his bag, and Jaje, tears in her eyes, picked up the pink overnight case, and life continued smoothly out the door and to the waiting car, as if the slap had never happened.

The soldiers didn't follow. No one tried to stop them. And as they drove on, it looked like the militia were leaving the streets. Jerry pulled to the curb and got out of the car. Artie slid behind the wheel. A few blocks later they played musical car again: Artie got out, McNatt climbed in the front and ordered Roger into the passenger side.

Roger sat, glum. Why hadn't he heard the thumps? Had they run over her or not? Was Jaje dead or alive or maybe hurting? He wanted to jump out of the speeding car himself and go find her.

He wanted to ask McNatt if he'd heard anything, but the major looked preoccupied.

On a side street on the northeast side of town, they abandoned the Buick. Roger followed McNatt to a sprawling house that overlooked the lake. Then walked with him through a thicket of palms and elephant ears to the servant's quarters.

McNatt opened the door, and by the time the door started to close—one, two, quick as that—he'd handcuffed Roger's right wrist. Roger jumped sideways. Let out a squeal like a hog. "Jesus! Oh, Jesus!" How had McNatt done that? Where had those handcuffs been hiding? Christ. Were those Marcel's death handcuffs, or not? Roger whipped his left arm around wildly, keeping it from McNatt's reach.

But McNatt was strong. He wrapped his arm around Roger's chest, and his muscles felt supernaturally hard, like if you shot him, the bullets would bounce off.

"Please, Dr. Lintenberg," the major said. "There is no need for this."

Where was the other guy? Where was Jerry? Oh Christ, oh Christ, where was the plastic bag? Roger wasn't as brave as Marcel—he was blubbering already.

"Please, Dr. Lintenberg."

McNatt pinned Roger's arms to his side and picked him up. When Roger's feet left the ground, he screamed.

McNatt carried him, still screaming, from the entranceway to the living room cum dinette cum bedroom. He forced him down on the parquet and locked the other half of the cuff to the bedframe. Then the major sat back, propped his hands on his thighs, and took a little breather.

"Please, Dr. Lintenberg. This location is soundproofed. Just . . ." He shook his head. Daubed at his mouth. The place Jaje had kicked him was bleeding again. "Please."

"Jesus Jesus don't kill me."

McNatt was still out of breath. He waved his hand. "No. I have no instructions on that. No, sir."

Instructions. Oh, shit. There was a phone on the wall. A god-damned phone on the wall. McNatt was waiting for fucking instructions.

"Would you care for a towel?" McNatt seemed nonplussed. "Or something?"

Roger wiped his face with his sleeve. His nose was snotty and running. His throat was raw. "Oh, no, thank you. I wouldn't want to be any trouble."

"Um." The major got to his feet.

"Any trouble at all."

Then—oh, Christ—McNatt was taking his shirt off. What the hell did *that* mean? He had one of those bodies that's not beefy like a weight lifter, but stronger, leaner, meaner. And he had these slabs of muscle over his sienna-brown belly, and striated muscles across his brown chest, like you see on guys in the movies. Shit, Roger hoped he wasn't going to take his pants off. Please. God. Not the pants.

McNatt folded his knit shirt carefully. Put it on the kitchen table. Pulled the gun out of his waistband, oh the gun. All Roger could see for a minute was that big black cannon of a gun. Ah. Good. McNatt put the gun on the table. Took off his shoe and sock—standing up, not sitting down. Then the major took off the other shoe and the sock, and he looked absolutely comfortable on one leg, like he could have run the Boston Marathon on one leg. Like if his other leg was fucking shot off or something, he'd never even notice.

Roger thought: *Not the pants.*

The major's eyes lost focus. His stomach and arm muscles clenched, the veins and tendons in bas relief. Taut body shifted, arms to the side, hands graceful as a ballerina's. What was going on? Roger broke out in a freezing sweat. His teeth started to chatter.

Lithe pivot. Body around, down, into a leopard crouch.

Staring transfixed, at the wall. Oh. Oh, right. Roger had seen this before.

"Uh. Tai Chi, huh? That's neat. You do it good."

Balinese dancer pose. Hold it. Hold it. Then release. New position, and, "Thank you. It helps to alleviate the stress."

"Really? Hey. No. I mean it. A body like yours . . ." Oh, if there was any vacillation to McNatt at all, there went the pants. "What I mean is . . . maybe you could teach me or something. If we're stuck here for a while. And I guess we will. Be stuck here for a while, I mean."

No answer. Why didn't he answer? Right leg rose, up, up. Then down.

"I guess you and me, we could get bored. Waiting." Oops. Not an invitation. Please. Not.

Controlled rotation. Eyes straight ahead.

"Well. So." Roger tested the handcuffs. They were, of course, firmly locked. "Guess it takes a lot of strength to do that."

"Not really." Arm swept to the side in slow mo.

"Hum. Interesting. I always wanted to . . . you know. I guess I was the typical ninety-eight-pound weakling. Well, not actually. Ninety-eight pounds, I mean. See? I studied. A lot. Four-point-oh grade average. Homework with Dove Bars. Cramming for tests with nacho-flavored Doritos. Never did get to the beach much. Maybe I missed out on a lot of childhood stuff, you think? We have these lakes in Minnesota. Lots of lakes. Thousands of lakes. Freeze your balls off, even in the summer. Well, come to think of it, I hated that. Probably childhood's . . ."

"The body's transitory, anyway," McNatt said, a dreamy expression on his face.

Whoa. Roger looked at the wall phone.

McNatt took a deep breath, and kept breathing in, breathing in, and the air had to be going somewhere, but Roger couldn't figure out what McNatt was doing with it.

Then he brought his hands together over his solar plexus. Closed his eyes. His breath came out, forever.

When he was finished, he said, "I've come to an interesting conclusion." His eyes opened. Roger had never seen eyes that dark.

"Oh?"

"I can tell you, because you'll understand. Both the science, and the metaphysics." McNatt wriggled his hands, rolled his head back and forth on his shoulders. Then he went into the bathroom and brought back a towel. "You care for one?" he asked as he scrubbed his cheeks dry, gently patted his mouth and puffy eyebrow clean.

"Uh, thanks. Maybe later."

The major put on his shirt, scooted a metal kitchen chair to the bed, and sat down next to Roger. "I am of the opinion that the entire universe lies inside us. And that includes Heaven and Hell."

"Hum."

"Take for example, when you kill someone. You know?"

"Yeah. That." A jingling. What the hell? Oh, the cuff. It was clinking on the bed frame every time Roger's hand trembled.

"There comes an epiphany at death. I tried to share Martinho's. It was just us two, alone; and when he went down, I went with him. He tried to tell me something, but of course he couldn't talk. So I put my mouth over his, and ate his last words, and—I know you will find this poignant—I could even taste the drug I killed him with. You see, Dr. Lintenberg, the drug couldn't kill me."

Roger's eyes stung. The room swam. He could not be hearing this. "No. Of course not. Not kill you. You're—"

"Perfectly nontoxic, taken orally."

"Hah. Yes."

"But it didn't work. I'm missing something. You know Henrique Freitas, the president's medium? I can't be certain, but I think that's what Freitas did. I think he killed his wife and then ate her death. Before he became what he is today, Freitas was not only a channeler, he was an outstanding psychic surgeon. I've learned quite a bit about him. I have spies, you know."

Joke. A joke. Should Roger laugh now? McNatt wasn't smiling.

"Psychic surgery, Dr. Lintenberg. I've seen studies on Zé Arigó, the one who died in '68. This man could walk up to a patient, and with the patient still standing, shove an ordinary table knife into the patient's open eye."

Roger wanted very much to squeeze his own eyes shut, but he was afraid he would miss something.

"Do you understand the significance? The absolute theft of the free will? I have tried this on myself, but cannot overcome the instinct to blink. I see I've surprised you. 'This is a reasonable man,' you're telling yourself. 'A Marine officer. How can he believe such superstition?' Well, Dr. Lintenberg, I have made this part of my life's study. One should always have a study, don't you think? Now, when I put my mouth over Martinho's . . ."

The phone rang. McNatt got up. Roger prayed for a wrong number. The major lifted the receiver. Grunted. Scratched his cheek. And hung up.

"Martinho, uh . . . we were just talking about Martinho, and you were telling me—wow—a fantastic . . . I don't mean fantastic. I meant awesome, but perfectly, absolutely believable. Psychic surgery, huh? So. Martinho. Was that Fatty? Oh, I guess you never knew—see? I didn't know their names. The, the guys. MUFON guys. Were they really MUFON?"

McNatt turned. His eyes were glazed, like he was going into his Tai Chi routine again. "What?"

"Martinho and, uh . . . Were they MUFON?"

He took out his roll of Tums. Popped one. "No."

"Man, they sounded real. MUFON real, I mean. Gulf Breeze. All the buzzwords . . ."

He ate another Tums. An absentminded, "They were briefed."

"Wow. Imagine that. And . . . so! CIA, huh? All the time. Had me fooled. Ha ha. So easy—"

McNatt, frowning, looked at Roger. Roger froze. "Teresa Solange seems to be all right."

"Teresa Solan—oh." Jaje was alive. The news made Roger feel almost okay. "I'm sorry. Look, I'm really sorry about what happened. It was Kinch. I wanted to keep her away from that dork Kinch, and—"

"It's perfectly all right, Dr. Lintenberg. It was just as well she got away. She was a problem, you see. I had no instructions on her." A third Tums. God. A third Tums.

"Ah. So. You had instructions, well . . . Instructions on Martinho and . . . uh, whozits. The bagged guy."

Roger finally snagged McNatt's attention. He came over, turned the metal chair around and sat, arms on the backrest, contemplating Roger. "They chose their deaths, whether they understood that at the end or not. Results like tragedy and success are inevitable. I always say: as we live our lives, we box ourselves into our destinies."

"Huh."

"First comes ego. Babies, Dr. Lintenberg. Neat packages of ego. And curiosity, the explorer in us. As children, if we encounter a dead dog in the roadway, we stop to look, don't we? And then we return the next day, and the next, just so that we may see what death is all about. I know you very well, Dr. Lintenberg, for despite skin color, despite upbringing—we are alike. And death, as sex, is forbidden fruit. They are what Gran called 'the nasties.' "

It was so quiet that the kitchen's dripping faucet sounded like funeral drums.

"So," Roger said. "Granny . . . uh. Mother's side, father's side?"

McNatt rested his bruised face in his hands. "Forgive me. I'm not explaining myself well. I realize, of course, that the theory may sound somewhat eccentric . . ."

"No, no! Not—"

"I very much admire you. A scientist's knowledge of nature, a metaphysicist's knowledge of the paranormal. I, myself, wanted to go into science, but I could not grasp the math." McNatt blew out a breath, let his hands drop. "I think about things, however. Deeply. Please, this is so formal. May I call you Roger?"

"Sure."

"And, please. Call me Doug. I need to nap for an hour. Would you mind terribly if I used the bed?"

"Oh. Be my—"

He yawned. Got up. Grabbed the gun. Oh the gun. And then he was lying down, the iron bed creaking and twanging, the pistol resting on his stomach. "Such a pity, Roger," he said to the ceiling. "Had I understood at eighteen what I understand now, I could have been a scientist. I could have been anything." His eyes closed. "The knowledge is there inside us, each and every one. Think of it—all knowledge there for the taking: faster-than-light travel, antigravity, what constitutes consciousness, and how life begins. Indeed, these are the very nuggets that Freitas is mining. If you will permit me to mix my metaphors: Freitas has picked the lock of Universal Awareness."

The next sound from McNatt's mouth was a snore.

CNN, Live

. . . sense of absolute helplessness—if you'll forgive the cliché—like a sitting duck. Only a few hours are left until the deadline expires. There is no word, none at all, that the Brazilian government will back down. You can see the shopkeepers taping windows here behind me. I've spoken with them, and they have little hope of salvaging anything. The truth has finally hit home. And I think it started with that accident in the Military Sector yesterday. Until then, the Brazilians simply didn't believe it could happen here.

How are the people holding up?

Sorry? The wind is—

How is the mood of the people, Susan? Are they frightened?

Yes. And oddly fatalistic. A woman came up to me yesterday. She lives in one of the apartment blocks which lie to either side of the Monumental Axis, just a few blocks from the seat of government. She saw the camera and realized I was with the American press corps. She asked me, 'Will they be careful?'

Careful?

Yes. She meant our Air Force. The Brazilians who can leave are leaving right along with the foreigners. The ones who have to stay, Bernie, can only hope that the American smart bombs are as accurate as everyone says.

20

How could you leave life so fast? A brief announcement over the jet's intercom that the tire was fixed; and that because of emergency scheduling, there would be no lunch served. The pilot hoped, sourly, that everyone would enjoy their flight. Then the turbines shrieked, and the jet began its lumbering race for the air. Dolores realized she'd forgotten something.

Harry. Harry needed his medicine. The iron was on. She needed to check the answering machine. The mail. God. The garden needed watering.

An instant of weightlessness. The nose lifted. In the front of the cabin, a baby started to scream. The plane struggled skyward, bearing its load of middle-class refugees.

When they banked over the city, the wing dipped twice. Clear-air turbulence, or the pilot's goodbye? Dolores looked down on the bird-shaped city, could see ruins in the northern section still smoldering.

Jack reached across the aisle and tried to grab her hand. She pulled away. She would leave just as she came, alone. It was safer not to count higher than one. Harry had taught her: men weren't company.

A chime sounded. Flight attendants unbuckled and stood. Passengers stirred. Then from the intercom boomed Ana Maria's song, "Vem Morena." A farewell gift from the cabin crew. The stewardess who was asking for drink orders paled, and walked quickly back to her seat.

Dolores looked at Jaje who sat, dry-eyed, beside her. Not callousness. Simple ignorance. Dolores had to remember not to lose her temper, must try her best to obey Ana's last order: give Jaje a family.

A warm tickle on her cheek. Oh. She was crying. She shouldn't, not over Ana. Not over Brazil. What did they matter? She was a Canadian tourist named Allison Morris, living with her husband Hugh who was not *moreno,* not mulatto, but black. And with her *café-com-leite* daughter, Tina, who would never again be a white girl's equal. Silly, simplistic—the color distinctions of North America.

She was flying to a black-and-white world. Political good and evil. Religious right and wrong. A two-choice place that she didn't want to return to. America's smug surety, its lack of ambivalence, scared her. Everything scared her.

She was afraid Canada would not be different enough. Brazil slipped away. Below, beige ground turned green and damp and wild, and soon the swamps would fold in on themselves, and the land would rise, and the Andes thrust up to meet the jet.

They were leaving too fast. Nothing would ever be as it was. Not freedom. Not career. Not contentment. Could she learn a new vocabulary? Jack reached across the aisle again, and this time Dolores let his hand stay.

Hiroshi vomited onto Xuli's clay yard, scattering the chickens. His bowels cramped, announcing a near-future return to the outhouse.

His vomit tasted of coffee. His shit stank of coffee. His sweat was the rank cheesy sweat of a foreigner. It frightened him, how he was losing himself. Yet, it was what he must do. Gingerly, he stood upright. Xuli was seated on the steps, watching.

"You doing good."

He ran a hand over his stomach. How many days had it been since he had slept? He had vomited so much that his muscles were sore. Shit so much that his ass burned, and it was hard to sit down. Yet he tingled with energy.

"Got to get all that old life out," she said. "Got to get clean for what's coming. And you know what that is, little one. Soon now, you'll have the Amazon and the Rio São Francisco in your veins. Your heart's going to pump *cachaça*. Your prick will be strong as mahogany, and your skin will smell of coconut and black beans and shrimp."

He nodded. When his mind wandered to the serene walled garden at his parents' home, he concentrated on multiplication tables. Twelve, twenty-four, thirty-six . . .

Xuli called, "Tell me who you are."

Aftertaste of greasy sausage, the caustic burn of gall, the acid sting of pepper sauce. He felt an urgent, undefined need to act. "The Warrior."

"Good. And where is your place now?"

Hot, arid air made his nostrils itch. The flat desert glinted and shimmered like a mirror. The strange far hills were blue. "With Oxalá."

"Yes," she said. "There's a great, dark evil on its way, and its name is envy, and its warrior is America. And if we don't beat it back, evil's going to cover the earth. You believe that?"

"Yes."

"And when that evil comes, who you going to fight for?"

So simple. Hiroshi felt the pull of the sun, and closed his eyes. Blind, he surrendered to the sweet drag of Earth. "Brazil."

"No need to be afraid. Not you. You got Xuli on your left side.

You got Oxalá on the right. One ball is Sugarloaf, the other, Corcovado."

Afraid? Not anymore. Xuli had given him direction.

"Tell me. How are you going to fight?"

His lips felt dry, and he licked them. "Alone."

Muller was asking something.

Edson pulled his attention from the car window. "What?"

"Do you wish me to take you to the office afterward, sir?"

"No." He upended the pint, let the last of the Scotch trickle down his throat. Then he dropped the bottle on the floorboard, and searched the glove compartment for another. There should be Gentleman Jack. Or had he drunk that already?

And where was Muller going? The road wasn't familiar. Bumper-to-bumper traffic. In the cloudless western sky, the sun was going down.

Edson unsnapped his seatbelt, felt around in the dust and grit under the seat. "Where in hell are we headed?"

A sigh. "Out past Candangolândia, sir. You remember. You are to meet with someone there."

No, Edson couldn't remember. He sat up. Out the windshield, taxis. He had never seen so many taxis. "Um. Traffic."

"All headed for the airport, sir."

Maybe there was a pint in the console. The traffic was making him nervous. "Everyone flying." It would be nice to fly. He rummaged through the papers in the compartment until he touched the cool welcome of glass.

"The U.N. has warned foreigners to leave. You remember."

He didn't. And it didn't matter. He'd discovered an unopened pint of Seagram's. He twisted off the cap and filled his mouth with whiskey.

Wait. Had something important happened today?

"What time is it, Gilberto?" Edson rarely called Muller by his given name, but people should try things. Life was experimentation, after all, and Edson was an explorer.

Someone had said that to him once. We're explorers, you and me. Where in the world had he heard that?

"About five o'clock, sir."

"When is the deadline over?"

"Midnight tonight."

Edson took another drink. "We will go down in flames. We will go down in history." Perhaps he should do something official. Make sure the hospitals had gasoline for their generators. The Americans could certainly knock out the power. Any six-year-old with a toaster could do that.

Something about children. Something . . .

The traffic came to a halt. A horn blew. Again, again. Edson leaned his head back, closed his eyes. "Ah, listen, Muller. The car horn: our National Musical Instrument. We should get to our feet. We should put our hands over our hearts."

Muller's exasperated sigh.

"We should cover our balls, Muller, before it is too late." He opened his eyes. Nearer the airport. Planes came and went, lights blinking red as maraschino cherries. "If I had a cherry," he said, "I could make a whiskey sour."

Traffic started to unclog. Muller hit the accelerator, then braked abruptly when the car in front came to a halt.

Edson bumped his forehead against the padded dash, and laughed. "If I had whiskey sour mix, and ice."

Planes. Something about planes. The memory darkened. Edson sat up straighter, took another drink.

And then the traffic was crawling off toward the spur to the airport, and their Mercedes was picking up speed. Edson closed his eyes again. Planes crashing? No, that wasn't it. A little plane. A baby plane with a broken wing. How strange. Memories hissed through his mind like static.

He dozed. Muller woke him. Edson sat up blinking. A sea of

beige grass. They were in the goddamned desert. Had Muller brought him here to shoot him? Edson fumbled for the door latch. "Where the fuck?" he asked.

"Way to the other side of Candangolândia." Muller sounded tired. He should take some time off.

The door opened and Edson fell out.

Strong arms caught him. "God, Edson." A sigh. Was everyone in the world tired? "What *schiesse*. You're drunk. Gilberto, he's drunk."

"I know."

Edson would have stood up and shown them, but he was tired, too. He perched on the ledge of the doorjamb, patted the velour seat behind him. Where had the bottle gone? "Bottle," he said.

"I need him sober. He has to okay a goddamned plan of mine, Gilberto."

Piehl? The voice sounded like Piehl's. But Edson's head was too heavy to lift. All he could see was scuffed dusty shoes, baggy tan slacks.

"Why is he sitting like that? Is he going to puke? Christ, Gilberto. Can't you make him pull himself together?"

The crunch of footsteps on dry foliage. Muller's voice. "There's no time. If you want a question answered, just go ahead."

Piehl. Squatting eye level now. Such blue eyes. "Like the sky," Edson said. He put his hand out to touch them, but Piehl jerked away.

"Edson," he said. "Listen to me. The Japanese is in the Valley. Do you understand?"

The Japanese? What were they doing there? Edson thought the Americans were supposed to invade. Piehl seemed to be waiting for an answer so Edson nodded, hugely. "Yes."

"Edson? This is very important."

Had he touched another man's face? Or . . . maybe that man had touched Edson's. A squeak—a door opening? No. The scrape of a beard against his cheek. Yes. That was it. God. And it had felt . . .

"He is with Xuli. You remember Xuli. The *mãe de santo*. Edson?"

He nodded. But no, that couldn't have happened. He was imagining a man's kiss. Give him a woman, now . . .

"I've figured out how to use our Japanese boy. We must consider the next few years, after the Americans have taken over. And how we can damage them today. Here is my idea. We use Sato to terminate Kinch and the CIA station chief. The Japanese government will be in the shit hole, and nothing can be traced to us. Clever, right? I will expect a bonus for this, Edson. Everything is set. Xuli has our boy programmed. I'm ready to order him activated, and all I need is your approval."

Brown girl. Nipples like maraschino cherries. But when Edson imagined touching them, the breasts elongated. Not breasts anymore, but . . . No.

Piehl was exasperated. "Edson, damn it. Can I have your verbal okay?"

What had he asked for? The Americans were going to bomb—sometime soon now. And Edson had received word that Japanese had invaded the Valley. Nothing mattered anymore. "Of course you can," Edson said.

Roger had looked at his watch for the fifteenth time when it happened: exactly one hour to the minute after the nap began, Mc-Natt's eyes popped open. He sat up and swung his feet over the side of the bed. His face wasn't puffy, and his eyes didn't look sleepy. His fucking clothes weren't even wrinkled. How'd he do that?

He picked up the conversation where he had left off. "The 'I want.' It's a human urge that . . . Oh. Forgive my poor manners, Roger. Do you need to use the facilities?"

McNatt was certain to go with him. Roger would have to whip it out and try . . . "Thanks. I can hold it."

McNatt went to the refrigerator and came back with a pair of Brahma Chopp. He held one toward Roger. Condensation beaded on the bottle's sides. A wisp of mist rose up from the open longneck. Over half a liter of Brazilian brew, stronger and heavier than the single can of Miller Lite Roger would nurse over the course of an evening. Half a liter. Jeez. That could set Roger on his ass. It could make him forget things. I want, Roger thought fiercely, and took it.

McNatt straddled the chair, propped his elbows on the backrest. "There are two kinds of love, really: one that is inward and body-fixated; and one that is outward and spiritual. Those pilotless UFOs? Those massless lights? Dr. Grabbel was quite taken with them. But I know that they are a part of Freitas which still feels a need to prevent violence. That is why we see them around military planes. They are Freitas's unconscious effort at salvation."

McNatt took another swallow of beer, propped his chin on his crossed arms. "Interesting, isn't it? To achieve what he has, Freitas must have had sainthood in him. Then something happened—I would certainly like to know what—and he became a romantic. Have you ever loved someone, Roger? Loved them very, very deeply?" A twinkle of mischief. "I think perhaps you were a bit smitten by Ms. Bonfim."

Roger took another drink. His sinuses buzzed. Drugged? He looked at the bottle and saw to his surprise that he had downed more than half. He realized, suddenly, horribly, that he had to take a piss.

"And when you love someone a great deal, you know how that love makes you ache, and therefore you hate the person, too?"

"Um." Piss very bad.

"And so you beat them sometimes, because of it. You hurt them to make yourself well again. That love makes you weak. And if you lose control of yourself, you are nothing. Absolutely nothing. You are so afraid of losing control, in fact, that if the person ever tried to leave you, you could kill them and it would be like self-defense. You see, Roger? The ultimate consequence of romance is murder. I have thought about this a great deal."

"Have you ever. And—Control, huh?" Aw, Jeez. Any minute Roger was going lose control. There was a firehose of a piss waiting impatiently in his bladder.

McNatt picked up the empty bottle, took it to the kitchen, and wiped the glass clean with a cloth. No. Stop. He was wiping Roger's fingerprints off. There would be nothing to show Roger had ever been in the house. He'd die without leaving a mark, be buried without a headstone. He wanted to leave something behind, if only his name carved in the wall.

McNatt tossed the bottle into a trash bag and brought Roger another. "You're letting me run on and on. Don't let me bore you," he said.

"No, no! Absolutely. This is just—wow. I mean. Fascinating stuff. We could talk all night. However long you want, Doug."

"So nice hearing a man of your caliber call me Doug, Roger. I mean that in the sincerest way."

The pants. Any minute, the pants. Then it would be over on the stomach, Roger, thanks for calling me Doug. Would you mind so very terribly putting your ass in the air and spreading your cheeks so I can give you some of that inward, inward love?

"Before you, I had never encountered anyone who had the intellectual capacity and the experience in the paranormal to follow what I am saying. It gets lonely for me."

"Understand. But you need to be strong, Doug. Fight that. Fight that urge. See—"

"Necrophilia, for example."

Whoa! Panic pumped freon through Roger's veins. He didn't need to piss anymore. He could hold gallons and gallons. An entire swimming pool of piss. And he was strong enough to pull the bed frame through that door. He could run faster than McNatt, even dragging the iron bed, and maybe even the house, behind him.

"After all, it's not a big step from romance to necrophilia."

Roger wanted to say something calming to McNatt, that he understood completely, that the theory was certainly compelling, but his throat was too dry to emit more than a sympathetic wheeze.

"If you love someone, you expect them to become a vessel for your wishes. But there's the free will problem. That stubbornness. And when you insist, the complaints. A corpse is so much more tractable. And there is another sort of allure. As I told you, I can clearly recall the first dead animal I saw. I literally could not pass it up, just as none of us can pass a car wreck without peeking. After my first dead cat, I began to explore the neighborhood for others. There is a process that the corpse goes through—I'm sure you're well acquainted with it."

"Absolutely." Roger's voice was back, albeit weak. "No question about it. Well acquainted, if not actually what you'd call friendly terms. Childhood? Where was that?"

"Philadelphia."

"Philadelphia!"

"Shame the insects eat it."

"Yes! Too bad about . . . Liberty Bell. Birthplace of—"

"And when the corpse is gone, you feel . . . I don't know, Roger. Such a loss. It hurts, losing it. Like losing a woman. And so you go out and make your own . . ." McNatt blinked. Then laughed uproariously.

"Ha ha," Roger said, and hoped he was smiling.

"Make a corpse just of your own, I mean. Not a woman."

"Um. I see."

"Although . . ." McNatt drained the last of his beer, went to get himself another.

Although. Although. The word walked on ten-pound hobnail boots across the floor of Roger's mind.

McNatt detoured to the bathroom. The sound of pissing went on for a long, long time. Roger tried to focus on something besides the bladder-tickling noise. At last a flush, the hiss of a faucet. McNatt emerged, straightening his zipper.

"Roger, I must tell you: it is such a joy to finally share these thoughts with someone."

"Joy. Yes. And sharing. Never know. Maybe we could take in a ball game. Do some bass fishing."

McNatt sat, leaned forward confidentially. "To squeeze something you love." His hands cupped a globe of air. "To squeeze the life out of it, as you would a kitten. That is the essence. That's what I tried to capture with Martinho, but I didn't—"

A sound at the door. In one fluid move, McNatt was on his feet, the pistol in his hand.

Jerry. Oh, man. It was Jerry coming through the door like a Vegas show-tune–humming guardian angel. Jerry. Roger didn't know when he'd been so happy. "Hey, somebody. Hey. I gotta take a leak."

But that's when Roger noticed that Jerry was carrying a familiar suitcase. And a camera case.

Jerry shot him a look. "How's he been?" he asked McNatt.

McNatt put the gun on the table. "Quiet. Tonight?"

Roger's Samsonite.

"Stroke of midnight," Jerry said. "I hear their Army chief of staff sent a quiet little word to the embassy that he wouldn't fight, and wouldn't put up any AAA. Shit. Leaving the city wide open. You believe that? Guy sees that Freightliner Super Chief barreling down the road at him, and he's crapping in his pants scared. The only one in this whole fucking country with a lick of sense. But General Davis doesn't understand shit from Shinola about Brazilians. He'll orchestrate the attack by the book. You know how that goes—you being one of the grunts." He looked around. "There's no TV in here, Mac. There's no TV. Shit. Spades."

"Gin," McNatt said.

"Hearts." Jerry put down the suitcase, took a pack of cards from his pocket, and tossed them on the table. He opened the refrigerator, got out a beer.

McNatt walked over—oh, shit—McNatt himself was coming to unfasten Roger's handcuff. Then it was up and to the john, McNatt giving Roger his normal taciturn treatment, like nothing had ever been said between them.

Roger hoped that whatever happened at midnight wasn't also going to happen to him. He saw Jerry kneel and wipe the Samsonite down.

ABC News Special

... *eerie. Brasília isn't a bustling commercial center like São Paulo, or an entertainment mecca like Rio. It has always marched to its own sedate drummer.*

Doesn't seem to be anyone outside. Are they pretty much keeping their heads down?

No, Peter. Actually there were a number of people in the streets earlier, ah, with cameras—a sight that I found very, very moving. Brasília is every bit as sophisticated as Washington, D.C., yet here were its citizens, wandering around like tourists, taking pictures of their favorite buildings—in effect, telling their city goodbye.

Um. The architecture is irreplaceable.

Yes indeed, Peter. And, uh, despite its youth, I suppose, quite historically significant. While I was at the plaza, there in the Monumental Axis, I passed a woman stroking the wall of the official pigeon house. Well, I suppose I should explain that, the Pombal. Ah, you see, Peter, when Brasília was built, there were no nearby cities—nothing for hundreds of miles—and they had to import their pigeons.

Funny.

At any rate, the woman was stroking the side of the Pombal and very, very earnestly instructing the birds that when the bombs began to fall, they should fly away. I tell you, Peter. I've covered other wars, but I've never lived through anything as poignant as this. And never has a city seemed as fragile.

21

Jack's performance was so flawless that Dolores felt at once proud and ashamed of him. A river of passengers streamed around their sidewalk island of baggage, while at a taxi stand Jack argued with a driver. The Peruvian stood propped against his taxi's door. Jack was down in his face. "Ho-tel?"

Dolores wondered if he was trying too hard. Only a Brazilian would be as loud. Only an American would be as demanding.

It was typical Lima weather—a day of almosts: not nearly sunshine, not quite rain. The city smelled of car exhaust and ocean. Mist beaded on the windshields of the rusting taxis; drops of moisture wormed down the windows.

In slow, patient Spanish the driver tried to explain again that the Lima hotels were full. All full. That if the *señor* wanted to pay for a trip to Callao, there might be a room there.

Jack looked exasperated. "Ho-tel?" He leaned his head on his folded hands and theatrically mimed a snore. "Ho-tel?"

"Oh, give me a break," Jaje said. "He's telling us to go down the road to Callao. That's not that far. We can afford—"

Dolores caught her wrist in a warning squeeze. "Let your father handle things."

Jaje *tsk*ed and pulled her arm away. She glared at Jack. "Oh, come on," she muttered under her breath. So far the spy game merely annoyed her.

Come get your kid, Ana, Dolores thought. *I'm tired of this.*

What had Ana said at Jaje's thirteenth birthday? Children are puppies—they take over your house, tear up your furniture, shit all over your life. Too cute to punish.

Cute. Jaje put her hands on her hips, tapped her foot, and pouted at the equivocal border where fog ended the world—a brat. Indulgent Brazilians bred millions like her. No wonder they grew up without a sense of duty. No wonder they grew up laughing.

The mist swaddled the airport, muted the honk of the horns, hushed the roar of the planes. Under the glare of the airport lights, it sequined Jaje's brown curls. When she shook her head, she struck rainbows. "Tell him to give it up. Please? Pl-eee-ze? I'm hungry."

"Ho-tel?" Jack waved a fistful of cruzeiros that would have been pesos had the *cambio* not run out.

Down the line of taxis, the bills caught a driver's attention. "America!" More Mexican than Peruvian, all wavy hair and swarthy skin and Cesar Romero moustache. "Hey. Over here, America. I espeak the English."

They picked up their bags and walked to him through the fading pewter day.

As they neared, the man frowned. "No dollars? Cruzeiros? After tomorrow, *sin valor, no?*"

Jaje opened her mouth, preparing for argument. Dolores butted her with the overnight bag.

Jack blinked, the picture of confusion. "Excuse me? After to-morrow—what?"

The driver tossed their suitcases into the trunk of his elderly piebald Chevrolet. "We stop on the way, no? You exchange. No cruzeiros, you understand? No Brazil money. Then I take you my wife cousin house. He go stay at my brother-in-law. Get in, you get in, pretty lady, please." He gestured to the sullen Jaje. "You esmile, no? So pretty when you esmile. And lady?" He gave Dolores's split lip a double take. A swift glance at Jack. Without another word, he got in the car.

The interior stank of mildew and stale cigarette smoke. The upholstery leaked a dingy fluff. Jaje sat next to Dolores, jiggling her leg. "If we're going to stop someplace, I need some mousse."

From the front seat, Jack turned around to look at her in astonishment. It was going to be an interesting next few days.

"Caught in war, America?" The taxi took off at breakneck speed through the fog, dodging suitcase-burdened wraiths.

"Not America." Jack held onto the bench seat so hard that his knuckles whitened. "Canada."

"Canada! You tell my wife cousin. He not charge you so much. Americans are pigs, no? And Brazilians are without shame."

Dolores could see it coming. She pinched Jaje's arm to head it off. The girl scooted out of arm's reach and gave Dolores a look before turning her face to the window.

Not quite a São Paulo taxi ride. When he was free of the airport traffic, and into the clay-colored houses and clay-colored streets, the driver slowed down.

Black vultures perched in knobby trees, overlords of Lima's dun Hell. It was a land without flowers, without a blade of grass. A maze of decaying churches and narrow alleys, where drab-clothed Indians shuffled.

"Go find Peru refrigerator, estereo, Inca Cola," the driver was saying brightly.

Jack looked exhausted, his eyes half-staff. He turned toward the streaked window and the row of darkened storefronts beyond, and yawned.

"Now it is only GE or Climax. Coca-Cola or Guaraná. Once we make Peruvian, but no more."

"Uh-huh," Jack said, his tone absentminded.

The sun, a tarnished dime in a nickel sky, was headed down. Day would slip from dim to dark. Dolores yawned, too, and wondered if she would be able to sleep once the lights were out, and silence returned.

The taxi driver shrugged. "Myself, I say, let Brazil and America fight. May they kill each other dead."

The shuddering of the house brought Roger awake. It was night. He'd been asleep, and now he felt almost sober. His head was stuffy, his eyelids swollen. He was lying on the bare mattress, belly down. His shackled hand was numb.

Another tremor. The iron springs jangled. Earthquake? Not a bad one, not a killer. Still, it went on too long.

He raised his head. McNatt and Jerry were dark shapes at a dark window where orange lightning flashed.

Jerry's soft, mumbled, "There . . ."

McNatt shifted. His hands were to his face. "See it." Oh. That was it. He had binoculars. A pair of binoculars.

The lightning flashed again.

Jerry's baritone, "Hey. Over there, Mac. No. Look east. See?"

McNatt's quiet, ". . . if Freitas can even help it." He took the binoculars from his eyes.

Jerry said clearly and with amusement, "So fucking weird. Swear to God, Mac."

Roger rested his cheek on a pillow that smelled of dust and feathers. A flash of yellow brightened the room, was followed by noise and rolling shudders and McNatt and Jerry's Fourth of July murmurs of awe. Roger drifted in and out of a beery doze where everything was fantasy: the hush, the man-shaped shadows at the window, the strobing dark.

"You ever get instructions on this guy?" Jerry asked.

"Yes."

Death threaded McNatt's voice. It tied up all of Roger's loose ends. Funny, how he couldn't feel frightened.

"After Cabeceiras. Then they say he'll be of no further use."

Jerry said, "Too bad."

The pair stood wordlessly for a while. Just two good friends at a window.

McNatt, the shorter shadow, gave the binoculars to Jerry, the tall silhouette. He turned to the table, toward the room. "I'm telling you, Jerry, those UFO lights can't hurt anything. They come directly out of Freitas. They're an autonomic reflex."

"Uh-huh. Except Machado says other universes."

"He doesn't know."

Silhouettes shoulder to shoulder now. "Standing next to the guy every formal occasion I've ever seen, and he doesn't know. So tell me, if he's not channeling some alien, how'd this Freitas get the technology?"

McNatt's voice, still as the shadows. "It's inside us—all of us. Everyone knows what Freitas knows. In fact, from working at meditation diligently, I myself have begun receiving glimpses. Didn't you notice that the Cessna we shot down could not have fired on our pilot? Its acquisition system was disconnected. Have you asked yourself why?"

A snort. "If you possess all knowledge, Mac, why the hell do I still beat you at cards?" The click of footsteps. Jerry returned to the window. "Man!" His cry was startling. "Oh, man! You gotta see this!"

McNatt stood upright. A calm, "That is really amazing."

"Goddamn, Mac. Goddamn. Flying saucers, some kinda weird soul shit—it doesn't matter. I've never seen anything so pretty."

Roger sat up. The bed creaked. He sensed, rather than saw, McNatt turn.

A soft, "Awake, Dr. Lintenberg? Would you like to watch your UFOs?"

"Oh, yes," Roger said. "Please."

McNatt came over, gently undid the cuff, and together they walked to the window.

Bombs fell north: on the Military Sector, through the campus of the Meteorological Institute. The spine of the city became embers. Above and through the smoke, gaily colored lights whirled like exotic jungle birds, like children's kites—Freitas's burning angels.

Beautiful, the death of Brasília. And somehow, not frightening at all.

An unexpected sound awakened Dolores to the sight of an unexpected room. An arm was wrapped about her. She and the person behind were lying, body spooned to body, like she and Harry had lain during the mild first years of marriage.

The sound was a car horn; the arm was Jack's. There would be a lot she would have to get used to.

Whispers. She sat up, chilled by wintry panic. Jack rolled over, snoring and oblivious. A shadow stood in the doorway.

"Aunt Dee?" Jaje. And such a small voice.

Blue flickering light from the neighboring room. Jaje always slept with the TV on.

"Aunt Dee?" Her fragile, newly learned sophistication had vanished. Jaje was sobbing. "I'm scared."

"Coming, hon." Dolores got out of bed, put Mrs. Nelson Albright's Republican-pink robe on over Mrs. Nelson Albright's floor-length gown.

Jack grunted a sleepy, "What?"

"It's okay, baby," Dolores whispered. Jaje put her arms around her. "It's okay, sweetheart. I'll come sit with you awhile. You have a bad dream?"

In the doorway Dolores halted. The nightmare was sitting in the living room: CNN playing to an empty couch a silent war movie.

*   *   *

The world ended with flashes of lightning, roars of thunder. The driver door of the Mercedes was open, and Muller was outside, screaming, "But where is the president?"

Edson sat up in his seat, scrubbed his face.

They were parked on Avenida das Nações. Through the windows Edson could see soldiers. A knot of Nando's soldiers. And over the thunder a captain was shouting, "I think at Alvorada. Perhaps at Granja do Torto."

"She can't be!" Muller had left his suit coat in the car. So unlike him. His tie was undone and hanging to either side of his neck, a limp, striped snake. "I just drove by there. Alvorada is rubble and the Granja is burning! Where is she?"

So Freitas is dead, Edson thought. The news orphaned him.

"I don't know!" The captain was beside himself. His voice was wild, his gestures disjointed. "In the Axis, all communication lines are being jammed. We can't find General Fernando. You must wake Director Carvalho so he can explain to the Americans that we are not shooting at them."

"He is *drunk*!"

A bad taste in Edson's mouth. He ran his tongue over his teeth, grasped the door handle, and got out of the car. Muller spun toward him as if he were seeing a ghost.

The time had come to put fear and whiskey away. Nando was missing; Ana dead. There was no one else to turn to.

The captain cried, "*Senhor* Director. Thank God! Please. We must do something. The Americans keep bombing. I think they believe the lights are attacking them, sir."

The lights. Edson held out his hand. "Give me those binoculars."

The captain took them from his neck and gave them to Edson. A few blocks away, fire sirens whooped.

South Embassy Row was perilously near the bombing, but the Americans had planned for that. The bombers were coming in so low that Edson could see their dark bellies reflecting the fire on the ground. What did they call that type of sortie? A milk run? Around the planes, brightly hued sparklers.

Freitas was still alive.

The captain screamed in Edson's ear. "Can't you tell them? Please tell the Americans we mean no harm!"

"No use." Edson shook his head. "They already know."

Bastards. An easy excuse the U.N. had. Probably captured by CNN and beamed live to a satellite hookup—UFOs were visual proof of Brazil's resistance.

A bomb struck too close. The captain ducked. His soldiers took cover by their APC. The wind shifted, sending oily smoke boiling down the street. Orange cinders flew upward like a swarm of Freitas's lights. Where they landed, they stung. The normally mild-tempered, mild-tongued Muller surprised Edson by brushing at his arm and shouting *"Pôrra! Pôrra!"* In the distance a row of palm trees flamed like torches.

It was time. Edson could do it. He told Muller, "Let's go."

Seeing them hurry to the car, the captain wailed, "But what are your orders?"

Edson cupped his hand to his mouth, shouted back, "Stay out of the bombs' way." He climbed into the passenger seat and closed the door.

Muller stared blankly at the shower of sparks. A nearby banana tree was suddenly pocked by blowing embers. "Where to now, sir?"

"Cabeceiras."

A flick of a look. A question.

There was no one else. "I am going to destroy the Door."

Dolores wrapped the blanket more firmly around them both. Entwined together on the couch, she briskly rubbed Jaje's ankles. "Cold legs. Oooh. Icy feet," she said.

A smile that had a short half-life. "Warm heart."

Beyond the unfamiliar living room, in a stranger's kitchen, Jack puttered. On the TV screen Brasília erupted in shades of night-vision green.

A rhinestone sparkle of bursting bombs. Then an explosion so huge that the cameraman twitched, and sent the view momentarily skyward. "No," Jaje breathed. "Was that Itamaraty?"

The CNN newscaster was saying so, her voice high pitched and helium-squeaky with excitement.

"They're way down at the Mirage Hotel. They can't tell, sweetie."

The picture dissolved. Sound became static.

Susan? the anchor called. *Susan? You still there?*

A last burst of static, then a picture of the dancing lights and the fires and a *That was close, Bernie. The TV tower went.*

Pan to show the direct hit.

Bernie? I wish you could see the colors of these lights, there in Atlanta. I know . . . the viewers at home. How do I describe this? They are magnificent. All colors of the rainbow. Bright blue. A deep purple. Orange. Just every conceivable color. And very, very fast. I imagine they're a distraction to the pilots of those bombers. I would think, ah, they'd have a hard time trying to avoid a midair collision. Very odd antiaircraft artillery, if it is actually 'triple A.' Long pause, so long Dolores could hear the ceaseless rumble in the background. *But in a strange way, very pretty.*

Jack came in balancing two bowl-sized coffees with milk, and set them on the end table. "You guys look comfortable."

"Where's yours?" Dolores asked.

"Um." A vague, sleepy gesture. His face was all lumpy hills and valleys, a topographical map of some rich brown land. "Later." And he shuffled back to the kitchen.

Jack. A man who knew poverty and crime, literature and art, and—more importantly—kitchens. Dolores smiled at his retreating back. The pajamas from the red suitcase were too small, the sleeves ending two inches above his wrist, the pants high as waders.

"You think Mom's okay?"

Dolores rocked her. Warm in the room, yet Jaje was shivering. "Your Mom's a survivor, honey."

Susan? Can you bring us up-to-date?

An overloud *Yes!* as she strained to be heard above the explosions. *It is now, ah, an hour and a half past the commencement of Allied bombing which began at one A.M. our time. We understand that most of the sorties are American, with some British and some French. Quite a bit of destruction in the Monumental Axis . . .*

Susan? We should explain here that Brasília was built in the form of an airplane . . .

Yes! The Military Sector is toward the tail of the plane, if you will, and the main government buildings comprise the nose. And Bernie, at this moment, um, two-forty-three A.M., those parts of the city seem to be in ruins.

"I want to call her," Jaje said.

Dolores stroked her hair. "You can't, baby. Maybe tomorrow when things settle down."

"But I didn't tell her I love her."

Kindness was what lies were made for. "She knows."

Cabeceiras sat in a white firestorm of floodlights, two armored companies surrounding it. Not militia, but career soldiers trained in riot control.

A guard stopped the Mercedes at the gate. "*Senhor* Director. All entry is forbidden by presidential orders."

Edson took a chance. "The president is dead."

The sergeant, a blue-black Bahian, flinched as if he had been slapped.

"Is General Fernando here?"

Shouted questions from troops near an APC. The sergeant called, "Dead! She is dead!"

"Damn you, soldier! I asked you a question! Is General Fernando here?"

The sergeant turned, still wearing his grief. "No, sir."

Then Edson had to. There was no one else. "I have taken charge of the presidency. Open up that damned gate."

Shock. A palm-out gesture to wait. The sergeant hiked his rifle higher on his shoulder and ran off through the floodlit evening, calling for a colonel.

Muller turned to look at him, probably wondering if he was still drunk.

Out of the lights' glare the colonel came, a gruff Paulista. "Director Carvalho. What is this *bagunça*? You give orders? No. This is an Army situation."

Edson got out of the car, trying not to stumble. "Why is this area lit when bombs are falling on Brasília?"

A *puh* of impatience. "By General Fernando's order. The Americans see at night as well as they can during the day. We don't fear bombs at this locale, *Senhor* Director. We fear the Special Forces. Get back in your car. Go home."

"Have you heard from General Fernando?"

A quick shift of the colonel's eyes. "No."

"I will not tell you that I have spoken to him." Edson put his hands to his chest, a show of candor. "I will not lie to you. But answer me this: when he said to keep visitors away from Cabeceiras, did he specifically mention me?"

The colonel seemed unaccountably interested in the tread of the APC. "No."

"Then why won't you let me in?"

The colonel hiked his hands on his web belt. "Bombers over Brasília. Cruise missiles at the factories in my beloved São Paulo. And in all Brazil, we are the only troops allowed weapons."

Edson looked around at the tanks. "As I can see."

"And this is by presidential order, with General Fernando's agreement. You seem absent in this equation. Let me be blunt. I have heard stories about you, and they seem to be true, since you come here stinking of whiskey. Drinking to forget? To celebrate? I don't care. The Army never broke faith with the people. Must I remind you that it was not a general who made us a dictatorship again? Now you tell us that *Presidente* Ana is dead, and this may even be true. But I will not obey your orders, or of anyone in O.S. If the office is to pass to someone, it must pass to the Army."

An instant of pique, then Edson laughed. "My dear colonel. How can I argue with the truth? I am a complete pile of shit, and not worthy to be president. I totally agree."

The colonel searched his face. "In writing?"

"Yes, yes, yes. I will agree in writing."

Quick orders, a scrawled note. Edson signed with a flourish, and the colonel waved the car on.

"Ah, Muller," Edson said as they passed through the gates. "The colonel didn't think I would give the country back, and I never really wanted it."

Muller didn't laugh.

Nando, the Army colonel, and finally Muller. Given time, they all despised him. When had Edson lost self-respect? As a São Paulo detective, he'd given up hope of redemption. Then O.S. hired him, and saved him from the streets. But power followed, and with it, compromise. Had he lost his soul by obeying Ana's orders? Or had he damned himself in his own house, on his way to see Freitas, when Muller begged him not to go?

Muller parked by the side of Hangar Eight. Edson got out, took the tire iron from the Mercedes's trunk.

"Shall I come with you?" Muller's blond hair was hot platinum under the halogen lights. Muller, the bright angel.

"Only if you want."

Muller got out of the car. Yes. Best that they do this together.

Inside the building, an empty, echoing hall. The single guard at the entrance let them pass without comment. At the end of the corridor waited the dark maw of the hangar. It wasn't too late. Edson could go back.

The double click of their steps on the tile. "Why destroy the

Door?" Muller asked when they had walked beyond earshot of the guard.

Because history demanded that he do something, and he wasn't brave enough to kill Freitas. Edson didn't even have the courage to tell Muller that.

The hangar was so immense, so hushed that Edson felt the urge to genuflect. He passed the steel chamber, the altar of the open Door, without a glance.

He halted before the control panel and hesitated, tire iron ready. Ask for the Disappeareds' forgiveness? How could he? Besides, better that the voices beyond the Door die. Safer that they be silenced. If Edson was to be expelled from paradise, let Muller do it. If he was to be accused, let him stand before God, not some American tribunal.

"Where do we start?" Muller had found a hammer, and he held it before the banks of controls like a sword.

Edson couldn't apologize to the voices. *Father, forgive me.* He took off his coat. *For I have sinned.*

He shoved the claw under the edge of the panel. One short, fast tug. The sheet of metal fell with a clang.

It has been twelve years since my last confession.

Nests of wires. A Medusa of cables from the power source. Edson knelt on the tiles. Muller knelt beside him.

Countless times, I have used the Lord's name in vain.

A box of square plastic plugs, colorful as toys.

As I have used His children.

Edson pulled out a salmon-colored plug, tugged the cable free. *Forgive me the sin of lust.* An emerald green. *And murder.* A lemon yellow. *And pride.*

The motors, the computer banks, fell silent. Edson looked up. Beyond the Door, the chamber was still dark, the light still supernaturally bent.

Muller was confused, too. "The power is off. How can it still be working?"

More plugs. "Help me," Edson ordered.

Both their hands busy. The answer was there someplace. A lavender. An orange.

Suddenly Muller fell forward onto his palms. They were face-to-face. He was staring at Edson, dumbfounded. Had he hurt himself? No. God. Had someone shot him?

And then Edson saw the finger. One square-nailed finger. It teased Muller's Adam's apple, then moved down, down, Muller's heated blush rising to meet it.

"I could take him now." Freitas squatted over Muller's back.

"He's not like me," Edson said. "Don't."

"They're all like you." Freitas explored beneath the waistband. Muller closed his eyes. "I can do anything I want," Freitas said. "No one tells me don't. Or can't. Or later." He pressed his body against Muller's. "Get up," he whispered.

When Muller did, Freitas spun him around, pushed him against the open panel. Freitas pulled his shirt free.

Then Freitas smiled at Edson. "Put your hand in him." Those blunt fingertips against Muller's stomach. "It's warm and tight and slick inside, like a woman. Come here. I'll show you."

To save Muller, Edson knew what he had to say. So dangerous. One wrong move, one wrong word. Freitas could do anything.

"Touch me," Edson said.

Instantly Freitas stood back. Muller swayed and blinked. When he started to leave, Freitas stopped him.

"Not until I tell you." Then Freitas turned his dark gaze to Edson. "Go in the Door."

Edson's knees went weak. It felt like he was falling.

Freitas came to Edson, stood belly to belly. He pulled his shirt up, and Edson, panic-stricken, tried to push him away. When Freitas touched his bare chest, he thought he could feel the fingers slip inside. He blundered back against the panel, wanting to scream. Muller. Muller.

"Do it," Freitas whispered. "Go inside me. Do it. The Door is just a mouth. I eat what I choose, anyway."

Edson wanted to fight, but his arms felt heavy, his muscles frail. His hands slipped, nerveless, off Freitas's shirt.

A quiet laugh. "A woman fought me once. She taught me everything, what I could explore—my tongue inside, how her bones tasted. And when she tried to leave, I kept her."

Freitas pulled him toward the Door. No. Dear God. Where was Muller? Edson's feet moved him to the dark.

Whispers there. Sighs of welcome. Before the emptiness could swallow him, he grabbed the doorjamb.

Freitas whirled him around, slammed him face-first into the steel wall of the chamber. Pressed his body against his back. Edson could feel the knuckle-hard prod of the man's erection against his buttocks, the heat of Freitas's breath against his ear. "No one hides from me. From living bodies I've taken blood clots like lumps of tar. Cancers like black sponges. Cysts like pink pearls." Freitas reached around him, stroked his lower belly. "And I ate them."

Whispers just beyond the range of hearing. And louder, the snap of a fastener. Edson flinched as his waistband loosened. Firm slide of elastic. Chill of the chamber's air against naked skin. That thumblike insistence just below the small of his back.

Cold whispers, and a single feverish voice. "Tell me you want it."

Edson thought of São Paulo. A dark alley. Three of his own troops laughing. On the ground a beaten, naked boy, blood pouring out his asshole. The smell of shit and sweat and sex. Two officers with their flies unzipped. One officer holding a nightstick, its tip smeared with offal and gore.

The lazy spread of his zipper. Exploratory fingers. Edson shivered, thought no, please, not that way, don't hurt me, don't let Muller see, and heard himself saying, "Yes."

Freitas wrestled him about until they were face-to-face. Wet lips met. A hot tongue pistoned into his mouth. Against his jaw, the scrape of an emerging beard. Fear froze him. It was fear that made Edson's thigh muscles loosen. Fear that made him tremble. Lips slid down jaw, down neck. A tongue left a snail path down his belly.

Then a tug, and his pants were to his hips. Cold air against hot swollen flesh—*please*—and it didn't matter, nothing mattered—*oh God please*—not that the mouth belonged to Freitas, not that he stood inside the Door. Nothing was important but having.

Then the mouth closed over him, and the hot eruption came up from his thighs, sent his soul with it; and he was gone, falling, tumbling into the dark. The dark was bottomless. It was warm and humid and tight, and as he plummeted, he felt blacker things brush past him.

And then it was over. He felt Freitas push away. Heard a laugh. Edson had come so hard that his balls ached. His penis burned, as if he had pissed acid.

Had anyone seen? Where was Muller? God. Dear God. He had to get out. Get out now, before Freitas called him back. He stumbled toward the exit, fumbling awkwardly at his zipper. Tucking in his shirt. Shaking so hard that his teeth chattered.

He blundered through the hangar, barking his shin on a chair. He kicked the fallen panel and nearly went sprawling. By the time he reached the hall, he was running. The guard stared at him as he passed. Had Edson, in that short few minutes, changed? Could the guard see on his face the shame of what he had done?

Edson lurched into the parking lot, straightening his shirt. He needed a shower. He needed a drink.

At first he thought the Mercedes was empty, then he saw Muller slumped behind the wheel. Edson couldn't get into the front seat and have another man's body so close. He opened the back.

Muller shot him a conspiratorial look of shame.

"Take me home," Edson said.

CNN, Live

. . . sun just now rising over Ipanema. Behind me you can see Corcovado and the Lagoon, still surrounded by protesters—mostly women—as it has been all night.

Very pretty sight, Ed.

Yes. Those lights on the water are candles in paper boats, offerings to the goddess of the sea, Iemanjá. Otherwise Rio remains in a blackout.

Quite a crowd.

Yes. The earlier rain certainly didn't drive them away. From the mood here, an invasion force won't either. People have come down from the favelas. From the high-rises at Copacabana. And, ah, do you have a close enough shot there in Atlanta to see the colored ribbons the women are wearing around their wrists? As I understand it, those are for the Bahian Nosso Senhor do Bonfim, Our Lord of Good Endings. Knots are tied for wishes. But today their ends have been left loose. Only one knot this morning, Steve: for the safety of the president.

Interesting coincidence, the name.

Yes. Brazilians also link President Bonfim to both the Virgin Mary and Iemanjá, sometimes respectfully, sometimes not. The patron saint of Brazil is Our Lady of the Appearance, and for a while there, Bonfim became known as Our Lady of the Disappearance. Well, Brazilians love a joke, but they're not telling that one anymore.

22

Cold brought Dolores awake. Sometime during the night, Jaje had pilfered the blanket. Now she lay curled in a corner of the sofa, as self-indulgent as a cat. On the television, a picture of the Lagoon, Corcovado in the background—CNN reporting from Rio. And in an easy chair nearby, Jack slept under the shelter of his coat, one foot exposed.

It was a perfect foot, really. Exquisitely formed. Dolores rose, crippled by morning arthritis. She limped to the television, switched it off. Then she bent over Jack, and tucked him in.

He stirred, blinked, smiled her a stuporous good morning. And grabbed her breast.

"Shit." She straightened so abruptly that a nerve in her back pinched. "Shit." She stormed off toward the bathroom.

Mrs. Nelson Albright had brought with her three new Reach toothbrushes—a testament to her faith in foreign oral hygiene. A sensible woman. Someone who always planned ahead. Dolores doubted Mr. Nelson Albright played much slap-and-tickle.

"I, uh . . ."

Jack was standing in the bathroom doorway. Against that new presumption, she pulled her robe tighter. She yanked a comb briskly through her hair, threw it in the sink, and pushed past him.

She wanted to be angry about the kitchen, but Jack had washed the dishes, scrubbed the counters, put everything away. She banged through the cabinets, searching for coffee.

Behind her a tentative, "Well. I guess it'll be a while before we're used to each other."

She unearthed the coffeepot. A filter.

"I don't understand why you're so mad."

Then the cups—one: a happy self-enclosed number. Two for enforced company. Three for the madding crowd. "I can't believe you did that, Jack. Treat me like a whore."

"God, Dee. I was playing."

"And in front of Jaje, too."

"She was asleep."

Cannister of coffee. A neat tin, an old-fashioned one, with decals. Something Dolores's mother would have spent an afternoon decorating. The creative urge was a maternal heritage, a longing for expression that Dolores's mother had chosen to spend, non-confrontationally, on the house.

"Did you ever think she might wake up when we started rutting, Jack? I mean, right there in front of her?"

"I wasn't going to—"

Dolores whirled. The can erupted, spilling coffee across the tiles, a fall of dark ash. "Then what was the point? I don't get the damned point."

"It was a sign of affection."

"Grabbing tit. A sign of affection."

Jack was a cautious man. He didn't nod or shrug. He didn't blink.

"Excuse me. I forgot all that romantic art: Botticelli's *Tit Grab;* Titian's *Zeus Copping a Feel at the Sink.* Jesus, Jack. Either let's fuck, or let's not fuck, all right?"

"I . . . well, I think this may be good, Dee. To get everything out on the table. I mean, we're not kids. We need to be blunt with each other."

She turned her back, began furiously spooning coffee. "What is it with you? Jaje right there on the couch. The whole goddamned world in flames. At least everything that's important. Everything that means something. What is it with men and their pricks? All you can think about . . ." She banged the cabinet door shut, again. Again.

She remembered Jaje, and froze. "I don't want this anymore."

Nothing. She couldn't even hear Jack breathe.

"It's too hard," she said.

A sharp intake of air. A sad, breathy laugh. "I'll be damned. All those years waiting for Harry to die. Thinking . . . Then it's like I win it all: win you, win everything. They give us money, a new life. God, Dee. This hurts."

"What are you talking about?" She looked around.

"I was kidding myself, wasn't I. A black man—"

"Goddamn it. Color's not the problem."

"Those folks up north see us together, all they can picture is some pathetic blue-haired scene from *Mandingo*. You're why I got in the spy game. You're why I stayed in Brazil all these years, even when I missed home so bad. But your choice, Dee. When we get to Cana—"

The words exploded from her. "It's not about you! Nothing's about you! Shit, Jack. I just got free from Harry!" The room blurred. The wall sucked her toward it. She slapped one hand against the cabinet, the other against the tile drainboard, to stay her fall.

Utter silence. The kitchen walls tugged her this way and that. If she didn't hang on, she'd be caught in the eddy, be dragged under.

Then a sleepy voice. Jack's reply through the thick, drowning air. "No, she's fine, honey. Your Aunt Dee spilled the coffee, that's all. I was just about to clean it up."

Faucet sounds. A grunt as Jack knelt.

"I turned on the TV. CNN said they stopped bombing."

The gravity of the walls was so strong that it began to pull Dolores's flesh from the bone.

From a distance, Jack. "That's good, sweetie. Tell you what. Let's all get dressed and go out to breakfast. Want to do that? When I was a kid back in L.A., my mama and daddy used to take me to breakfast of a Sunday. We didn't have much money, but we had enough for an eat-out breakfast every single week. My daddy always said, bad as life was, a big old restaurant breakfast helped take your mind off things."

Kinch answered the knock dressed in polo shirt and shorts. He seemed surprised to see him. "What're you doing here?" He leaned out into the hall. Looked both ways. Adjusted his glasses. "Come on in. You have a problem getting through?"

The peroba wood door of the penthouse closed with a solid click, encasing them in silence. From somewhere in the huge apartment came the soothing trickle of a fountain. Kinch's foyer was floored in green marble; its walls were brass. The air was heavy with the scent of ginger flowers.

"Sorry about the mess. Maid quit. Is that a kick in the ass or what?" They walked past an atrium: mossy waterfall, spills of bright pink impatiens, and orchids: a flashy purple, a green one as spotted as a snake, a thick-stemmed vanilla vine. "Hey. You want something? Mineral water? Coke?"

"*Cachaça.*"

Kinch looked at him. "Hm. Heard you were on sick leave. Thought they were going to send you back to Japan."

Another atrium, birds flitting like spirits through a blue shaft of refracted sun.

"Naturally they would tell you that. I was put on a special project."

The suspicion in Kinch's face became petulant envy. "Cool," he said.

Only the kitchen mourned the maid. It was in upheaval. Dirty dishes. Empty bottles of Antarctica. Of Jim Beam. "*Cachaça*." Kinch rummaged the cabinets. "*Cachaça.* Know I got a bottle somewhere. Ah-ha!" He turned, bottle in hand. And paled when he met Hiroshi's eyes. "Uh. Something wrong?"

"No."

" 'Cause sometimes a game'll weird you out a little. Make you a little wonky. Happened to me once." He twisted off the cap. Inspected a line of glasses dubiously. Picked one. "You want something in this? *Maracujá?* Cashew juice? Lime?"

"No."

"So. This game finished, or what?"

He took the offered glass from Kinch. Drank the raw *cachaça* down. "Almost." He held the glass out again.

"Hey, just take the bottle." Kinch flicked another look. His glasses caught the light, and for a dizzy instant the frames looked empty. Then he bent and took a beer from the refrigerator. "What say we go to the living room?"

In a second atrium, finches dashed, branch to branch. A sun conure, all the colors of fire, chattered madly.

"Pisses me off, the way the maid quit. Bitch just walked. No note. No nothing. Stole all kinds of shit. Really cleaned me out. Well, my own damned fault. I'm just too trusting. You want a toke?" He took a joint from an enameled box, offered the box.

"No."

"You're really hitting the liquor. Never known you to do that. Don't get drunk on me."

"Drunk is a matter of mind."

"Don't go ass-over-end crazy on me, either, like McNatt. Guy freaks me the hell out." Kinch lit his joint, took a drag, fidgeted. "Hey. What about that bombing? You see that? I had a ringside seat. Put some Sinatra on the headphones. Got on the telescope.

Man, shoulda been here. Saw the bombs take out that fucking head of Kubitschek, the one that stuck out of the side of the museum. Broke it in half. Didn't think anything could do that to basalt. So, what's up?"

"They have sent me to give you a message."

"Oh?"

From the atrium, a cascade of song so haunting that the other birds hushed. Even Kinch went still.

When the *sabiá* was finished, Hiroshi said, "Japan will share the rewards now, as will Germany and France and Great Britain. We have helped a great deal."

"Yeah. So I heard."

"But it is a pity—don't you think it so?—to have earned the Brazilians' resentment. It is a shame about your maid."

An instant of confusion. Kinch put out his joint, half smoked. "Yeah, I guess. I thought we had something going, too. More than the master/servant kinda shit. Although, hey, there's something to be said for that, know what I mean? Anyway, I treated that nigger like the Queen of fucking Uganda. You think she cared? Fixed up her room. Gave her all sorts of stuff. Expensive clothes. Nice jewelry. A good watch—not a Rolex, mind you. But you can't give them something like a Rolex. When you let them go home for a visit, the family steals them blind. You want some . . . ah, chips? Nuts? Nothing? You sure? You had that maid one time. Right after the baby. Good looker, too. You ever, you know?"

"It was a small apartment that we lived in."

"Yeah. Oh, yeah. And the old ball and chain. Man, I don't know what I'll do if they send me stateside. I mean, can you picture me back home playing hide-the-sausage with some fifteen-year-old nigger chick? Huh? Without her mean old gang-banger brother shooting my ass?" He laughed. Shrugged. "Well, anyway. For a while I thought it was love. But you know those favela cunts, they use and abuse you, right? Like the song says, take your heart right out, and throw it away. Hey. You nearly got you a dead soldier there. Sure you don't want anything to eat?"

If Kinch would turn around. If he would shut up. If the sabiá would sing again.

"Another one, then? You brought a hollow leg?"

"Show me the statue."

"The . . . ? Oh. Oh, sure."

They stood up. And the sabiá sang. It sang them through the living room, and out to the sunlit balcony. It sang as Kinch pulled a chair to the telescope's tripod. And then it stopped.

The wind blew, tickled a set of nearby wind chimes. Hiroshi sat down in the chair, looked in the eyepiece. "Where?"

"No. To the right. More right."

"I don't see."

"Get up. Come on. Get up, guy. Lemme get it focused for you."

Kinch sat down, peered in the eyepiece.

Hiroshi slipped the garotte from his pocket. He stepped forward until his belly pressed the back of the chair.

"Almost, almost . . . There! I—"

Hiroshi whipped the guitar string around Kinch's neck. A grunt of fear. Kinch clawed at his throat. His glasses fell, hit the stone with a click. He bucked. Heaved.

Hiroshi fought to hold on. The wire cut into his palms, nearly pulled free. The chair squealed against the polished limestone floor. And Kinch fell hard to his knees.

Hiroshi went down with him. Kinch's dry hacking, less like the gurgle he expected, more like a simple cough. The guitar string birthed a shallow bloody river that cascaded down Kinch's neck. Their two bloods mingled. Hiroshi's was peppery palm oil and *cana*. Kinch's was whiskey and weak American coffee.

Between Hiroshi's spread legs, Kinch shuddered. The American's death trembled up Hiroshi's thighs. From the sabiá, a liquid trill. From Kinch's throat, a mist of crimson. His shit was a sharp-smelling tea-colored stream that pooled on the white stone.

Hiroshi released the guitar string and let the body fall. "The message is," he said, "that the god-in-goddess Oxumaré has turned woman for the last time."

The wind chimes rang. "Never again will she be man, not even when the seasons change and the rains leave."

He looked up. There. From a nearby balcony, a woman—a spirit—watched, face blurred by distance. Orange and purple dress. Crimson ribbon around her wrist. The loose ends of the ribbon and her long dark hair fluttered in the smoky breeze.

Hiroshi spoke loudly, so Maria Bonita could hear. "Oxumaré says that because of shame she has thrown away her cock. She says she would rather be a rainbow, or a river, than wear it."

When Jerry left to scout lunch, McNatt walked over to Roger. "Are you comfortable?"

The floor tiles had turned Roger's butt to ice. The handcuff had chafed his wrist raw. The night's beer throbbed through his temples. "You bet. No prob."

McNatt sat on the parquet next to him, propped his elbows on his bent knees, his back against the bed. "I appreciate the fact that, with Jerry in the room, you have not alluded to our little talks. I hope they are as precious to you as they are to me. But I'm afraid that I will now shock, and certainly offend you."

The ice in Roger's butt moved upward, froze his chest.

"It's my belief that mediums in fact channel themselves." McNatt looked at Roger expectantly.

"Hum," Roger said.

"Heretical, I know. I have watched films of the Brazilian psychic surgeons. They are so much more than the Filipinos. It's possible to palm cotton soaked with blood; but how does one fake shoving a tablespoon into an eye? Pushing a table knife into a chest—a knife that, I might add, came directly from the plate of a university researcher?"

Lunch. Oh, Jerry was going to come back with lunch. Roger's stomach bobbled.

"No amount of will can overcome instinct. And that is the answer: the psychic surgeon actually steals the patient's free will."

In one fluid move, McNatt was on his feet and pacing. Roger practiced the Zen of becoming one with the wall.

"What a wonderful, wonderful . . . Well, I tell you, Roger. I must admit to a great deal of envy. Still, think of the tightrope they must tread. Safer to imagine that a higher spirit takes over. Dangerous to know the raw power one holds inside oneself." He halted. "This said, follow the logic: if we are angels, we are also devils. And murder is simply a collusion between perpetrator and victim."

Whoa! Time to say something.

"For years I believed murder sprang from hatred. Now I know that it comes from love."

Say something before it was too late. "Uh . . ."

"Yes?"

"Uh. All the same to you, Doug, I'd rather not."

"I don't . . ."

"I'd rather not die, okay? I mean, if it's all the same to you. Consider this sort of a conflict we have here, although, I want you to understand, a very minor, ah, friendly conflict."

"Certainly."

"Nothing to upset yourself about. And, please . . . please please please. Don't hold it against me."

"Not at all. I welcome debate. Oh! Oh, my. You overheard Jerry and myself talking last night, didn't you? I was wondering if you were awake. Well, I suspect that you might find this difficult to believe now, but when the time arrives, there will come a welcome feeling of surrender. I've seen it in so many faces."

He sat down beside Roger, put a hand on his knee. Roger nearly came up off the floor screaming.

"I'd never do anything that you didn't ask for first."

Tears came then, and there wasn't any sound to them. No sound at all. Just that brimming heat, and the warm wet slide. "Please. Please don't. I mean, if it's all the same to you, you know—? I mean, if we're taking a vote here? Put my request in on the side of never, ever wanting to die."

"Shhh." McNatt leaned close. Roger wanted to push him away. Wanted to run in place. Shriek. "I know you don't want it. Not yet. Not now. But seeing is my gift, and when your special moment comes, I'll take you."

No. Christ. McNatt was going to do something weird. Torture him until he begged for a bullet. Poison and then French kiss him. Jesus. Store his body in a closet for a few weeks so he would watch the insects chow down.

"I'm gonna be sick," Roger said.

McNatt took the key from his pocket, reached for the cuff.

"Oh, shit." Roger's voice was thick. "I'm gonna ralph."

Up and to the bathroom, McNatt at his elbow. At the commode Roger dropped and bent over. A noise between a whine and a moan came up, and suddenly Roger was sobbing.

McNatt handed him a wet towel, patted his shoulder. "Perhaps I shouldn't have been quite so forthright."

Roger's teeth chattered. His shoulders shook. He bent over, opened his mouth, and once more brought up nothing but an anguished wail. "Ooooh. That's okay. Really."

"Sometimes I forget myself. That was unforgivably insensitive. A Coke, perhaps? To settle your stomach?"

"Yeah." McNatt would leave him here. Would go to the refrigerator. Give Roger enough time . . .

"Up-sie daisy," McNatt said cheerfully as he helped Roger to his feet.

Now or never. Do or die. Roger gave it everything he had. He slammed his shoulder into McNatt and bounced off, thought for a confusing instant he'd hit the wall. Then a battering ram connected with his stomach, and he went down, gape-mouthed and mute.

"Are you all right, Roger?"

Roger tried to draw a breath. Couldn't. Dark stars swarmed in his vision.

"Goodness. I hit you rather harder than I intended. Instinct and training. One just can't escape it. Well. The pain will go away in a moment. You—that's right. Just lean back and rest a little."

Roger held onto the toilet bowl. He was breathing now, shallow unsatisfying pants.

"That's it. Just take your time. And again, let me apologize . . ."

"Me," Roger wheezed.

"Sorry? I didn't catch that."

The dark stars swam away. "Me. Fault." He waved a hand earnestly. "Please. Forgive. Don't know. What came over . . ."

"Oh, misunderstandings like that are to be expected. Let's go have that Coke, shall we?"

Roger couldn't straighten. McNatt held his elbow. He couldn't do this. Couldn't face . . . God. He had to hold on to life and never let go, so that if McNatt took him, he would have to take the room, the house. Roger grabbed the doorjamb. His eyes seized every piece of litter, every stick of furniture.

"I thought you wanted that Coke."

Roger started to sob again. His thighs went watery, and he sank to his knees. The doorjamb was smooth and hard against his cheek. How could it happen? Holding on to something. Breathing one minute, then dropping into the void.

And that's when Jerry walked in, humming "Gigi." Roger heard the humming stop. Heard the rustle of paper. "What the fuck's the matter with him?"

"We had a little accident."

"Um."

"I think he overheard us last night."

"Why don't I just go ahead and do him now?"

Fear reduced Roger's prayer to basics: no no no no no.

"Otherwise he's going to be a problem. Just look at him, Mac. Blubbering like that. You want to do one of your weird things, don't you?"

"We cannot do him now. Where would we stow the body?"

"I could—"

"No. He must go to Cabeceiras. Those are the instructions."

"Uh-huh. You and your instructions. Come on. We can say one of the Brazilians got him. Let me do it."

A sharp snap that made Roger jump in place. The sound of a silencer. Was he still alive?

"I'll do him that fast," Jerry said. Another dry snap. "He's gone, just like that. It'll all be over. I'll take care of the disposal. I gotta tell you—what you do, Mac, sometimes it really makes me sick."

A *tsk*. "You are so pedestrian."

McNatt knelt, put his hand around Roger's shoulders, stroked him, and how could Roger leave? How could anyone take him? Was McNatt right, or would he feel terror at the end? Would it hurt? God. Would leaving life be like a fall into dark? And after, no touch, no sound, no smell at all, the whole wide world turned empty.

"Roger?" McNatt's voice was concerned. His stroke was gentle. "Come on. Don't pay any attention to Jerry. Let's you and me go have that Coke."

At the zoo a dying elephant rocked, dull-eyed and fretful, too old or sick to lift his head. Jack looked back over his shoulder at Dolores, then turned his attention to Jaje. Poor Jack. He should have stayed near his wife and kids. Should have been at least a part-time husband and father.

Conversation trailed the two. Mist blotted the sound.

". . . true?" The word hung in the gray, manure-fragrant air. The innocence of the question made Jack lower his head.

Up a slick clay trail. At the top, a line of bushes. Below was a square carpet of grass where a multitude of silent, black-shawled Indians sat with their silent children.

"Yeah," Jack said. "But people do things for complicated reasons. And nothing ever turns out like you expect."

Not Harry. Harry had been a surprise. A whoopie cushion.

"They were friends first," Jack said.

The lion cages, cats the same color as the bare ground. Two females side by side, an elderly male by them.

"Your mom was in Congress, then."

Dolores halted. The ground sucked at her feet.

Jack turned. "You okay, Dee?"

"I'm fine. Just fine. Leave me alone."

Something between a shrug and a nod, then they were walking past the pretty llamas, with their obdurate lantern jaws. Ana's delicate beauty disguised her meaness, too.

". . . they approached her. Just to have a politician in their pocket. That's the way the CIA works. And Dee thought she could handle them. And your mom thought she could exploit them. But one thing led to another . . ."

Love to marriage. Marriage to hate. Connect all the dots, step back, and you'll see the prison.

"They never meant to hurt anyone."

A ripping pain in her midsection. Dolores stopped.

"Dee? You okay?"

She would vomit blood. "Goddamn it, Jack. Leave me alone. I'm fine."

They walked on without her.

She watched them leave, thinking she was about to die, that the pain she felt was a bursting heart. But then the pain subsided. She should have known. Empty as the Tin Man. When she took a step, she found to her surprise that her legs were steady.

". . . me?" Jack was asking with a smile. "No, sweetie. When I got to know your Aunt Dee real well, I decided to work for your mom.

Always have worked for her. Always will. Like I said, it's a big old complicated world."

Jaje murmured a reply. Jack put his arm around her shoulders. She leaned her head against him, and he hugged her tight. Dolores looked away.

Someone had deposited walk-through dioramas on the zoo's plain: huge concrete turds, painted in colors too frenetic to be happy. Indian children ran through the crude structures, chasing each other, never laughing. Moisture beaded on Dolores's sweater sleeves, on Jaje's hair, on the llamas. A fog not heavy enough to be rain.

Her legs ached. How far had they walked now? Miles. Decades.

Jack stopped, turned. "Let's wander around the city a little. You want to?"

Dolores met a tiger's apathetic gaze. Along its striped side, a baby-pink patch of mange. Best to keep moving. You could always outrun it. If the tiger would just get up . . .

"Dee?"

"Why not?" she said.

What was the number? Had he written it down, or had Muller? No. That's right. He had fired Muller. Sent him back to Rio Grande do Sul, back to Novo Hamburgo or one of those tight-assed German places.

Ah, here.

Done the right thing for once. Sent Muller to a cleaner, brighter life than Edson had a right to. Sent him away quick, before . . . Edson sat in his easy chair. On the television screen, a smiling American reporter was interviewing a smiling British captain. Edson pulled the phone toward him, dialed.

Over the receiver, a ring. Edson pulled his bathrobe close, tucked his legs under him until he was a terry-cloth cocoon. Not that he was any safer. Not that he could be clean. The skin of his hands was wrinkled from the shower, and still he felt . . .

It rang again.

He'd scrubbed until his skin turned pink. Until the flesh of his groin had chafed. But only a knife could clean deep enough. Only a bullet. And Nando had taken his gun.

Was there some weakness in him, like a hidden embolism or a cancer, a flaw that he had never once suspected? Did Muller have the flaw, too? That look he'd given him as Edson got in the car.

Edson put the fifth of Maker's Mark to his lips, took a drink.

"CNN," the voice from the receiver sang. How American, that flat nasal. Like they had their noses up the asses of the world.

"Hello?"

"Tem alguém aí que fala Português?"

"I'm sorry?"

Edson sighed. "I don't espeak the Engliss."

"Uh-huh?"

Was his pronunciation too poor? Had whiskey slurred his words? More than memory, then. Memory kept its edge. "I espeak from Brazil."

"Thank you. Please hold."

Edson understood "hold" only the instant after the music began. A strangely familiar melody, but Edson needed eight bars to recognize it. *"Dores de Coração,"* "Heartbreak." The classic *mod-inha* they stole for that American movie.

A click, and then a new voice. A young woman's happy chirp. *"¿Pronto? No hay alguien aquí que habla portugués. Puede usted hablar español?"*

Americans. They stole it all, and never bothered to learn the language. He took another drink, gave a resigned *"Sí."* And then he told her to speak slowly.

"Bueno. ¿Puedo ayudarle?"

"Yes." Help him, yes. Roll back time to before Freitas. To before

Brasília. Before the murders in São Paulo. "My name is Edson Carvalho," he said. "And I wish to make a confession."

He looked into the plate glass window, was surprised to see that he cast a reflection. "*¿Señorita?*"

"Yes. I—wait . . ." Muffled conversation from the other end. Fast, panicked English. Then the girl and her Spanish again. "Uh, sir? Sir? The Carvalho who is the head of the secret police?"

Was he that? So sinister-sounding. The midnight knock on the door. The fatal drive. "Yes."

"*Señor* Carvalho? They're telling me, uh, they want to record this conversation. Is that all right?"

"Nothing matters."

"I'm sorry?"

"I said, nothing matters, *querida*. It hasn't mattered since I was twenty-seven years old, you see? And my country did not have a death penalty and so what do you do then? Please. Can you understand me? Sometimes the Portuguese words are different."

"No, it's fine. I—"

"We were prudent. Only the third time they were caught— never the first, because we might have made a mistake, neh? And never the second, because the second was sometimes enough warning. No. We waited until the third time, because then we were sure that we had the guilty man, and we were certain that the man would never learn. And the only thing left was to kill him. And we did that, you see? Took them to the swamps and killed them. They cried, but softly. And they struggled, but they were handcuffed. They fell down in the mud, and made you dirty with them. Still they were human, I suppose. In the same way that a feral dog is a dog."

She cleared her throat.

"What is your name, please?"

"I'm sorry?"

"Your name."

"Rosa."

"No, child. We share secrets. Give me your name so I have something of yours to hold on to."

"Rosalinda Teresa de Concepción Herrera Gonzales y Peña."

"Rosa." In the patio, sun glinted on the palm trees, filtered through the grapevine and cast dappled shade. On the TV, the reporter and the captain were still smiling. "Are you a reporter, Rosa?"

"Uh, no."

"What do you do, then? A producer?"

"I'm, uh, a secretary in the Marketing Department. We're trying to get hold of one of our Spanish-speaking reporters right now. Uh. Oh. Okay. They tell me he's on his way. In the meantime—there's a crowd here—they're sort of passing me notes and things, so I know what to ask you. It's a little confused on this end. I'm sorry."

"But it's you I want to speak with, Rosalinda Teresa Gonzales y Peña."

"Oh? All right."

"Because I have never to my knowledge killed a reporter. But I have killed secretaries, I think. And I have killed children half your age. And that, too, was a crime against humanity. Although I have always been of the opinion that the Church sinned first. All those children. No one to care for them. They were hungry, the children. They were wild dogs. You couldn't turn your back. Feed them, and they would bite you. The gangs fought each other, and it was good to find their bodies on the sidewalk in the morning. Good to find a boy whose throat had been cut. A bullet would have come from a shopkeeper. Or another officer. That's when my wife left me and took my sons. I don't think she ever knew . . . Well, yes. I suppose she did. Even when you wash them, cordite stays on the hands." He took a drink. "Rosa. Rosinha. Are you from Atlanta?"

"No, sir. Not originally."

"Where?"

"El Paso, Texas."

"And is it pretty? El Paso, Texas?"

"Well, it's desert."

"A hard beauty, then. I tended cattle, growing up in the *sertão* when I was half as tall as a zebu's shoulder. Huge, the color of caramel custard, with horns longer than my arms. Alone with them, just me and my stick. But no need to beat them. When I called, they followed my voice. The cattle were smarter than the men I killed. They were kinder, and I loved them for that. They could have gored me. Me, such a baby. And them so gentle." He looked down the hall, at the hanging Christ. His eyes watered. "Rosa? Do you think that God is sweet, like the cattle?"

Whispers.

"Rosa?"

"Just a minute, *Señor* Carvalho." More whispers. Angry ones.

Edson's tired face in the patio door. A squeak . . .

"Sir? I didn't catch that."

Oh. Had he cried out? The snap of a fastener. Hands on his belly, moving down. His own hips thrusting eagerly up.

"Sir? Sorry. I was trying to get them to stop recording, sir. But they wouldn't."

"This should be recorded. I want you to play it for your president. For all the American people."

"Do . . . ? Okay. Okay. They're nodding."

"You must promise."

"Yes, sir. The executives here are all nodding."

"I told you the rest so that you would see the sort of man I am, for I have done an unpardonable thing. I am responsible for the Disappeareds. I alone. I arrested them. I took them to a place, and I killed them."

The "why" was so quick, so shocked, that it had to have come unprompted.

Because Freitas was hungry.

He took a quick breath, held it, closed his eyes, and said, "Because I could."

Was this how it felt to fall, helpless, in the swamp? Before he left, he wanted to make Freitas dirty. Perhaps he would forget things, then. If God was sweet.

"Rosinha?"

"Sir?"

"I am not fond of the Church, but even so, thinking it might be possible to die and to awaken to cattle . . . please. Would you say a Rosary for me?"

On the television, the airport and helicopters. And a frantic reporter.

"Sir? *Señor* Carvalho? Sir?"

Gently, he hung up. He went into the bedroom and put on his jeans, a shirt. He picked out a light jacket, a fresh fifth of Jim Beam. And then he walked outside to the Mercedes. It was an easy road. A wide road. Even drunk, he could remember the way. Cabeceiras was an inevitable place. If he simply stood still, the world would tip east, and he would fall there.

CNN, Live

. . . helicopters! Hundreds of . . . Can you—Oh! God! Too close. A helicopter directly overhead. Just deafening. And that rotor wash . . . Amazing, Bernie! They . . . All the helicopters. Can you still hear me?

Ye—

Right overhead! Flying so low they shake the ground! All flying toward the airport, looks like. And—Quick! Quick! Get a picture of that! Down the way. Right there! We're trying to get closer. Bernie? Can you see this? The Brazilian soldiers in the next block are dropping their weapons. They are dropping their weapons, Bernie, and—I don't believe it. This group of soldiers here by the zoo . . . I don't know, maybe fifty or so men—they marched up from where they were blocking the highway cloverleaf earlier . . . they're just putting down their rifles, and sitting in the middle of the street. They've put their hands on their heads. All very orderly. The officers are standing around near them . . . can you get a picture of this yet?

Yes. Yes, we can, Susan.

But they must be putting up resistance elsewhere, Bernie. I'm hearing rifle fire. Repeat. I'm hearing a lot of rifle fire. And still no word from the government. At least, from whatever part of the Brazilian government still exists . . .

23

She turned from the shop window and the television screens.

"Dee!"

The quick tap of footsteps, following.

"Hey." Jack sounded exasperated. "Wait up."

She had to keep moving. Down a winding alley. Past dun steps and black vultures with tattered capes for wings. Nimble, weightless, they fought over a fish, and the pink of those guts was the only color in the world. She passed shuttered shops and high garden walls. Life had to go on someplace in Lima, didn't it? In Brazil, even the slums had color. The slums had samba.

Jaje's: "Well, just ignore us, you know? What's the matter with her?"

Jack's: "She gets in a snit sometimes. Best to just leave her be."

It was Harry who got into snits. Didn't Jack know that? Of course he did. Men stuck together.

Jaje's: "Come on, Aunt Dee. Please? I want to go back now. It's gonna rain."

It never rained in Lima. Hadn't for one hundred and fifty years. But clouds kept the sun hidden, like the people behind Lima's walls.

Another alley. Everyone Oriental. Japanese? Chinese? They stared as she passed.

Jack's weary: "Dee. Please."

Around another corner, moving fast. Furniture shops. The day so dark that they'd lit the lamps. Open doors invited. Plate glass windows. Light gleamed on ornately carved wood, on plump satin cushions, on the faces of the waiting hucksters.

Not furniture. Coffins. To every side were shops and shops of coffins.

Close your eyes. Here it comes. They say you never hear the one that gets you.

The cold of the gun barrel against her temple, and that was the last time she cried. Never again would she let Harry see that he frightened her.

Let's do roller coaster. Huh? Whaddya say?

Fine, she'd tell him. *Go ahead.* Because he'd do it anyway. Go ahead, turn off the headlights at the top of the mountain. Race the darkness and the hairpin curves down. Had to be strong to face Harry every day for the rest of her goddamned life. Why didn't she kill him? God. Why didn't she just leave?

Jaje's small, frightened: "This is too weird here, you know?"

And Jack's: "Come on. That's enough, Dee. Let's go back."

She could sense it coming. Not flesh, not bone. It would swallow you if you let it. Cold, dark mouth, and you couldn't escape it. Couldn't kill it, not ever.

Jack's: "You okay, hon?"

Jaje's: "Yeah, I guess."

"In a minute we'll go back to the apartment, have us a nice cup of hot chocolate. Saw some chocolate back in the cabinet. There's enough milk in the fridge. And tomorrow night we'll be in Vancouver. How about that?"

Faster. The echo of her steps. Windowless walls to either side, an intestine of a place. Then suddenly the cobblestones ended. Black-shawled Indians. The gloomy silence of Indians. And a claustrophobic clay path—shining path—a rivulet of sewerage down its center.

Jack: "This is far enough, Dee. This is dangerous."

After Harry, nothing was dangerous. She'd had the vaccine.

Someone came up behind her, grabbed her wrist. She pulled free and whirled. In Jack's face, no surprise, only desperation.

She hissed, "Don't touch me! Never touch me like that!"

Jack's soft: "Please, baby. If not for me, for her. We've got a responsibility—"

And Jaje's: "Oh, get over it, Aunt Dee. He just wants to help."

Get over it. A responsibility you could never get rid of. It stank of medicine and its own incontinence and stale hate. Dolores seized Jaje's upper arms. How could those perfumed arms, those perfumed hands, know? Dolores shook her so hard that her neck whipped back and forth, that her brown hair flew.

"They kill you, Jaje! Damn it, they kill you! They take everything, and we always let them do it. Two steps behind. That's where they keep us. Harry had to get sick before I could have my career. Sneaking around the house. Apologizing. Like painting was a goddamned lover. I lost my life being cook, nursemaid, resident twat. And, you know? You have to ask yourself if it's worth it. Don't you, Jaje? I mean, at some point? Harry wasn't even good in bed, and I let him control me. Isn't that pathetic? Paulo was lousy in the sack, too. Or so your mom always said. But still, her twat must have thought he was worth taking the beatings—"

Jack's startled shout: "Stop it!"

Two Indian children were staring. Jaje was sobbing.

Oh. Dolores was sobbing. She was trembling. Cold here. Too cold. If she didn't keep moving . . .

She let Jaje go and rushed down the foggy alley, around the next dim corner. This time Jack didn't follow.

*   *   *

The invasion was noisy. McNatt and Jerry played hearts while Roger sat chained to the bed, counting helicopters. Big helicopters: transports. And huge transport planes. Where the hell had they come from? Leapfrogging up from Paraguay, through the unpopulated Mato Grosso. Bringing their own fuel, appropriating it. Everything timed to the second. Now the soundproofed cottage trembled as they passed overhead, flying south.

Cabeceiras would come next. And after that . . .

The phone rang. Roger flinched. He watched McNatt get up from his game and—oh, Christ—here came the instructions.

He picked up the receiver, turned his back to Roger. Not the back. Please. Not the silent treatment. McNatt listened intently, and hung up.

Roger's own back was so tense that it felt like he'd been shot between the shoulders. McNatt walked to the table and stood, looking down.

Roger wanted to go home now. Wanted to get on one of those transport planes and fly to Houston. Wanted familiar smells to surround him: the pine trees, the smog, the oil refineries.

"What're the instructions, Mac?" Jerry asked.

Roger wanted to be in his own living room so badly that he could feel himself sinking into the leather sofa.

McNatt frowned at the tabletop.

Oh, Christ. Roger wanted to go home. He thought about the little nick in the fireplace mantel. The original lava lamp he'd paid big bucks for.

McNatt said, "You looked at my cards, Jerry."

"Did not."

"Don't lie to me."

"Mac, you're so full of shit."

McNatt sat down, swept the cards into a pile, tapped their edges straight. "You're on point."

"Get oughta here."

Sunlight glared through the kitchen window, spotlighted Mc-

Natt's strong hands, loaned Jerry a halo. Helicopter forty-two—or was it forty-three?—raced south, the vibration of its passing tickling through skin, through muscle, all the way down to Roger's bones.

"I said, you're on point, Jerry."

Scream of metal against tile. Jerry shoved back from the table. His hands hung relaxed and loose between his jeaned thighs. His face was tense. "I'm not one of your candy-ass Marines, Mac. You don't get mad at me, and then tell me to drop it and give you twenty."

Roger plotted trajectories, wondered if he could escape the line of fire.

"Get your weapon," McNatt said.

Uh-huh. Under the bed was good. McNatt and Jerry would kill each other. He could gnaw his arm off and leave.

"Get your weapon, Jerry, and stand point. Please." McNatt straightened the cards again. Dug a roll of Tums out of his tee shirt pocket, popped two.

A swift, alarming move. Jerry was on his feet. In his face, an eerie calm. Three fast steps. He grabbed the Uzi from against the wall and turned.

Roger froze in place. Where the fuck was the U.S. Army when you needed them? Please, God. Make some grunt come busting through the door, an M-16 at his hip.

McNatt put the cards into their box.

"Mac?"

McNatt looked up. The Uzi was pointed straight at him. Slowly Roger tucked his body into the alcove between the headboard and the bedroom's half-wall. No sudden moves. But, Jesus. The bullets were sure to go through the plaster.

He heard Jerry say, "I'm gonna go stand point now."

And McNatt said, "All right."

"I'm going to protect us against all those marauding rich people out there."

"Good."

"I mean, the diplomats—our neighbors—who happen to currently be our allies. And their maids. I forgot the maids."

"I appreciate that, Jerry."

"I think the dog next door's onto us."

Roger peeked around the corner. McNatt was cleaning his pistol. The strap of the gun hung over Jerry's right shoulder. The Uzi was pointed in McNatt's general direction. Suddenly, as if he knew Roger was looking, Jerry glanced his way.

Roger ducked into the alcove, gave it a count of fifty, then looked again. Jerry was peering out the window. Had he seen something? He was nodding. Some sort of signal? Then, strap secure on his shoulder, hand braced on the top of the gun, Jerry started to bounce. Jesus. How weird. Point the foot. The other foot. Talking to himself, expression dreamy. Jerry planted the muzzle of the Uzi on the floor and, Christ—he started a mincing dance around it. Roger could hear Jerry's breathy words: "... my-y-y own ..."

Jerry moved like he was weightless, like his joints were perfectly oiled, more effortless Fred Astaire than athletic Gene Kelly. McNatt was still industriously cleaning his gun, but one foot tapped rebellion.

Jerry soft-shoed Roger's way. He swung his arm, the barrel of the Uzi still clutched in his right fist. He'd obviously forgotten the lyrics, but that didn't stop him from belting out the tune. "... la la LAH la la, ta-dum-da da da DAH da ..."

A familiar melody. One that was far too sugary for the circumstances. It reminded Roger of music halls and the 1930's. Something 'Doll.' What the hell *was* it?

A loud knock. McNatt sprang out of his chair. Instantly, both guns were pointed at the door. McNatt peered out the window. Jerry opened the door a crack.

"Help!" Roger screamed.

Louder. And now. Now! McNatt was rushing toward him. At the door, Jerry turned.

Roger gave it all he had. "Help me!"

Then Jerry opened the door wider and this Oriental guy in a jogging suit sauntered in, his hands shoved in the pockets of his cotton jacket. McNatt abruptly relaxed.

Oh. Not the Army after all. The CIA had sent Roger someone special.

The guy looked at Roger. "Why is he handcuffed?"

Wait. Not CIA. Too much sushi in that accent.

"What are you doing here?" McNatt asked back.

"Ah." One of those Japanese half-bows. "I have been on assignment, and—"

"I heard you were on sick leave."

Jerry closed the door, stepped behind the guy, neatly sandwiching him between two guns. Uh-oh. Some kinda weird shit going down.

"Yes, Major. If I am on special assignment, that is what they would tell you. I was actually in Blumenau, tracking an old KGB agent. And when I returned—"

McNatt's brusque, "Why?"

Mr. Cucumber Cool, that Japanese. He slumped into a chair, his hands still in his pockets. "To see if he knew something about the Disappeareds."

"Oh," Jerry said. "Oh. Is this the guy, Mac? The one who got the Japanese's shorts in a wad about the missing Brazilians?"

"Who was the KGB agent you talked to?" McNatt asked.

"Piehl."

"Right. Piehl." McNatt was so blasé that Roger was sure he didn't know Piehl for shit. "And what did you find out?"

"Where is Kengo?" the Japanese asked.

Whoa! So cool! The guy sat in his conversational bunker, lobbing questions at McNatt like grenades.

McNatt: "Don't you know?"

"Why should I know? I was in Blumenau, and I came back to find American paratroopers and attack helicopters. It is too dangerous to go to the embassy, and I cannot call. Your bombs brought down our secure system."

"What did you find out about the Disappeareds?" McNatt asked.

The Japanese guy shrugged. "What I found was that I went to Kengo's apartment and he had disappeared, too. It has been a long walk. Do you have something to drink?"

A Pearl Harbor of a comeback.

"They sent Kengo back to Japan."

"Yes?" The guy sighed tragically. Nodded. "Ah."

Jerry said, "You fucked up his career, man. And you royally screwed the Company's rep, too."

"They believed you." McNatt tucked his pistol into his waistband. He went to the refrigerator.

Jerry laughed. "Hey. Someone who fucks Kengo's rep totally can't be all bad." Then he was humming, this time so softly that Roger couldn't pick out the tune.

The Japanese could. "Very nice. One of my favorite songs."

Jerry spread his arms and assumed the serenade position. "What the —"

The Japanese pointed at Jerry. Pop. Jerry fell. At the refrigerator, McNatt spun. His face. God, the shock in his face. Beer and glass hit the tile like bombs. He grabbed for his pistol. Too late. Pop. McNatt dropped to one knee, a red bloom on his white tee shirt. Pop. His head snapped back, spraying crimson.

Before McNatt's face hit the floor, Roger was already screaming. "Jesus Jesus Jesus!"

The gun was barely larger than the Japanese guy's fist. And the toy barrel was pointed at him.

"Aw, please!" Roger cried. "I don't know anything! I'm NASA! Not CIA! Not!"

"I know," the guy said. And lowered the gun to his lap.

Roger couldn't believe it. His mouth hung open, his lungs full of another scream.

The Japanese leaned his head back against the rest. That's when Roger noticed that the guy's palms were bleeding.

"Uh . . ."

He opened his eyes. Looked at Roger questioningly.

"Have we, uh, met?"

"No, Dr. Lintenberg. We have never met."

Aw, jeez. "You, ah . . . you're a spy, aren't you? You're a spy, too."

The guy sat up, put the gun on the kitchen table, wiped his hands with Jerry's beer napkin. It came away soaked with red. There were deep cuts down the guy's palms, like he had picked up knives the wrong way.

The guy was bleeding a lot more than Jerry. There was only a quarter-sized spot of red at the center of Jerry's chest. He didn't look particularly dead, old Jerry didn't, except for those empty eyes.

McNatt, now—he looked so dead that Roger didn't dare sneak more than quick glances at him. The head shot had drilled Mc-Natt's cheek, and then came bursting out the top of his skull, bringing brain and bone and hair with it. Jesus. To die like that. Almost embarrassing. One minute breathing. *Gee, Roger. Thanks for calling me Doug.* And the next minute you're all over the refrigerator. All over the kitchen cabinets. All over . . .

"That was one of my favorite songs," the guy said sadly.

Shit. Not again.

"Do you think the world needs love, Dr. Lintenberg?"

Please. Oh, please. Not again. And the way the guy mangled the word 'love.' Roger would sooner cut out his own tongue than laugh. "Uh. Yeah. The two of us, say. One would like an alibi. And the other guy would just love a handcuff key . . ."

"Where is it?"

"McNatt's front pocket."

Just like that, the guy went and got it. He apologized for the blood that dripped on Roger as he unlocked the cuff, and Roger told him it was no big deal, no biggie at all. Then another helicopter went over, and Roger remembered the paratroopers, and he wondered where he was supposed to go, and what he was supposed to do next.

When the guy started to leave, Roger realized that he was as scared of being lost and alone as he had been of being handcuffed with company.

"Hey! Mr.— Uh, sir?" Roger said. "Wait up! Mind if I come with you? Just till I meet up with the Army or something? Hey, thanks. I appreciate that. Uh, just . . . lemme get my stuff, okay?"

Hollow concussions of mortar fire. Hiroshi didn't stop, didn't bother to take cover in the empty streets. His fault. If he had killed Kengo as Xuli had ordered . . .

The American sounded out of breath. "Where we going?"

There was no place left.

"Wait a minute! Please? Just a minute! Jesus! You ever take a breather, or what?"

Hiroshi glanced back. The American had stopped on the sidewalk. He was panting, hands braced on his thighs. His suitcase was scuffed and ragged along the side he had been dragging it.

Distant mortar fire again. Hiroshi lifted his head. Nothing moved in the street but wind-buffeted branches: palms, jacarandás, almonds. The flagstone breezeway nearby reminded him of his own apartment building; but it was the sound of helicopters and small-arms fire that drew him. That is where he needed to go. *Baka! You stupid.* If he had done things right, the invasion could have been prevented.

"Oh, wait! Please, okay? I gotta get my passport. Just . . ."

The American left his suitcase open on the sidewalk, was shoving papers into his camera bag. He hurried to catch up. "I don't want to be too much trouble, but you know? I mean, you know?"

Hiroshi would die in battle. No one to trouble themselves, not for his sake. No one to perform *kuyō* for him, no one to offer spirit food or pour hydrangea tea. And then his soul would wander, and that would be best. He had been made so foreign that, if he returned home, family ghosts would not know him. Japanese spirits would think him a stranger. Besides, this way was easier. When dead, he could walk where he wished. Do what he wanted. Travelers incurred no shame.

"Could you, uh, slow down, maybe just a little?" the American was asking. "If it's not too much trouble or anything. I'm wiped out. What a vacation, huh? Captured by spies. See some flying saucers. Oh, man. And what great flying saucers. I fall in love with the president's daughter. Yeah. Bonfim's daughter—who, I kid you not, has the world's greatest-looking ass. Then to top things off, a little icing on the cake, I do a revolution. Just wait till I get home—although, well, I guess I can't talk about everything. And, oh. Hey. I won't mention you. Hey. Count on that. Come on. 'Fess up. In there with McNatt the Weird and everything . . . I mean, right now, even as we speak, we could have been part of his dead body collection. Weren't you just a teeny bit scared?"

The dead don't fear. And that was a good thing, too, for Hiroshi had nothing to live for. Oxalá did not accept him as The Warrior even after he had, with bowed head, asked the gods to save him. Even after he had filled himself to bursting, made himself sick, with Brazil.

Baka.

Hiroshi had been given two *buns*. The first he had stupidly thrown away. The second he had carelessly put in his pocket, and lost on the road.

"So you think I'll get in trouble with the Army? Maybe I shouldn't tell them anything, right? Although I don't guess the CIA's going to buy that I killed McNatt. Me? Do McNatt? Store him in the closet. Keep a leg hung on my mirror to remember him by."

A helicopter growled in the distance. South. All the tumult was south, by the airport. He walked faster.

Around the corner, the American still chattering. Odd. There were people on the next block. A crowd of women. Ribbons trailed loose on their wrists, red and purple and blue.

"Wow," the American said. "Cool." He dug in the camera bag, brought out a Canon AE1. A camera flash. Some of the women looked startled.

Then Hiroshi was swept up by the crowd and pushed toward the mouth of a nearby plaza, all individuality absorbed. The jostle soothed him.

"Excuse me," the American was saying, behind him. "Excuse me, ma'am. Hey, lady? Coming through."

Something nearby was burning, and Hiroshi let himself be assimilated by the smoke, by the movement. The sound of mortar fire was louder, the wind black.

"Mega-cool," the American said as he came up alongside. He snapped another picture. "Good news. Here come the Marines."

Through a screen of smoke, soldiers, and the firecracker pop of gunfire, so harmless-sounding that everyone stopped as if to listen. Then, in the quiet of the tree-shaded plaza, screams. And the women started to fall.

Hiroshi gave himself to it: the shouts, the cries, the clatter of people running. It was over quickly; and when it ended only Hiroshi was left standing.

It was quiet but for the soft mewling of the wounded. Blood splattered the decorative planters, dripped off the stone benches. Amid the flagstone field of bodies lay the debris of curtailed life: purses, string shopping sacks. The breeze blew smoke into Hiroshi's face, and made ribbons on dead wrists flutter.

Beside him the American engineer lay, clutching his belly. His eyes were wide. He was trying to speak.

Hiroshi bent down.

"Oh, man," the American whispered. Blood pumped from between his fingers, pooled thick on the flagstones. "It's—it's . . ."

The American had dropped his camera. Hiroshi picked it up. The American grabbed Hiroshi's pants leg and held on.

"I will bring it back," he promised, but the grip didn't loosen. In the end, Hiroshi had to pull himself free.

Across the plaza, camera held high. The platoon of soldiers milled, confused, at the other end. A shout—the lieutenant ordering them to leave. At the camera flash, three of them turned and raised their guns.

"The people had no weapons!" Hiroshi told them. "I see! I see what you have done!"

He was very close, shoving the camera into their faces. They were younger than he had thought. And scared. "I see you. You killed them."

Flash. Startled blue eyes, shamed eyes.

"I will tell the world how you killed them."

Flash. The angry brown eyes of the lieutenant.

"Sergeant," the lieutenant said. "Take care of this." He herded his men down the street.

Flash. The resigned hazel eyes of the sergeant.

And the world went black.

There was so much blood that he thought he had been shot. Blood over his hands, over his face, over the broken camera.

Hiroshi sat up, felt around the gash on his cheek. The plaza was silent now, the cries of the wounded stilled. Corpses lay strewn across the flagstones, and the sun was going down.

He picked up the pieces of the Canon AE1 and took them back to the American; but the pool of blood was already drying, and the American was dead.

Hiroshi squatted, put the broken camera into his hand, folded the limp fingers around it. Then Hiroshi sat with him awhile, hoping his soul would find its way to Houston. It was happier to die and be prepared. More suitable. A fly landed on the American's cheek. Hiroshi brushed it away.

The camera bag had spilled its contents: a telephoto lens. Filters. Yellow rolls of Kodak film. A jade-green passport, its pages riffling in the breeze.

And a second camera. A tiny gray one. Hiroshi picked it up, turned it over. It was full of film.

"Thank you," he told the American. He stood and bowed deeply.

Photo of the NASA engineer, dead near his passport.

Stop at the next body, to bow permission. Snapshot of a woman, her forehead spilled hot red, cooled by the striated blue shade of a palm.

The teenage girl beside her, contorted in agony, body stiff, colors brilliant as a macaw. Pepsi-Cola tee shirt. Bloody Guess jeans. Yellow sandals. Hiroshi bowed forgiveness for the intrusion.

"I do this so you do not wander," he said to each corpse. "I do this so you are never lonely." And he moved through the hush of the plaza, gathering souls.

There was panic at Cabeceiras. In the orange afterglow of sunset, just past the main entrance, Edson parked. He was immediately surrounded by soldiers.

"Out of the car!" a sergeant shouted.

"I am Ed—"

"Out of the car!" A dry rattle of guns. Rifles pointed at Edson's face.

He raised his hands. The sergeant opened the door.

"I am the Direct—"

"On the ground!" Voice high-pitched. Hysterical. "Face on the ground!"

Something clubbed Edson's back, knocked the breath out of

him. He dropped. Dirt in his mouth, his eyes. A jab on the back of his skull. The unmistakable touch of a gun barrel. So this is the way it would end.

"Call the captain!" the sergeant said.

"Orders were to shoot intruders on sight, sir."

"Damn it. Call the captain now."

Edson tried to get up, but a booted foot shoved him down.

And then a gentle voice. "Are you all right?" Nando, shaking his head with consternation, helped Edson up.

"Where is Ana?" Edson asked.

"At your safe house in Villanova. Go home, Edson. You are drunk."

"I will go home when you give me my whore of a pistol."

Nando sighed. "Get in the jeep," he said. "Come on."

They drove through kilometers of fortifications. An entire regiment was there, too much for the Americans to tackle with Special Forces. And, despite the accuracy of their smart weapons, they would be afraid to bomb.

"Where is Freitas?" Edson asked.

Nando shot him a look. "Don't go in there. I have already tried to get that boy away from him, but you can't make that bastard do anything he doesn't want. He's too dangerous to approach. If he shows his face outside, my soldiers have been ordered to shoot. Without warning. Without question."

"You left him with the boy?"

"Don't lecture me, Edson. Not after what you have done."

They pulled up outside the first building. About them was chaos and noise: grumbling engines, tank sprocket squeaks.

Nando shouted to a major, "Is it ready?"

"Nearly, sir."

"Damn it, son. Get it ready. We don't have much time."

Edson tugged on Nando's sleeve and raised his voice to be heard over the rising scream of a helicopter. "Get what ready?"

Nando shook his head, leaned over, cupped his ear.

"What are you making ready!"

A nod. "Yes! We will raze these buildings!"

Nando started to get out of the jeep. Edson grabbed him. "Did Ana give the order?"

The general pulled out of Edson's grip. "She is the president. All the other orders she gives me, I follow. And I expect you to follow them, too. Your pistol's in the glove compartment. Take it. Shoot yourself. Or if you feel like living, wait here." And he stalked off.

The gun was too easy. And not oblivion enough. Edson would go into the chamber and gather the Disappeareds. Lead them to freedom, if he could. Enter nothingness with them, if he could not.

Edson climbed out of the jeep and walked past a baffled guard. When the door was firmly shut behind, he could hear it in the air of the complex—the sad, eerie quiet of abandonment.

Not much time left. He broke into a trot. Past rows of modified Cessnas in Building One. Shortcut through the abandoned offices in Five, where red drops on the floor made him slow his pace. Farther on, near a filing cabinet, a lump of maroon jelly. No. A liver. Blood made a dribbled pathway past gobbets of mealy yellow fat. Edson followed the gore to Building Eight, the main hangar, and stepped in.

His footsteps echoed. Nothing there, except for the open welcome of the Door. Except for the grotesque Hansel and Gretel trail. More trickles of blood. A pink kidney in a fist of blue veins. A pale ribbon of intestine.

And a smell. The cloying smell of the butcher shop. A fetid stench from punctured guts. José Carlos had been tossed indifferently near the Door, his torso and groin plucked empty.

A whisper from the shadows. A familiar voice. "Now I'll give you what you want."

Run in the Door. That was the payment Edson had to make for heaven. Go where he had sent the others, if only in the interest of justice. If only for the love of God. But too many promises had been broken. Between Edson and the Door José Carlos lay, pudgy child limbs, body cavity picked clean as a nutshell. Edson didn't dare try to lift him; couldn't leave him behind.

Then Freitas was there, close. And it was too late. A touch on his shoulder. Edson's body went helpless. He felt himself sink.

On Freitas's shirt, small rusty handprints. A bulge at the front of the jeans. Two huge hands, a stern father's hands, with spatulate fingers. Butcher's dregs caked under the nails.

The small-caliber pop of the brass snap, the spread of the zipper. Freitas took Edson's hands in his own, ran soiled thumbs down the center of his palms. Lust surprised Edson. It was surprise, in fact, that held him there on his knees, flush rising, breathing quickened.

Then Freitas scrubbed Edson's hands against himself, and Edson shut his eyes. He would never hold another man like this. The smell of blood came from a simple beating, and in his hands was a rubber hose. That was all.

He turned away. Freitas took Edson's arms, pulled them around his buttocks. Against Edson's cheek, a scouring of coarse hair, the smell of the swamp.

Edson tried to push him back, tell him no. He wasn't strong enough. That aggressive cock, like a jabbing finger. Freitas was too aroused not to be careless. Edson would strangle in his own blood, choke on his own teeth.

Rhythmic heaving, ponderous as the sea. Edson fell into dark. He fell dizzy and fast, and suddenly it didn't matter, to die. Against his cheek the nudge of something velvety and swollen. Edson opened his mouth for it, like a baby.

A blast echoed through the hangar, and that didn't matter, either. Freitas shivered, bone-deep; made a small, apologetic sound. Then he was leaving, the swollen nub pulling away, the buttocks slipping through Edson's hands. Edson couldn't let go— wouldn't. He followed Freitas down.

Freitas was slippery. The limp weight of him was hard to bear. Edson wrapped one arm about his waist, tore at his jeans with the other, until he felt the warm ejaculation fill his hand.

Startled, he let Freitas drop. Flaccid, loose-limbed, the body hit the floor. Too much blood. In Edson's palm, all over Freitas. Bright, arterial blood, and Freitas was dead. Oh. Edson hadn't meant to do that.

He shook him. Screamed his name. Freitas's shirt flapped open. There was a puckered mouth in the man's side. A bullet hole.

Edson looked around. Nando stood in the shadows of the hangar, Edson's own .45 still aimed. All Edson could see was the well of that barrel. He imagined the long fall, felt the tug of that gravity. And he wanted. He was hungry enough to do anything to make that need stop.

Nando's once-familiar face was grim. Edson knew that it was desire that made him a stranger. More than soul, more than life, Nando wanted to pull the trigger.

So Nando finally realized what Freitas had made Edson into. Now he and Nando would fall together in the swamp, and Edson would make him dirty. Edson meant to shout a warning. Only a sob escaped. His shoulders heaved. He lowered his face into his bloody hands.

God forgive him. Not for the sins of commission. Not for the executions, for who could blame justice? Not even for the spy tricks, or the lies. What he wept for were the things he hadn't done: how his life had been a waste; and how in not fighting to save himself, he would take Nando down, too.

A loud clatter. Edson flinched, dropped his hands. The .45 lay nearby, where Nando had thrown it.

"Get out," Nando said. "Get out."

Edson nodded.

"Fifteen minutes."

A whispered, "Yes."

"I swear I will give you what you want, Edson. I will bring this whole damned building down on you." Boot heels clicked, receding through the hangar.

Edson wiped his face with his sleeve. Freitas's eyes were open, vacant of appetite. For the first time Edson noticed how small the man was. How truly ordinary.

Freitas had the beginnings of a paunch. His jeans were pulled to his hips. The tip of his cock peeked out of leopard bikini undershorts, a purple-faced puppet. Who had bought those silly undershorts for him—Ana? Freitas was a man like any other, hiding secrets behind a zipper. Anyone's uncle. Someone at a bus stop. At the grocer's.

Tired, shaken, Edson stood. He retrieved his gun; thought about shooting himself, but that seemed pointless. Thought about going in the Door, but that was no use. Dr. Lizette and her Donato were gone. Light from the hangar flooded the chamber, brightened the corners. The floor was dusty, the painted walls shabby.

Just a room, really.

Just a man.

CNN, Live

. . . minutes until dawn here in Brasília. The heart of this great city, the Monumental Axis, has sustained an overwhelming amount of damage. But as you can see behind me, Itamaraty still miraculously stands. And that is where, a few hours from now, Ana Maria Bonfim will officially surrender to Fredrick E. Davis, the American Marine general serving as U.N. Coalition Commander.

Ah, perhaps we should note here for our viewers that CNN will be reporting the signing ceremony live, beginning at eleven o'clock Eastern Standard Time.

Susan? Have you found out anything about the destruction of the military base at Cabeceiras?

A U.N. team is already at the base, sorting through the wreckage. But the destruction does seem, at least at this moment, to be complete. General Davis supposedly plans to question Brazilian chief of staff General Fernando Machado, ah, at some length. Gossip has it that Davis is upset. Aides tell me the general is notorious for his temper. They call him 'Ferocious Freddy' behind his back. I've met him. Davis is a Marine's Marine. He doesn't have much of a sense of humor. I would not like to be in Machado's shoes when he calls him on the carpet.

Any radioactivity out there?

The inspectors have been sent in with protective clothing, but the fears about a radioactive release into the atmosphere seem to be groundless. Privately, I've been told that, extensive as the damage is, and as hot as it is out there, the site will eventually be cemented over, and a fence thrown up around it.

Can we expect some arrests today?

I assume so. Machado, although those charges may be dropped. Carvalho, who, as you know, has confessed to murder. And, of course, Bonfim.

And now I can just see the sun rising over the horizon behind you, Susan. And the building. Quite dramatic.

Yes, Bernie. All the glass was blown out in the bombing, but otherwise, it seems to be in good shape. Since Itamaraty is just a glass box inside a huge colonnade of arches, there has been a lot to clean up. Can you see the trucks lined up outside there? To my right? Those are Brazilian maintenance vehicles. Crews have been here since late last night, ever since the announcement was made that Bonfim had telephoned the White House.

And let us note here, that telephone call was logged in by the White House switchboard at ten forty-seven P.M., Eastern Standard Time. White House spokesperson Dan Rosen has informed us the call lasted a very short four minutes. Again, as one of her last acts, Bonfim has been brief. Well, Susan. Quite a few clouds there. Are the weather reports calling for rain?

No. Those are fair-weather cumulus. Very common this time of year.

Uh-huh. Looks like you're in for another beautiful day.

24

BLACK TURNED GRAY. BUILDINGS LOOMED OUT OF THE FOG. MIST CON-densed, wormed down windows, glossed the cobblestones. In the trees, vultures stirred in their roosts, shook themselves dry. Head down, she kept going. The one thing Dolores had always known was direction: straight ahead. Never turn aside. Never, ever look back. If you looked back, you would see it coming. Don't stop, or it would catch up.

But she was tired; and if there wasn't a home on the next block, at least there was rest, a place to put her feet up for a while. She nearly missed the steps—secretive, Lima steps, narrow and unfriendly. And at the top, the door.

She stood there, hair and blouse soaked through. She'd forgotten the key. If the door was locked, she would have to knock and rouse them.

She put her hand to the knob, and turned.

It was waiting for her there in the darkened living room, in the blue flickering light of the TV. Had been waiting for her all along, painstakingly furnished while Harry lay dying: Jack's comfortable little world. He looked up. And the concern in his face lured her, as exhaustion would lure her to a feather bed. On his left, Jaje lay curled asleep. On the right side of the sofa, a hopeful place, her place, had been left empty.

She closed the door, hermetically sealing herself in family. For a panicky moment, she couldn't breathe.

Cups and plates littered the table. When Jack was in doubt, he cooked. A woman's solution. A mother's. Dolores tiptoed to the sofa and looked down at Jaje. Egotistical little girl. A smart girl, and lucky. Growing up without demons of sacrifice or self-denigration.

Dolores said quietly, "Get some sleep, Jack. We need to be at the airport by ten."

In his face, a touching relief. How could he stay with her, when she hurt him? How could she have stayed all those years with Harry?

"Can't wake the girl up," he whispered. "She just dozed off about two hours ago. I'm fine. You?"

A question with layers. She didn't answer. And she didn't take the place he had saved. She sat on the floor by his legs. The television sound was off. On the screen, pink sunrise and Itamaraty.

A gentle touch at the back of her hair. "You're wet," Jack said. "Need to get dry."

She reached up, caught his fingers. In Brasília, two American soldiers were raising the Stars and Stripes. "I love you."

He didn't say it back. Instead, he cleared his throat, the way men do. When he spoke, his voice was almost steady. "Snows up in Vancouver. I know how you like snow. You can paint, baby. You know you can always paint. The ocean's right there, and they have those big old fir trees. And mountains. Oh, you'll just go crazy painting those mountains."

The warmth of Jack's fingers. Through them, his slow steady pulse. She wasn't Ana, and it wasn't with men that she made her mistake. She had loved only one thing without check, without balance.

For thirty years she let Brazil grow wild inside her. Its lushness root-bound her heart. "I can leave you anytime," she told Jack but, as she had learned with Harry, duty was probably strong enough to make her stay.

A hesitation, then a kiss to the top of her head. "I know."

Galleon clouds voyaged the sky: heavy gray bellies, sun caught in the tops of their sails. The breeze in the plaza was an ocean sort of breeze, one that felt as if it had traveled a long way, unchallenged.

He walked, trying to use up the last of his restlessness. Perhaps later, when it was spent, he would sleep. His wandering took him by Kengo's apartment. Then to the place he had killed Kinch.

Wide tile breezeway. Palms and eucalyptus shivering in the wind. He spotted the orange and purple dress first. Maria Bonita sat on the steps, legs tucked beneath her. The red ribbon on her wrist fluttered.

He stopped at her side. No magic, but that was all right. She was older than he had thought, and every bit as pretty. She looked up, tucked her dark hair behind her ear. The wind teased it loose again.

"*Olá, querido.* Your face is hurt. But I guess you know. Would you like a cigarette?"

"I have given up smoking," he said.

She made a space for him, patted the step. "Come. Sit down. I gave up smoking, too. But the Americans have invaded. Think of it: an army of camouflage tourists. I will kill myself slowly. I will eat foods high in cholesterol. I will not wear my seatbelt anymore. I was at the Cathedral when the bombs hit. Ceschiatti's metal angels fell from grace, and glass shattered on the floor like ice. I ask you again: are you sure you don't want one?"

She offered him the pack. He tweezered a cigarette out with his fingertips.

"What a mess you have made of your hands," she said, and lit his cigarette for him. "Tastes good, neh? Small sins."

Good? He wasn't sure. But he supposed that small nostalgic sins were forgivable.

"I've seen you before. You're the one who killed the American."

The smoke made him light-headed, made his eyes water. To escape her direct gaze, he looked down. There was blood on his pants cuff: a handprint.

"Don't worry. I won't tell," she said. "I didn't like him, that American. I applauded your good job when you were finished, but I suppose you didn't hear."

Kinch. She was speaking of Kinch.

"He always had parties, that one. People went for the food, for the American whiskey. But then after a while not even that could make them go, and I guess he ate the food and drank the whiskey alone. He thought he was funny, but he had no *jeito*. No way of dealing with people. And among the women, he was a joke. He squeezed my breast once, that pig, and with my husband right in the next room. I think he was a spy. Are you a spy, too?"

Hiroshi looked up. Hidden sun outlined a cloud with bright. "Yes."

"I thought at first that you were American. Then I thought you were Brazilian, until you spoke. And now I would think you Japanese, but the Japanese have won the war and they should be happy. Who do you spy for?" she asked.

The wind snagged a thread of smoke from the cigarette. It unraveled down the sidewalk, thin and white. "I don't know."

"Oh, every spy knows who they spy for. That must be the nature of the business."

"Yes," he said. "That is the nature of it."

"My husband, he knows the nature of his business. He is an architect. We could have lived anywhere, Petrópolis, Cabo Frio. But architects, you know, they worship the light. Light rains down here, he told me once. Light showers down in Brasília."

Hiroshi lifted his head. Washes of sun through the trees, splashes of bright on the tiles.

"I take photographs," she said. "Mostly for travel guides. Houghton Mifflin. That one. I've been in *Paris Match*. And *Life* magazine. A little reporting, too. But I like photography best. Form and space. Shadow and light. That is what my husband and I manufacture. I can understand taking a photo. I can understand building a building, for no other reason than wonder. But to spy for no reason seems pointless."

He yawned, tried unsuccessfully to hide it. At last he was ready for sleep. He took one last drag from the cigarette, dropped it, ground it out on the tiles. "I served one master all my life, and then he died."

"Oh," she said quietly. "I'm sorry."

He shrugged. "Now I spy for wonder."

He got up. He would curl up on a park bench somewhere. When the banks opened, perhaps in a few days, he would take his money out. When he was rested, he would know what to do.

A tug on his jacket. He looked down. "What sort of wonder is there in spying?" she asked.

"Take care," he said. He took the small gray camera from his pocket and pressed it into her hands.

Itamaraty stood suspended over its own reflection. Muller waited on the pool's walk, clouds at his feet.

Irked, Edson approached. The boy should have left. Edson pulled at his lapel. Pulled again. The .45 under his jacket felt heavy. The shoulder holster pinched. Everything that was ordinary seemed strange.

Muller stepped toward him, and his shadow fell over Edson: looming, masculine, and hungry. Edson instantly lowered his eyes and stumbled back.

Muller retreated. "Sorry, sir. I'm sorry."

Edson straightened his jacket, looked up in time to catch Muller's pity. Edson took a steadying breath and tried to smile. "Well, you look familiar. So well dressed. So prosperous. Have we met? Novo Hamburgo, perhaps. Or Caxias do Sul. One of those gaucho places."

"Sir. I've learned they plan a tribunal: Americans, Germans, British, Japanese."

Standing over that reflecting pool of sky, Edson felt weightless. Another breath of wind, and he could float free. "I passed by the

ministry," he said. "It is a loss. The Americans outfinessed themselves. Go home, my esteemed gaucho. Take what name you wish.
Buy a little ranch for yourself in the mountains, for that is what gauchos should do."

"Please. There is no need for this, sir. I can hide you. I have everything in place . . ." His voice trailed off when Edson shook his head.

Eight years together. It should have ended with an *abraço*. Instead,
Muller let Edson walk away.

Four steps later, Edson looked over his shoulder. Muller hadn't
moved. He called back. "My last order."

"Yes, sir?"

"Raise some cattle. One or two. Treat them gently." When Edson
looked back again, he was gone.

Bombs had opened Itamaraty to the wind. Edson made his way
into its shade and through its interior gardens. He passed papaya
trees with fruit like ponderous breasts; passed the dangling purple
phallis of a banana bud. Waiting on the polished floor of the foyer
were two gatherings: Nando's officers and pigeons. Across the huge
room Nando stood, ankle-deep in birds. Edson waded through the
flock to reach him.

A quick embarrassed look. Smells of bird shit and disinfectant.
Nando lowered his head, tore a hard roll into pieces. Edson found
himself looking for blood under Nando's nails.

"Nando."

Some tone in his voice. Nando jerked his head up.

"I had to tell you—"

"Don't, Edson. Don't say it. Freitas is dead. We sent the thing back
to its own universe. The Door is closed."

Down the hall, an anteroom door opened. Ana stepped out with
her aides.

"Can it be closed?"

Edson's voice shook. "You said once you recognized Freitas's
emptiness. You saw the same hunger in your brother-in-law. Nando,
listen. What if there are no aliens? No devils? What if the thing inside—"

Nando's eyes narrowed, his cheeks flushed. "Damn you, it is *over*." Unlike Edson, Nando had been left an option—and he chose not to know.

Shouts from Nando's officers. The Americans had arrived. Edson could see them striding their businesslike way past the courtyard's wide-hipped stone women.

Nando crumbled the last roll, and left him. Breeze blew through Itamaraty's open walls, vibrated empty window supports, sounded a continuous bassoon.

The American soldiers looked sinister: wide shoulders, beefy faces, shaved skulls. They walked like automatons, tuned to the same frequency; all in unintentional step, and yet no rhythm.

At the door, Nando was trying to herd his officers into a line. Each seemed to have his own idea of where to stand. Edson sensed someone at his shoulder. He looked down. Ana.

She was watching the Americans. "I knew he was dead when the lights in the sky went out," she said. "And I imagine that the Door opened, too, and that the spirits of all the people he had captured went on. When Nando finally ordered his soldiers to release me, he wouldn't tell me what happened. Before he died, Edson, were you there?"

A pause, then Edson nodded. Through the bassoon solo of the wind, a restless stirring. The Americans entered, news people trailing like scavenger birds. The American general halted, spun to Nando, and stood, arms at his sides. His men stopped, attentive, behind.

From Nando, an impish smile. He lifted his arm, whirled, brought it down with a flourish. His officers opened their mouths. "Weee-geeve-eh-aaapuh-you-eesss-tuuu-peed-ah-maaa-there- foook-airs."

The Americans blinked. The cameraman lowered his minicam. Edson began to smile.

In Ana's face was a weariness as profound as despair. "Everyone has always made my decisions for me. First Paulinho. Then Dolores. And finally Nando."

A frustrated shake of Nando's head. He whirled, lifted his hand again. From the choir: "Weee geeve-eh aah-puh . . ."

She said, "I need your gun."

Edson brought the gun merely to keep Americans off him. But Ana was used to the effects of hunger, and oblivion was the only shelter she had ever known. He took hold of her fingers. Her hands were like ice.

The officers' gleeful ". . . you estuuuu-peed . . ."

The gun was too big for her. Too heavy. He folded her fingers around it. "Both hands," he said. "And not in the heart." The heart had always been her weakness. "Don't put it against the side of your head. You can't help but tremble."

Edson lay his cheek against hers. Her skin was already cold. "In the mouth," he whispered. "So deep, you will think you choke." And when the explosion came, he prayed she would not swallow emptiness. "Please . . ." *Don't make a mess of it,* he thought.

A rousing finish. ". . . maaa-there-fooo-kairs!"

A final squeeze of her hand. He let her go, and turned.

The slam of the anteroom door caught the crowd's attention. Nando was staring. The American general was staring. They were all staring at the place where Edson stood guard.

The boom was so pure a sound that it sent a shiver racing through Edson. It made the Brazilian officers flinch, and made Nando cry out. It was so powerful that it halted the Americans in their tracks.

And in the emptiness of the foyer, a dry snap of feathers. A confusion of light and dark. The flock found direction, stormed the breezeway.

Clear of the shade of the overhang, birds ascended, free and fast. For a single heady instant they blazed with sun—a host besieging heaven.